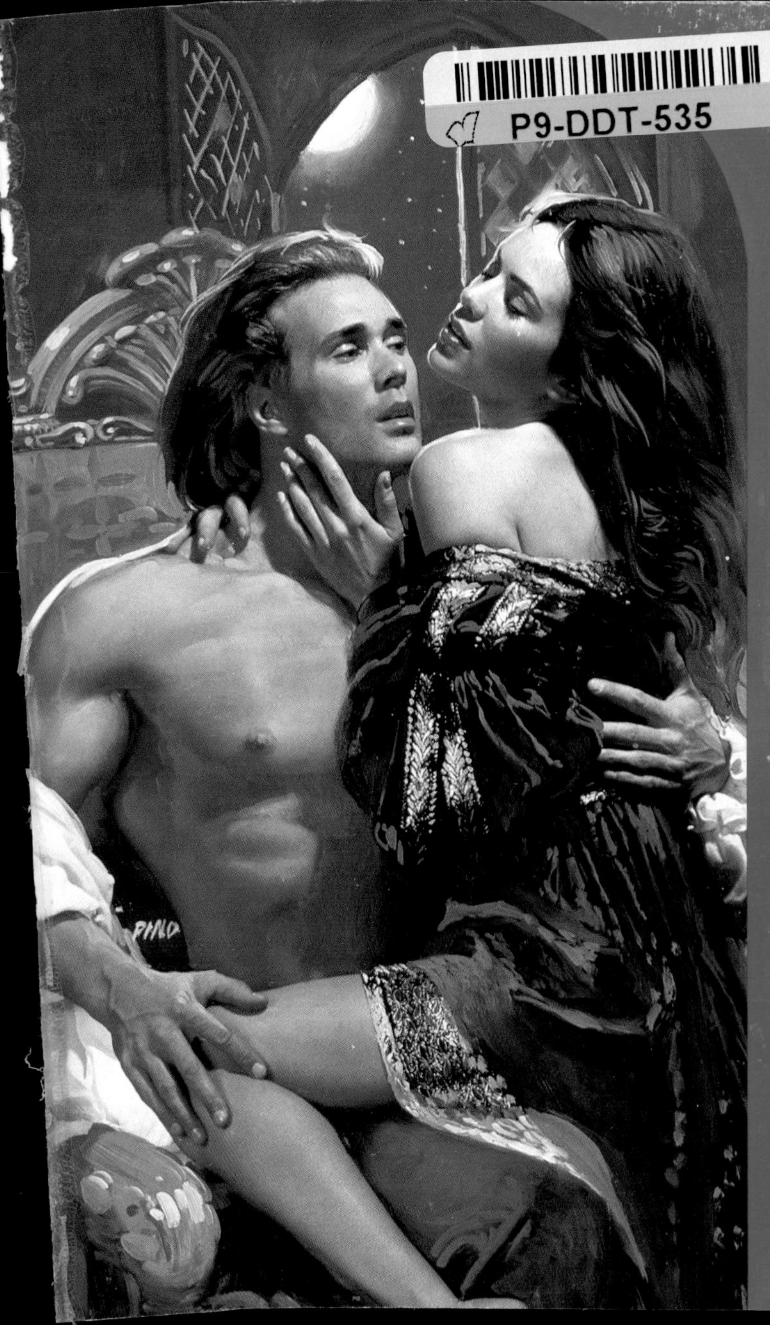

Mistress Anne Blanchemain was not only wealthy, she was beautiful. The men in the room were watching her like a pack of hunting dogs surrounding a wounded heart, each vying to be the one to make the kill. Kit blinked. He stared. Why hadn't he realized that every man in all England would have an interest in her?

A tiny frown pleated her brow, and she caught her lower lip in her teeth. At this sign of nervousness, pity unwound from some hidden portion of Kit's gut. How well he remembered his own dread over his presentation at court.

For the brief instant that Kit's eyes met hers, her gaze stayed on him. The sensation was unnerving and oddly intimate, stirring the most carnal of his desires. This was no Puritan miss after all, for no religious woman looked at a man like that. My, but lust was a fine thing to feel. The seducing of Mistress Anne was going to be pleasant, very pleasant indeed.

Deep in the core of Anne's being, an answering flame woke, stirring her long banked desires. As the heat grew, it brought with it the image of this man pressing his mouth to hers. Warmth flowed through her. Although it had been almost seven years since the beginning and end of her fall from innocence, her body had not forgotten the pleasure of a man's touch. But she drove all such thoughts deep within her. 'Twas dangerous to indulge herself in any emotion at all until she was certain she'd found the man she needed. . . .

Lady in Waiting

Denise Domning

A TOPAZ BOOK

TOPAZ
Published by the Penguin Group
Penguin Putnam Inc., 375 Hudson Street,
New York, New York 10014, U.S.A.
Penguin Books Ltd, 27 Wrights Lane,
London W8 5TZ, England
Penguin Books Australia Ltd,
Ringwood, Victoria, Australia
Penguin Books Canada Ltd, 10 Alcorn Avenue,
Toronto, Ontario, Canada M4V 3B2
Penguin Books (N.Z.) Ltd, 182–190 Wairau Road,
Auckland 10, New Zealand

Penguin Books Ltd, Registered Offices:
Harmondsworth, Middlesex, England

First published by Topaz, an imprint of Dutton Signet,
a member of Penguin Putnam Inc.

First Printing, January, 1998
10 9 8 7 6 5 4 3 2 1

 REGISTERED TRADEMARK—MARCA REGISTRADA

Printed in the United States of America

This book is dedicated to my mother,
Joan Domning, who held my hand
throughout its production. Without
her patience, advice, and gentle prods,
it would never have been written.
I can't thank you enough, Mom.

Prologue

Master Christopher Hollier stirred in his sleep, straining to awaken. Too late! The nightmare wound its steely tentacles around him and dragged him down to hell.

He was eight again, wearing the black doublet, breeches, and coat that had marked his grandsire's passing. The child Christopher smoothed his fingers over his coat's velvet surface. He loved his coat. 'Twas just like those his lord father wore, with a soft fur collar and long, dangling sleeves.

As he had all those years ago, Christopher stood in Graceton Castle's kitchen, with its brown stone floor worn to gray along concave paths wrought by a century worth of footsteps. The fireplace filled the far wall, its mouth wide enough that two tall men could walk into its opening, side-by-side, a tiny step separating its bed from the kitchen's floor. Mutton sizzled over the roaring fire at the hearth's back wall, while a wee black iron pot stood in a pile of white-hot embers at its forward edge, the pot's lid chattering as the sauce within it bubbled.

'Twas a ten-year-old Nicholas who appeared beside the child Christopher. Christopher's elder brother wore clothing identical to his. Nick was crying.

Christopher offered what sympathy he could. "I wish

our lord grandsire hadn't died and you didn't have to go to serve the heretic king."

His brother wiped his nose upon his sleeve as he looked up at Christopher. "If I do not go, Kit, we'll be poor and I'll never be Lord Graceton."

Kit wrinkled his nose. Such a thing was impossible to comprehend, when there had always been a Lord Graceton. With the next breath he shook off these deep thoughts. This was their free hour, a time for enjoyment, not worries.

Leaping to the wood stacked near the fireplace, he snatched up a stick, then threw out his chest and pranced to and fro like some high-strung pony. "On your guard!" he warned Nick, wagging the branch before him in challenge.

Just as Kit expected, the prospect of play soothed Nick from his sadness. His brother grabbed himself a weapon and took a defensive stance. Kit thrust first, still owning that right, even though they were now of a height and he no longer needed the advantage. 'Twas the only thing in which they were equal; as a second son, he was far less important to his family. His attack drove his brother into a brief retreat.

Nick stopped to eye Kit down the short length of his nose. "How dare you attack the lord of this castle! Now I shall have to slay you for your impertinence."

Sticks clashed. Bark flew. Two years more experience told the tale. Nick's weapon cut through the air more quickly than Kit anticipated, and the blow caught him on the shoulder with a solid whack. "You're dead," Nick crowed as he scrambled back beyond the reach of Kit's weapon.

Kit yelped as much in anger as in pain. It wasn't his turn to die, and Nick knew it. "Nay, I was but injured and went away until my wounds were healed," he said, *trying to force the game back to its familiar pattern as he skipped behind the cook's worktable to play out his departure and subsequent recovery.*

With his stick held before him, he darted out to again confront his brother. "When I was well, I came to find you, so we might duel again."

"And I stabbed you again," Nick said, thrusting for his brother's breast.

Dodging the blow, Kit's eyes narrowed. This was a flagrant breach of their rules. "But you missed," he said, "so I hired me four to help drub you proper." He waved his stick-cum-sword to call these newly employed mercenaries to his side.

Nick only sneered at this paltry threat. "Then, I called me eight of mine own retainers to beat your four."

Kit set his fists on his hips in outrage. " 'Tisn't fair, Nick. You can't have more men than me."

His brother's mouth tightened, and a superior look twisted his pretty face. "I can do anything I want. Even if our house is bankrupt and I will be but a squire, I am still Graceton's heir, while you are only the second son. Not only do I have more men, my swords are the finer." Accompanied by his larger and better armed imaginary force, Nick charged his younger brother.

Kit glared at him. If Nick could cheat, so could he. He stuck out his leg. "Then, you stumbled," he said. Nick did just as commanded, tripping over his younger brother's outstretched leg.

Trapped in sleep, the adult Kit moaned, trying to call back his ancient actions. 'Twas useless. There was nothing for him to do but watch his brother stagger toward the hearth. As it always did, the only sound the dream let him hear was the scuff of Nick's shoes on stone. The flailing of Nick's arms slowed to an eerie pace.

"*Nick!*" the younger Kit screamed as his brother's foot caught on the low hearth step.

Nick dropped face first atop the wee pot. As the tiny cauldron toppled, scorching mist exploded in the fireplace's arched mouth. Nick's coat's fur collar and his dangling sleeves burst into flame. Graceton's heir shoved himself upright off the searing hearthstone, his mouth opened in a silent scream.

Kit stared in horror. Nick's golden hair was a stinking, blackened mass. Gone were his eyebrows; the skin on his face was shredded.

Chapter One

Graceton Castle
England, 1569

"Nay!" Kit burst out of the nightmare, coming upright in his bed as he did so. His heart pounded, his arms were outstretched into the inky darkness as if he could reach back through time and stop his brother's destruction.

He let them fall, empty and useless, into his blanketed lap. No matter how much he wished it, such a thing wasn't possible. Nor could he return to Nick what his childish trick had taken. Because of that day, his brother had never left their home to seek favor in the royal court and the monetary recompense that such favor brought with it. Without additional income to offset their grandsire's debts, Nick's title had gone into abeyance. There was no longer a lord at Graceton.

From the floor outside the open doorway to Kit's bedchamber, Herbert Babthorpe snorted and stirred on his cot. "Who comes! Where are you?" his servant demanded, his panicked voice yet thick with sleep. Kit could hear him scuffling around on the floor for his dagger.

" 'Tis only me, Bertie," he called to his servant.

Bertie huffed in relief, his joints popping and snapping as he stretched. The servant's bedclothes rustled. "That dream of yours again, was it Master Kit? I should have expected as much," the man said around a yawn as he settled back into sleep. "It's always worse when we're home." His words faded into quiet.

Worse? 'Twas the nightmare that kept Kit from returning to Graceton for any length of time. As long as he stayed here the dream plagued him at about the same hour on each and every night. Each incident was followed by an irresistible urge to visit the kitchen. So consistent was Kit's torment that the servants were warned against his midnight prowls.

With a sigh he leaned back against the bed's head and forced himself to remain abed. Bertie worried about these nightly jaunts, thinking it unhealthy for his master to brood so over what had happened almost a score of years ago. Kit didn't wish to argue over it, not this night. If the queen's business had taken him away from court, 'twas his own business that made his route extend to Graceton. As always happened when he reached the lowest points in his life, he needed to see Nick. Visiting his brother gave him the strength to face what lay before him.

Rain spattered against the room's mullioned window. The wind gusted, then moaned its way along what had once been the old castle's outer defenses and was now the exterior of the house. Bertie's breathing descended into the rhythmic pattern of sleep.

Kit thrust back the bed curtains, then turned on his mattress. Without moon or stars to shed their silvered light, shadows cloaked what had once been his and Nick's childhood room. No matter. 'Twas long habit that led him across the room to the peg where his bed robe hung.

With that garment drawn on atop his shirt, Kit crossed the small sitting room for the suite's exit. He pulled gently on the door handle. There was a creak as the door's tenons swiveled in their mortises; the burly panel swung wide. Kit glanced over his shoulder at his servant. Bertie was naught but a dark mound in even darker surrounds. The man sighed and rolled over, dragging the blanket with him as he went.

Leaving the door ajar, Kit stepped out into the gallery. Worn by time, the wood was smooth beneath his bare feet. Wide, with windows along its length, the gallery extended the length of the house, offering access to both the family's living quarters and the guest apartments. To Kit's right, was the door to what had been his sire's apartments. Two doors to the left was the door of the chambers his mother had used, the ones in which Nick now made his home.

Light seeped out from around Nick's door, outlining its arched form while it left the nearby corners as black as ink. Something shifted in that darkness. Kit caught his breath. He had no wish to encounter Graceton's ghost this night.

'Twas a man's form, not a woman's that appeared out of the shadows. "Is that you, Kit?"

Kit relaxed as he recognized Master James Wyatt's voice. Jamie was his brother's closest friend and Graceton's steward. He also served as gentleman attendant to the man who would have been his lord, if not for the child Kit's petty need for vengeance.

"Aye, Jamie," he replied, tensing in dislike. Such was the consistency of his dream's torment that Nick had known just when to send Jamie out to await him.

"Nick was sorry to have slept through your arrival. He says he cannot wait until the morrow to see you," the steward said.

Worry for his brother woke beneath Kit's guilt. "Jamie, he shouldn't be about in the middle of the night. Nick won't win out over what rattles in his lungs if he doesn't get his rest."

Jamie's quiet laugh echoed down the stairs that led to the hall. "You're right in that, he'll not win out over what rattles in his lungs. Each bout weakens him. Someday it will take him."

The man's words were like a knife thrust to Kit's heart. Nick couldn't die; he wouldn't let him. He couldn't let him. If that happened, Kit was certain the guilt would kill him, as well.

"That's not true," he snapped, sorry he had nothing but a scold to wield against the man who should have been his inferior. It was because he'd sent Nick tumbling into the hearth that he was but a gentleman and not the squire he should have been. "Nick's no weaker now than he was two years ago."

"So you would say." There was a shuffling, then a scrape. 'Twas Jamie catching up the stool he'd used as he waited for Kit's all-too-predictable appearance. "Come, Kit."

The gentleman's footsteps echoed across the landing. The door opened, then candlelight tumbled into the open space, gleaming golden against the plasterwork that covered the stone walls. The light glinted in Jamie's dark red hair and marked the straight line of his nose. Dark hollows hung beneath his pale eyes and tired lines marked his lean cheeks.

That Nick's steward yet wore his shirt and breeches, stockings and shoes, suggested he'd been sitting the night away at his master's side. Kit's guilt tried to consume him. 'Twas he who should have been sitting beside his brother, tending Nick in his many illnesses. Instead the dream kept him away.

"He should rest," Kit protested again, even though he knew it was useless. "Tell him we can speak in the morning. There's no need for me to leave at first light. I'm not expected in London for another few days."

Jamie shook his head. "Kit, you know how he gets when you refuse him. Agitation can only make matters worse."

"Christ." Aye, Kit knew just how bad things could get when he refused to do Nick's will. Padding down the landing, he stepped into the apartment that now defined the limits of Nick's existence. Not even the Yuletide could bring the man who should have been Graceton's lord into the public areas of his own house.

Like their childhood apartment, this suite had an antechamber and two private bedchambers, although the size of the rooms was far larger. Here in the sitting area, Nick had two tables, a great branch of candles standing upon one of those narrow pieces, and his desk. Papers, quill, ink pots, along with other writing implements, cluttered the desktop. 'Twas the management of what remained of Graceton's estate that occupied Nick's hours. There was only one chair set aside for the rare visitor permitted to view the master of Graceton Castle, face-to-face.

"Is that you, Kit?" Nick called from his bedchamber, his voice made hoarse and thready by the lung infection presently plaguing him.

"Aye, Nick," Kit replied, striding into his brother's inner sanctum with Jamie close upon his heels.

As Kit stopped beside the bed, Jamie went on, claiming one of the two small chairs that faced the flames. The fireplace stood in the river wall, flanked by the two tall, arched windows that allowed Nick his only view of the outside world. The massive crucifix that had once hung in Graceton's chapel now decorated the abutting wall with Nick's private altar set beneath it. His brother's illegal Catholic prayers were marked by flickering candles.

Framed in blue-green bed curtains, Nick sat upright upon his mattress, papers strewn atop the blankets and a cup clutched in the bony remains of his hands. If the smell could be trusted, the concoction within it contained horehound. As always, 'twas welcome that glowed from Nick's eyes, their green color being the only feature Kit and he shared between them. "I heard you shout, Kit."

Knowing his brother would tease him over the dream made it easier for Kit to hide his reaction, but it didn't stop the words from tearing into his heart. Rather than admit to his hurt, Kit let Nick spill the same jest time after time, simply grateful that his brother yet lived to say the words. He managed a smile. "Liar, if you'd truly heard me, Jamie wouldn't have been sitting in the gallery waiting for me to pass him on my way to the kitchen."

If Nick's mouth could not do it, his eyes returned his brother's smile. "Ah, Kit, I know how difficult it is for you to come home, but glad I am that you're here. 'Tis good to see you."

Would that Kit could say the same. The nightmare never let him forget how Nick had looked before the burning. Where Kit owned the Graceton face, long in the nose, narrow in the cheeks, and sandy-brown hair atop it all, Nick had promised to be a truly handsome man, with fine features and hair like gold.

No more. Scars now webbed from the bridge of Nick's nose across his cheeks, this second layer of skin so stiff it made talking a chore and smiling out of the question. Nick's eyebrows and eyelashes, like his hair along his brow line and around his ears, had never returned.

"How are you, Nick?" Kit demanded gently.

"Me?" his brother replied as if surprised that anyone would ask. "I am well."

This only made Kit's eyes narrow. "Liar," he repeated. "I can hear you struggle for breath."

Anger flashed in Nick's eyes. "If you do not like my answers, then do not ask me how I do. I said I am well. Leave it be, Kit."

"How can I leave it be," Kit persisted, "when you dismissed the physician I sent you. Why? He could have helped you." No matter how he tried to return to Nick some of what he'd stolen from him, his brother ever threw it back into his face.

A touch of sadness filled Nick's gaze. "So that's what brought you here. I should have guessed it wasn't me you came to see."

Stung that he should think this, Kit reached to lay a hand on his shoulder. "That's not true. You are precisely who I came to see. Am I not seeing you now?"

"Nay," his brother retorted with more than a little irritation in his voice, " 'tis my ghost you visit, not me. Look at me, Kit. Can you not see 'tis still me behind my scars?"

Kit frowned in confusion. "Of course I see you." How could he help but see the brother upon whom he'd laid these scars?

Nick sighed. "He still doesn't see me, Jamie."

"He cannot," the man replied from his chair near the fire. "The past holds him."

"What are you talking about?" Kit demanded, looking from one to the other. "All I asked is why you dismissed the physician."

"The man was a fool," his brother retorted. "Everything he did to me left me weaker still. 'Twas for your sake I let him stay as long as he did."

The scars on Nick's face shifted into what passed for an expression of wry humor. "Besides, there's nothing wrong with my bowels, and he was obsessed with them."

"You cannot know if what he planned would be effective after only a week," Kit protested.

Nick opened his mouth to retort, but his breath caught as a coughing spasm overtook him. Clutching a hand to his chest, he bent against what wracked him. Kit took the cup from his brother's hands, then rubbed at Nick's back until his breathing calmed.

"Ach, Nick," he said, "all I want is for you to be well, once more. I thought the man might help."

Nick leaned into his pillows, still struggling for breath. "What you want would take a miracle," he managed, "and only God can offer you that. Here, give me the cup."

He extended his hands toward the cup. With most of the flesh burned off them, his fingers were skeletal and without flexibility. Rather than give it to him, Kit lifted the container to his brother's lips.

Nick didn't need his face to move to let Kit know how irritated he was with this attempt at pampering. Resentment burned in his eyes. "Give it to me," he snapped, "then tell me why your creditors have come tapping on our gate."

Startled, Kit dropped the cup. Nick ably caught the container between his scarred palms, only a little of the thick, dark liquid sloshing over its rim.

"May God take those damn tradesmen," Kit snarled. "How dare they come here!"

Nick sipped at his brew, watching his brother over

the cup's rim. "I suppose they dare because they want to be paid."

"Well, they'll have to wait," Kit growled. His position as gentleman pensioner to England's queen was compensated at only eighty pounds a year. 'Twas hardly enough to cover his basic needs, much less pay his present debts. It certainly didn't come close to the fortune he needed to see Nick's title restored.

His brother tilted his head to one side. "What happened? Last you were here, you'd invested in a shipping corporation and thought it showed potential."

"So it did." Kit turned to drag a chair away from the hearth, placing it before Nick's bed so he might sit as they spoke. Although the floor was covered by a plaited rush matting to stop the drafts, his bare toes were chilling.

With a sigh he folded his long frame into the seat, then braced his feet against the bed. "Indeed, if not for politics, it might well have turned a profit."

Now knowing how closely his brother followed the doings of the country here at Graceton, Kit set himself to explaining. "In November past, four ships filled with treasure bound for Spanish forces in the Lowlands took shelter in Plymouth Harbor." He offered his brother a wry grin. "I fear our queen couldn't resist; she confiscated them, keeping the silver that lay within those holds. In retribution the Spanish confiscated my corporation's ship, which was at harbor in the Lowlands at the time." The only fact Kit wasn't willing to share with his brother was that the loss of the ship left him so deeply in debt, his creditors were set on throwing him in prison.

Nick tapped a scar-hardened finger against his cup in thought. "How much do you need?"

"From you, nothing," Kit said, his words sharp.

"You'll not pay my debts when you have your own mortgages to worry over." Kit wanted nothing to interfere with the paying of those mortgages. The sooner Graceton was free of its debt, the sooner Nick could claim his rightful title as its lord and the sooner Kit would be rid of guilt.

"You speak as if we were bankrupt," Nick started irritably.

"We?" Kit interrupted. "Graceton is yours, not ours, and I'll not take your coins. If you're worried about the tradesmen, don't be. They can wait, they always do." Only they wouldn't, not this time.

The green of Nick's eyes hardened into an emerald brightness. "What you need is an heiress to marry." 'Twas a jab, meant to repay Kit's refusal to take his aid.

Kit stiffened. No matter the conversation, it always came back to this. Well, he'd have none of it. "Me, marry? You know full well I cannot. 'Tis the elder son who must wed first."

Even beneath the scars there was no missing the stubborn jut of Nick's jaw. Jamie stepped forward to once more place himself between them. "Not again, Nick," he warned. "There's no reasoning with him on this issue. If he doesn't wish to wed, let him be."

Nick turned his hard gaze on his steward, just as determined to force Kit where he would not go as Kit was to resist him. "If you'll not have me speak about this again, then tell my pigheaded brother he has no choice over marriage. Aye, and after that tell him he is no longer a younger son, but my heir. When you're done telling him that, remind him that if neither of us marries, Graceton will go to our second cousin."

"Do you think throwing Sir Robert into this conversation will change my mind?" Kit snarled, his muscles tensed against this ancient battle. "You hate him more than I do. If you don't want Graceton in his hands, wed and breed yourself up children to keep it from him."

"I am too frail for that." 'Twas a flat statement and a terrible dodge.

Kit lifted his brows in scorn, the twist of his lips smug. "I think not. There's nothing wrong with your chest and arms, torso and legs. Save for the constant illnesses that eat away at your body mass, you are as much a man as any other. I know about Cecily."

Cecily was the daughter of the woman who'd nursed Nick back to health after his burning. As she was long accustomed to his appearance, she was the only woman with whom Nick was comfortable. "If you can bed Cecily, you can bed a wife," Kit said. "Marry first, Nick, and I vow I'll follow your lead."

A garbled sound that was neither laugh nor cry escaped Nick's stiff lips. "Who would I marry, brother? Look upon my face, and name me one woman at our queen's court who would take me as I am." Pain filled his words.

So Nick said every time they spoke of marriage, refusing to see that if Cecily could accept him, other women could do so as well. "You're a good man, Nick. There are many who would put aside appearance if they were assured of a gentle and kind husband."

"Nay," his brother's voice rose until he coughed. "You'll do your duty to our family and wed."

'Twas an empty threat. Six years ago, when Kit had been but one and twenty, Nick had tried to force marriage on him. Rather than give way, Kit left England for the Continent to battle the Spaniards for the Protestant Dutch, his choice of sides a statement of rebellion against his yet Catholic brother.

"Do as you must, knowing I'll do as my heart de-

mands," Kit said with a shrug. "Who knows? I might
well come home from the Lowlands this time with
a knighthood and the two hundred and fifty pounds
attached to that title." Or suffer far worse than a slash
that made for a long scar across his chest.

Rising from the chair, he stretched, the motion far
more relaxed than he felt. "Now, I think we've argued
enough for one visit." He leaned into the bed to press
his lips against his brother's rough and ridged brow.

"Leave my monetary problems to me, and I'll see
that my creditors no longer plague you." He turned
and started from the room.

"Kit," Nick called after him, "I will find a way to
force a wife on you. You cannot win."

Kit didn't bother to reply as he closed the door to
his brother's apartment, then slipped back through the
darkness to his own familiar room.

Since the last thing he wanted was to become master of Graceton Castle, marriage was out of the question. Kit's heart twisted. It was the fear that Nick
would give way to his ailments and die once he was
wed that kept him from it.

'Twas this that sent him seeking other routes to the
fortune needed to restore Nick's title. Of the two Kit
had found, soldiering and royal favor, he'd tried and
failed at advancement through war. That left only
royal favor.

Kit sighed. After four years at Elizabeth Tudor's
court he'd proved himself neither handsome nor
sprightly enough to dance his way into the realm of
her favorites. Indeed, instead of winning a fortune he
was now so deeply in debt he feared there was no
hope of rescue.

Chapter Two

Mistress Anne Blanchemain threw open her parlor window. Borne into the chamber on the day's cold breath, rain spattered the front of her black bodice. Droplets caught on her modest ruff and plastered her fine cotton shirt to her skin. From Owls House's courtyard harnesses rattled and leather creaked. Tired horses stamped and blew. Men spoke, their words inaudible against the low moan of the wind.

Balancing her hips on the window ledge, Anne leaned out the window as far as she dared and peered around the corner of the house. 'Twas an army that filled the square before the door. At their head was a tall man, a great ruby pinned to the band of his flat black cap.

Anne threw herself back into the parlor and slammed the window shut so hard the diamond-shaped panes rattled in their frames. Whirling, she faced the room's narrow fireplace and her mother, sitting in the high-backed invalid's chair beside it.

Lady Frances Blanchemain wore black, as did Anne, against the recent death of the third of her four daughters, but her attire was more bed robe than gown. Indeed, aside from Frances's tiny ruff, her only nod to fashion was the attifet perched atop her graying chestnut hair. That cap's heart-shaped front framed a face once lovely enough to cause her banishment from King Henry's court by a jealous queen. Ah, but Frances's beauty was long gone, stolen by the fit that had frozen the right side of her body and robbed her of her tongue, even if it hadn't dimmed her intelligence. Just now Anne's mother's hazel eyes, as expressive as her lips were mute, were filled with question.

Long accustomed to her mother's silent communication, Anne loosed a steaming breath. " 'Tis Sir Amyas. Who does he think he is, rapping upon our door without warning?" she snarled.

Frances's left brow dropped in chiding at this, while half her mouth thinned to a demanding line. Her yet functional left hand clenched, and she rapped her knuckles on the arm of her chair.

Anne glared. A persistent faith and the words of the apostle Paul gave her mother the ungodly notion all women must submit to the rule of men. Raised as she was without a man to command her, Anne owned neither her mother's deep faith nor her ability to submit. She crossed her arms in refusal.

"You are wasting your breath, Mama. I will not apologize, not when each time my grandsire comes he takes another bite from your jointure. I give thanks that there's little left for him to take, save me."

Fear twisted on half her mother's face.

Regret tore through Anne. Flying across the parlor, her skirts and petticoats rustling on the floor's plaited matting, she crouched beside Frances's chair. Her mother caught Anne's hand, squeezing as if she never meant to let go, terrible shadows filling her eyes.

Anne pressed a swift kiss to her cheek. "You worry where there is no need. If he comes for any reason this day, 'tis to announce that he's found me a husband, now that I am Owls House's sole heir. Since he vowed I should never leave you, the man he chooses must abide here and, thus, must accept you as you are."

This time, Frances's eyes widened in a wholly different concern.

Shame touched Anne's answering smile. The isolation of her life here hadn't proved a perfect barrier to sin. She gave a halfhearted shrug. "Any man who can accept you will also be accepting of me as I am."

From the hall outside the parlor door, wood scraped on the stone flooring. Sir Amyas's men were setting out the tables and benches, coughing and spitting long hours of cold travel from their throats as they did so. Anne came to her feet, Frances's hand yet clasped in hers, and glared at the door. Sir Amyas never waited for hospitality to be offered. Instead he behaved as if Owls House were still his and not bound in trust to his second son's daughters.

Someone tapped. Anne's anger swelled, but there was no point in refusing to answer. If she didn't admit her grandsire, he'd simply barge into the room. "Come," she called out.

Cold, damp air gusted in as the door opened. Candles flickered in their sconces, while the flames on the hearth drew new life, leaping far up on the fireplace's brick wall. 'Twas Lucy Malvin who entered, their housekeeper yet wearing a stained apron atop her workaday attire and no veil beneath her cap. Without that shield, not even candlelight could soften the bubbled, pocked ruin smallpox had made of her face.

"Sir Amyas Blanchemain," she announced, then dropped into a deep curtsy.

Anne's grandsire strode into the parlor, his sodden cloak yet dripping, mud spewing from his boots. At three score years, Sir Amyas was still a handsome

man, being fine-featured and olive-skinned, his hair
pure white beneath his black cap. He didn't greet his
second son's widow or her daughter. Instead he took
inventory of the parlor.

Anne's lip curled as she watched him check to see
the room's most valuable assets were still in place: the
expensive carpet that covered the parlor's narrow oak
table, the golden bowl at the center of the walnut
mantelpiece, and the Flemish tapestry on the far wall.
A touch of triumph joined her scorn. The tapestry was
Frances's, brought with her into her marriage, thus
beyond his reach no matter how much he coveted it.

Lucy rose, careful to keep her face turned away
from their auspicious guest. Sir Amyas's religious beliefs were far less forgiving than Frances's. He named
Lucy's scarring a sign that God marked her for dam-
nation. "Might I take your cloak, Sir Amyas?"

He didn't glance at her as he slipped his outer garment from his shoulders. Beneath it, he wore a knee-
length brown coat trimmed in black fur and, beneath
that, leather riding breeches and a black doublet studded with pearls. The thick gold chain across his coat's
breast and the pearl pendants pinned to the center of
his scarlet garters, which held his boot tops to his
thighs, made certain no one mistook him for less than
the shire's wealthiest man. As he tossed his cloak
toward the housekeeper, firelight sparked in the gem-
stones peeking from his glove's slitted fingers.

"See to it my party is served a goodly meal and is
accommodated for the night." 'Twas a cold command.
"We'll leave with morn's light."

"As you will, Sir Amyas." Lucy retreated into the
hall, leaving the door ajar behind her.

When she was gone, Amyas looked to his granddaughter, his mouth but a thin crack in the granite

slabs that were his cheeks. Beneath his tangled brows, his eyes narrowed. 'Twas here that Anne found their resemblance; his eyes were like hers, almond shaped and so dark a brown they seemed black.

"I see you yet staff this place with cripples and sinners, despite my command to the contrary."

Anne lifted her chin. "I do as my mother wills." 'Twas a lie. Although Frances didn't deny her daughter's penchant for rescuing those on whom society had turned its back, believing that such a thing befitted one of God's elect, 'twas Anne who pleased herself by doing so.

"Your mother?" her grandsire replied in scorn. "What little wit she ever owned was taken from her during your birth, two and twenty years ago."

Outrage burned in Anne's cheeks at the cruel reminder that she was the cause of Frances's crippling. As she opened her mouth to protest, her mother was but motionless, not witless, Frances's hand tightened on hers. 'Twas a warning against impertinence. Where Amyas could not command, her mother could; however reluctantly, Anne held her tongue.

Amyas started toward them, the pendant pearls on his garters swinging with each step. Halting before the hearth, he reached out and caught Anne by the chin.

"What are you doing?" she cried, and jerked free of his grasp.

Anger sparked in his eyes. "I'll handle my heir as I please."

"What sort of nonsense is this?" Anne retorted. "My sister's death made me my father's heir, not yours. 'Tis my cousin who will take all you own when you're gone."

Amyas's expression flattened. His gaze shifted to the dancing flames on the hearthstone. Lifting a foot, he toed at the logs, until one split in twain with a pop. The pieces dropped to either side of the grate, its exposed heart glowing bright red.

"The damn fool went and broke his neck in a fall from his horse a week ago," he told the hearth, his voice harsh and cold.

"My cousin is dead?!"

Even as the frantic words leapt from her lips, Anne shook her head in refusal. She couldn't be Sir Amyas's heir. A man of the lower gentry, the kind she might marry as heir to Owls House, would welcome a quiet, rural life. Not so the sort of man who panted after Sir Amyas's vast properties. That man would expect a far more social lifestyle, one in which her mother could never be included.

Anne snatched for the only possible escape from this fate. "Even if he is dead, his wife is pregnant. 'Tis her child you want, not me."

Her cry prodded her grandsire into raising his head. For the briefest of moments, his face seemed to be touched with emotion, as if he might truly have been grieving. With his next breath, his expression regained its usual stony lines.

"The stupid cow wouldn't heed me. Upon hearing the news, she grew hysterical and shocked herself into an early labor. Both she and the babe followed him into the grave. She failed me, just as did he, his brother, and your useless sisters. They all failed me: not one of them leaving a child behind them for me to use. You, such as you are, are all I have left. And," he said, reaching out to again catch her chin, his grip unbreakable this time, "I will look upon my heir."

Too shocked to resist, Anne stood still and let Amyas take inventory of her features. The movement of his eyes marked the tiny peak of dark brown hair at the center point of her forehead, the gentle arch of her brows, the short length of her slightly too wide nose and the lush curl of her lips. Lifting his thumb, he touched the wee mole at the corner of her mouth. As he released her, satisfaction glowed like bits of gold in his dark eyes.

"I thought I remembered you as a pretty thing. It will serve you well in your new position."

Anne blinked. Chambermaids and governesses had positions, not gentlewomen. "You mean my wedding," she corrected.

"Do I?" Her grandsire crossed his arms over his chest and rocked back on his boot heels. Smug satisfaction glowed in his dark eyes. "As the final Blanchemain and my sole heir, I can afford to look high for your husband, even into the nobility. 'Tis to attract such a man that I've made you a maid-of-honor to Her Gracious Majesty, the Queen of England." He added the slightest sneer to this, as if he thought Elizabeth Tudor neither gracious nor majestic.

His words struck Anne like a blow. Gasping for air, she whirled on her mother. 'Twas her own panic reflected on half of Frances's face.

Except for her mother's distant cousin, Mary Radcliffe, who was near to Anne's age and had served her queen for almost nine years, Elizabeth's maids-of-honor were mere babes. More importantly, all of them, Mistress Radcliffe included, were virgins. If Anne's age might be forgiven, her lack of purity would not.

She opened her mouth to tell Sir Amyas what he wanted wasn't possible, then bit back the words. His response would be no less violent than the queen's when she told him his only remaining heir was spoiled goods. If he didn't kill her for it, 'twas a sure thing he'd permanently remove her from Owls House. Who, then, would tend her mother?

Terror shot through Anne. If she didn't speak, she would go to court, which meant she'd have to lie to the queen. Elizabeth Tudor was not only England's ruler, she was also the supreme governor of its church. What if the queen could divine that her new maid was spewing lies, then saw her punished for attempting the position under false pretenses? Anne's youthful sin might see her Tower-bound, that's what.

Frances grabbed Anne's hand and tugged. The need to protect her only remaining daughter blazed in her hazel eyes. Staring at her former in-law, she pulled Anne's hand close to her chest to show possession. Her lips moved as she fought to speak. Spittle filled the drooping right side of her mouth.

"Maaan." The slurred sound that left Frances's lips was barely recognizable as the word she meant: mine.

Love and pride filled Anne. Her mother held tight to what little dignity life had left her. To humiliate herself so before Amyas had cost her dearly. That she had done so on behalf of the child whose birth had left her in this state, the same child who had betrayed her love by giving way to lust, was precious.

Bolstered by her mother's sacrifice, Anne set aside her panic and prepared to battle her grandfather. "My mother says I belong to her," she told him. "She has already mourned for three daughters and does not wish to lose another one. She would remind you that you vowed she could keep me for her life's time."

Sir Amyas's brow creased in scornful disbelief. "All that from a single, slobbering sound? I say you put words in her mouth for the sheer joy of defying me."

" 'Tis only her tongue that does not work," Anne flared back, ready to tell him her mother spoke as eloquently as he, using a board with letters painted upon it to communicate her complex thoughts. Ach! This was nothing but an attempt to divert her from the issue at hand. "You gave your word, and we will hold you to it."

The imperious motion of Amyas's hand waved away the whole issue. "What I said all those years ago is now moot. The queen has called for you to come. Would you have me return to court alone, saying you will not serve?"

Anne's eyes narrowed at his clumsy trap. "Tell the queen what you will, then tell her the truth, that you had no right to promise me to her."

Frances tugged on her hand, demanding her attention. Rather than respond, Anne shook free of her grasp, already knowing that her mother wished her to relent. Instead she crossed her arms, denying Frances any further control of her tongue.

Turning, Amyas strode to the parlor's window. Despite the rain that sheeted the thick glass, he stared out at Owls House's garden, his hands folded behind his back. "You are the only one left to me. That promise was offered when I thought your mother was not long for this world," he finally said, his voice quiet.

Anne glared at his back. Damn him, but he was going to break his word and couldn't bear to look upon the one he meant to betray as he did the foul deed. "You are the shire's justice," she said to remind him of the honor expected of a man in his position, the same honor he was forgetting here. "Do this, and I'll name you 'oath breaker.' "

Her grandsire whirled, anger flaring red along his jutting cheekbones at this insult. "Dirty my name at your own peril." There was a dangerous edge to his voice.

Gone too far to back down now, she gave a haughty lift of her brows. "How can the truth be a slur? My mother needs me. I'll not let you take me from her."

Anger didn't disappear from Sir Amyas's face as much as it slid into hiding beneath an icy expression. He almost smiled. "So, 'tis you and you alone your mother needs, is it? If that's the case, then you can do without all the cripples and undesirables who reside here. What a shame that will be. Some of your servants seem so capable. Indeed, your stable master has quite the gift with horseflesh, despite that he wears a cutpurse's slitted ear. That housekeeper is adept, but her face, well—" He shrugged, as if it were quite beyond his ability to prevent Lucy's dismissal.

"You would not." Anne stared at him in horror. Without their employment at Owls House most of their servants would be begging at the crossroads before the week was out.

Amyas flicked at a spot of drying mud upon his glove, a sly smile playing about his lips. "Now that you're my heir, Owls House is under my control until you're wed. I'll not have such servants on one of my properties."

As Anne stared upon defeat, her arms opened, hands returning to her sides. "How could you?" she cried in futile protest. Her high pitched words rang against the delicate white plasterwork covering the parlour's ceiling.

He smiled at her. "The better question is 'How could *you*,' when 'tis but a simple thing you need do to save them," he returned without much passion.

"Nay, you'll not break your word. If you're so needful of an heir that you must steal me from my mother, you should wed again and sire yourself up another batch of brats to use."

As Anne's voice rose to a shout, Amyas's breath hissed from him, his face whitening to a deathly pallor. "What sort of surly bitch speaks so to her grandfather, the man to whom God commands she give her obedience and loyalty?" he barked, his angry words echoing away into a new quiet.

The fire crackled. Rain drummed upon the windowpanes. Outside the parlor's slightly open door, the hall was silent. Sir Amyas's men had closed their mouths and turned their ears toward this argument between their betters.

Frances caught Anne's hand and pulled, seeking her daughter's attention. Anne ignored her to press the point. "Aye, Grandfather, wed again. Truly there is nothing so uncommon in a man remarrying when he must beget more heirs, even a man of your age."

His eyes widened until his dark irises were fully ringed in white. "Say no more," he bellowed.

Again, Frances yanked, this time hard enough to make her daughter gasp in pain and shoot her a startled glance. Anne caught her breath in surprise. Half of Frances's mouth was lifted in a twisted, malicious smile, while in her mother's eyes lived the belief that Amyas was incapable of begetting children. Loosing a strangled sound of amusement, Frances shifted in her chair to look upon Amyas. With her left hand she made a motion to chide him for his lack of manhood. Sir Amyas jerked as if she'd struck him. 'Twas something deeper than rage that filled his face.

"Lying spawn of Satan!" His shout thundered in the quiet room as he launched himself at Frances. The sound of flesh against flesh was loud in the quiet room. Anne screamed in wordless rage as her mother's head slammed against the chair's back.

As Frances cupped her hand to her bleeding lips

and bent, her sobs soundless, Anne thrust herself between them. "What sort of man strikes a cripple?"
she shouted as she drove him back from her mother's
chair with pushes and shoves.

With each backward step the terrible emotion pos-
sessing her grandfather ebbed. As color returned to
his lean cheeks, he grabbed her by the arms and gave
her a shake. "Enough," he snarled. "I'll tolerate no
more impertinence from you. You'll fold your hands
and bow your head before me."

"I think not," Anne sneered, too deep in rage to
think at all. "I tell you now, if she sickens because of
your attack, I'll name you beast. If she dies, I call you
murderer to every man who listens!"

The power of his backhanded blow sent Anne stag-
gering, pain exploding along her jawline. Stars swam
before her eyes in a sea of tears. She fought them
from her eyes. She'd be damned before she cried in
front of him.

Steadying her footing, Anne drew herself up to her
tallest and glared at him. His eyes were mere slits, the
glint within them daring her to give him a reason to
lay more than one blow. Her jaw tightened. Let him.
Better to suffer his beating than to have him think
her cowed by his violence.

Aye, better for her pride, but not for Owls House.
Once he was convinced she wasn't afraid of him for
her own sake, he'd use the residents of her home
against her. If she resisted, she would lose, no matter
what tack she took.

Anne bowed her head and glared at the tawny matting beneath her feet. "My pardon, Grandfather. I was
wrong to speak so to you. I place myself at your command." The false words seared her tongue as they
dropped from her lips.

Sir Amyas freed a pleased hiss. "So you can behave as a proper woman should."

"I pray you, Grandfather, take pity on my mother." She almost choked. There was no pity in this man. "If I am to depart Owls House, she will need familiar faces around her. Leave our servants as they are, and I will be as compliant a maiden as you could desire." It was a promise no truer than the one he'd made to her mother all those years ago. She was neither compliant nor a maiden.

This time, he huffed in disbelief. "You insult me, then beg favors? 'Tis fortunate that I am a charitable man, quick to forgive. As you will, the servants stay."

How easily he returned to her what he had no right to take. As much as it galled her to do it, she gave him what she knew he expected. "My thanks, grandsire."

"Prettily said," he replied as if she were but three and not a woman full grown. "Know you, if I find one harness ring missing from even the meanest of saddles, I'll see the cutpurse hang for it." 'Twas a heavy-handed warning that he meant to hold his threat against Owls House's servants over her head, no doubt until the day she was wedded and bedded.

"Your servants should pack your clothing, your bed, and any chairs you own. We leave for London upon the morrow," he said.

Anne's head shot up out of her meek pose. So soon?! She needed time to think and plan, time to prepare herself to utter blatant falsehoods to her queen.

Her grandfather's lip curled in disdain as he eyed her rain-spotted bodice and plain black skirts. "If all your garments are as poor a quality as this, your clothing chest can remain empty. I'll have a London tailor fill it."

His sneer pricked Anne's anger until it ate her fear. "Will my maid travel with me?" 'Twas more goad than question. Rosalee's nose had been snipped for whoring.

"Nay," he replied, an unwitting victim of her sarcasm, "none of your servants will do. Instead I have employed an upstanding woman as your governess."

"She is here now with you?" Anne asked in surprise. She'd seen no woman in the courtyard. Then again, she hadn't truly looked for one.

This only made Amyas's scorn deepen. "Do you think I'd have you ride without a proper chaperone among so many men? I hope you place more value on your virtue than your words reveal."

Turning, he strode to the parlor door and threw it open. "Mistress Watkins!" he called.

Mistress Watkins scooted into the room, her every movement tight and uncomfortable, dressed from head to toe in modest brown save for the simple white cap atop her mouse-brown hair. She wasn't unattractive, 'twas only the way the woman held her face that made her seem so. When she stopped at the parlor's center, she curtsied, then bowed her head over hands that were more clenched than folded. "Sir Amyas," she said in a proper woman's meek voice.

Amyas made her no response as he turned to Anne. "This is Mistress Patience Watkins. She is a widow who hails from a fine, religious family, a woman of impeccable character." His tone inferred that Anne was not. "I confidently place you in her care."

His words brought Mistress Patience's head up far enough so she might look upon her new charge. Beneath the self-righteousness living in her pale blue eyes was vindictive triumph. Dislike filled Anne. 'Twasn't a governess Amyas had procured for her, but a jailer. Her grandsire's upstanding woman was relishing the idea of holding power over one who was her better in rank. Anne had no doubt Patience would prove to be nothing more than a sanctimonious spy.

"Now, begone from me, taking Patience and your mother with you as you leave," Amyas said. All emotion drained from his face, leaving him looking sallow and old. "I will keep mine own company for the remainder of the day."

Once again, he strode for the window, putting his back to the room. Anne ignored her new keeper to fly to her mother's side. There was a rush of air behind her as, without invitation, Lucy raced into the room. The housekeeper darted past Mistress Patience to join Anne at Frances's chair. Under Anne's new jailer's sharp scrutiny, they lifted the invalid between them, then carried the sobbing woman to the door.

Pain tore through Anne as her mother's head lolled onto her shoulder. Emotional upset was always dangerous for Frances, often being followed by weeks of illness. What if she died whilst Anne was gone? The thought was almost more than she could bear. There had to be some way to escape court attendance and return to Owls House.

Anne's lips curved. There was. Amyas had given her the key to her return when he told her that Owls House would remain under his control until she was wed. 'Twas a husband she needed and where better to find one than at Queen Elizabeth's court? Using her grandsire's wealth as the lure, she'd sift through the offerings seeking the man courageous and powerful enough to resist Sir Amyas, yet compassionate enough to care about those not so fortunate as he. Once she found him, she'd wed him, even in secret if need be.

Aye, but to find this paragon, she would have to deceive her queen. Terror again tried to rise. Anne slaughtered it. If protecting those she held dear required that she lie to God, Himself, then lie she would.

Chapter Three

The setting sun shot rusty beams of light through the small London house's slatted window shutters, presently closed over precious panes of glass. 'Twas illumination enough to explain to Kit why the homeowner rented his abode to trysting courtiers. The place, with its two rooms, one facing the street, the other behind, was as plain a house as he'd ever seen.

Here, in the foreroom, there was no mat upon the floor, and the fireplace was so small its glowing coals barely offered light, much less cheer. What made this all the more astonishing was that, without a kitchen proper, the homeowner did all the cooking at this hearth, or so said the few small pots that sat upon the mantel. Upon the small cabinet beside the hearth stood two cups and a wooden trencher, along the various items needed to maintain a fire and add light to a darkened room.

For seating there was a plain wooden bench and a chair made from a used barrel, sides cut into the appropriate armed form with a bit of planking for a seat. A slab of wood leaned against the plastered brick wall, the legs that would turn it into a table resting on the floor beside it. Indeed, the only thing of value was the writing desk.

The pretty walnut piece stood atop a stool near the

hearth, a lock at the base of its sloping top and a new candle in the wooden holder at its back. A quill lay beside the ink pot, as if Kit's arrival had driven the owner from his room just before he started on his accounts.

Cloak swirling about him, Kit made his way to the reworked barrel. Taking care to drape the edges of his outer garment over its makeshift arms to avoid splinters, he sat, stretching his legs out before him, ankles neatly crossed. A stripe of light from the shutters fell across his lap, making the brown breeches he'd borrowed from Bertie gleam like new.

With nothing to do but wait, Kit watched the light descend with the sun. When it reached the garters at his knees, impatience grew beyond all toleration. He lifted his head to stare at the doorway. God's wounds, but where was the lady?

Perhaps she'd decided not to come. The relief that filled him at this thought put a bitter smile upon his lips. There was a good reason he knew Lady Mont-mercy least of all the queen's ladies-in-waiting. Those who fell into her tender care often found their lives a shambles after she was finished with them.

With a harsh sigh, Kit folded his hands behind his head and leaned back in his chair, his eyes closed. Through the house's cracks and crevices, twilight's breath sighed into the room, London's air rich with the smell of rotting garbage, coal smoke, and the filthy Thames. As the room darkened, so did the day. The folk on the street were hurrying now, trying to finish their last tasks before night was upon them.

Cart wheels squealed. Roosting pigeons purred from just outside the window. Nearby a mother and daughter were shrieking at each other in anger, while from some greater distance, children laughed in play.

Metal scraped on metal: a key being fitted into the front door's lock. Kit straightened in his chair as the street door groaned open. A becloaked woman stepped into the darkened room. She knew her way well, treading with ease through the darkness to the cabinet beside the hearth. There, she took a taper and held its wick to one of the still warm coals on the hearth. The twist of cotton sputtered and hissed, then came to life.

Straightening, Lady Elisabetta Montmercy pushed back her cloak hood, her face bathed in the candle's golden glow. Kit sighed. That evil should own such beauty!

The lady had a doll-like perfection of feature, as if her face was sculpted of glass. Despite her more than two score years, no lines marked her skin and there were few strands of gray in the fair curls that lay against her cheeks. Her eyes gleamed as blue as the Montmercy sapphires.

As their gazes met, the noblewoman's lush mouth lifted into a smile. "Why, Master Hollier, you came." Her voice was sultry and deep.

Kit forced himself to return her smile. "When a woman offers to pay a man's debts, it behooves him to come when she sends for him."

"So it does," she agreed.

Crossing to the desk, she lit the second candle with her own. When she'd set the one beside the other, she loosened her cloak, letting the garment slip from her shoulders to puddle upon the floor around her belling skirts. Kit frowned. She yet wore her court attire, a green doublet, a mannish style the queen was presently affecting, atop pink and green skirts. Christ, she hadn't even removed the wee gem-studded cap upon her head.

If she was going to be so open in conducting their affair, then he'd have none of it. Elizabeth Tudor blinded herself, expediently so, to the immorality in her court, but this she did only so long as the sinners were circumspect. Those exposed in their misdeeds could find themselves disgraced, banished from court, or occupying a chamber either in the Fleet or the Tower.

Stiff fabric crinkled as Lady Elisabetta sat upon the corner of the bench. She tilted her head to the side, her eyes narrowing as she peered at him through the gloom. "What, do I receive no thanks for saving you from incarceration?"

He leaned forward in the chair to brace his elbows on his knees. "My lady, I am at loose ends as to how you even knew of my need. Dare I ask?"

She offered him a tiny smile. "At court for four years, and you must yet pose me such a question? People are talking about you, Master Hollier."

This but confirmed what Kit expected. 'Twas gossip that was the source of her information. "Ah, then, I expect my next point would be to remind you we are but talking about a promise to pay my creditors, not actual payment. I came this night to discover what it is you want from me that would cause the transfer of coins from your hands to theirs."

Her laugh was quiet and deep, the very sound of it an invitation to intimacy. "How impatient you are! I'm not yet ready to discuss business. First, I must chide you for using that goldsmith. Heavens, but he's worse than a highwayman, charging so much for his work. From now on you must use my man."

When Kit said nothing, she spoke on. "Tell me of yourself. I know so little, save that you are close to my son. Of all the gentlemen pensioners our royal mistress keeps, you seem the only one disinterested in making an advantageous marriage. Why did you come to court, if not to promote yourself?"

Kit saw no reason to offer a truthful answer. "I need more than a position as the queen's pensioner if I'm to attract a wife," he said with a shrug, then paused. 'Twas the cultivation of power, not loyalty, that made Lady Montmercy her queen's servant. It could hardly hurt him to seem as if he had no liking for their royal mistress.

"Fool that I am, I came to court believing I could make my fortune from the Hollier name, even if we no longer own our nobility. Little did I know I would be but one among so many other young and impoverished men, all of us dancing to gain our queen's attention so we might suckle the tit of her generosity."

He gave a studied, scornful snort. "Now, is that not a useless exercise? Our fair princess's tits are as dry as her womb is barren." Of all the foul things said by the gentry and peers who disliked their queen, this one was true. When it came to coin, Elizabeth Tudor was as miserly as her grandsire, something of which Kit was all too aware. 'Twas rare when even her faithful secretary, Sir William Cecil or her pet, the earl of Leicester, received more than a word of praise in payment for their efforts on her behalf. This was quite dismaying to her nobles who were accustomed to royal favor coming in coins, not fine words.

This time Lady Montmercy's laugh was pleased. "Indeed, I think our gracious Oriana enjoys watching her courtiers tear each other apart over the mere promise of her favors. No doubt she finds it a more entertaining sport than bear baiting."

Her amusement faded into a small and secret smile. "By the by, I am not diverted. I cannot tell you how

I ache to peel back that crust and discover what it is you conceal beneath it."

Kit snapped his teeth shut on a foul word. She'd not pry into his life with impunity. "What could I possibly have to hide?"

A wicked gleam took life in her eyes. "Surely not shame because your family has lost its nobility?"

His jaw stiffened. This was no meeting, it was a battle. Armed with her verbal daggers, Lady Montmercy was thrusting at him, seeking out vulnerabilities to exploit.

"What shame?" he retorted in mock surprise. "The Holliers have lost and restored Graceton's title as often as the Montmercys have seen theirs slip from their fingers. All the court knows my lord grandsire squandered my brother's inheritance as he sought to rescue displaced monks and save other papists from losing their lands to confiscation. If my brother were willing to sell off the better part of his estate, he'd be a lord once more. But, without the lands, there's no point to the title, is there?"

Her smile took a triumphant twist. "Ah, yes, the reclusive Squire Nicholas Hollier. Odd, but when I think of the two of you I find myself reminded of Cain and Abel."

Kit caught his breath as guilt shifted in his gut. How could she know? He reined in his reaction. She didn't. Most of England believed Nick was crippled. If some might know about the scarring, no one outside of Graceton knew the truth behind Nick's face: 'twas a secret carefully guarded by both family and loyal servants.

When he made no reply, she motioned him forward. "Come and kneel before me so I might better see you."

Rising, he left his cloak in the chair and crossed the room to drop onto one knee before her. Lady Elisabetta studied him, brushing her fingers through his hair as she straightened the golden-brown strands to her own satisfaction. After a moment she nodded. "You're attractive enough, I suppose, although there's too much power in your features for my tastes. I like a prettier man."

Kit cocked a brow at this. Did this mean he didn't have to couple with her to win the repayment of his debts? "You knew my appearance before you made your offer."

Amusement touched her face, and she made a sound of mock concern. "Poor man, have I piqued your vanity by telling you I do not swoon over you?"

With the tip of her finger, she outlined his mouth in a sultry caress, then traced the carefully trimmed beard at his chin. She let her fingers trail down the curve of his neck to rest her hand upon his shoulder. As she fingered the collar of Bertie's blue doublet, the corner of her mouth lifted in scorn. "Good heavens, whatever are you wearing?" she asked, when she knew full well he meant to disguise himself.

Indeed, so concerned had he been at the thought of discovery that he'd untied the ribbons on his shirt's high neck and spread his collar wide, the way a workman might. She toyed with his dangling shirt strings, then used her fingertip to draw a circle on the skin exposed in the vee of his shirt.

"Now then," she said, her voice soft and seductive, "on the morrow our dear monarch will officially accept a new maid-of-honor to serve in her Presence Chamber. 'Tis a strange appointment, this, for the lass has lived her life in isolation from all society. Not only is she a regular Puritan, but she's past a score of years in age, which makes her more spinster than maid."

"What has this to do with me?" he asked in some confusion. As a rule, he kept his distance from the virgins Elizabeth used to emphasize her own supposedly pure state. All save one of those maids were interested in husbands, while he did not wish to wed.

Once again, she trailed her fingertips across his exposed skin. Her lips quirked in pleasure when she drew a shiver from him. "I am wondering if she will find you attractive, this young woman."

He eyed her warily. This was the strangest meeting. She said she didn't wish to bed him, then seemed to be trying to seduce him. "And if she does?"

'Twas a delighted smile bent the noblewoman's fine lips. "Why, you'll take her maidenhead for me, then tell all the court what you've accomplished."

Her words hit him like a punch. Kit sat flat on the floor. "Are you mad?" he cried out. "Those maids have the queen's protection. Elizabeth will throw me in prison for using her. That is, if the girl's male relatives don't kill me first."

"Did I say there'd be no risk?" the lady asked, a glint of vicious laughter in her eyes. "This is what you must do if I'm to pay your debts."

Kit stared at her. If there was one thing in life of which he was absolutely certain, 'twas Lady Montmercy's capability to hate. She was notorious for seeing those who injured her paid in double the coin. He wracked his brain for something he might have done to her that required his destruction. No matter how he worked at it, there was nothing he could put his finger to. Then again, it wasn't beyond her to ruin a man just for the sheer joy of it.

"Why me?" It was a blunt question.

"Because you have no connection to me," she replied. "No one must know 'twas I who engineered the girl's downfall."

So it was the girl she wished to ruin, not him. The noblewoman simply didn't care he might also be destroyed in the process. A touch of pity woke in Kit. What in God's name had that poor country lass done to Lady Elisabetta to warrant so harsh a revenge?

Who cared what the girl had done? All that mattered was how much Lady Montmercy was willing to pay for the wreaking of her vengeance. She'd been right to name this business, for the haggling was about to begin.

He shook his head. "Nay, I'll not do it. Take back your promises. If I'm going to die or rot in prison, I'll do it for my own sins, taking no innocent along with me."

"May God damn all honorable men and you doubly so," she snapped, anger bringing a new pink to her alabaster skin.

This teased a single bark of laughter from Kit. Here was a woman long accustomed to a lackey's panting agreement. "Honorable? Nay, 'tis only that I can see no profit in dying after my debts are paid. What you name rescue, my lady, is no rescue at all."

She frowned and plucked at the great golden brooch pinned to her doublet's breast. As the quiet stretched between them, night crept into the room, curling around the circle of candlelight like a contented cat. Most of the street sounds had stilled. A dog barked as two men sang their way home, pausing to laugh at each other's false notes.

At last her hand fell to her lap. She smiled, but there was no amusement in her eyes. "Do this for me, and I will assist you in the restoration of your family's title."

It was the offer he'd awaited. Deep in Kit's being, the door leading out from under his guilt opened. Even as his heart urged him to lunge for freedom, his head resisted. So far, all she'd offered were words.

"Now, here is something for which I have use, but before I go blithely off to risk my life on your behalf, you'll need to tell me how you intend to achieve this miracle. By the by, if you suggest wedding my brother, I fear I could not countenance such a match." He sent her a chiding look. "The whispers about you, madame. Tut, but I dare not repeat them."

'Twas a nasty little smile she sent his way. "Since you've been listening to rumors, you should also know that my daughter is newly widowed. If I wed Arabella to your brother, her dowry along with her jointure from her previous union will do all you desire."

Kit froze. It would, indeed. Moreover, Lady Arabella Purfoy was her mother's opposite, being sweet-natured and plain. All in all, she would make a perfect mate for Nick.

Even as he reached for freedom, it slipped from his grasp. Nick would never agree to this, and not just because of his scarring. Unlike Kit, who was now comfortable with the queen's religion, Nick would never accept a Protestant wife.

With that, the door in his heart slammed shut. As it closed, Kit saw himself for the desperate and careless fool he was. How could he believe, even for a moment, that Lady Elisabetta would squander her only daughter on the destruction of some unknown Puritan miss?

"You'll do it, then?" she prodded.

"Did I say that?" His voice was choked and hard. "Nay, I was but sitting here on this cold floor waiting for you to explain why some innocent virgin's downfall is worth your daughter's value on the marriage market."

She shot off the bench, her eyes blazing. "You'll die in prison before I explain myself to you," she shouted. "Get you gone from me!"

Kit's brows rose. Well, well, well! He wasn't the only desperate soul in this room. Perhaps all was not as hopeless as he'd thought. He set himself to testing the limit of her need to see the girl destroyed.

Coming to his feet, he brushed the dust from the back of Bertie's breeches, then fished the door key she'd given him from his dagger's sheath, the thing too bulky to be confined in his purse. Setting it upon the mantel, he swept Bertie's short-crowned hat from his head and offered the lady his deepest bow. As he straightened, he winked.

"By God, my lady, but you're lovely when you're angry. My heart fair breaks at the thought that I am to be no longer in your company." He crossed the room to fetch his cloak from the chair, then started for the door.

"Stay." 'Twas a cold command.

Kit paused a beat, then looked over his shoulder at her. Only the slight rise and fall of her breasts within the confines of her bodice testified that she wasn't statuary. "To what end?" he asked. "I'll not do your deed unless you explain why you trade your daughter's hand in marriage for the ruination of a single girl . . . and you'll not tell."

Pain came to life in her eyes as her gaze shifted to the room's far wall. "Call it idle curiosity on my part." Her voice trembled. She stopped to clear her throat. "I wish to know if Puritan maids can be seduced in the same way as those who are not so holy."

Astonishment exploded in Kit. Her dodge said far

more than she knew. Someone had hurt her deeply enough that she was willing to marry her daughter to Nick in order to revenge herself.

He turned back into the room. "To marry my brother, Arabella must agree to convert to the Roman faith."

Lady Montmercy shrugged. "In the last twenty years, we've all shifted faiths a time or two with this king or that queen. I doubt my daughter will protest."

Kit nodded, accepting this. 'Twas a common complaint among the more fervent of England's Protestants that church services were still filled with Roman imagery, making it too easy for the weak-willed to regress into the realm of popish evil. "You'll also pay my creditors."

"God's eyelid, but you want it all," she snapped.

"Not so, madame," he replied with a grin. "I can hardly go about a seduction if I am confined for my debts. Aye, and we'll have a written contract between us. In it, you'll list exactly what it is I do in trade for using your Puritan miss. Until my debts are paid and you've scribed your name and set your ring upon such a contract, I'll not even glance at this lass of yours."

She freed a short, sharp breath. "This is the problem with clever men."

Taking a far smaller key from her purse, she turned to the householder's desk and opened the locked top. From its interior she retrieved a length of thick paper, which she handed to him. "You'll find I was prepared for you."

Kit sat upon the corner of the bench, dropping his cloak over its back, to scan what she'd written. He drew an astonished breath. It was all here, the betrothal of her daughter to his brother, the repayment of his debts.

"How?" he demanded, looking up at her.

"I have my sources," she replied, adding a tiny smile to drive home just how resourceful she'd been.

As he again turned his attention to the contract, he took care to read every word of what she'd written. In return for Nick's marriage and the coins to repay his debts, he was to seduce and publicly reveal the ruination of one Mistress Anne Blanchemain. His eyes caught on the family name.

Last he'd heard all the Blanchemains were dead, except for Old Amyas, the remaining grandson having passed only the previous month in a hunting accident. And good riddance it was. Walter Blanchemain and his brother had been officious boors, while their grandsire spouted too much religion for Kit's taste, Sir Amyas having been converted by the Calvinists whilst in exile during the reign of Mary Tudor. To Kit's way of thinking, such zealotry combined with the ruthless persistence of a social climber made for an unholy mix.

"Is this maid of yours related to Sir Amyas Blanchemain?" he asked.

Lady Elisabetta nodded. "She is his sole, surviving grandchild."

With that, a piece of the puzzle the noblewoman presented to him fitted into place. Kit pursed his lips as he looked up at her. "So you will use the girl to wound Sir Amyas?" Nay, 'twas a deathblow not a wound she meant to deal the old man. Kit doubted Old Amyas would survive the shame of being made a laughingstock by the impoverished scion of a Catholic family.

All expression left her face. "Best that you keep your mind on the deed at hand." The coldness of the lady's voice suggested it would be dangerous to pry for more.

"Just so," Kit agreed, " 'tis none of my affair." That

was, none of it was his affair if he wanted to force Nick into marriage. "What happens if I fail?"

She arched a perfect brow. "For your sake, pray that you do not. As my debtor, I'll have no choice but to see you imprisoned for what you owe me. I doubt you'd find your stay in the Fleet conducive to your health." The threat was clear. The price of failure was the same as the reward for success: death.

Kit nearly laughed. What did he care? Whether he succeeded or failed, Nick would have to wed, but only in success was he guaranteed that Graceton's title would be restored to Nick. He handed the paper back to her.

"One clause wants addition. You must write that Arabella cannot refuse my brother because of physical deformity, frailty, or scarring."

"As you will," she replied without hesitation. The quill scratched across the paper. When she was done, she scrawled her name at the page's bottom and handed him the quill. "We'll both put our names on this."

A tiny breath of a laugh left Kit. She wasn't about to let this contract of theirs out of her sight without being certain they'd both be ruined were he to expose it. But what was there to guarantee she'd not try to retrieve it and renege on her part of the bargain, should he die in success?

Slow, cool amusement filled him. She could hardly do so, if someone other than himself held the contract. Aye, and the man to do it was Lord Andrew Montmercy. Lady Elisabetta's son hated his mother. The young nobleman would see his dam paid dearly should she try to misuse his friend.

Secure in that thought, Kit stood to add his name beneath hers. Once he had and she'd sanded the ink, she folded the sheet, then dribbled wax onto the fold.

She pressed her signet into the hot mass, then moved aside so Kit could do the same.

When it was done she nodded, pleased. "On the morrow, you'll arrive early in the Presence Chamber and stay near the queen's chair. I want you at hand in case an opportunity appears whereby I can tie you to the girl."

"As you will, my lady," Kit said as he took the packet. The feel of the paper against his palm was startling, almost wondrous. So this is what life without guilt was like.

"You may go." Lady Elisabetta gave a dismissing wave of her hand. "From this point on, you'll not so much as even glance toward me at court. I want no one to suspect our connection. If we must meet again, it will be here. Send your servant to the one who dwells here, and she'll arrange it."

Kit came to his feet. "Shall I send my man to escort you to your destination?"

Surprise flashed across her face as if his offer startled her. Her face softened for the briefest of instants, then returned to its previous static perfection. She shook her head. "Nay, I am staying the night."

Kit's brows lifted. Did this mean there'd soon be a better-looking man keeping her company? 'Twas an odd mingling of relief and regret that washed over him. He caught himself wondering if he was missing anything by not bedding her. Temptation dissolved with his next breath. Some things were better left unknown.

"Then, I bid you a good evening, my lady, and take my leave." Grabbing his cloak up from the bench, he made his escape, his goal the alehouse three streets down where he'd left Bertie seducing both the brewer's daughters.

Chapter Four

Kit yawned as he strode along the long gallery leading to Whitehall's Presence Chamber. The dream had returned last night with more clarity than he usually suffered in London. He put this to how much Mistress Blanchemain's arrival at court meant to him.

As always, there was a crowd before the Presence Chamber door. Of these folk, some were servants waiting upon their betters, while others were those whose rank was below that of gentleman. This lack of stature meant they had to wait until they were called into their queen's presence.

Stopping before the door and its two guards, dressed in uniforms of scarlet and silver, he pulled at his doublet's hem. Bertie had nearly murdered him before he'd finally settled on his green doublet atop his better gold and yellow slashed breeches with tall brown boots gartered above his knees. 'Twas a rust-colored coat he wore thrown over one shoulder, as was the fashion, and a brown cap upon his head. Bertie's nerves aside, Kit was glad he'd fussed, for confidence glowed as brightly in his heart as did the golden beads that decorated the front of his doublet.

When the usher didn't immediately appear behind

the guards' crossed pikes, Kit frowned in impatience. "Can you let me in, Dickon?" he asked of the guard to the right.

As were most of Elizabeth's guardsmen and gentle-men pensioners, Dickon was tall and fair of face; the queen liked fine-featured men of height. The man winked. "You'll owe me and Will a bit of something wet, then," he said as the two of them raised their pikes to allow him entry.

"Tonight, it is," Kit grinned. Such was the value of including the guardsmen among his drinking companions.

Confidence shattered as he stepped into the chamber. Kit came to an abrupt halt to stare. Caught in the bright light streaming through the chamber's tall, paned windows, the crowd within these walls glowed. There were doublets of the deepest of orange, pale green, and cherry-red paired with breeches of deep blue or scarlet or clear yellow. Bright ribbons tipped with precious metal held embroidered and slashed sleeves in place, while a king's ransom in jewels deco-rated hatbands, ears, fingers, and fronts of doublets.

Against all the satin and silk in the room, his attire seemed dull as lead. How would Sir Amyas's grand-daughter ever notice him in all this glitter? 'Twas with the potential of failure nibbling at him that Kit set himself to finding a place in the room that was both near the queen's chair and in the heiress's line of sight as she entered the door.

Three years ago, such a thing would have been eas-ily accomplished. Not so this season. Elizabeth was keeping those peers she least trusted trapped in atten-dance. Since no nobleman went anywhere without a goodly retinue, the Presence Chamber was unusually crowded.

Near the entrance to the queen's Privy Chamber, he caught the glimmer of golden wall hangings where no one stood. Although somewhat distant from the public door, it would have to do. He started toward it, making his way with care through the crowd.

"Kit!" At ten years younger than Kit's seven and twenty, Lord Andrew Montmercy's voice still tended to slide between a youth's tenor and a man's depths.

The lordling, dressed in blue and red beneath his fur-trimmed coat, stood midway across the room. Although his hair was almost black and his eyes so deep a blue they sometimes appeared brown, Lord Andrew's features were the masculine reflection of his mother's beauty. Aye, and well he knew how his face affected the opposite sex, being already the father of several bastards.

"You will come stand with us, Kit." The lordling shouted his command across the room.

At this display of arrogance, Sir Edward Mallory pressed a hand against his brow in dismay. Ned was the younger brother of Sir Richard Mallory, Lord Montmercy's warden. Like his elder sibling, the young knight despaired over Lord Andrew, fearing he would never learn control. It was for the purpose of encouraging the start of sense in Andrew that Sir Richard had asked Ned, Kit, and their friends to wear the Montmercy badge.

Ned's brows rose, his hazel eyes filled with a silent plea for aid with his charge. Kit gave way with a sigh, working around the earl of Pembroke's party to stop before them. Doffing his cap, he offered them a brief bow as was due their higher rank. "Good morrow, my lord. Ned."

"Have you heard?" Lord Andrew demanded, the diamond in his earbob glinting as he looked up at Kit.

"Old Amyas's heiress is to be presented this day. I wonder if the parvenu's granddaughter is fair of face. If so, I may woo her, just to spite him." As did others with ancient titles and noble names, Andrew scorned those families newly come to the gentility, many of whom had their roots in trade as did Sir Amyas, the lawyer son of a London draper.

"Bite your tongue, my lord," Ned commanded his charge, his eyes narrowed as he set a hand on his hip, his fingers splaying on the flared hem of his yellow satin doublet. Beneath that garment Ned wore a pair of short, ballooning breeches in the newest shade, called "goose turd" green. Of all of Kit's companions, the golden-haired knight tread closest to being a popinjay. "Need I remind you that Sir Amyas is a friend to your warden, my brother?" the young knight chided.

'Twas generations of inbred arrogance that put the snarl on Andrew's face. The youth slapped his side where his sword would have hung, had the queen allowed weapons in her presence. "You dare to so speak to me?!"

Hiding his amusement at the lad's bluster, Kit lay a restraining hand upon the young nobleman's shoulder. Even though there was no longer a lord at Graceton, the Hollier name retained shades of its ancient nobility, thus Andrew tolerated more interference from him. "My lord, are you so hotheaded that you cannot see our Ned is trying to save you from yourself?" he asked, his voice soothing. "Mistress Blanchemain is to be the queen's maid. Trifle with her, and you're liable to find yourself either sitting in the Tower or wed to her."

Lord Andrew's jaw was yet stiff with damaged pride. "If you say so, Kit," he replied.

"And so I do," he replied, "but that doesn't mean we cannot all look our fill upon this newcomer. I think I know a spot near the Privy Chamber door that will give us an unobstructed view of the room. Will you stand there with me, my lord?"

"Aye," the lordling said, his pique replaced with anticipation of the newcomer's arrival.

Kit glanced at Ned. "Left?"

Needing no further explanation than this, Ned nodded and slipped to stand at Montmercy's left, while Kit stood at his right. "This way, my lord," Ned said, once the young lord was caught between them.

They made this seem a friendly escort rather than the guard it was as they led him along the windows, then behind the queen's cushioned chair with its cloth-of-silver canopy. The route was the one least likely to bring the lad to blows.

Kit had barely pressed his back into the golden draperies when Lord Andrew lifted a hand. "There's our John," the lad said as he waved.

Tall, even by the queen's standards, Master John Fayrfax's shoulders were broad beneath his blue doublet. A month ago his garment had been trimmed in silver buttons; now they were brass. John had invested in the same venture as Kit. Although his finances weren't quite as desperate, he'd had to surrender his buttons to pay his gambling debts. The gentleman smiled as he saw his companions.

Excusing himself from the group of men with whom he'd been chatting, Master Fayrfax started across the room, threading his way through the crowd with all the finesse of rampaging bull. As each man he struck whirled and reached for his nonexistent weapon, John would pause long enough to bow in apology, his broad

face and well-made features displaying naught but a
congenial innocence.

"My pardon," he'd say, his south country accent
heavy in every syllable, "but 'tis so close in here."

Ned laughed and shook his head. "Someday a man
will comprehend that this jostling of his was no accident and our Johnnie will die for his game," he whispered to Kit.

Kit loosed a snort at the very concept. "Not as long
as he owns his face and that accent, he won't. No man
can ever think him anything but a hopeless country
bumpkin."

"This is the perfect spot in the room," John said in
approval as he stopped before them.

"For what?" Ned asked.

"Why, to see the heiress." Avarice flared in John's
blue eyes. "I hear she's worth a thousand pounds a
year, and I mean to make every shilling of it mine."

Kit's confidence sagged like a pair of ungartered
stockings. It hadn't occurred to him he'd have to fight
off a friend in order to make use of the girl.

The usher stepped into the room and there was a
break in the general tumult of voices. One by one,
groups quieted as Master Bowyer banged the foot of
his staff against the floor. As the chamber was car-
peted with thick matting, stained a rich brownish hue,
all he achieved was a dull thud. "Sir Amyas
Blanchemain and Mistress Anne Blanchemain," he
shouted in announcement.

His words echoed into a new silence so deep Kit's
ears rang with it. To a man, the occupants turned to
watch the heiress enter. He stared. Why hadn't he
realized that every man in all England would have an
interest in Old Amyas's granddaughter? Indeed, even
those already married were ogling, no doubt thinking

on the rich fee they might win if they could arrange her union to some friend or relative.

Confidence took a mortal wound, then bled to death on the matting beneath Kit's feet. With so many men offering her honest marriage where he was not, what chance would he have for a seduction? His stomach soured. None, unless Lady Montmercy worked some miracle.

It was a moment before Sir Amyas moved into his field of vision. The old zealot wore a fur-trimmed, floor-length black robe belted atop his doublet and breeches, with a black cap upon his head. Kit leaned forward, peering around the man in front of him.

At his first glimpse of Amyas's granddaughter, all hope of restoring Nick's title via the bedchamber shattered. Mistress Anne was not only wealthy, she was beautiful. Framed in the semicircular flare of her scarlet headdress, her face was a smooth oval, her dark brows peaking over eyes so deep a brown a man could lose his soul in them. From her center part, gentle wings of brown hair swooped against her cheekbones before being caught into the confines of her headdress. 'Twas a cunning little mole at the corner of her mouth that drew attention to the full line of her lips.

"By God, but Sir Amyas spared no coin in dressing her," John whispered in awe.

Kit blinked. How could he not have noticed her attire? Mistress Blanchemain glittered, her bodice and underskirt made of golden brocade strewn with tiny rubies, her red velvet kirtle trimmed with thick, golden lace. A massive brooch set with more tiny rubies held the one piece overdress closed at her waistline.

A tiny frown pleated her brow, and she caught her lower lip in her teeth. At this sign of nervousness, pity unwound from some hidden portion of Kit's gut. How well he remembered his own dread over his presentation at court. What had been difficult for him must be horrifying to one who had been raised in isolation from all society. Moreover, where he'd found welcome from the other young and impoverished men at court, she could hope to find no quarter from those watching her. The men in this room were more like a pack of hunting dogs surrounding a wounded hart, each vying to be the one to make the kill.

She glanced at the party to the right of Kit's, her gaze sliding from man to gawking man. Her look skimmed John, lingering just a bit, then slipped past Lord Andrew, skipped Ned completely to rest on him. For the brief instant that his gaze met hers Kit let his lips lift into what he hoped might be a reassuring smile. It wasn't much, but this bit of friendliness was all he had to offer her.

Rather than move on to the next man, her gaze stayed on him. Her lips parted slightly. New interest shimmered in her dark eyes.

Kit's smile faded. There was something strange in the way she watched him, as if she thought to find some message hidden in his eyes. The sensation was unnerving and oddly intimate.

Still, she watched him, until her gaze felt like a touch against his skin. Kit drew a swift breath as her strange interest stirred the most carnal of his desires. Lady Montmercy was wrong, Sir Amyas's granddaughter was no Puritan miss, for no religious woman looked at a man like that.

Triumph rose from the ashes of what only moments before had seemed certain defeat. She found him attractive.

'Twas a different sort of smile that turned his lips this time. My, but lust was a fine thing to feel, especially when the bedchamber was just where he needed to be with this woman. The seducing of Mistress Anne Blanchemain was going to be pleasant, very pleasant indeed.

Anne stared at the gentleman in the gold-spangled doublet. Unlike every man around him, 'twasn't greed that shone from his marvelous green eyes. Instead what she saw was a welcoming kindness, as if he were commiserating with her on the ordeal of her introduction. This compassion of his teased her into further study.

What an interesting face he had, not truly handsome, but compelling. His features were long and thin, his nose arching forcefully out from below his brow. Perhaps it was in an effort to soften the harshness that he wore his golden-brown hair slightly longer than was the fashion and kept his chin beard neatly trimmed so his well-made mouth might be emphasized. She liked his eyes best of all. Set beneath gently arching brows, their color was a deep and true green.

As she stared at him, something dark and warm glimmered into life in the depths of his gaze. A slow smile uncurled along his lips, then his eyelids lowered, just a little. As his mouth softened Anne caught her breath in surprise. He found her attractive.

Deep in the core of her being, an answering flame woke, stirring her long banked desires. As the heat grew, it brought with it the image of this man pressing his mouth to hers. Warmth flowed through her. Although it had been almost seven years since the beginning and end of her fall from innocence, her body had not forgotten the pleasure of a man's touch.

She stomped on her reaction, driving all such thoughts deep within her. 'Twas dangerous to indulge herself in any emotion until she was certain she'd found the man she needed. Tearing her attention from him, she forced herself to survey the rest of the crowd in the chamber.

The corners of her mouth lifted in amused disbelief. Someone had let a rainbow run riot among England's highest born men. The courtiers gleamed jewel bright, one man in a coat, doublet, breeches, all but his tall-crowned hat, of the most incredible shade of lavender. Now, if only they smelled as sweet as they looked. The room reeked of too many warm bodies in too small a place along with scent of a hundred different perfumes.

Anne coughed lightly against the mélange. Although 'twas but a small sound, it seemed to jar those who stared at her from their greed-induced trances. As one, the courtiers turned their fickle attention back to their comrades and enemies. In the space of a breath, the Presence Chamber once again thundered with the sound of their voices.

Now that she was no longer the center of attention, Anne let her gaze skip around the room a second time, more interested in its furnishings than its occupants. Her attention came to rest upon the cushioned chair beneath the silver canopy. Here would England's queen sit.

Anne's stomach set to tumbling and jumping like a hare with the hounds after it. If only she were familiar with the face of her mother's cousin, Mistress Mary Radcliffe. Mistress Mary had been a friend, kind and true, to Anne's recently departed sister, Eliza. To have even a potential companion among all these strangers would have been calming, indeed.

She sneered at herself. Her kinswoman was no more likely to forgive her her lies than was England's queen.

The certainty of doom settled heavily on her shoulders. What sort of fool thought she could deceive God's chosen monarch?

Sir Amyas leaned close. "Smile," he hissed, jerking his head to the left, "here comes Lord Deyville to meet you."

Anne looked in the direction her grandsire indicated. Dressed all in black, a man with a crooked nose worked his way through the crowd toward them. His black cap wasn't big enough to hide his balding pate, his hair having receded to naught but a narrow, silvered ring around his head. Despite his age, Lord Deyville's shoulders were yet powerful beneath his coat, his build still trim. Given that his pale gray eyes were aimed at her grandsire, not her, Anne dismissed him as a potential suitor. It was just as well he wasn't interested. Rightly or wrongly she had her heart set on a younger man, one with whom she could share the better part of her life.

As the nobleman stopped before them, Sir Amyas swept his cap from his head and bowed as deeply as his aged joints would allow. Anne dropped into a respectful, but brief curtsy. When they rose, Sir Amyas extended a friendly hand in a far more intimate greeting.

"My Lord Deyville, it has been too long," he said with a broad grin. The motion of his mouth made time peel away, revealing just how handsome a man he'd once been.

Anne stared. She hadn't even known her grandsire could smile. That he did so for Lord Deyville could only be a sign of how deeply he respected and admired this man.

Lord Deyville answered Sir Amyas's grin with a weaker expression of pleasure, just wide enough to show he yet owned all his teeth, something Amyas could no longer claim. There was no spark of friendship in his eyes, saying he expected Amyas's respect, but didn't return the emotion. "Indeed, it has," he replied as he caught the knight's hand in his.

With these pleasantries addressed her grandfather crossed his arms over his chest, and his expression took a mournful twist. "My lord, as much as I regret the need, might I offer you my condolences on the loss of your son? He was a man of virtue, who will be sorely missed. I do not doubt that he now dwells with the elect in our Lord's house. I pray your faith gives you the strength to endure his passing."

Lord Deyville gave a deep sigh. "My thanks, Sir Amyas. Would that I did not need to offer you the same sentiments upon your grandson's passing. Such is the bane of folk who live too long, as we have. We must sometimes watch those we cherish reach heaven before us." His gaze shifted from Amyas to Anne, and new heat flared in the cool depths of his eyes.

Revulsion roiled in her. 'Twas one thing for the young man across the room to lust after her. In so old a man as Lord Deyville, it seemed nigh on sinful.

" 'Tis fortunate you yet have your granddaughter to serve as an heir," he told Sir Amyas without removing his gaze from that man's granddaughter. No sign of what his eyes told her was reflected in his voice.

"Hardly a triumph, that," Sir Amyas replied with a harsh snort. "Despite that I am His most faithful of servants, our heavenly Father sees fit to leave me with naught but this weak and foolish woman, incapable of carrying forward my name."

At the same time he offered Anne this insult, Amyas's fingers tightened on her arm, the pressure meant to force her into extending her hand. Only by the

barest of margins did Anne manage not to roll her
eyes in frustration. Did he think she meant to court
disaster by insulting her betters? Nay, 'twas more
likely her grandfather believed she'd already forgotten
yesterday's lecture over how she must behave while
in the Presence Chamber. Anne set her kidskin-clad
fingers into the cup of Lord Deyville's gloved palm.

"My lord, may I present Mistress Anne Blanchemain,
the fourth and only surviving daughter of my second
son, Richard," Amyas said.

'Twas Anne's cue to drop into a deep curtsy with a
graceful bend of her knees. The nobleman's hand
closed tightly around hers, his thumb moving in a soft,
suggestive circle atop her knuckles. Anne came bolt
upright at this intimate caress.

Lust and amusement tangled in Lord Deyville's pale
eyes, his smile widening into the grin of the hunting
wolf. With a frown, she gave her hand a tiny tug to
prod him into freeing her. He didn't. Instead, with her
fingers yet trapped in his, he let his gaze drift from
her face down past her shoulders to the deep, square-
cut neckline of her bodice.

As was the custom for unmarried women, Anne
wore her shirt open, baring a triangular patch of skin
from the bottom of her ruff to the top of her bodice.
This left the tops of her breasts exposed almost to
their nipples. Until this day the style had never made
her feel uncomfortable. Now, as Deyville occupied
himself in a pointed study of those generous curves,
she fought the urge to spread her free hand across her
exposed chest.

She glanced at Sir Amyas, certain he would be outraged with his acquaintance's bold and inappropriate
behavior. Although Amyas's jaw was tense, his eyes

were decidedly blank. Anger joined Anne's revulsion. He was blinding himself, apurpose!

"How now, Amyas, but I see why you saved her for last. She's the best of the lot," Deyville said to Anne's cleavage.

Setting aside any facade of politeness, Anne yanked her fingers from his grasp. Twisted pleasure flared in the man's eyes, fed by the thrill of the chase. Anne's anger grew. Here was another man like her grandfather, one who believed her easily used and helpless to stop him. More fool him for misjudging her.

Now that he'd finished toying with her, at least for the moment, Deyville glanced to her grandfather. "Did I tell you my wife ails? May God preserve her, I fear her illness will be fatal."

Anne gaped at him, stunned. The cad! What sort of man attempted a seduction while his wife lay upon her deathbed? Not the sort with whom she wished to have an acquaintance.

"Is that so?" Sir Amyas replied.

At his speculative tone Anne turned her even more shocked gaze on her grandsire. His mouth was pursed in consideration. "Have I told you I've acquired new properties of late?" he offered, his eyes narrowing into a horse trader's squint.

Lord Deyville straightened at his words. Greed washed the lust from his expression. "Indeed? Where and how many acres are attached to them?"

With that, the two of them circled into a strange dance of words, where the profits of wool and wheat, along with new modes of architecture, became a way of discussing a marriage contract without openly admitting the groom was not yet a widower. Within minutes 'twas clear that, should the nobleman's wife pass on to what was certainly the poor woman's deserved heavenly reward, Anne would be the next Lady Deyville.

Anne's heart went through the floorboards. Perhaps Sir Amyas was not as deluded as she thought. Revulsion grew at the thought of wedding Lord Deyville.

This could not be. In her need to escape this fate, Anne bowed her head and begged God to spare Deyville's poor wife, at least long enough for her to find the man right for her and Owls House.

At the back of the room, a door creaked open and a man entered. Another usher, or so his baton said. Like the man who stood at the public door, this man banged his staff upon the matting.

"Her Royal Majesty, Elizabeth, Queen of England, France, Ireland, and Wales!" he shouted, then dropped onto one knee.

Chapter Five

As the call resonated 'round the chamber, Anne's stomach once more set to dancing in a dreadful mixture of excitement, awe, and terror. All around her, men removed their headgear. Fabric rustled, bones creaked, and joints snapped as every one of them bowed before the unmarried woman who ruled them, leaving Anne and the few other women in the chamber to curtsy. Even though Anne bowed her head as she knew she must, that didn't stop her from peering up at her queen.

On this day Elizabeth Tudor was a study in black and white. Pearls played out a whimsical design on her black overskirt and black sleeves, while the same pattern was repeated in black embroidery and jet beads on her white underskirt and bodice. Her ruff fitted perfectly beneath her chin and jaw. A tiny, brimless cap thickly sewn with pearls and jet sat atop the queen's upswept fiery red-gold hair.

A smile lifted the corners of Anne's mouth. Elizabeth's bodice was styled like a man's doublet, being high necked and close-fitting, and her cap did not cover her hair. Both were fashions Amyas denounced, proclaiming any woman who dressed so an abomination before God.

A small group of women followed England's monarch to her cushioned chair. Anne eyed them in consideration, knowing these were the ladies-in-waiting and Elizabeth's maids-of-honor. 'Twas a simple thing to tell the married from the unmarried women. While the ladies all dressed in bright colors, the virgins wore white kirtles atop more colorful bodices and underskirts.

Among this purer set only one was close to her own age. The young woman was plump, with dark hair gleaming beneath a green headdress trimmed with golden threads, her bodice and skirt made of a green and gold fabric. A golden belt set with amber held her white kirtle closed at the waist. Anne watched her, certain this must be Mistress Radcliffe.

As England's queen settled herself atop the cushions filling her chair, curling her slender, silk-clad hands over its thick arms, the occupants of the room straightened. This left nothing for Anne to see but the backs of men's heads. Folding her hands before her, she stared at her entwined fingers and stoked her courage for the coming ordeal.

"Call them," Elizabeth said, or at least Anne assumed it was the queen. So strong and impatient a female voice could only belong to royalty. "We'd be done with this as soon as possible. 'Tis too fine a day to spend within doors."

Anne pitied the persons toward whom the queen's impatience was aimed. There was something in the royal voice that said England's ruler wasn't the forgiving sort. Again the crowd shifted as men moved back from the queen's chair to leave an open space for the coming stream of penitents and plaintiffs.

The motion seemed to be a signal for those courtiers with no interest in the queen's business to return to their conversation, albeit with voices somewhat lowered. In the room's far corner, someone set to plucking at a lute. Of the queen's women, a few moved out into the crowd, greeting men they knew. Fewer still clung to the chair's back to listen, while the rest, the dark-haired maid among them, dropped to sit behind their royal mistress's throne, finding seats upon the low chairs or cushions that had been placed there. One produced a deck of cards, and a game began.

The same usher who announced the queen's arrival stepped to the center of the room. "Come forward, Sir Amyas Blanchemain and Mistress Anne Blanchemain."

Anne started. It was toward *her* that her monarch's impatience was aimed! Panic surged through her. This was an omen, portending naught but disaster. She should run whilst she still had the chance.

Before she could turn toward the exit, Sir Amyas caught her arm and drew her close to him. He took a step. Fighting to breathe, Anne tried to follow him, but her feet refused to leave the plaited floor matting. Amyas's jaw stiffened, and he leaned his head to the side.

"Is it your intent to make me drag you to that royal bitch's feet?" he breathed to her through the corner of his mouth. "If you force me to make a spectacle of you, know that it won't be only you who rues the day you shamed me."

Resentment steadied Anne's fluttering stomach, while anger pinned her heart into its proper place. This time, when he started forward, she strode boldly at his side. By God, she'd see 'twas he who rued the day he forced his granddaughter into so dangerous a position. Never mind that it was her own sin that created the danger.

As they stepped into the open area before the queen's chair, Anne took stock of the woman who would be her new mistress. In the midst of her third decade of life, Elizabeth was still handsome, despite her somewhat thin lips and slightly hooked nose. As was usual with those whose hair was so fiery a red, the queen's skin was delicate and pale. Her brows were bare wisps of red-gold hair, her eyes large and almond shaped. Anne blinked in surprise. She and the queen shared the same almost black eye color.

"Ah, there you are, Sir Amyas," Elizabeth said as they approached, her lips lifting into a smile that was neither warm nor welcoming.

Anne glanced behind the queen's chair at the plump maid, the one she hoped was Mistress Radcliffe. The dark-haired woman's amber eyes glowed as she smiled in what was surely welcome. There was no time for Anne to return the gesture as she and her grandfather knelt before their queen, Sir Amyas once again removing his cap as Anne bowed her head.

So they stayed, waiting leave to look upon their monarch's majesty. The queen said nothing. As the quiet stretched, Anne shifted. Even through her many petticoats and her farthingale, the rubies that trimmed her skirt were biting into her knees.

"So, Sir Amyas," Elizabeth said long after the silence had become uncomfortable, "you would bring your final grandchild to serve us." A touch of sardonic amusement colored her voice. "How amazed we are at this turn of events. After all, you've called our court a den of iniquity, because the woman who rules remains unwed against what you say is God's ordained order."

This comment provoked a low rumble of laughter from the listening courtiers. Beside Anne, Sir Amyas stiffened. She shot her grandsire a sidelong glance. Eyes narrowed to mere slits, Amyas's gaze was burning holes through the hems of his monarch's skirts. His mouth twisted in disgust.

Beneath worry for herself, a touch of satisfaction woke in Anne. How it must gall him that a woman should hold such power over him. Yet here he must kneel in impotent silence as his queen speared at him, while he was incapable of lifting a hand to shield his pride from puncture.

"I fear mine enemies have carried tales to Your Majesty's ears, meaning to discredit me," he said, his voice low.

"Tales?" Elizabeth gave the word an actor's dramatic emphasis. "We have always considered things said in Parliament as even more public than what is uttered before our royal person. You not only complained about our court, you decried our services as papist and called our chapels blasphemous, filled as they are with what you call popish symbols."

Sir Amyas drew a swift breath as he struggled for some way to deny opinions Anne had heard him express often enough during her few weeks with him. His shoulders sagged when he realized he could not. "Majesty, you know me as a good and loyal servant, with the crown's interest ever in my heart. If in speaking my mind, I have rendered myself detestable in Your Majesty's eyes, then I beg you to deprive me of my position as your justice. I place myself at your mercy."

Anne gave her grandsire credit for his courage, then despised him for his stiff-necked pride. Rather than an apology, his words were an attempt to call his monarch's bluff as he nigh on dared her to do her worst to him.

"As you should," Elizabeth agreed. "Indeed, as every man in this room should place themselves at our mercy." Her voice rose as she gave odd emphasis to these words. " 'Tis fortunate for you that we are a most forgiving and patient prince."

Anne could almost feel her grandsire sneer at this. "Know you, Majesty," Amyas assured his monarch, "my prayers ever beg our Lord God to keep you, preserving your life and health. Madame, will you look upon my granddaughter?" he asked, plowing gracelessly into an attempt to steer his queen where he willed her to go. "I am certain you will find she is more than a fit servant for you, with years of service to her invalid mother to recommend her."

Those of the queen's women who listened gasped, while in the room, men chuckled. Anne sagged in disbelief. How could her grandfather not realize what he'd just said? If he didn't take care, Amyas would see them both dead for his unfortunate tongue.

"So you think we need the assistance of one experienced with invalids, do you?" Elizabeth's question was flavored with sharp amusement, rather than anger.

As Anne gave thanks to God for His mercy, Amyas ground his teeth in frustration. "Majesty, you twist my intent."

The queen laughed at this, the sound of her amusement light and silvery. "Poor Sir Amyas, your faith leaves you humorless. Let us look upon your precious heir. Raise your head, Mistress Anne." 'Twas a steel command sheathed in silk.

Anne did as she was bid and lifted her head. Elizabeth Tudor stared upon her prospective servant. Something flickered through her dark gaze as if she found Anne's face familiar but could not place the resemblance. Anne knew the moment recognition came. The corners of Elizabeth's mouth drooped a little, and her brow creased. Leaning forward in her

chair, the queen touched a gloved fingertip to the
flared band of Anne's red velvet headdress.

"You have the look of my mother about you," she
said, her voice so low Anne could barely hear her
words, "especially dressed in red as you are. So is she
dressed in my favorite portrait of her."

"I did not know, Majesty," Anne murmured, bowing her head to hide the terror that washed over her.
Not only was she certain her grandsire had known of
her resemblance to the ill-fated Anne Boleyn, Anne
was utterly convinced he'd played upon the likeness
apurpose. After all, he had been adamant that her
presentation attire be red velvet. Was every manipula-
tion Amyas undertook so ham-handed? What if the
queen took insult at his attempt? Anger roared
through Anne. She'd pay his price along with him,
that's what.

"Do you, indeed, have years of service to recommend you as your grandsire claims?" The queen's
voice was once more regal, but, blessedly, no more
impatient or cooler than it had been in the previous
moment.

So great was Anne's relief at escaping the queen's
wrath she forgot everything save her need to protect
herself from Amyas's not so subtle stratagem. "Aye,
Your Majesty, I do," she said, her entwined fingers
clenching as she strove for a meek voice. "For all of
my life I have lived with my mother, the Lady Frances
Blanchemain, widow of Sir Richard Blanchemain. In
that time I have served her as both companion and
attendant."

The queen made a noncommittal sound. "How you
must resent the woman who thus bound you to her.
'Twas wrong of her to deny you the company of
your peers."

However casual Elizabeth's voice, there was nothing offhand about the question; 'twas a trap, pure and simple. Anne blinked in understanding. Elizabeth disliked Amyas and was seeking some reason to refuse her new servant, so as to punish her outspoken and abrasive subject. Should that happen, Anne had no doubt Amyas would happily retire, holding his granddaughter close until Lady Deyville died and that poor woman's husband was free to wed again.

Caught betwixt and between, Anne considered her options. If she said she had no resentment, the queen would express disbelief, leaving her new servant to defend herself. To do so against a monarch could be deadly, indeed. Yet to admit resentment was to give Elizabeth just cause to despise her as a feckless, uncaring daughter.

"Madame, my mother is crippled, incapable of walking or speaking," Anne said at last, picking her way with care through the queen's traps. "If I entertained moments of resentment, they were in my early years, when the impatience of childhood didst blind me. With age came wisdom. As I grew, I understood how much my mother sacrificed on my behalf. Thus it is with joy in my heart that I have served my mother, just as I would serve you."

This time, the queen's laugh was a wondrous thing, filled with amusement and life. Anne dared to glance up at her. Elizabeth Tudor's smile was pretty, with only a few of her teeth touched with blackish rot. Her dark eyes were bright in pleasure and filled with the welcome that she'd earlier refused.

"Well said, Mistress Anne," she cried out in obvious pleasure, "well said, indeed. Tell us of yourself. Have you any education?"

This surprised Anne. Surely the queen's councillors

had told her all there was to know about the
Blanchemains. Nonetheless, one did not refuse a royal
command. "My mother has always found joy in the
arts, Madame. Thus she saw me tutored in many subjects, including Latin and Greek, mathematics and
grammar."

Sir Amyas watched her as she spoke, worry creasing
his brow. He'd hoped she wouldn't have to confess
her educated state in public. He believed all any
woman needed to learn could be gained from God's
Holy Book. It was a sign of his arrogance that he
thought all other men might despise an educated
woman. Anne found herself praying Lord Deyville
was one of those who shared his belief.

"Well, now, this is a surprise," the queen said, her
voice growing warmer by the word. "Have you an ear
for any modern tongues?" It was almost an eager
question.

Anne breathed in relief, recognizing another step
back from disaster's edge. "French, Madame," she
told the lush folds in her queen's black and white
skirts, "and Italian, although I have only begun my
study of that language and cannot say with any truth
that I speak it."

"We are liking you better and better, child. We
must convey our praise to your invalid mother. She
has cared well for her daughter, despite her disabil-
ity." Elizabeth was making no attempt to disguise her
approval now. "Here we thought you might be as your
grandsire is, sour and filled with condemnation for
those who are not as holy as he."

Sir Amyas released a quiet, angry breath as the
woman he referred to as the royal bitch sent another
insult his way.

"Of course, you play an instrument." There simply

was no question in the queen's voice. "The virginals, perhaps?"

"I fear not, Madame, although this is not for lack of effort on my mother's part. Much to her chagrin, I prefer the strings of the lute to the keyboard." Anne glanced up to gauge Elizabeth's reaction to this in time to see her monarch wave her hand, dismissing the lute as an inconsequential instrument, despite the young man who played his in the room's corner.

"The virginals are far more suited to a woman of your consequence. Perhaps, we can be your tutor. We have been told that we have a bit of a talent for the instrument."

Once again, Anne's gaze shifted to her queen's hems, this time to hide her mouth's twist at the thought of more practice on the virginals. She hated the instrument. Her fingers always seemed to knot as she sought the proper notes upon its keyboard.

"And how well do you dance?"

"Not at all I fear, Madame," Anne replied, so relieved that they would speak no more of musical instruments that the words left her lips unconsidered.

"What?!" The exclamation erupted from the queen's mouth, the sound sharp and startled.

"You do not dance!" Sir Amyas cried in stark surprise as he sat back on his heels. His fisted hands rested on his thighs. "Why did you not tell me?" This was a pained demand.

"You never asked." Anne added a harsh and condemning look to her reply. The hypocrite. He decried dancing as the first and most sinful of the queen's activities.

"This simply cannot be," Elizabeth protested, seeming truly shocked to discover so great a fault in one she'd begun to admire.

Anne turned her boldest gaze upon her monarch. If she didn't want to live as a prisoner with Sir Amyas until Lady Deyville died, she'd best catch a position as the queen's maid. "Madame, I know it must seem strange to you, but there is no dancing at Owls House. Once long ago, when my mother served your Majesty's stepmothers"—she paused a beat after this to make certain the queen would be reminded of her mother's past service—"she was lauded for her fine footwork. It seemed cruel to force one who so loved the activity to watch others caper and skip to a tune, when even the smallest step is beyond her. Thus I never pressed to learn."

Elizabeth's face softened at this explanation. "Noble, indeed. In this, your mother's blood reveals itself," she said, referring to her mother's connection to the Radcliffes and the earl of Sussex, while dismissing Sir Amyas's far more plebeian roots.

"Still," she continued with a frown, "we cannot have a maid who does not dance."

"Majesty, might I offer a suggestion?" The woman who spoke was one of the queen's ladies-in-waiting. Dressed in green and gray, she was beautiful, being fair of hair and fine of feature, with eyes as blue as the sapphires glinting in her earbobs.

Beside Anne, Amyas caught his breath so sharply that she thought for a moment he was in pain. He straightened, coming upright on his knees once more, his head bowed. Fingers clenching into his thick gown, he stared at the floor's matting, his lips moving as if in prayer.

Elizabeth shifted upon her cushions until she could gaze upon the beauty. Although no emotion colored the royal face, the queen's fingers were tight on the arms of her chair. If not for Anne's years of reading her mother's unspoken messages, she would have missed the signs of dislike that touched Elizabeth's body, for they did not show in her face. New appreciation for the queen's subtlety woke. Where Elizabeth ably hid her feelings toward this lady, she had been openly impatient with Sir Amyas. This could only mean his public rebuke had been part of what it cost him to place his granddaughter into royal service.

"And what might your suggestion be, Lady Montmercy?" 'Twas a bland question.

The noblewoman dropped into a deep curtsy. "Mistress Blanchemain seems a worthy enough maid," she replied, her head bowed, "and an inability to dance seems a flaw easily rectified. While a tutor could be hired for her, you have often said there are many men at court who turn their legs with great skill. I find myself wondering whether there is any difference between the skill transmitted by a man who teaches dancing as his trade"—a touch of scorn colored the word—"and one who dances for the simple joy of movement."

Interest sparked in the queen's eyes. "A suggestion worthy of consideration," she agreed. "Who might you suggest for this experiment, my lady?"

Anne glanced from her princess to her noble servant. The queen's words were like unto the starting thrust at a match in arms, an attempt to discover her opponent's strengths and weaknesses. Now, why would a queen keep one near her whom she did not trust?

The noblewoman shook her head. "Madame, I am not the one to ask. Well you know that my skill at dancing is but marginal. You are better seeking names of candidates from those who are nimble on their toes." His words set a pair of the queen's youngest maids to giggling and whispering between them.

"That's got you hissing." The queen threw this not unkind comment over her shoulder at the two. "Does this mean one of you has a recommendation to make?"

Elizabeth's words brought the pair of highborn maids around the corner of her chair. They clutched together as if one needed the other to stand. The instant they were within their queen's eyesight, they knelt, bending heads over bodices yet undisturbed by womanly curves.

"Madame," one offered, her golden curls resting against her sweet nape, "what of Master Christopher Hollier? 'Twas he you complimented last week for how finely he turned his leg to music."

Amyas gasped. "Nay, I'll have no papists near my heir!" Even as the words exploded from him, her grandfather cringed as he recognized his mistake.

In her chair Elizabeth's eyes widened. Her neck tensed until Anne could see the blue of her veins. "God's teeth, but you do tread roughshod over ground where you should not tread at all," she shouted at the one who claimed to be her good and faithful servant.

"We have had enough of you and your pompous ilk, all of you thinking to command God's chosen monarch to your will. It is ours to decide who serves us and how they will serve." With every word, Elizabeth's voice rose until the sound of her rage echoed about the now still and breathless room. "Not even our councillors have the right to demand otherwise, although God knows they have dared to try. We say Master Hollier is your granddaughter's tutor, and so it will be!"

As the echoes of the queen's shouts faded, Kit

straightened out of his slouched stance against the wall. All around him, men cleared their throats or coughed, the more daring whispering to each other. No matter their reaction, every one of them was giving thanks he wasn't Old Amyas. God knew, Kit was.

Although Amyas's head was bowed, his back was stiff in eloquent declaration of how deeply he resented his queen's tongue-lashing. Poor old man. There was no way for him to know the sort of morass into which he'd blundered. In Amyas's arrogant outburst Elizabeth had found just what she'd been needing, a whipping boy on whom to vent her yet simmering rage over the actions of those more highly placed and powerful than he and a pulpit from which she could inform her courtiers just how she felt about her council's attempt to usurp her authority in February, two months ago.

The corners of Kit's mouth lifted. How that parvenu must be eating at his heart right now. Amyas had to know that, save for his protest, the queen would have asked the onlookers to submit names for Mistress Blanchemain's dancing master. Indeed, the appointment would have become like unto a tennis match, hours passing as the highest nobles at court swatted names about like balls until the strongest faction settled the chore upon their favorite.

Against Lady Montmercy's admonition not to do so, Kit glanced at her, his respect for her ability to scheme rising. It had been a stroke of genius to use a maid to proffer his name, all the more so since to the best of his knowledge the queen had never offered him a word one way or the other over his footwork. It was Kit's fellow pensioner of the same name, Master Christopher Hatton, who received all their mistress's praise for his dancing. Now, how was it that a devious,

amoral viper could know a devout old man so well
that she'd been certain he would explode at the mere
suggestion of the Hollier name?

John clapped Kit on the back, the congratulatory
blow so powerful it nearly knocked him from his feet.
"By God, that was a neat trick," John cried in quiet
awe as he gave up pounding on his friend to come
around Kit, grab his hand, and pump vigorously.
"Who did you have to pay and how much did it cost
to arrange that?"

"I had nothing to do with it," Kit declared, glad his
words could ring with truth.

Lord Andrew appeared from around John's back to
catch Kit by the arm. "In honor of your appointment,
I will *not* pursue the woman," he offered in his own
version of congratulations.

Kit stifled his laugh. "Magnanimous of you, my
lord," he said, sarcasm almost dripping from his
words.

Ned's laugh rang out. "I fear this generosity of
yours has more to do with the color of Mistress
Blanchemain's tresses than our Kit's good fortune,"
he said to his charge. "We all know you prefer fair-
haired lasses."

"So I do," the boy replied with a grin so charming
it drove all arrogance from his face.

Near the queen's chair, Sir Amyas was mumbling
his way through the appropriate humble apologies.
Once he was done, the usher called Mistress
Blanchemain forward to recite her oath of service.
John looked at Kit.

"Since you're vowed not to marry, do you think you
can whisper a good word to her about *me*? I can even
help you with your lessons, being as light on my feet
as you."

Dismay filled Kit. Those lessons were to be his opportunity to seduce Mistress Anne. Lord Andrew chose that moment to again thrust himself between his taller and older friends. Rather than chide the lordling for his rude interruption, Kit breathed in relief as it served to distract John from his request.

"Look there," the youth said, his voice low as he shot another glance toward the body of the room. "Leicester's making his way to the queen. What will you wager, friends? I have a good red angel that says he speaks to her of the maying, reminding her we are late in repairing to Greenwich for that celebration. Aye, and after that, I've a pound that says he does so good a job at wooing her, we find ourselves Greenwich-bound before the morrow's sunset."

"That's too easy a wager," Ned scoffed. "Everyone can see she's finally ready to be soothed into it."

Shoving past his friends, Kit stared toward his royal mistress's chair. That parvenu of all parvenus, Robert Dudley, now Lord of Denbigh and Earl of Leicester, was already on one knee before his queen. Elizabeth's handsome favorite shone like the bright star he was, his doublet yellow, his breeches green and red beneath his brown, fur-lined coat. Bright diamonds served him for buttons, while his buckled garter proclaimed his status as a Garter Knight.

Mistress Blanchemain and Old Amyas were nowhere to be seen. Kit cursed himself for allowing his friends to distract him. With so many men certain to pursue the new maid-of-honor and despite that Amyas could but hate him, Kit wanted to make his introductions now. There was a flash of red near the Presence Chamber's doorway. It was Old Amyas, taking his heiress from the room.

Panic spiked. What if Lady Montmercy's ploy was

more than the old man's arrogance could tolerate and Amyas now sought to completely remove his granddaughter from court? Although the queen would be furious, her vengeance was more likely to be heavy fines than a request for the girl's return. If Mistress Blanchemain departed, all chance at reclaiming Graceton's lordship went with her.

"Pardon," he told his friends, already pushing through the courtiers to intercept Amyas. His path took him close enough to Leicester to overhear his words to the queen.

"May Day will soon be upon us, Madame," the earl was saying. "Give way to pleasure, sweet Gloriana. Too long have you shielded your brilliance from us, trapping us in winter's drear dullness. 'Tis time to celebrate the coming of summer. Be you our goddess and lead us into gaiety."

'Twas a coquette's smile Elizabeth offered her Master of Horse as she reached out to trail the royal fingers along her earl's cheek in a caress that was but a hairbreadth this side of being too intimate for public display. At that moment Kit wouldn't have cared if Elizabeth bedded her favorite before all the court; he had his own bedmate to catch.

"You are right, My Eyes," the queen replied, new huskiness in her voice, " 'tis time we were done with all this animosity and strife. Activity is what we need to clear our livers. What say you?" the queen asked, raising her gaze to the many men whose only job was to adore her. "Are we for Greenwich on the morrow?"

Her announcement sent a pleased rumbling rolling across the room even as half a room ahead of Kit, Old Amyas and Mistress Anne exited this chamber for the gallery beyond it. Kit put wings on his feet. If he didn't catch them now, the chaos of the court's move would forestall his introduction until after they were settled at Greenwich. 'Twas as sprightly a dance as he'd ever done as he wove through this party and that to catch his quarry.

Chapter Six

As Amyas pulled Anne toward the Presence Chamber exit, she opened her mouth to protest that leaving the queen's presence before being released was rude, if not dangerous. But as she glanced up at her grandsire, she thought the better of it. Amyas's breaths came in quiet gasps; sweat beaded on his brow. His face was so pale his skin held a greenish tinge, just as had happened during the attack on her mother.

Anne chewed her lip in worry. What if the queen's tirade had caused some sort of damage to his mind? Were Amyas to be adjudged incompetent, she would become Elizabeth's property to grant to any man the queen pleased. Although this wasn't as horrid a prospect as marriage to Deyville, it certainly wasn't what Anne planned for herself.

Amyas shoved her out of the Presence Chamber door with enough violence to make her stumble. Anne bit her tongue on her complaint, fearing any word might cause him to lose what little remained of his control. She even managed to smile at the startled guards as if such an exit were a normal occurrence for her.

In the area beyond the Presence Chamber, her grandfather's pace slowed as this space had filled to overflowing in the short time they'd been in the queen's presence. Although some were the servants of the highly placed, there were a goodly number of merchants and artisans hoping for the chance to bend their monarch's ear. No matter their rank, all of them gleamed to the full limits of their purses; one did not appear before the queen in less than his best.

The only drab note in all this splendor was Patience Watkins dressed in her persistent brown. Anne's keeper was huddled against the wall, her arms tightly crossed before her as if she feared contamination from a nearby group of laughing men. As Patience caught sight of them, she started through the crowd at the moderate pace she insisted was a woman's proper stride. This made her too slow to meet Amyas as he pulled Anne down the long gallery. Anne bit back a smile as astonishment at being abandoned by her patron played across Patience's face. Sending the woman her most helpless of looks, Anne watched from over her shoulder to see how the sniveling creature would resolve her dilemma, since, by Patience's standards, both running and calling out were the actions of a forward woman.

Flustered, the young widow hurried her pace to what was almost a trot. When she realized it still wasn't fast enough, her worry deepened until she almost gave way to crudeness and waved. So intent was she on Sir Amyas, she didn't see the young musician, if the gittern across his back was an indication of employment. When they collided, the man dared to smile at her in forgiveness.

'Twas more than the poor creature could bear. Patience yelped at his unwanted attention. "Sir Amyas, wait," she cried, her voice sinfully shrill against the deeper thrum of masculine conversation. "I cannot keep pace."

To Anne's surprise, Amyas stopped, thus proving that whatever his state he could yet hear and comprehend. Although he swung his head in Patience's direction, Anne doubted he saw anything. Lifting a hand, she touched his fingers where they curled into her upper arm. His hold on her loosened. Patience came to a stop beside them.

"What is it?" Anne's governess cried, her expression stricken as she glanced from her employer to her charge.

"He's had some sort of fit," Anne replied as she freed her grandfather's hand from her arm.

He sighed, then swayed as a man stunned. "Jezebel," he muttered, "Delilah!" he clenched his fist and set it against his heart. "Be strong and hold firm upon the path of righteousness."

Patience gasped, then pressed her fine, frail fingers to her lips to conceal her smirk. There was nothing she could do to disguise the vindicative triumph that glowed in her pale eyes. 'Twas Anne she thought Amyas named as temptress.

Ignoring her, Anne studied her grandfather, eyes narrowed in consideration. Was it the queen he meant? Nay. For no reason she could name, she knew it was the other woman, Lady Montmercy, at the root of Amyas's present distress.

Curiosity pricked at Anne. What connection could there be between that noblewoman and her grandfather that could generate so deep an emotional reaction in Amyas? This was something that deserved further investigation.

Of a sudden it seemed the doors to the Presence Chamber had been thrown wide. Courtiers flooded

into the gallery, each man calling to his servants, until
the noise became a roar. As folk whirled into action,
Anne grabbed her grandfather's hand and led him out
of the traffic. He followed dumbly, stopping when
she did.

Anne frowned. She was far more comfortable with
him when he was hateful and overbearing. If this state
of his persisted, there was the danger she might become concerned about him. What, then, would happen
to her and her goals?

"Grandfather, you must gather your wits," she demanded, trying to prod him back to lucidity.

"Is he ill?"

Whirling, Anne looked upon the gentleman with the
green eyes. It surprised her to discover how tall he
was, for the top of her head reached only a little beyond his jawline. Against the size of the Presence
Chamber, he hadn't seemed so large. Just now concern filled his wondrous eyes, the emotion directed
toward her grandfather. This pleased Anne well, indeed. Anyone who could be concerned for Amyas
would be capable of feeling pity for her mother, and
possibly be able to forgive her lack of purity.

Amyas turned toward the sound of the young gentleman's voice. He blinked. Life returned to his eyes
in the next instant. With awareness came anger, and
his face flushed a bright red.

"You," he spewed the word as if it were a mouthful
of poison. "No papist will be my granddaughter's
dancing master."

There was more than a little pleasure in the surprise
that tore through Anne. "*You* are Master Hollier?"

"Indeed," the man replied with the same slow grin
that had so beguiled her only half an hour ago. "Since
your grandfather does not seem inclined to do the

honors, I must introduce myself. Master Christopher Hollier, at your service Mistress Blanchemain."

Sweeping his brown cap from his head with one hand, Master Hollier caught Anne's fingers in the other, then extended his leg. 'Twas a graceful bow he made over her hand.

As he straightened, he lifted her fingers to his mouth. Thin leather was no barrier to sensation. Anne drew a sharp breath as the touch of his lips sent languid heat spreading to every corner of her being. Even as he raised his head from her hand, his fingers moved in the cup of her palm in a secret caress. Anne sighed as the heat in her gave way to deepening pleasure. Here, her body whispered to her, was the man she wanted.

And here, her mind countered, was one man she dare not take. Anne sighed again, this time in disappointment. Even if Master Hollier should prove accepting of her mother, all the servants at Owls House, even herself, she dared not wed him. Sir Amyas would never accept their union and not just because he thought Master Hollier a papist. That the queen had forced him upon her grandfather doomed any relationship she might wish for them.

It wasn't proper for Anne to allow him to continue holding her hand. Still, the desire to savor a last moment of enjoyment before she removed his name from the list of potential husbands was too strong to resist.

Patience was quick to note this breach of convention. "Mistress Anne," she squeaked in complaint, then whirled on Sir Amyas as if to urge him into confronting his kin's misbehavior.

She wasn't swift enough; Sir Amyas had already thrust between Anne and her new tutor to force them apart. His eyes blazed, his fists clenched. "How dare you behave so in my presence?" he snarled at Master Hollier.

His words reawoke Anne's simmering anger. It was a relief to let it consume what remained of her concern over her grandfather's strange state. Here was a man worthy of her hate, the hypocrite who warned away one man's untoward advances while tacitly encouraging another man, that one yet married, in an immoral pursuit.

"Your appointment is an outrage," Amyas snarled. "You can be certain I will protest this to Sir William Cecil. I'll see you driven from court before I give you the opportunity to take some advantage with my heiress."

Master Hollier only offered his better a brief bow. "Do as you must, Sir Amyas," he replied, his voice calm and confident, "but until the moment my royal mistress commands me differently, I am bound to be your granddaughter's tutor."

"I look forward to our lessons, Master Hollier," Anne said, to let him know she'd not inherited her grandsire's idiocy.

"I am at your convenience, Mistress Anne," he said, with a final quick bow.

As he retreated toward the Presence Chamber against the tide of gentlefolk pouring from that door, Amyas whirled on her, eyes wide and mouth harsh. "Do you dare to speak to him in your own right? No decent woman encourages a man after her rightful kin tells him he must leave off!"

His words sent Anne's rage exploding past her ability to contain it. "You dare to chide me, when all of this is your fault?" she hissed. " 'Twasn't me that shouted 'Nay' to our queen!"

Patience's face paled at such boldness, then her lips

twisted in anticipation of Anne's comeuppance. To
hide her reaction, she folded her hands before her and
bowed her head as if in prayer.

Amyas opened his mouth. When no sound came
forth, he closed his lips and frowned at her. 'Twas the
acknowledgment of wrongdoing that lived in the
depths of his dark gaze. While there was more than a
little satisfaction in this, it wasn't enough to soothe
Anne. She leaned toward him to keep her words private between them.

"I thought my heart would stop when our queen
said I had the look of her mother to me," she whispered. "You used me, playing upon that resemblance
in full knowledge of what it could cost! As it was, she
was set to refuse me, and would have, had I not managed to win her interest. What if she had understood
your ploy and taken insult before I could soothe her?"
Even remembered, Anne's terror over matching wits
with the queen was strong enough to make her
voice squeak.

There was a subtle softening to Amyas's face. "Aye,
it was a risk, but she wasn't insulted. All worked out
for the best, save that a recusant was named as your
tutor. If it calms your fears, you may take lessons with
the man until I have his appointment revoked."

This was the closest thing to either an apology or a
word of thanks Anne would ever get from him.
"Praise God for small favors," she replied, irony thick
in her words.

"Aye, praise Him well, but heed me," her grandfather retorted, his voice rising to its normal, imperious
tone. "You'll spend no time in Master Hollier's presence without Mistress Watkins at your side. Not only
is he forward with women, as you have seen, his family
is in disgrace, the estate ruined, their title lost."

"Master Hollier is a peer's son?" The question leapt from Anne's lips, even as she dismissed the notion. Nay, he couldn't be noble. As the son of a lord, he would have been knighted. Even as a younger son, he would own the higher title of "squire," not the simple "master" of a gentleman.

"Did I not just say as much?" Amyas returned sharply, not the least bit pleased by her question. "God in His divine plan stripped the family of their nobility, then crippled the elder son to prevent them from forcing Roman rule back upon God's holy kingdom."

Anne stared. Master Hollier's older brother was crippled? Her gaze leapt to the Presence Chamber's door, into which her tutor had disappeared. Despite her grandsire's hatred for him, she couldn't afford to turn her back on a man who might comprehend her mother's needs.

"I beg your pardon, Sir Amyas." 'Twas the young woman, the one Anne hoped might be Mistress Radcliffe, who came to a halt before them, bobbing a quick curtsy. "Mistress Eglionby begs me lead Mistress Blanchemain to her, claiming custody of your granddaughter as is her right as Mistress of the Maids. She says she must have her as we are to prepare for our departure to Greenwich."

"A moment," Amyas demanded, catching Anne by the arm before the maid had a chance to answer.

He pulled Anne far enough from Patience and this newcomer so neither could hear, then pressed his mouth close to her ear. "Take heed and be warned before I release you into the queen's custody," he whispered. "That recusant lusts after my wealth, thinking to restore his family's estates. I daresay he'll ply you with flattery and evil suggestions, wanting secret marriage with you, for he knows I'll never approve any union between you. Should you give way and wed with him, I'll see you dead for it. 'Tis better that I am left without an heir, thus allowing all I own to go to that royal bitch, than let some papist enjoy what was once mine."

His warning delivered, he set Anne away from him. "Go with Mistress Radcliffe, granddaughter, taking Mistress Patience with you whilst leaving the matter of Master Hollier to me. I will see your belongings forwarded from my house to Greenwich."

Chapter Seven

Anne ignored his departure to whirl on the young woman. "You are Mistress Mary Radcliffe?"

"Indeed, I am," her mother's distant cousin said with a smile. Mary was as pretty as her dam, the London merchant's daughter who'd won herself the earl of Sussex's uncle as a husband.

For her departed sister's sake, Anne dropped into a deep curtsy. "I cannot tell you how glad I am to meet you, Mistress Radcliffe," she said, her head yet bent.

"Nay, now," her kinswoman said, catching Anne by the arm and forcing her to rise. "I'll not have such formality between us. You must call me Mary, just as I will call you Anne, or Nan, if you will it." She pressed a swift kiss of greeting against Anne's cheek.

Anne couldn't have been more pleased. "Nan, it is, for I'll have no other name between us, not after the great kindness you showed my sister. Eliza's letters always spoke of you with such fondness, may God rest her sweet soul."

Sadness dampened Mary's eyes. "Poor Eliza. I yet miss her dearly. She deserved more happiness from life than four dead infants and a husband who loved her so little. Sometimes I think 'tis her experience in wedlock, more than my vow to remain a maiden as

long as our sweet mistress owns that state, that keeps
me from the church door."

With a final sigh for the recently departed woman,
Mary looped her arm through Anne's. "Come, then.
We are off to the maids dormitory." The two of them
started toward the gallery's end and the more residen-
tial areas of the palace, Mary's pace forceful, indeed.

"Mistress Anne," Patience protested, following
them in that modest, measured tread of hers, "you
must slow. Only a forward woman moves so swiftly."

Mary shot a sharp glance over her shoulder at Patience, the twisting of her features saying she didn't
think much of servants who corrected their betters.
"Is this your maid?"

"My governess," Anne replied. "I fear she finds immorality in all I do." She lowered her voice to a whisper. "Have a care with what you say, she's also my
grandsire's spy."

Mary choked back a quick laugh, then her face
came to life with the need to do mischief. "We must
give her something to report, then. Faster, cousin,"
she urged, stretching her legs as they started down
the gallery.

Anne laughed and kept pace, leaving Patience to
trail ever farther behind them. 'Twas good to have a
friend in this strange place, but 'twas even better to
know an insider, one who might understand the
strange interplay that had happened between her
grandfather and the noblewoman. The need to probe
for information grew until she spilled her question.

"Mary, I am wondering if you noticed how my
grandfather reacted when Lady Montmercy made
her suggestion."

"Ugh," Mary replied, her mouth pursed in disgust.

"Now, there's a woman who could use your Patience. Lady Elisabetta is as immoral and evil as they come."

This startled Anne. "If this is so, then why does our royal mistress tolerate her presence as a lady-in-waiting?"

Mary offered an arch smile. "Of what use is it to keep only friends close?" she asked. " 'Tis her enemies who bear watching. She keeps them close, giving them less opportunity to do harm."

Anne frowned at so strange a concept. "It cannot be easy for her to live so."

Her kinswoman nodded. "Easy, nay, but 'tis safer. As for your grandsire's reaction, I cannot say I saw anything, since everything he does seems so odd. Why, what do you think you saw?"

Their pace had slowed as they talked. Anne glanced behind her to see if Patience could overhear. Amyas's spy was several yards behind them.

Anne only shrugged as if she were helpless to prevent Mary from dragging her along, then turned her attention back to her kinswoman. "He seemed overcome by her presence, as if he feared her. Now, my grandsire has no regard for the weaker sex. That any woman should affect him so, well, the mystery of it is more than I can bear."

'Twas the joy of prying into others' secrets that came to life in Mary's face. "If there's a mystery to be solved, I can help, doing so for your sake as much as against Lady Elisabetta. I cannot tolerate that woman."

Anne laughed. "I see there was nothing weak-kneed about your opinions. Aye," she said with a nod, "I would welcome your assistance, as I know nothing and no one at court, save that it wasn't my grandsire the queen meant to chastise this morn when she spoke to the room." Here, she paused, tilting her head to the side in question. "So if not him, then who and why?"

"Well, now, if we're to talk about that, we best move like your maid, as it will take me a few moments to explain," Mary replied, slowing to a modest walk as she spoke. "Once Mistress Eglionby has a hold of us, there'll be no time to speak, as we'll be packing for the move.

"You are right to think our mistress meant to wound more men that just Sir Amyas, although I say he got no less than what he deserved for his blunt speech." Mary's eyes gleamed with amusement. "Take a lesson from his experience. Our mistress doesn't much care for criticism, especially not just now."

"What is different about now?" Anne asked as they strolled at near to a snail's pace.

"It's her council. February last, those arrogant fools tried to remove Sir William Cecil. That's our mistress's secretary," she said and was right in thinking Anne didn't know the name, "and as good and true an adviser as any prince might want, although she's not respectful of his advice. At any rate, they plotted in secret, trying to raise the support of both nobles and commoners against him and see him Tower-bound before our mistress knew aught about this. 'Twas his head on a pike they wanted."

"They obviously failed," Anne said as an aside, "for my grandsire told me he meant to speak with him."

"Aye, so they did." Mary gave a satisfied smile. "Sir William now has proof of her loyalty to him. Having already lost two beloved friends at the new year's turning, my sweet mistress wasn't willing to let her council strip her of another. It will be a long while before she forgives their attempt to force their will upon her."

Anne's brow creased as she struggled to absorb all this. "What was it he did that caused them to hate him so?"

Mary made an impatient sound. "The council claims Sir William intends to make war with Spain and form an alliance with the cursed French. At least that's how it appears on the surface."

"But you think there's more to it?"

'Twas just the prod her cousin wanted. "Aye, and the more of it is Her Eyes, the Earl of Leicester." Hatred browned and curled the edges of Mary's words.

Anne drew a quick breath. Not even Owls House was so isolated that she'd missed the rumors about Leicester and Elizabeth. 'Twas said the earl murdered his wife to make way for marriage to the queen. The gossips also said Elizabeth had born him a son, although such a thing seemed unlikely, indeed.

Having caught but a brief glimpse of the favorite as Amyas had led her from the chamber, Anne could understand the queen's fascination. Lord Robert was a handsome man, with even features and hair and eyes of brown. Apparently, his charm didn't extend to Mary.

"I take it you don't much care for our mistress's favorite," Anne said in wry amusement.

Her cousin huffed in disgust. "If ever there was a more dastardly schemer I cannot think of one. I vow he believes once Sir William is removed, our sweet mistress would wed with him, making him her consort."

The thought of such a scandal made Anne's eyes widened. "Would she?" she breathed.

"Praise God, no," Mary retorted in relief.

"How can you be so certain?" Anne asked.

Mary's face softened with a touch of pity. "No matter how deeply our mistress might love that man, she'll never give way to marriage. To do so is to threaten her grip upon the throne. 'Tis the memory of her time in the Tower during her sister's reign that does this. Mark my words. Our mistress will never again give anyone, not husband, council, or Parliament, the opportunity to hold her life in their hands."

"But if she doesn't wed, there'll be no heir to take her place after," Anne cried in protest.

Mary made a face. "Now you sound like Parliament, for the members, your grandsire among them, ever harp upon just that subject. I say there are already too many heirs for England's throne. Think on the Scots queen." Mary Stuart had sought refuge in England early in the previous year, after escaping imprisonment on the charge of murdering her husband.

"She's not only in line, being a blood royal cousin to our mistress, but she has a son to follow her. Indeed, some nobles, especially those who yet cling to the Roman faith, mutter that Queen Mary's claim is more legitimate than our mistress's, not only because she's Catholic, but because Elizabeth was once declared a bastard by her father."

As she said this, Mary glanced behind her and gasped. "Look, your Patience is catching us. Hie, cousin," she cried, and once more dragged a laughing Anne down the passageway.

Chapter Eight

'Twas a glorious spring day, made all the sweeter by the memory of last winter's unusual cold. Kit drew a deep breath, filling his lungs with air spiced with the tang of the Thames. Gulls soared overhead, birdsong rose from every copse and thicket. The sun was warm against his leather riding jerkin, while beneath him, his gelding strained at the bit, begging to be allowed to run. Aye, 'twas a fine day for a ride, even if his duty saw him riding with the some three hundred wagons that followed the queen to Greenwich.

Kit grinned to himself. It was last night's dream that had his spirits soaring. Rather than his persistent nightmare, it had been Mistress Blanchemain who had visited him in his sleep last night.

With a sigh, he savored the imaginary, wondrous sensations her dream form had made in him. Even remembered, the things they'd done left him breathless. Would that he'd not drawn baggage duty for the day. He stared up the road. Men on horseback filled the narrow throughway. The farthest he could see was the hundred gentlemen who rode with Thomas Howard, Duke of Norfolk. He only recognized that 'twas Norfolk's men because the sun gleamed off their velvet attire. Mistress Anne rode ahead of them, in the maids' company and protected by the queen's lifeguard.

"Huh! 'Tis just as well she cannot see you now," Bertie Babthorpe said, riding at his master's side, the baskets containing their belongings bouncing against his horse's rump.

Startled, Kit turned in his saddle to stare at his man. Bertie couldn't have discovered his involvement in Lady Montmercy's plot, not when Kit had taken such care to keep all covert. For all that was good about him, Bertie had a tendency to talk. "Who?" he demanded.

Bertie's smile was dazzling. Although short as men went, he owned a face so handsome half of London's wives were panting after him. The other half were also panting, or so Bertie claimed, their gasps elicited by the memory of his prowess between their thighs.

"Why, whoever it is that has you so heated," his man replied, his bright blue eyes gleaming from beneath the tumble of dark hair upon his brow. "Have a care, Master Kit. If she catches one look of your face, she'll know every detail of your plan for her."

Kit frowned. "What plan?"

"What, indeed," Bertie scoffed. "Yesterday, you nigh on drove me mad picking over your clothing to find just the right attire. Now, this morn, you're sniffing up this train of ours, like a leashed dog after a bitch in heat. You're after a woman, of that there is no doubt."

"I vow, Bertie, I'll have to dismiss you one of these days. You are hopelessly impertinent."

So empty a threat drew only a rude sound from Kit's man. It was a lifetime's worth of familiarity that gave Bertie the confidence to speak so to his employer; the Babthorpes had been Graceton men almost as long as the old keep tower had existed. "If I'm impertinent, you're too eager and wholly inexperienced in this sort of hunting," he retorted.

It piqued Kit's masculine pride not a little to have Bertie think him an inept lover. "Hardly so," he snapped. "If I'm not as promiscuous as you, I've seduced a woman or two before this day."

"Nay," Bertie laughed, "you only *think* you've seduced them, when in truth 'tis they who've had you. It's just the way you are, Master Kit, too blind to know they're setting their traps for you, until you've been snared. Do you remember Mistress Bridget, the cobbler's wife?"

Kit drew a swift, sharp breath. Remember her?! Breasts round and ripe as melons, hair the color of gold, lips as rich as Madeira. Even as a memory, Bridget could wake his body.

"How could I forget?" he said, then banished her image from his mind. 'Twasn't she upon whom he needed to focus. As the lovely image of Mistress Blanchemain again formed before his inner eyes, the sensations of the dream returned. Lust was a fine thing to feel this day.

Kit shot Bertie a chiding look. "By the by, if this is your example of a woman having me, then you're proved wrong before you start. I saw Bridget before she even knew I existed. She was walking through the market at Saint Paul's. It took me days to discover where she lived."

A sly grin twisted Bertie's finely made lips. "You'd have saved yourself all that time and effort if you'd but returned to Saint Paul's the next day at that same hour. She was there, waiting for you."

Kit's chin jerked up as he turned in the saddle to

stare at his manservant. "How do you know that?" he demanded.

"You jest!" Bertie cried. "A woman like that doesn't go unnoticed by any man. I went back the next day, hoping she'd be there, and there she was. Sweet Jesus knows I tried, but she was very definite. 'Twas you and no other she wished to attract."

"She told you that?" Kit gaped at him.

His servant shrugged. "Not as such, but there are some things that need no words. Suffice it to say, she was already at the hunt and you were her prey."

The look Bertie bent on his master was that of the hoary, aged tutor upon his foundling student. "Now, if you wish to be the hunter, you must do as the shoemaker's wife did. Appear to be disinterested, but make your presence known and felt. Oh, and I warn you, if your quarry glimpses even a flicker of what's been filling your gaze this day, Venus's gate will be barred to you for all time."

"Well, then, I'm doomed already," Kit snapped, even as he resolved to be more distant when next he and Mistress Anne met. "My 'quarry' had a good look at me outside the Presence Chamber yesterday."

Bertie held up his hands. "Master, I was only trying to aid you," he cried, a shade too much laughter in his voice to carry off his protest of innocence.

Well and truly wounded by Bertie's attempt to school him in the lover's art, Kit glared at his servant. With the next breath came the means to give Bertie just as good as he'd given. So hard did laughter strain at Kit's throat, he had to return his gaze to the road, staring at the narrow line of muck as if it were the most fascinating thing he'd ever seen.

"Since you are so eager to aid me in this, there

might be something you could do," he said, baiting the trap.

"What might that be?" his manservant asked, new interest in his tone.

"Nay," Kit said, creasing his brow as if in consideration. He let the quiet drag out long enough to tease Bertie's interest, then shook his head to convey that his yet-unspoken request was quite beyond his man's capabilities to achieve.

"What?" Bertie prodded, circling Kit's hook, but not quite ready to bite.

"Never mind. 'Twas just a wayward thought and wouldn't serve at all."

"What?!" Bertie cried out, now eager for a chance at the bait.

"Well, I suppose there's no harm in telling you my thoughts," Kit said, "although 'tisn't the sort of thing one man asks another to do."

"Speak," his man insisted.

Kit paused, then said, "Bertie, you've always said if a man's to win his way into a woman's heart, he must find a way around the barriers she sets to discourage others, thus forcing himself into her mind. In this woman's case, I think there's but one barrier, and that's her servant. I was thinking what a boon it would be if you were to win her maidservant's heart, thus opening that door for me." Kit offered his man a sorry smile as he waved away his own request. "Foolish of me, I know."

Bertie stared at him in blatant surprise. "You want me to seduce a woman? You, who is ever chiding me that I will lose my cock if I'm not careful where I put it?!"

Kit sighed sadly. "Did I not tell you 'twas but an errant notion? Besides, 'tis quite impossible, even for a man of your talents." However honest this warning, Kit knew well enough it would firmly fix the hook in Bertie's mouth.

His man came bolt upright in his saddle. "Impossible?" Bertie cried, blind to the fact that he was now swimming to the end of Kit's string. "There's no woman in the world I cannot conquer."

Such arrogance deserved its comeuppance. Kit formed his face into an expression of grateful innocence. "Glad I am to hear it. How long do you think such a thing would take you? A week? Two?"

"Two weeks?" Bertie scoffed, sounding insulted at the notion. "It hasn't taken me that long to win a woman since my twelfth year."

Kit let his breath gust from him, as if deeply relieved. "Glad I am to hear your confidence, for I was certain this woman might be immune to any man's charm, even yours."

· A flash of concern shot through his servant's pretty eyes. "Why?"

Kit rubbed his gloved hand over his mouth as he fought to contain his grin. "Perhaps, 'twould be best if I showed you. Follow me," he said.

Turning their horses, they trotted down the long line of wagons that creaked and groaned their way down the road, their big wheels squealing through the muck. Numbering near three hundred, they were pulled by massive dray horses or teams of bellowing oxen. 'Twas furnishing that filled their boxes, chairs, chests of plate, trunks of linens. And beds, whole wagons worth of disassembled beds. What didn't belong to the queen, belonged to her courtiers, for no man with a rank high enough to claim a bedchamber went abroad without his own furnishings.

Kit pointed to the cart belonging to Old Amyas.

"There, do you see that woman in brown walking beside yon wagon? That is Mistress Patience Watkins, companion to Mistress Blanchemain."

Bertie caught his breath as he recognized the name. "Are you mad?!" he cried. "Mistress Blanchemain is one of the queen's maids. You cannot mean to seduce one of those virgins!"

"Hush, Bertie," Kit snapped. "Who said anything about seducing? All I want is a chance to spend time alone with her. Can I help that my heart is given?"

"If it's your heart you intend to give her, then I'm the lord of Graceton," his man snorted, turning in the saddle to study the frail, flat-chested woman.

Kit looked as well. Having seen the fire in Mistress Anne's eyes, he didn't wonder why Sir Amyas had set such a pinched-faced jailer on his granddaughter. Mistress Anne's keeper was as tight in mind as she was in body. He'd seen her twice chide those around her for giving way to laughter, proclaiming that such explosions of gaiety opened the doors of their hearts to Satan.

"Look how her mouth moves, as if she's speaking to some invisible companion," Bertie said after a moment, his voice weak. "What is she doing?"

"Praying, no doubt," Kit replied. "Sir Amyas would hardly supply his granddaughter with a servant of low morals, now, would he? I'll wager the woman believes as he does." He grinned at his servant.

"But, he's a Calvinist," Bertie cried, a worried line destroying the perfection of his brow.

Kit reared back in his saddle in mock outrage. "What is this, Master Cock-too-big-for-his-codpiece? I thought you were expert in the seduction of unwilling women. Have I been led astray?" He pressed his hand to the front of his jerkin to display how much the very notion of Bertie's incompetence shocked him.

"Imagine how stunned your companions will be when I tell them there is one woman in the world who is beyond your charms," he continued, "one woman who will not even look in your direction."

Bertie's eyes narrowed. Only now did he feel himself flopping and flapping at the end of his employer's string. "You wouldn't."

Kit's grin widened in triumph. "Wouldn't I?"

"I should have known this was naught but a prank on your part," the man muttered.

"A week, was it you said?" Kit asked, savoring his victory.

Bertie once more turned his gaze on the tightminded woman, then heaved a martyred sigh. "I will think on it as the challenge of a lifetime."

Chapter Nine

'Twas the maying and what a glorious day it was! Early this morn all the men connected to the queen, from highest courtier to lowest scullery lad, left Greenwich Palace to hide among the rolling hills. Later, the queen and all her women, Anne among them, came to find them. Now reunited, the party set to gathering their flowers and celebrating summer into being with music, dancing, and laughter.

Anne swept along the woodland path, seeking another hawthorn tree to strip. With her every step her hems stirred last year's foliage and released the rich scent of a fertile earth, the aroma so potent her heart was fair drunk with it. The air above her was alive with birdsong, the sweet notes twining with the sounds of lute and flute rising from the nearby meadow.

Aye, 'twas a joyous day, and for more reason than just the festivities. A note had come from Owls House this morn. In it Lady Frances wrote she was fully recovered from Sir Amyas's attack, although the bitter tone of her sentences suggested Anne's mother hadn't forgiven her former in-law his assault.

Her heart soaring against the knowledge that her mother was well, Anne spied the next hawthorn. This one was a gnarled oldster, rising from a bed of velvety green moss, sweet violets blooming at its feet. May's advent left its horny branches clouded in fragrant white blossoms.

As she left the path to reach it, Patience squeaked. "Nay, mistress, you must not!" Anne's governess caught her charge by the arm to stop her. "We've already gone too deep into the shadows."

Irritation nibbled at Anne's fine mood as she yanked her arm free of her keeper's hold. She shot the woman a narrow look. The morn's bright sun had added a wide-brimmed straw hat to Patience's usual brown attire, but not a single ribbon broke the plainness of her headgear and woe to anyone who offered her something so festive. "Patience, we're only a few dozen yards from the clearing."

Without a backward look, Anne thrust through last year's foliage to stop before the hawthorn. Taking her clippers from the basket she carried, she prepared to relieve the old tree of a few of its branches. Patience followed, making tiny, fearful sounds as her skirts caught upon the dried bracken.

She sidled close to Anne, her gaze darting about this sunlight glade. "Mistress, 'tis bad enough that the queen requires us all to attend the maying, the day being Satan's tool for claiming ownership of our souls. Why must she send us to wander unprotected in this dank wildness?"

"You know well enough I have no choice but to do as my royal mistress commands," Anne said, rolling her eyes in frustration. Upon their arrival in the meadow this morn, Elizabeth had declared her bower not festive enough. Her maids were dispersed into the fields and woodlands to gather more flowers with which to decorate it. It was Anne's chore to find the mayflowers. "What I cannot understand is how you can call newborn foliage speckled with sunlight a dank wildness."

"What else would I call it?" Patience replied, her eyes narrowing and her arms crossing as she gathered momentum in her complaint. "Men and women are wandering unchaperoned among these trees. They could be doing—things—in the shadows."

"I'm not," Anne retorted, wishing to God she was doing anything other than keeping company with her governess. She thrust an arm into the tree. Thorns snagged at the fine cotton of her shirtsleeves as she cut a flowering branch.

"I daresay it won't be long before you are." Jaw set, Patience waited until Anne laid the flower-bedecked bough into her basket along with the others, then reached out to yank at her mistress's oversleeve. It dangled beneath Anne's arm by the ribbons that tied it into her bodice.

"Has not the day's evil already tempted you into untying your sleeves?"

Anne shot her keeper a nasty look. No matter how right Patience might be about the impropriety of loosening her oversleeves, she had no intention of refastening them. "I'll not have the thorns ruin them, not when this is the first chance I've had to wear them."

Nay, she wasn't about to let anything ruin her attire, not when she knew she looked so fine. In accord with the day's pastoral theme, she'd paired sleeves and overskirt made of a fragile sky-blue silk with a white bodice and underskirt embroidered with tiny flowers in every color of the rainbow. Her hair was covered with a pearl-strewn red caul, while a wide brimmed hat trimmed with bright ribbons sat upon her head.

Again, Anne thrust her arm into the hawthorn. The clippers closed on the next branch with a satisfying

snap. Would that it were Patience's neck. This helped
to ease her irritation, then woke her need to tweak
her keeper.

"You're wrong if you think this maying sinful," she
said, laying the branch atop the others. "I find the
queen's celebration far tamer than those I knew at
home. 'Twasn't to display cold foods that the folk in
the village near Owls House spread their blankets. I
can think of four lasses who came to childbed nine
months after." She cast a knowing look upon Patience.

Patience's eyes widened in shock. "Nay," she
gasped, mortified.

"Good morrow, Mistress Blanchemain."

Both Anne and Patience started at this unexpected
greeting. Together, they whirled to face the pathway
behind them. Three men stood upon that thread of
dirt, all awaiting the chance to present themselves to
the heiress.

As the oldest of them bowed, his belly jiggled beneath his red doublet. "Mistress, we were introduced
yesterday. I am Sir George Fulmerson." Only then did
Anne remember he was a widower looking for a wife
to mother his young children.

The handsome man at the other end of the wee
group swept off his cap. "Master Richard Newton,"
he said. Anne nodded. Mary had spoken of him, saying he was a good Protestant, although apparently not
so strict that he shunned celebrations. More importantly, he was connected to the duke of Norfolk.

As he rose from his bow, a charming smile bent his
lips. "I'd offer you my services in your quest for
branches. No doubt you'll find my assistance more
beneficial than that of others." The slur found its target as Sir George shot him a snarling look.

Caught between them like a grain between the millstones was young Master Kelway. Although this was a day for tromping about wood and field, the slight lad wore silken attire more appropriate to the Presence Chamber. Anne didn't doubt he'd chosen the more formal dress in the hopes his otherwise meek appearance would be disguised.

"I would aid you as well," the youth proclaimed, grimacing as his voice squeaked up an octave.

Patience glowered, finding evil intent hidden in their innocent offers. This pleased Anne well indeed. With a smile, she beckoned them to her. "But you must all help me in my first official duty for Her Majesty," she told them.

Once through the bracken Sir George elbowed his way past Master Richard to snatch up her basket, then held it out so Anne might lay her next branch into it. "I understand your life was quite isolated with your mother, Mistress Anne," he said. "Could it be this is your first maying?"

"Of course it isn't," Master Newton snapped, before Anne had a chance to speak. The young man's narrow nose nigh on quivered at the indignity he perceived done to her by Sir George's question. "How can you conceive of anyone in all England who hasn't been a-maying?"

Anger shot through Anne. How dare he speak for her? As she clipped another branch she crossed Master Richard from her list of potential mates. "Owls House is not so isolated as to leave me ignorant of such things," she said, trying not to give Master Newton the satisfaction of confirming his arrogant statement.

Sir George scowled at the man, then his mouth took a sly twist. Vindictive pleasure sparked in his eyes as he set to driving off the competition. "Speaking of ignorance, 'tis said your master, the duke, isn't content to own half of England. I hear Lord Thomas plans a wedding that will give him all of Scotland as well, although I doubt his choice of wives will please our Gloriana."

Anne drew a quick breath and turned to look at the middle-aged knight. Three days at court and she'd already heard the rumors that Thomas Howard, Duke of Norfolk, meant to wed the Scots queen. Her gaze darted to the duke's man, as she awaited his answer.

Master Newton's eyes narrowed, while his hand had dropped to rest where his sword might have been, had it been buckled atop his velvet attire. "Gossip is for old women," he warned, his voice low and harsh, "and ancient men, like you."

His challenge sent new worry tearing through Anne. Another thing three days at court had taught her was that Elizabeth's courtiers owned tempers hotter than any coal. "Peace, gentlemen," she said to them, trying for a soothing tone. "I pray you, do not argue before me or I vow my heart will break."

Her words came too late. Sir George's face reddened, the second of his chins disappearing as he thrust out his jaw. Dropping Anne's basket, his hand flew to his nonexistent sword's hilt. "Do you dare insult your better?"

"Better?" Master Newton snarled. "If you are, 'tis in title only. Why not try me and then we'll see who is the better man."

Anne glared at them. She'd rather remain unwed for all her days than choose a husband from these sorts of men. The desire to encourage them to fight each other to the bloody end rose. To her way of thinking, the world would be a much safer place without either of them in it.

"Enough," she snapped, "begone with you, taking your argument with you as you leave me."

Both men started at her commanding tone. While Sir George stared in shock, Master Newton's eyes narrowed in disgust at such forward behavior in a woman. "As you will, mistress," he said, then turned on his heel and strode away without a backward look.

"Mistress Anne," Sir George tried to protest.

Anne shook her head, no longer caring what he thought of her. "Nay, Sir George. I will not tolerate such violence in my presence."

The knight sighed, then bowed. "I beg pardon, mistress, praying the insult I have done you won't ruin what remains of your day." 'Twas with sadness in his step that he started toward the meadow.

"Good riddance," Patience muttered beneath her breath.

"That leaves only me," Master Kelway crowed quietly, nearly wriggling in his satin at such good fortune. He turned to Anne. "I am your servant, Mistress Blanchemain. Cut your branches." He snatched up the basket and awaited the chance to collect his bounty.

His solitary state didn't last long as brush rattled from beyond the hawthorn. 'Twas Master John Fayrfax who pushed his way through the dry bracken. "Why, Mistress Blanchemain," he cried as if startled to find her here.

"Surprise, surprise," Patience said irritably, not the least fooled by this seemingly chance encounter.

Anne offered Master John a welcoming smile, then caught the glint of gold from over his shoulder. As she looked past him, her breath snagged in her chest. 'Twas sunlight gleaming on Master Hollier's hair as he followed his companion through the woods.

The man who would be her dancing master looked

fine, indeed, with a soft leather jerkin atop his blue doublet and gray breeches. There was a sprig of hawthorn in his cap. Like many men this day, he eschewed a ruff and opted to wear his shirt collar open, revealing the strong column of his neck.

'Twas only as her new dancing master came to a stop beside Master John that Anne noticed the youth walking between them. This youngling was a pretty dandy no older than Master Kelway. Anne stared at him. He seemed familiar, although she was certain she'd never before seen him.

"My Lord Montmercy." Master Kelway bowed toward the young fop.

Anne hid her smile. Now, why hadn't she recognized the noble lad's arrogant pose for what it was? No doubt this was what she recognized. All the lords held themselves so. "My lord," she said and bobbed him a quick curtsey.

As she rose, a tendril of curiosity unwound within her. How strange it must be for Master Hollier to see another nobleman receive the respect he could no longer claim. Her gaze again slipped to him.

He was studying the foliage around him with an air of disinterest. There was an odd prick in Anne's heart. It seemed her grandsire's warnings had been more effective than she'd thought.

"You are looking fine this morn, Mistress Blanchemain," Master John said, his broad face fairly radiating his plea for the invitation to tarry a while with her.

Again, Anne's gaze slipped to Master Hollier. Her dancing master was now inspecting his gloved fingers as if bored by this whole encounter. The pricking in her heart worsened.

As if he felt her look, Master Hollier lifted his attention from his fingers. Their gazes caught for just an instant. There was nothing in his eyes for her to read, no clue as to why he no longer found her worthy of pursuit.

Anne's eyes narrowed. Nay, she'd not ask them to stay, not if he was going to ignore her. She forced her gaze back upon Master Fayrfax. "You are kind to say so, Master John," she told him, smiling at his compliment even as she refused him what he so craved.

The big man's face fell. He bowed with great flourish to hide his disappointment. "Enjoy the day, Mistress Blanchemain."

"Mistress," the young nobleman said as he also bent to bid her adieu.

Anne waited for Master Hollier's farewell. He barely inclined his head in her direction, then turned toward the young nobleman. "What say you, my lord, shall we return to the meadow?"

"Aye," the handsome youth replied, already moving away ahead of his companions. "You were wrong to think there was anything within these woods worth seeing. I say 'tis more likely my warden set you to distracting me whilst he removed Berta." There was a note of accusation in his voice.

As Master Fayrfax followed his companions, his steps dragging, Master Hollier laid his arm over the lordling's shoulders. "Why, the very idea, my lord," he protested as they made their way to the path. " 'Twas naught but exercise we sought in our walk. I'm certain your return will find the maid right where you left her."

Anne frowned as she stared at his receding back, the pricking in her heart growing worse with each breath. Master Hollier seemed almost eager to part company with her. Well, if that's how he felt she'd have no dancing lessons from him.

Master Kelway turned toward her and thrust out the basket. "I'm ready for your branches, Mistress Blanchemain," he prodded.

Struggling to hold onto even a shred of her previous joy, Anne returned to the task at hand. As she again put her clipper's mouth to a branch, Patience leaned toward her so suddenly their hat brims collided.

"Did you see how that big one nigh on gaped at you?" her keeper whispered, her reference to Master Fayrfax making him sound more ox than man. "This is all your fault. Did I not warn you? Men will think you shameless for going about with your shirtsleeves exposed."

What remained of Anne's fine mood evaporated. She yanked on the newly cut bough. The branch burst free of the tree in a shower of white petals and a rending of fabrics. With an angry hiss, she whirled on her maid.

"Look upon this and cease your nagging," she snapped, displaying the new tears in her sleeve and glove. "I'll not ruin my attire to please your ridiculous standards." That said, she thrust the slender limb at Master Kelway, the vigor of her offering driving the slight man into a backward step.

He steadied himself, his gaze darting between servant and mistress, then cleared his throat. "Mistress Anne, you may tell your maid there's no wrong in a woman exposing her shirtsleeves," he assured her, his expression earnest. "Why if there were, no woman at court would wear oversleeves of tissue so fine the garments seem invisible."

Anne's mouth tightened as anger escalated into rage. 'Twas bad enough he'd listened to what should have been private. Now he dared to contribute! Well, 'twas a pitiful day when she needed someone so mouse-meek as him to defend her. With a bold swipe of her imaginary quill, she crossed his name off her list of potential husbands.

"I think I am finished cutting branches for now," she told him with a curt nod of dismissal.

Hurt flashed through his eyes and he clutched her basket close to his chest in refusal. Flowers showered the front of his doublet, one fragrant white petal floating upward to cling to the faint line of his eyebrow. This only served to make him look all the more young and foolish.

"You think me a stripling barely able to carry his own purse, don't you?" In his words lived the deep shame of one who knows he'll never be as much man as those around him.

Anne's conscience twinged. "Of course not," she lied. " 'Tis only the thorns that concern me. They've done me damage enough. I'd not have your attire ruined as well."

Confidence returned and he beamed at her. "Mistress, I would shred all I own if I could but be of use to you."

Instantly the image of this girlish man dressed in nothing but tatters and a petal on his brow filled her. "Pray, do not," Anne cried, half in jest, half in horror as laughter roared through her. She clenched her teeth against it. "I vow I would never ask such a thing from any admirer."

His eyes took light in unfounded hope. "If not that, then what would you have of me?"

In his words Anne found the way to escape him without doing further injury. "Would you give me time alone to straighten my thoughts? The others and their argument have soured my mood. I will walk with you to the wood's edge," she offered as a sop.

Although it wasn't much of a gift, not with the

meadow so near, pleasure blossomed on his face. "I am your servant," he assured her as he handed Anne's basket to Patience.

As she took it, Patience glared at Anne. 'Twas the opportunity to commit sin she saw in her mistress's harmless offer to an equally harmless man. Anne made a face at her and dropped her clippers into the basket.

Master Kelway extended his elbow in invitation. Anne wound her arm into his, still trying to ignore the wayward flower on his face. At her touch, his eyes came alive with a new sort of joy.

"Mistress, I cannot tell you how your touch pleases me. Say you want more of me than this simple stroll," he begged quietly as they started toward the meadow.

Wicked delight rushed through Anne. Oh, but 'twas heady having so many men at her feet, even if she knew their pretty compliments were nothing but empty air. Each time any one of them threw himself before her, she took a wee taste of the power the queen wielded over all of England's men. "How you tease," she laughed.

With that, the need to rid Master Kelway of the offending flower merged with her need to tweak Patience. Lifting her hand, Anne used the tip of her finger to dislodge the petal from his brow. Patience gasped at her charge's forward behavior, while Master Kelway's face came to life with the belief he'd gained the heiress's favor.

He dropped to one knee before her. "Sweet mistress, you do honor me with your touch," he cried, claiming her hand as his own. "I vow, my heart is given, my body yours." As he spoke, his fingers slipped up along her wrist to probe beneath the loose band of her shirtsleeve, his caress belying his earlier assurances of propriety.

Anne laughed at such daring from one she'd assumed meek. "First your clothing, now your body?" She let her voice lower into a husky, suggestive tone. "Pray tell, whatever would I do with your body?"

His eyes glazed. Whether 'twas images of her beneath him or visions of Sir Amyas's fortune that danced in his mind, Anne couldn't say. His eyelids lowered, his mouth softened into a girlish curl. "Use it, use me as you will, mistress. I am yours," he murmured.

"Mistress Anne!" Patience's shrill cry pierced the woodland quiet.

Anne's keeper thrust herself between them, toppling Master Kelway in the process. Pushing Anne back a step, Patience turned on the startled gentleman. "Such behavior! Get you gone from her!"

Anne laughed, spring's exhilaration once more pulsing in her veins. There was joy for her in this game, for she could play it with impunity as long as she had her keeper to guard her. Indeed, she was doubly guarded, for she dared never give way to any man on pain of her secret's exposure.

"Be off with you, now, knowing I will keep your proposal in mind," she told Master Kelway as she turned back to the tree and her task.

Anne froze. Lord Deyville now stood beside the hawthorn. Although the old man still wore mourning attire, today's doublet was relaxed in cut and his slashed breeches were made of soft leather. A great golden pin set with a green stone held his massive golden chain in place upon his breast. Even though the nobleman grinned at her, 'twas anger she saw flashing in his gray eyes.

"What a tease you've become, Mistress Anne," he called. "Why not come play that game with me? I daresay the outcome will be different."

Chapter Ten

"How dare you speak so to my mistress!" Patience cried, sweeping past Anne to confront this next menace. Hands on hips, she commanded, "Begone with you!"

Lord Deyville's gaze did not even flicker in the servant's direction. Instead he stared at Anne, his lips held in a taunting twist. Lust's heat warmed beneath the anger in his gray eyes. 'Twas adultery he would commit with her. Anne hid revulsion behind a cool mask. Here was one sin Patience need never fear she'd commit.

Bowing her head, Anne bent her knees just far enough to acknowledge his superior rank. "My Lord Deyville, you honor me with your presence," she said, the coldness of her voice belying the compliment of her words.

"My lord?!" Patience cried.

Anne's gaze darted to her keeper. Amyas's lackey stared at the nobleman, her expression awestruck, then the hostility drained from her. Patience plummeted into a curtsy so deep her brown skirts puddled on the forest floor around her. "Oh, my lord, I am so sorry, but I didn't know 'twas you."

Her apology was wasted. Deyville's gaze never left Anne.

"My lord," Master Kelway said, offering his better a brief bow as he came to stand beside the woman to whom he'd promised himself, heart and body.

The nobleman shot the youth a harsh look. " 'Tis private business I have with Mistress Blanchemain. Be off with you." Master Kelway stiffened, his already aching self-image injured anew.

Anne wound her arm into Master Kelway's. "There's no need for you to go," she sweetly told the youth. "Whatever business he has with me can be uttered in your presence."

"Go, boy, unless you'd prefer to lose your position at court," Deyville retorted, the calm coolness of his voice adding weight to his threat.

Master Kelway shrank into himself. He glanced from the nobleman to Anne. Although shame colored his cheeks, his fear was greater than his pride. With a sorry nod of his head, he removed his arm from Anne's and did as his better bid.

Her stomach souring, Anne watched him abandon her. More fool her for thinking there might be even the slightest truth in his pretty words. How many of the men at court were like him, all breath and no backbone?

New anger followed. Who did Deyville think he was, sending away her suitors? They weren't affianced, nor would they ever be if she had her way. The sooner he understood that the better.

As if he'd read her thoughts and found in them no threat, Lord Deyville's lips parted. The baring of his teeth was not quite a smile. Passion burned in the new color that touched his lean cheeks.

"Come, mistress," he urged, his voice low and vicious, "ply your wiles on me as you did that stripling. Come see how a true man plays your game."

Anne let her eyes widen in an expression of innocence. "I cannot imagine what you mean, my lord," she lied.

Sharp amusement darted through his gaze. "Oh, but I think you can. 'Tis this I most admire in you. Your fire would be wasted on the mealymouthed or the meek. It's a man who's not afraid to use the whip when necessary that you need, a man like me." 'Twas a promise for their future.

Only they could have no future. Of all the men to discover her secret, Deyville was the one most likely to kill her for it. He would never believe she'd come to court no maiden, thinking instead that she'd given herself to another if for no other reason than to spite his claim on her.

Anne stared boldly into his eyes as she set a barrier between them. "Pray tell, my lord. How fares your wife?"

His brows lifted, his expression saying he thought little of her puny effort. "She has not improved since last we spoke. How charmed I am that you should remember her. Know you, I will not soon forget it of you."

Here was another promise. Nay, 'twas a threat. He would see she paid dearly for her defiance once they were wed. This only fed Anne's anger. Did he think her so weak that she'd stand still and allow her grandfather to force her into such a marriage?

She threw his threat back in his face. "Indeed, my lord, I have thought of her often since our meeting, even including her in my prayers."

"This is true, my lord," Patience dared offer as she sought to amend her earlier error while aiding her employer's cause. Anne's daily prayers, one hour each morn and one each eventide, were the only thing about her charge that pleased Patience. "I have oft-times heard her mention Lady Deyville's name in her devotions."

Her assurance didn't provoke even a glance from Lord Deyville. Instead the nobleman crossed the glade to Anne and caught her hand. Startled, she yanked, trying to free her fingers. His hold tightened until she winced. Left with no other option, she retreated to arm's length from him.

He smiled at her, the goad in his grin. 'Twas a fight he wanted. He wanted her to run so he might chase her, the thought of hurting her as he forced himself upon her thrilling him.

"Such kindness and caring on your part shouldn't go unrewarded," he said, although unpunished was what he meant.

His thumb moved over the ridge of her knuckles. "Mistress, whatever have you done to your glove?" Deyville cried in mock distress as he looked at the rent the thorny branch had left in her thin hand covering. He tsked. "Why, 'tis torn to bits and your skin is cut beneath it. My heart breaks to see you so injured."

So saying, he lifted her hand to his mouth, keeping his gaze locked on her face. His eyes were hungry for more than a simple kiss upon her knuckles. Fear stabbed through Anne. He meant to do rape, right here!

As she tensed to battle him, she caught the echoes of laughter and festive music that rose from the nearby meadow. Her shoulders relaxed. Nay, he was but trying to frighten her. With the possibility that someone might come upon them at any moment, he'd do nothing more than fondle her. She steeled herself to endure his caress without feeding him the reaction he wanted.

The tip of his tongue probed the tear to taste her skin beneath it. Anne's jaw clenched against so lewd a caress. Pleasure made his eyes darken to almost blue.

Patience squeaked as what should have been a brief touch stretched into something altogether different. She swept forward to stand alongside Anne. "My lord, you must release her," the servant told the nobleman.

Straightening, Deyville caught his other hand around Anne's wrist, then turned her hand in his to unbutton her glove. As he did this, his lips parted. The new color burned along his cheekbones. Again, panic shot through Anne, sharp and deep. If someone didn't come soon, there was no telling how far he'd go with his torment.

"Release me, my lord," she demanded, again yanking on her arm as she sought to reclaim ownership of her hand.

He gave her arm a cruel twist. Anne gasped as stars burst to life before her eyes. All resistance relaxed as she fought to regain control of her spinning senses.

Patience gave a small shriek. "My lord, what are you doing?" she cried, wringing her hands. Again she might as well have been invisible.

As he began to peel Anne's glove from her hand, she managed to curl her fingers, preventing its complete removal. Still, her palm was bared. Lord Deyville pressed a kiss to the cup of her hand.

"I cannot help myself," he murmured against her skin, peering up at her to gauge her reaction to his attempt at lovemaking. He pressed his lips to the sensitive skin of her inner wrist, then pushed up her shirtsleeve to kiss her inner arm.

"Do you know what torment it is for me to watch all those other men sniff at your skirts? Mistress, my heart is yours, my body given to you to use as you see fit." 'Twas a profane mockery he made of Master Kelway's harmless words.

Straightening with a laugh, he jerked her toward him. She fell against his chest, her hat tumbling from her head. Bracing her hands on his chest, Anne pushed. He latched his arm around her back to hold her against him. Aged he might be, but there was no breaking his hold.

Panic gave way to terror. What if no one walked by to stop him? Anne opened her mouth to scream for help. Deyville's eyes took light in the hope that she would.

She snapped her mouth shut on her shout. Why did he want her to call attention to what he did?

Her breath hissed from her as she understood. If the queen learned of his attack, it wasn't the nobleman Elizabeth would send from court. Nay, the queen was keeping her peers close. Instead it would be the newest maid of honor who departed, no doubt under the mistaken notion that her removal would protect Anne from Deyville's unwanted attentions. Then Amyas would keep Anne prisoner until Lady Deyville was buried and properly mourned.

"My lord!" Patience cried in protest, her shrill voice echoing in the glade. "You must release her."

Rage exploded in Deyville's eyes as the servant at last forced herself into his awareness. "For God's sake woman, hold your tongue," he snarled. "There's nothing that happens between us now that won't occur once we're wed. Hinder me further, and I'll see your employer beats you for it. Now, if you wish to wait upon your mistress until I'm finished, go yonder and sit."

Patience yelped. Since she was powerless to stop the nobleman, she did the only thing left to her: she turned on her charge. "Did I not tell you to fasten your sleeves? See now where your bold ways have brought you?!" Her voice quaked.

As Anne realized she was well and truly abandoned, rage roared through her, tearing panic to shreds. She splayed her fingers across Lord Deyville's chest and shoved with all her might.

Trapped in resentment, Kit strode into the woodlands toward the glade where he'd last seen Mistress Anne. If it weren't bad enough that he'd had the dream again last night and lost the better part of his rest, the queen had proclaimed today as the day for her maid's first dancing lesson. Christ, but that meant every eye in the field would be upon them. Although Kit's footwork was vastly superior now to when he'd first come to court, he was no Hatton or Leicester. New worry followed. What if Sir Amyas's complaints had already been heard and he was to lose his appointment? The easiest way for the queen to remove him without leaving herself open to criticism, was to publicly expose his lack of skill.

At the glade Kit stopped. His eyes widened. Lord Deyville stood with his arms about Mistress Anne as she thrust away from him with all her might.

"Aye, fight me, love," the old nobleman laughed, yet holding her with ease in the entrapment of his arms. "Fight me and I'll still have my way with thee. Come, sweet, but press your lips to mine and I vow I'll be satisfied."

"What is this?!" Kit shouted, then wondered why he'd wasted his breath. He could see what it was! 'Twas that worm-eating son of a bitch trying to steal the very thing Kit needed to restore his brother's title, that's what. Aye, and by the look of it, the old man would have been between Mistress Blanchemain's thighs in another few moments.

Deyville looked at him, murder in his eyes, while the hope of rescue filled Mistress Anne's dark gaze. Not that his appearance had stopped her battle. Nay, she yet strained and shoved at her captor, trying to free herself from a man half again her size and her better in rank.

Respect stirred. In that moment Kit knew without doubt she would have battled Deyville to the bitter end, had Providence and the queen not sent him to her. The thought of one so lovely battered and torn by Deyville's evil made Kit's heart twist. Ah, but freeing her from her captor wasn't as simple as barging in and demanding Deyville release her.

Sweeping his cap from his head, Kit offered the peer his most formal bow, as if coming across a nobleman forcing himself upon the queen's maid was an everyday occurrence. "A thousand pardons for the intrusion, Lord Deyville," he called out in his best fawning courtier's voice, "but I've come for Mistress Blanchemain."

The old man still held tight to the maid. "Begone with you," Deyville commanded, as if Kit were some lackey.

He nearly smiled. 'Twas a ploy, meant to prick a man's pride. Deyville wished to goad the intruder into striking the first blow. Since doing so would result in Kit's banishment from court, Mistress Anne would be neatly deprived of the witness she needed to corroborate her claim of assault. Nay, Deyville would have to do better than words if he wanted to provoke an attack.

"My lord, I fear I cannot go. I am commanded to return with Mistress Anne. You'll simply have to give her up," he replied, ladling a goodly dose of sardonic amusement onto his words.

'Twas a far better weapon than any blade, drawing something more precious than blood from an arrogant lord. Fury twisted in the nobleman's face. Deyville's hold on Mistress Anne loosened as he reached for the sword he didn't wear.

The queen's maid was ready. With a great shove Mistress Anne propelled herself out of her captor's arms. Off balance, she staggered backward, until her maid caught her about the waist. Clutched together, they eased to the edge of the glade. There, the servant turned to run, but her mistress caught her by the arm. With a shake of her head Mistress Anne refused escape.

The frail woman moaned, then collapsed to sit on the ground. Mistress Anne looked at Kit. Although her face was yet pale in shock, 'twas the offer of support that filled her eyes. Kit's conscience ached. She meant to see he came unscathed out of her rescue.

Deyville glared at him. "How dare you interfere in what is none of your concern?"

A tiny breath of amusement left Kit. Ah, but preventing Mistress Anne's rape by another man was very much his concern. He plastered a simpering smile on his face. "Once again, I do beg your pardon, but the queen sent me to find Mistress Blanchemain."

"So you would say," the nobleman retorted, filling his words with disbelief as he threw the unspoken charge of "liar" at his opponent.

'Twas a second prod for reaction. Had Kit been a different man, Deyville might well have succeeded, but Kit had waited too long for the chance to restore Nick's title. To give way to an excess of conceit now would mean he lost all, when all he hoped to achieve was within reach. Aye, and the only thing that stood between him and his goal was an aging nobleman.

Now that Deyville had done his worst, 'twas Kit's turn. He pressed his hand to his chest in an actor's portrayal of astonishment. "My lord, if you do not believe me, you need only come with us and ask the queen yourself. You'll soon see what I say is true." However carefully cloaked, his challenge was there. Kit waited to see if the old man's arrogance was so great he'd agree to confront the queen with them.

Deyville took Kit's slap poorly. His face reddened, his hands clenched. So heated was his glare, the air between them fair seethed. What filled the old man's almost colorless eyes was the promise of Kit's ruination at the court.

The threat came too late. Participation in Lady Montmercy's revenge had already put Kit on a course for ruin. With nothing left to lose, he dared to drive his knife just a little deeper.

"Shall we go, my lord? I'd not keep my royal mistress waiting any longer than I must."

This was more defeat than the old man's pride could tolerate. Deyville's breath hissed from him. Without a word; he turned away from the glade.

Rage tore through Kit as he watched the nobleman stalk deeper into the greenwood. What sort of man raped a woman? Again, his conscience twinged. The sort who meant to use the weaker vessel for his own purposes—in other words, his sort. His stomach twisted, not much liking the comparison between himself and yon vicious old man.

He glanced at Mistress Anne. She was watching him, her hands neatly folded before her. Such courage she owned. Although her face was wan, there were no tears, no swooning. She smiled in gratitude.

Christ, but she was lovely. He gazed upon her face, drinking in her beauty, until he realized he was staring. So much for Bertie's recommendation of indifference. Even as he tried to look away, his gaze caught on the wee mole at the corner of her lush lips. Small and dark, it was a lure, calling him to come kiss her.

Desire's heat rushed through him, the sensation so powerful his shaft filled. Rage returned, almost blinding in its intensity. By God, he'd kill Deyville if that sordid old man ever again tried to touch his woman.

His woman? Kit catapulted out of a tangle of anger and desire into stark confusion, the transition stunning. What was wrong with him?

This wasn't his woman, nor could she ever be his, not if he wanted Nick's title restored. To harbor even a moment's care for her in his heart was to render himself incapable of using her as he must. With that, he set himself to slaughtering every bit of softness she'd made in him.

Chapter Eleven

Yet giddy in relief and with Patience still sobbing softly near her feet, Anne stared at Master Christopher. Gone was his earlier disinterest, leaving only the kindness she'd first seen in him. Her heart swelled. Even though Lord Deyville had tried to drive him away as he'd done Master Kelway, Master Christopher had stayed, doing so even after it was plain he earned the nobleman's hatred for doing so.

Not only was he a man of honor and bravery, but clever as well. 'Twas with words, not swords, that he'd battled Deyville and won. Anne's gaze slipped to the line of his broad shoulders beneath his doublet and jerkin, and a tiny thrill of desire shot through her. Not that he would have been outmatched had the meeting come to blows. He was a well-made man, and there was much more than safety for her to find in his arms.

As Master Christopher started across the glade toward her, Anne's eyes drifted to half closed. She willed him to put his arms about her so she might press a kiss to his lips. The image of her hand touching his bared chest followed.

Anne's eyes flew wide in disbelief at herself. What sort of idiot was she? There were only two men at court with the power to hurt her. She'd just escaped rape at the hands of one, now here she was planning to give herself over to the other!

Fighting to tame her wayward emotions, she watched him stoop to retrieve her hat. He halted before her, still holding her headgear in his hand. His brow was knit, his green eyes dark with concern for her. Against all her warnings to the contrary, her heart dared to sigh at this.

"Are you unharmed, mistress?" he asked.

She smiled at him. "I am, a fact for which you have my undying gratitude."

That slow smile of his played across his wondrous lips. "Dare I say 'twas nothing?"

Anne's heart melted, vanquishing all sense as it went. Her list of potential mates was doomed. From that moment onward, every man would be held to Master Christopher's standard. She very much doubted any other could match him.

"You will not say so, for it was not," she returned stoutly.

He laughed, the sound of his amusement deep and warm as his angular face softened. "Well, then," he said, "I only give thanks that our royal mistress sent me to find you when she did. I will add that she did, indeed, send me and is even now expecting our return."

That bit of news launched Anne out of her thwarted lusts. "Then, we must be off."

As she reached out to claim her hat from him, her shirtsleeve slid up along her arm. Where Deyville had held her wrist, the skin yet flamed a bright red, although portions were already bruising. Master Christopher stared at her arm.

Panic shot through Anne all over again. She snatched her hat from him, pulling it close to her side

to hide her arm in the folds of her skirt. The attempt
came too late.

When Master Christopher raised his gaze to her
face, new tenseness touched his jawline. Fiery lights
glowed in his eyes. "He hurt you," he said, his voice
low and harsh.

Even while Anne gloried that he should rage upon
her behalf, she dared not make an accusation. "Nay,
'twasn't Lord Deyville who did that," she replied,
" 'twas the snipping of hawthorns. I caught my arm
among the branches and was hurt when I pulled free."

His brows jerked upward at so implausible an explanation. For a moment he struggled with the polite
convention that demanded he accept this lie as her
explanation. He couldn't.

"Why this pretense?" he demanded quietly.

Anne bowed her head, not wanting him to see her
face as she told him only part of the truth. "Were the
events of this day to be revealed, I fear the queen
might send me from court."

"So she might," he agreed.

When she looked up at him, she found questions
still lingered in his eyes. He was too clever by far. It
was a long moment before he set aside his curiosity
and shrugged. "Then, we will keep this as our secret."

To share even something as horrible as Deyville's
attack with him filled Anne with unaccountable pleasure, as if in doing so they were somehow bonded.
She set her hat upon her head, then caught one of
her dangling sleeves and thrust her arm into it. With
its ruff and ribbons again tied at her wrist, her bruise
would be concealed.

"Again, you own my gratitude," she told him as she
donned the second sleeve.

Master Christopher's mouth lifted into a smile.

"Best you have a care with what you offer me. For all you know, I might be no different than yon nobleman." The jerk of his head indicated the direction Lord Deyville had taken as he departed.

Anne laughed at so absurd a notion and turned to Patience. Yet seated on the ground, her keeper looked up at her. The woman's face was bloated and red from crying. There was no trace left of her superiority. "You must rise," Anne commanded. "The queen has called for me, and I need you to fasten my sleeves."

Rather than come to her feet, Patience sat where she was, her eyes dribbling tears as another sob hiccoughed through her. "Mistress, I was so frightened, I couldn't even run," she whispered. "If not for Master Hollier, he would have—" Patience's chin trembled so violently she couldn't finish her sentence. At last she hung her head. "I failed you."

Startled by this admission, Anne stared at Patience, the dislike she bore her keeper daring to soften. She tried to squash it, reminding herself this was the same Patience Watkins who spied for Amyas. Come the morrow, her snide superiority would return. Instead compassion grew, until it no longer mattered where the woman's loyalty lay. Anne sighed as her heart's need to comfort overwhelmed all else.

"Will you give us a moment?" she asked of Master Christopher.

He nodded and backed away a few feet. Anne crouched and lay a hand on Patience's arm. "You did your best to stop him," she told her governess, keeping her voice low. "Lord Deyville is both a nobleman and my grandsire's friend. 'Tis he who has done wrong, presuming upon both those relationships to take advantage where he had no right."

"Aye, but," Patience muttered, "I should have run, calling for aid."

Anne gave thanks to God she hadn't. "Nay, now you mustn't blame yourself. Take heart. No harm's been done," she assured the woman. "In the future we'll have more care when we're near him."

This wrung a sodden nod from Patience. " 'Tis wrong that such a man should try to do you so when he's already wed. Such a man isn't worthy of marriage's holy estate."

Deep in Anne hope flickered to life. Perhaps, with the right cultivation, Patience could be turned into an ally in her fight to escape Deyville. "That's true enough," she agreed with all her heart.

The woman drew a shuddering breath, as if this bit of assurance lent her new strength. Patience struggled to rise. Anne put an arm around her to aid her. When they stood side-by-side, Patience wiped her eyes on the back of her sleeve.

"I must tell Sir Amyas what the nobleman's about," Anne's keeper said. She glanced about her, as if expecting to find her employer here, when they both knew he was in his London house.

However strong Anne's desire to inform Patience that Amyas already knew what Deyville intended, she bit it back. Patience wasn't capable of believing such evil of her employer. "How can we?" Anne asked instead. "Think how hurt my grandfather would be if he learned what his friend had attempted. Nay, this is best kept between us."

A terrible sadness filled Patience's eyes. Her lips quivered anew. "You are right," she said in a tiny voice that spoke of ancient hurts. "When it comes to their friends, no man believes what a woman says of them."

Anne stared at her. Pain radiated from the frail woman. Now, who would have suspected Patience could harbor such depth of emotion?

As if startled by what spilled from her mouth, Patience gasped and grabbed Anne's arm. Pulling her mistress a step closer, she worked at the oversleeve's ribbons. Her fingers trembled so badly the bow she made was loose and misshapen. At last she freed a shaken sigh and opened the knot to try again.

"Perhaps you will pay closer heed to me when next I tell you that only a hussy goes about with her sleeves undone," she said in a weak and toothless scold as she worked. Anne let it pass without comment, content to let Patience reclaim her former self.

Once Anne's sleeves were again fastened, Master Christopher offered his arm. "Mistress?"

With a smile, Anne accepted, winding her hand into the crook of his elbow. Her fingers rested against the curve of his upper arm, his muscle hard beneath the fabric of his doublet and shirt. He lowered his arm, drawing her a step closer to him as he led her out to the path. Their nearness set a shiver to making merry upon Anne's skin. Patience followed in silence, yet too distraught to complain over such closeness.

As they moved together toward the meadow, Anne's thoughts spun. Even as Amyas's threat against Owls House insisted she slam her heart's door upon Master Christopher, the memory of his crippled brother rose. How could she turn her back upon the one man who might accept Lady Frances for what she was? She couldn't, at least not until she knew how he felt about his brother.

Or was that just the excuse she used to put him at the top of her list of potential husbands, when the truth was she was attracted to him? Dismayed at herself, Anne eased a step away from him. 'Twas time to settle the matter of his brother, before things became any more complicated. No matter that she knew him too little to ask so personal a question.

"Master Hollier, I have heard it said your brother is much like my mother, being crippled." She let the blunt words drop from her mouth.

His arm tensed beneath her hand. When he glanced at her 'twas guilt and sadness that filled his gaze. "I cannot say Nick is like your mother, not knowing your mother," he replied, and fell silent. There was a finality to his quiet that suggested she'd heard all he would say on the subject of his brother.

Anne didn't need another word to recognize her answer. Master Christopher not only cared deeply for his brother, he blamed himself for his brother's crippling, just as she held herself responsible for her mother's state. Against all logic, her heart swelled in the certainty that this was the man she needed.

"Nan!" Mary's cry came from the meadow's edge. She and Mary both wore blue and white this morn, but Mary's sleeves and overskirt were in a darker shade, her white underskirt and bodice trimmed with silver. Quite a variety of wildflowers now sprouted from the band of her black, short-crowned hat.

With a wave, Mary started up the path toward them at her usual forceful gait. As they met, she smiled up at Master Christopher. "Oh-ho, so this is who's been delaying my cousin."

"Not at all," Anne retorted. " 'Tis slow me, who doesn't walk as fast as you, who is keeping him." The words reverberated through her. Would that she could keep Christopher as her own.

Master Christopher grinned down upon Anne's kinswoman. "I fear your place in my heart is in jeopardy, Mistress Radcliffe. Tell me you tremble at the thought I might replace you with your cousin."

This teased an amused snort from Mary as she looped her arm through Anne's. "Cousin, have a care with this one. He's all flattery and no action. Our Master Christopher is long at court but never married. Why is that, Master Bachelor?" 'Twas a taunting question, sparked with laughter.

Master Christopher moaned. "Must you harp upon this every time we meet?"

"Aye, and I'll continue harping until you give me an answer," Mary retorted.

"I always answer you," he cried in feigned distress, "but you never listen."

Releasing Anne, he dropped on one knee before his tormentor. " 'Tis you, Mistress Mary, who keeps me from marriage to any other, and well you know it. My heart was given from the first moment I saw you. Since you so cruelly refuse me, I can but pine away in chaste loneliness, loving you without hope of ever requiting that dear affection." He pressed one hand to his breast as if his heart were broken, while the other shielded his eyes to stop his tears. 'Twas the very picture of misery he portrayed.

"One day," Mary warned, shaking her finger at him, "I will win the truth from you."

"She wounds me again," Master Christopher cried, both hands clutched at his chest now. "Am I so poor a swain you cannot believe me smitten? Mistress Blanchemain," he looked at Anne, laughter quivering at the corners of his mouth, his eyes bright green with the pleasure of this game, "tell my sweet Mary that you can see proof of the heartbreak in my face."

"Oh, aye, I see it," Anne agreed, aiding him in his lie, when what she really saw was a barrier, no matter how amiable. He would play this game as long as Mary persisted in delving into something he had no wish to share.

Disappointment deepened. It just wasn't fair. Not only did her grandfather hate him, but the only man she felt qualified to be her mate did not wish to wed.

Mary giggled, sounding younger than the youngest of the queen's maids. "You shouldn't encourage him, Nan. Get up, you great buffoon," she commanded of her supposed lover.

"You have no appreciation for fine drama," Master Christopher grumbled as he rose. Slapping the grass from his knee with the back of a hand, he once again took Anne's arm.

"Come, then," Mary said, and started toward the meadow, pulling them all along with her at that nononsense pace of hers.

"In all truth, Mistress Mary," he said to Anne's kinswoman as they walked, "if I were to wed anyone, 'twould be you. I like your forthright nature. It must be a trait carried in the Radcliffe blood, for I suspect Mistress Blanchemain is much like you."

Anne glanced up at him. He watched her, desire glowing like bits of gold in his green eyes. The challenge rushed through her. Could she make him want her enough to win him?

"My, but he is clever with his compliments," Mary told Anne, her grin wide and pleased. "Should I worry that you've been learning flattery from 'Her Eyes'?" The maid gave sneering emphasis to the pet name her royal mistress had given the earl of Leicester.

"What?!" Master Christopher retorted as if shocked at the thought. "And have you despise me as you do that poor earl? Never."

Mary wagged a chiding finger at Master Christopher. "Best you hope your footwork is as clever as your words for my cousin's first dancing lesson."

Anne stopped, forcing her escorts to a halt as well. "What lesson?" she asked, dreading what was sure to be the answer.

Master Christopher tilted his head to one side as he confirmed her worst fears. "Her Majesty feels 'tis wrong that all others are enjoying the day's dancing, while you cannot."

"Not before all the courtiers and servants," she cried out, glancing between her kinswoman and her tutor in horror. Her heart pounded so hard, she swore it lifted both her bodice and the corset beneath it.

"Nan," Mary said, patting her arm, " 'tisn't so bad that you should panic over it."

But it was. It was worse than enduring Deyville's attack. Why, she'd die of embarrassment were she to stumble before all the court. Everyone would think her graceless and fumble-footed.

"Nay," Anne pleaded, even though she was certain she was beyond reprieve. She freed her hands from both maid and gentleman, then took a backward step. "Nay, I cannot do this."

Master Christopher caught her bruised hand with its tattered glove and pressed her palm to his chest. Anne felt his pulse against her fingers, while her skin tingled where his hand held hers. He smiled that slow smile of his.

"Mistress, anyone who can survive an encounter with a maid-eating hawthorn can weather with ease something as mild as a dancing lesson," he told her, then once more tucked her hand into the crook of his arm to lead her into the meadow and certain shame.

Chapter Twelve

Kit hoped his assurances eased Mistress Anne's mind, for they did nothing to change his own resentment over this impromptu lesson. With the certainty that a single misstep meant he'd be Mistress Anne's tutor no more, he led the two young women into the meadow. At this end of the field stood the wagons and horses that had carried them to the meadow. Nearby lay what had once been a fine, straight tree. Now stripped and wrapped in ribbons, it waited to become the morrow's maypole. Alongside it was a full wagon load of birch and sycamore boughs.

The pasteboard giants lay nearby. Gog and Magog, they were, each nigh on as tall as a house when manned. Right now, their fearsome painted faces were turned into the sod. By custom, they preceded the queen's party to Greenwich at the maying's end.

Would that the time for departure was nigh. Kit shot a hopeful glance into the sky. The sun yet held its own, although clouds billowed in the east. Aye, there'd be rain, but not soon enough to save him.

Beyond the wagons, the meadow opened up, its expanse awash in sound and motion. Folk sat about upon the grass, gamed or strolled, enjoying the fine day. Music rose from not one, but three flower-bedecked wagons, each group of court musicians vying to outplay the others. Near one, a stomping, shouting ring of folk turned, the gentlemen in their finery dancing shoulder to shoulder with servants just as vibrant in their brightly dyed worsteds. Screaming with joy, royal pages forgot their status to run with the grooms and scullery lads, whilst a full pack of tiny lapdogs chased them, nipping at their heels.

Bertie appeared out of the crowd. Dressed in his better blue doublet and brown breeches, with sprigs of hawthorn thrust into his hatband, Kit's servant looked handsome, indeed. He sent but the briefest glance toward his master, then began to carve his way through the crowd toward Mistress Anne's governess.

The intensity on his face surprised Kit. Not even when three lovely young things tittered, their voices rising as they sought to attract his attention, did Bertie waver. Kit glanced over his shoulder at the frail Patience Watkins. Her shoulders were bent, her head bowed. Where Deyville's attack had failed to quell Mistress Anne's spirit, it had broken the spine of her servant's pomposity. It seemed almost a shame to set Bertie on her now, when her resistance was so low. Still, he supposed she could say "nay" as well, if not better, than any other.

He led the maids toward the queen's tent, near the field's opposite end. The construct was made of fabric but seemed a woodland bower, so heavily was it decorated with flowers and leafy branches. This illusion was aided by the trilling of songbirds in cages hanging from the tent's supports.

There was but a single small chair beneath its canopy, set with thick, embroidered cushions. Given the day's relaxed atmosphere, this wee seat was enough to satisfy the royal need to be lifted above all others. After all, even the highest nobles were taking their ease upon the ground or on small stools as they drank the summer into being from their bejeweled cups.

At the moment the chair was empty. Elizabeth was dancing with Sir Thomas Heneage before her musicians' cart, encircled by her admirers. The tune was a quick one, requiring much fast and furious footwork. The queen's yellow skirts flashed as she moved. The gems on her white bodice glinted, the color nearly as fiery as her hair. Beneath the narrow brim of her brown hat, Elizabeth's face was alive with joy, her dark eyes sparkling.

"Faster," Mistress Mary cried out in pleasure, dragging Mistress Anne along beside her, "so I can watch."

Kit stretched his legs to keep pace with the maids, then glanced over his shoulder. Mistress Anne's servant trailed far behind them. Her gaze was on her mistress's back, her brow furrowed in concern, as Bertie circled in upon her like an eagle on carrion.

Once they reached the crowd around the queen, Kit used either a look or a shove, depending on the man, to cut a swath through the watchers. At last they stood behind Leicester's group. Where Kit dared not trespass, Mary didn't hesitate. With a gay laugh she inched her way between the earl's men, going with ease where Kit's passage would have provoked violence.

Once at the crowd's forefront, Mary clapped to the song's beat. "La Volta!" she cried along with all the rest. 'Twas the cue for Sir Thomas to lift his queen by her waist, turning as he did so. Held aloft, her hands braced upon her partner's shoulders, Elizabeth threw back her head and laughed.

Instant appreciation fired within Kit, his resentment forgotten for the moment. No matter what a man said of her politics, England's monarch was every inch as fascinating as any woman he knew. Almost any woman.

He looked at Mistress Anne. Now that Mary was no longer at her side, she'd moved as close to him as her hat brim would allow. Was it her dread over their forthcoming ordeal that brought her near, or a liking for him? Either way there was a great pleasure to be had in it.

As if she felt his look, she looked up at him. She tried to smile, the motion of her mouth faint. A crease marked the perfection of her brow. 'Twas dread, then. Oddly her worry over their upcoming dance worked to ease his own resentment.

The crowd called "La Volta" once more, indicating Sir Thomas should lift his queen for the last time; then the musicians brought the dance to a halt with a flourish of sound. Both Kit and Mistress Anne watched as the yet gasping Elizabeth laughed and curtsied to handsome Heneage. The crowd burst into applause. Together the twosome turned once about to accept this worthy accolade. Calls for another dance were met with a shake of the royal head.

"Nay," the queen said, " 'tis time for another brace to take the field and do their worst."

Plying her fan with vigor, Elizabeth's gaze darted ever so briefly toward Kit. 'Twas look enough to both acknowledge his presence and warn him to await her forthcoming command. With that, England's queen retreated to her tent, followed by her faithful Mary.

Kit looked past his retreating monarch to see who it was she'd collected about her to observe this lesson. Stiff and still, the Earl of Arundel sat near the tent's back, his thin face set in harsh lines. Like Nick, the earl yet clung fervently to the Roman faith. Not far from him sat his former son-in-law, Norfolk. The duke, a man only a few years older than Kit, looked unusually tense. Beneath the fringe of dark hair crossing his wide brow, Norfolk's dark eyes held worry in their depths.

Worried wasn't all Kit would be feeling were he the duke. Despite that Elizabeth had directly forbidden England's highest-ranking nobleman to have any further concourse with the imprisoned Scots queen, rumor said Norfolk persisted with his wedding plans. A quiet breath huffed from Kit. Since Norfolk was too honorable a man to be a betrayer, this made him a fool, for one queen or the other was sure to have his head should he dare to wed.

Leicester occupied the space nearest his royal mistress. Although Kit knew Norfolk and the earl were no longer sworn enemies, it was startling to see them sitting so near to each other.

Accepting the praise of her nobles with a gracious nod, Elizabeth settled into her chair. After fetching her royal mistress a cup of wine, Mary retreated to stand behind the queen's small chair. She smiled at Kit.

Just as Elizabeth nodded in his direction, the musicians pealed into another quick tune. All around Kit, the crowd yelled in approval, surging forward as everyone hurried to join the ring dance. Mistress Anne yelped as a man jostled her with enough force to knock her hat from her head. As she staggered to the side, Kit caught his arms around her, pulling her into his embrace to steady her, her back to his front.

His senses filled with her nearness, his body alive with the feeling of her in his arms. He need but turn his head and he could press his cheek to her hair, where it swept back into the containment of her caul.

A shudder wracked him as his gaze dropped to the swell of her breasts above her bodice. With her shirt parted, the sun gleamed against her exposed skin. Dear God, but he wanted to touch his lips to her flesh.

"My pardon, Master Hollier." 'Twas a fiery-haired gentleman, a man Kit knew to be attached to the Earl of Northumberland. The rough-hewn northerner held Mistress Anne's now ruined hat in his hand. "I meant no harm to Mistress Blanchemain."

The man shuffled nervously, no doubt hoping his apology would stave off any insult Kit might take. He needn't have worried. Kit was too busy taming his desires to attack some hapless stranger.

"No harm is done," Mistress Anne said for him. She stepped out of Kit's arms to take the battered remains of her headgear from the man. She gave it a sad shake. "At least not to me."

"No matter," Kit said, trying to smile. " 'Tis time to take it off, for our lesson is at hand."

She groaned, her eyes softening in pleading. "Do you think we could disappear into the crowd?"

This made him laugh. In the arms of a rapist, she fought like a tiger, but a dancing lesson left her knees knocking. "Nay, we cannot. Our royal mistress has already seen us and awaits our approach."

With that, Kit extended his arm in the formal manner required to lead a woman into Elizabeth's presence. There was usually an awkward moment or two when he didn't know his partner well as he sought to match his stride to hers. Not so with Mistress Anne. From their very first step, their movements flowed with startling ease. This boded well for their ability to dance together. As if they'd practiced for years, he and Mistress Anne knelt as one before their monarch.

"Ah, there you are," Elizabeth cried out as if she'd

not seen them until that instant. Her voice was still breathless with exertion. "Mistress Anne, how pleased you must be that we will oversee your first lesson."

"Madame, I am overwhelmed that you should spend your precious interest on one so unworthy," Mistress Anne replied. If her voice was filled with reverential awe, beneath it hid the hint that it did the queen's image no good to take on the menial task of her maid's dancing lesson.

Kit blinked and fought his laugh. Lord, she was a bold thing.

"As you should be," the queen blithely agreed. Mistress Anne's effort was wasted. So enamored was their monarch of dancing, Kit doubted it was possible for her to imagine anyone could dread the activity.

Elizabeth looked at Kit. "So, Master Hollier, what do you think appropriate for her first lesson?"

'Twas an easy test to pass. "I think something slow, with simple steps. What of a pavane, Madame?"

Well pleased by so sensible an answer, Elizabeth smiled and nodded. "A fine choice."

She clapped her hands and the musicians left off playing as they awaited her command. The dancers looked to see what had caused this halt to their pleasure.

"We'll have a slow tune," Elizabeth called out, "but nothing deadly dull. A pavane, something for one who has not danced before this day."

Anne tensed as her backward state was announced to the world for a second time. 'Twas without complaint that folk gave up their own amusement to come and witness this debacle. The muttering behind her grew until she peered over her shoulder. Her heart dropped. It wasn't just any folk, but every man who aspired to wed her standing at her back. Aye, and while they watched from that side, the country's highest nobles sat directly before her to watch upon the other.

"Up, up," Elizabeth exhorted teacher and student. "Give heed to your tutor, Mistress Anne, and dance," she commanded.

With that, Master Christopher took Anne's hand and drew her to her feet. He was smiling. If it wasn't enough to inspire confidence, his tight grip on her kept her from fleeing like the coward she was.

Only as she regained her feet did Anne realize she yet held her poor hat in her hand. She swung around, meaning to give it to Patience. Her keeper stood at the edge of the crowd, utterly unaware of her mistress's need as she spoke to a breathtakingly beautiful, if short, man. This paragon was smiling and nodding, as if whatever Patience said was fascinating.

Anne turned helplessly back to the queen. However did one rid oneself of a hat before a monarch? It was Mary who came to her rescue, stepping out from behind the queen's chair.

"Give it to me, cousin," she said. As she claimed the battered bit of straw, she leaned near to whisper, "Take heart, you'll do fine."

"Where would you have us, Madame?" Master Christopher asked of their royal mistress.

"Here," the queen said, an imperious wave of her hand indicating the forward portion of the tent before her own chair.

As the way cleared, Master Christopher led Anne to stand at the tent's far end, facing the musicians. The lute player plucked a few notes, then cocked a brow. Her teacher nodded in approval, and the man set to playing in earnest.

Anne's heart pounded. Her pulse thundered in her

ears. She clenched her jaw to keep from whimpering. Shame was bad enough. She wasn't going to give way to hysterics atop it, at least not yet.

Master Christopher lifted her hand, then eased a bit to the side. "Now, then," he said, "when I give the word, you'll turn toward me, offering me a small honor. We'll then turn to stand shoulder to shoulder. It'll be a series of the same steps that will take us all the way to the tent's end. Stand with your left foot behind you, as so." He pointed to his own feet.

"When we step out, it will be one step forward with your left foot, while the next step is meant to bring your right foot even with the left. This is all done to the tune's beat, so listen for the rhythm."

Although Anne nodded as if she understood, his words tangled and tumbled in her head. A small curtsy, a slow step. Back foot front with the left, then a second step. She stared at the tent's opposite end. It seemed a mile distant.

The music played. Master Christopher nodded slightly. She kept her gaze locked on him, waiting.

"And now," he told her, turning to offer her a small bow.

Anne curtsied too deeply. Before she'd risen, he had turned to face front and was preparing to take his first step. Her gaze leapt from his face to her feet as she straightened and turned. In the time it took to do this, he was already stepping. She hurried to catch up, but something was wrong. Off balance, she collided with him.

Master Christopher halted. A tiny rumble of laughter rippled across the crowd. The music stopped. Not daring to look at the watchers, Anne kept her gaze locked on her tutor as she fought off horror.

Although he didn't smile, amusement glowed in his

green eyes. "Nay, try again, starting with your other left foot this time."

Shame burned in her cheeks. She'd stepped right, instead of left. How could she have erred on something so simple? Anne steeled herself to make no more missteps.

"And the honor," he said, as the music began again.

She followed his instruction, feeling as wooden and gawky as a pasteboard giant. At least she used the correct foot this time. Up the length of the tent they went. Not once did they move as one.

"Mistress Anne," the queen cried, clapping time to the music, "heed the rhythm."

Rhythm? Anne couldn't hear anything except humiliation pounding in her ears. Once again laughter rippled over her observers. From the corner of the tent came a derisive titter. Anne glanced toward the source. 'Twas a group of ladies, among them Lady Montmercy and the viscountess of Hereford, who shared the fiery hair color of her royal cousin.

Still giggling, the youngest maid among them came to her feet. "Here, Mistress Anne, watch me." With the grace of a swimming swan, this babe glided up the tent's length, doing with ease what Anne could not.

"Turn and start again," the queen commanded.

Master Christopher's hand shifted until his fingers intertwined with Anne's. With this more intimate touch, his heat flowed into her. Her frozen soul began to thaw. He leaned his head near her ear. "You can do this if you but relax."

"I cannot," she moaned softly.

"Try this, then. Think of nothing but me next to you," he told her, his voice low. "Watch my feet, not yours, only listening for my commands. I'll tell you what to do with each step."

As listening to him was infinitely better than listening to folk laugh at her, Anne did as she was bid.
Once again the music played. She was ready this time.

"The honor, step, together," he whispered, his
words keeping time to the music.

Up the tent they went. She kept pace.

"Step, step, step, and together," he said, changing
the order of their steps. "Step to the right, together.
Now the left and together." Not a cue did she miss.

Only as the tent's wall nearly slapped Anne in the
face did she realize she'd gone the entire length of the
construct and made no error. She whirled on her
teacher, her eyes wide in joy. For the second time
that day, Master Christopher had saved her. He was
grinning, seemingly as relieved as she.

The ladies who'd laughed were now nodding. The
queen clapped, long and loud. "Well done," Elizabeth
cried, her voice echoing against the fabric walls, "well
done, indeed.

"Look here, my lord of Norfolk," Elizabeth called
to the nobleman. "Mistress Blanchemain again proves
herself a clever lass. This is the sort of woman any
man should be proud to take as his wife. Were we a
man, we'd look no farther."

Anger roared through Anne as she understood.
Elizabeth must know her noble cousin was yet considering marriage to the Scots queen. This hadn't been a
dancing lesson, but an opportunity for the queen to
drive home a subtle warning to the duke. What right
had even a queen to use another being as her tool!

She whirled on Master Christopher, rage spiraling
as she readied herself to protest such abuse. He
shook his head. " 'Tis her prerogative; we are hers
to command," he whispered. "Now, bank that fire

in your eyes, and we'll go bid her thanks for her compliments."

At Master Christopher's third rescue of the day, gratitude swallowed up Anne's anger. This was the man she needed at her side. With that, she tossed aside all the reasons she could not have Master Hollier as her husband. All that remained were the details, such as what he would think of her when he discovered she was no maiden. Ah, but that was a worry for later.

"I am ready," she told him, and together they started up the tent's length toward their queen's chair.

Chapter Thirteen

May God take the queen and her penchant for early morning walks and surprise audiences. Yawning, Kit leaned against the cold stones of Greenwich's garden wall, cloaked in what remained of night's shadows and the grayness of what would soon be a moist morn. Only servants and the queen were up and about, leaving all sensible gentlemen and nobles to their beds.

Shivering, he crossed his arms. Even with his coat draped over his shoulders, dawn's chill was deep. At least he wasn't alone in cursing the queen's odd habits. 'Twas Mistress Anne he awaited, to lead her into the queen's presence.

With that, worry over being replaced as Mistress Anne's tutor returned. In the four days since the maying, Elizabeth had kept him busy, sending him to London on what seemed a make-work chore. 'Twas almost as if she meant to keep him away from Mistress Anne.

Kit almost smiled. If so, then she'd failed, at least in the spirit; on every one of the past four nights, he'd visited Mistress Anne in his dreams. He ought to be grateful, since their lustful nightly visits kept his nightmare at bay.

Bertie was faring no better. His servant was gnashing his teeth over Mistress Patience. Instead of giving way to seduction, the woman was doing her best to convert Bertie to her Calvinism.

Men whistled and women laughed. Kit peered down the red brick length of the queen's residence, so called because 'twas in this building that old King Harry had housed his queens. Near the kitchen at its far end, the laundresses, already hard at boiling their linens, were speaking to the huntsmen.

He watched them, the scent of baking bread filling his lungs. All but one man climbed the kitchen's back stairs. The master of the hunt made his way toward Kit and the garden gate, nodding as he passed Kit, on his way to inform the queen of the day's quarry.

When he was again alone, Kit sighed back into the shadows. What concerned him most was that the queen hadn't arranged for any more lessons. This, despite the fact that she'd been more than a little pleased with the outcome of her charade. Where he'd hoped success would settle his position, here he was again wondering if Amyas had won his dismissal. And if he had? Angry frustration at the thought of yet another failure in his quest to restore Nick's title gnawed at Kit's vitals.

Usually this feeling could plague him for days, his sense of ineptitude lingering for weeks. This morn it gave way to a strange sort of relief. Startled, Kit pondered the feeling, only to come bolt upright.

May God take his soul, 'twas on Mistress Anne's behalf that he was relieved! When had he begun to let himself consider her pain as a factor in the restoration of Nick's title? Well, this simply could not be. Whether Amyas stood in his way or not, he'd use Mistress Anne as he must, giving no further thought to the cost of her downfall. Jaw firm in his resolution,

Kit shifted his coat over his shoulders as the huntsman reemerged from the garden.

"Her Majesty awaits you at the garden's end," the commoner said to the gentleman. So great was the huntsman's value to his royal mistress that he need offer Kit but the barest nod, before he strode away. 'Twas Elizabeth's love of the sport that brought her court here from May until her summer progress started, despite the palace's somewhat rustic condition.

Kit turned his attention on the long bank of stone buildings that followed the Thames, running perpendicular to the queen's residence. 'Twas from this part of the palace compound that Mistress Anne would come, as that was where Elizabeth kept her quarters. Unfortunately, all he could see of it was the water gate, a massive square tower studded with tall windows that allowed river egress to the palace. The windows were flat and dark, as dull as the day. It would be hours before the sun broke through the clouds, if it ever did.

At last Mistress Anne trotted through the narrow passageway that separated the two sets of royal residences. She paused, her cloak billowing open around her. Kit's brows rose in surprise. Even in the weak light he could see her bodice, sleeves, and skirt were all the same rich orangish-brown color. Such monotony of color was very much against fashion. Upon her head she wore a headdress of black velvet. Rather than detract, this plainness of color served to draw attention to the perfection of her face.

Peering past her, Kit waited for her escort to appear. There was no one, not her governess, a guardsman, or even a page. He frowned at her. Hadn't she learned anything from her encounter with Deyville?

By God, but he'd give her a good chiding for such idiocy!

Kit nearly groaned at his own foolishness. Here he went again, worrying about her, when vulnerable was just how he needed her. He watched her scan the garden's darkened wall. Her gaze slipped right past him without reaction. He smiled. As the wall was yet cast in deep shadow, she hadn't seen him. He considered stepping out to reveal himself, then discarded the thought. Like the predator he had to be, Kit stayed still and awaited his quarry's approach.

The queen had called for her, and she was late. The words kept repeating in Anne's head like some horrible litany. What if her tardiness caused the queen to lose her temper? Anne shuddered at the thought and squinted at the darkened wall, trying to remember where the garden gate was. So frayed were her nerves, she could barely see, much less discern the arch of stone that marked it. As she located her target Anne lifted her skirts with one hand, clamped the other upon her headdress to hold it in place, and ran.

This was all Patience's fault. Elizabeth's unexpected command left Anne no time for her usual morning prayers. When Patience's angry protests that duty to God came before that to earthly rulers went unheeded, Anne's keeper turned the act of dressing into the punishment. Laces were drawn with aching slowness through eyelets. Bits of attire were misplaced, only to be rediscovered long moments later.

Anne skidded to halt before the gate, the tiles that paved the pathway being slick with moisture. More fool her for ever feeling any softness toward that stubborn chit. Anne would have dismissed Patience at once had she owned the power. One thing was certain, if the queen punished Anne for her tardiness, Patience would pay as well, she'd see to it. She reached for the latch.

"Hoyden, did your mother never teach you 'tis unmannerly for a woman to run?" a man asked.

With a squeak Anne leapt back from the gate. Fear exploded in her. Idiot! Why hadn't she waited for a page to escort her? Because Patience had made her late and a page would expect her to walk.

The man shifted in the shadows. Anne took another backward step, half fearing it was Deyville, although she'd heard he'd left Greenwich. Instead Master Christopher appeared out of the darkness.

His breeches, coat, and hat were all a pewter color, while his doublet was a muted blue-gray, the color bringing out unexpected blues in his green eyes. Its collar was so tall, it forced the lacy folds of his ruff to follow the strong line of his jaw. This morn a tiny earbob dangled from one ear.

"Oh, 'tis you," she said in breathless greeting, trying to stem the delight that flooded over her at this encounter. She'd nigh on eaten her heart out these past four days thinking he was avoiding her. "Where have you been?" The words were out before she could stop them.

The pleasure that filled his face at her question was almost worth the possibility of the queen's wrath. "I was in London on the queen's business."

He turned to open the gate, then stood aside so she might precede him into the northernmost of Greenwich's two pleasure gardens. Anne strode a few feet into the enclosure, then stopped in dismay. Unlike the southern garden, which was arranged in a series of squares marked out with walks, each plot filled with low-growing herbs planted in careful designs, this side was far wilder. Apple and pear trees, their branches clouded in delicate blossoms, stood upon small hillocks thick with a velvet carpet of grass. Crowded at their feet, daffodils nodded with heaven's every sigh, humbly accepting the shower of cast-off blooms that snowed down upon them.

Bees droned, birds sang. Panic soared. How was she to know where the queen was? Anne turned right and trotted toward the far wall along the narrow paved pathway, all the while peering through the foliage as she sought something that might point her in the right direction.

Master Christopher strode alongside her. "Where are you going?"

"The queen has called for me, and I'm late," Anne cried out without pausing as her belled skirts jerked through the thick grass.

"Ah, so that's what has you dashing," he said, his voice filled with gentle teasing. "I heard our mistress has been a bit sharp of late." Friendly amusement glowed in his green eyes.

"This is no jest," Anne snapped.

"Aye, you're right about that, the queen's anger is no jest," he agreed. "Now stop. You're not late."

"How would you know?" Anne stretched her legs as she tried to escape him.

He caught her elbow and pulled her to a halt. "Did no one tell you that the queen called us both to her?" he asked, a frown marking his brow. "I can but guess we're to speak of dancing lessons. As for being late, you can't be. We weren't expected for another quarter hour."

Anne froze in relief. There would be no royal raging. 'Twas a sign that God forgave her for missing her prayers, even if Patience never would.

Master Christopher smiled. "Feel better, now that you know she'll not be angry with you? Frankly, I'd not have thought you one so easily frightened."

"Anyone who does not fear our mistress's rages is a fool," she told him, with a shake of her head. "Yesterday, Mistress Brooke dared speak boldly to Her Grace, something that well and all deserved a chiding. But so wild and wicked was the tongue-lashing she received, the poor lass collapsed."

Still awed by the event, Anne's voice grew hushed. " 'Twas like nothing I'd ever seen. The things she said, I vow, my ears burned. No one dared come near her for an hour, not even Mary, for fear she'd start again."

He winked at her and offered his arm. "You tell me nothing I've not seen with mine own eyes. Ah, but where there's storm and thunder, there's heaven as well. 'Tis one of our princess's smiles that everyone at court covets."

"I suppose," she replied as she settled her hand into the bend of his elbow.

With the feel of his arm against hers Anne's resolve to wed him firmed anew. Well, then, if she was to have him, the sooner she began to chip at his defenses, the swifter the deed would be done. She shifted nearer to him until their upper arms touched and set herself to charming him as best she could.

"You may lead me to my mistress, Master Escort," she said, then smiled, "but only if there'll be no more nagging over my manners or lack thereof. That, I have in plenty from my governess."

"Nag?" he protested, his lips held in a half smile as he gave a cocky lift of one brow. "I'd never nag. You're much too lovely for something so crass as that. This way." He turned and led her back toward the gate.

Yet clinging close, Anne laughed. "Glad I am you were sent to wait for me, else who knows how long I'd have wandered in this wilderness."

"Sent?" His face was the picture of righteous indignation. "I'm wounded to the core that you should think 'twas necessary for any man to send me into your company. I, mistress, am your faithful servant, my hands and feet yours to command."

Anne stifled her groan. A week at court, and she was already swimming in body parts. This was followed by a terrible need to do mischief. "Haven't you anything better to offer?"

He came to an abrupt halt. So complete was his surprise that his mouth opened, his brows high upon his forehead. "I beg your pardon?"

Anne fixed an innocent expression on her face. " 'Tis just that I've no need for either your hands or your feet, having been offered so many of these by other men. What of your liver? Might I have that, or has some other woman already laid claim to it?"

The most incredible series of emotions flashed through Master Christopher's eyes. There was shock that she should tease him whilst he was in the midst of flattery, then appreciation for her jest, followed by a flash of fear so brief that Anne wasn't truly certain she'd seen it. At last the corners of his mouth lifted. Golden lights sparked in his green eyes, and fine lines of amusement creased his cheeks.

"My liver, is it? A kidney would not do?" He tilted his head to the side as he spoke, his mouth pursed and one eye closed, as if he were dickering over an item at the market.

Anne knit her brow to show she was considering this trade, then shook her head. "Nay, 'tis the liver or nothing."

"I see," he said. "Well, then, my liver it must be. However, since that organ is more precious to me than my hands or feet, I fear I cannot simply give it to you. I must have something in trade."

Disappointment shot through Anne. Was he so single-minded in his pursuit that there was no imagination left to his flattery? "And what would you have from me that might be its equal in value?" she asked, bracing herself for what would certainly be the suggestion that she give him her heart, trading one organ for another.

He drew her into his embrace, his arms held loosely around her. "A kiss," he said, his voice almost hoarse with his need for her. "You may own my liver in trade for a kiss."

A tremor tore through Anne with his words. Beneath her palms she could feel the steady thud of his heart. Heat spread from where his arms touched her to every corner of her being.

How she wanted to feel his mouth on hers, but it was his walls she meant to breach, not to let him through hers. "Nay, I fear that would not be an even trade," she told him, keeping her tone light and teasing. "My kiss is priceless, or so I've been told. You'll have to add something to the bargain if you're to have it."

"What might that be?" he demanded softly, lifting a hand to brush his fingertips against the curve of her cheek.

Even wearing gloves, his touch was enough to make Anne's knees shake. With a laugh she turned and danced out of his reach, skipping a few steps up the path. Master Christopher stood where she'd left him.

"I'm not certain. Let me think on it some," she called back over her shoulder. "Are you content to wait until I've calculated the value of my kiss, no matter how long that might be?"

"Mistress, I would wait for you until the world ends," he said. Pretty words, belied by the disappointment in his gaze.

Anne's smile broadened. "And so you very well may."

"Why, you little tease!" he cried, the sound stained with laughter.

He started after her, but Anne skipped away, her swinging skirts tossing cast-off petals with every step. She turned toward him, her hands on her hips. "Nay, I'd call it tit for tat. 'Tis nothing more than payment for you calling out of the shadows this morn and frightening me near to death."

He came to a stop before her, then swept his hat from his head to offer her his most graceful bow. "I am justly repaid. Since you'll not kiss me, I suppose there's nothing left to do save kneel before our mistress and see if we keep our heads attached to our necks today."

Chapter Fourteen

Behind his smile Kit's teeth were clenched in frustration. How could he be wanting her so badly he could barely think, when she seemed untouched by the slightest pang of desire? Bertie was right. She'd seen his plan for her on that first day and was now warned against him.

At least there was no hesitation on her part when he again offered his arm. Nay, no hesitation at all. Dear God, but it was both heaven and hell to have her so close to him. While he stewed in his own juices, she glanced happily around her, savoring the garden's beauty as he led her to its far end.

'Twas Mistress Mary, along with the prim-faced countess of Warwick and pretty Lady Scrope, who bore Elizabeth company this morn. These women already wore their green and brown hunting attire, while he and Mistress Anne had to wait until after this audience to change for the day's sport. Without farthingales beneath their skirts, the women's clothing clung strangely close to their legs.

Mistress Mary pointed to them, and Elizabeth turned. As with all her other garments, the queen's attire set her above the rest. Her forest-green doublet was decorated with golden ribbons and a great pin set with emeralds, while a tall white plume waved from her hat.

"Why, here is our Mistress Blanchemain, looking fine indeed this morn," she called out, sounding as pleasant and sweet as any woman might. Whatever had soured the royal mood these past days seemed to have eased.

As Kit and Mistress Anne reached her, they began to kneel. Elizabeth waved her hand. "Nay, I'll have none of that this morn. Here, walk with me a moment."

Startled, Kit glanced at Mistress Anne. She was as surprised as he that they should be allowed such intimacy. There was nothing for them to do save join their queen as she strode a few yards back into the garden.

"You should be aware that there is a wager," Elizabeth said without preamble as she stopped. She glanced between them. Even in the day's rain-grayed light, the jeweled pins that held her curls in place glinted.

Her gaze settled on Mistress Anne. "It seems the earl of Leicester believes it will take all the summer for you to become adept in the slower dances. Indeed, he swears a galliard will be out of your reach before Yuletide."

"Madame?" Mistress Anne asked softly, the hesitation in her voice saying she wasn't certain what response was expected of her.

"I, however, have more faith in you, lass," Elizabeth went on, a touch of a smile lifting her thin lips. "I wagered against him, saying you'll not only be capable of all the dances by July's end, but be expert in the La Volta as well."

The queen turned her attention on Kit, her dark

eyes afire with the need to best her favorite. "Have you the skill to accomplish this?"

'Twas the opportunity of a lifetime she handed him. Although he had no hope of ever trading on it, Kit couldn't resist fixing his face forever in his monarch's memory. "Fie on you, Madame," he dared to tease. "You are attempting to alter the conditions of the wager by this meeting."

Elizabeth's fine feathery brows lifted as she grinned. "Fie on you for pointing that out. Think on it as naught but a bit of a hedge." The intensity returned to her dark gaze. "In all truth, even if I said nothing to you, I'd remain convinced she can swiftly learn to dance. At the maying I saw she owns the ability, but an apt pupil needs a clever teacher. Now, tell me true, can you do this?"

Kit glanced down at Mistress Anne. There was worry in her gaze. She feared what might happen to them were they to fail in this endeavor. Bitter amusement filled him. That wasn't where she needed to spend her worry. If he had his way with her, they'd both be gone from court before July's advent. He looked back to his monarch.

"Madame, I think if we practice on a daily basis without interference from others, I'll have her dancing the La Volta by July," he lied.

Mistress Anne's hand clenched on his arm, her nails digging into the fabric of his coat, doublet, and shirt. Although no trace of it showed in her face, she was furious with him.

Elizabeth's grin was wide and pleased. "But of course it must be private. 'Twouldn't do to have Leicester think I had any hand in this, now, would it?"

With her words the queen doomed any appeal Old Amyas might make for Kit's removal. More than that, she gave him reason to spend time closeted with his intended victim. Thoughts of failure in his quest for Nick's title gave way, leaving Kit's spirits soaring.

"Madame," Mistress Anne cried, almost dropping into a curtsy as she spoke, "will folk not think me forward for spending so much time alone with Master Hollier?"

Too caught up in her need to win the wager, the queen waved away her maid's concern. "No one, save for a select few, will know you are alone together. Moreover, Master Hollier is my gentleman and will behave as such." There was a note of warning in this. "You'll also have the musicians and your governess as chaperones."

This time, when England's monarch glanced between them, the joy of scheming showed on her face. "Now, here is the how of it. I'll see a place set aside for your daily use, but once a week you must still practice within sight of all others. In those practices Mistress Anne must seem clumsy and flat-footed."

She paused to look at her maid. "I saw how your pride ached at the maying, and know this will gall you right smartly. Take heart and let them think you clumsy, content that you will prove them wrong, come July."

Kit felt Mistress Anne's start of surprise at this; she hadn't been to court long enough to realize there was little that Elizabeth missed. "Aye, Madame," she replied. "I will look forward to that day. What of my duties?"

Elizabeth smiled, delight beaming from her. "Your schedule will be arranged around your time with Master Hollier. Now, be you also warned that the earl will ask you to dance in the coming weeks, testing you. Take care and reveal very little of what you've learned. Step upon his feet if you must." The thought of her maid treading upon her favorite's toes made her smile again, the movement of her mouth owning a certain sly satisfaction to it. "Need I warn either of you that no one should know of this conversation or our plans?"

"Your secret is ours to keep, Majesty," Kit assured her. God knew, he wasn't going to invite the court to watch him seduce this woman. Mistress Anne only nodded, as if she dared not open her mouth for fear of what might leap off her tongue.

"Aye, then, we're settled with this," the queen replied, more than satisfied with all that had occurred. "If you feel you need a tutor to aid you, but slip me notice and I'll see the man hired. These lessons will begin upon the morrow, for on this day, we hunt. Now, hie with you both and be off to prepare. 'Tis the fair roebuck we're after."

"Majesty," Kit said with a bow. Beside him, Mistress Anne offered a small bob. Even before they'd begun to back away, the queen whirled and strode to her companions.

"Hie with all of us," the queen cried out. Whether her voice was light in anticipation of the day's exercise or at the thought of hoodwinking her favorite, there was no telling. " 'Tis time to rouse the house and be at our pleasure."

"Come with me," Mistress Anne hissed, catching Kit's arm in both her hands. She nigh on shoved him down the path away from the queen's party.

He let her drag him nearly halfway to the garden gate without protest. Why complain, when he could happily enjoy the angry jerk of her skirts as she stomped? When the path forked, she turned into a secluded leafy grove.

Even though he knew she was furious with him, pleasure woke as the branches closed around them. Soon he and she would be lying in just such a place, doing more than sharing the kiss he'd promised her. The anticipation of their lovemaking was enough to send his desires winging anew.

Once she was certain they were private, she grabbed him by the arms and stared up into his face. "What are you thinking!" she cried softly. 'Twas terror and anger over what she thought lay ahead of them in her question.

Kit almost laughed. The last thing she needed to know was what he was thinking. Instead he set out to soothe her into his clutches as best he could. "Do you not see this opportunity can do us both good?" That was not quite true, as laying with her would do him more good than her.

"By God," he continued, "have you any idea how many men would slit my throat for a chance like this?"

Mistress Anne's eyes widened as anger overtook fear. "You've traded my safety and well-being for a chance at royal favor!"

Kit blinked in surprise. If the queen won her wager, her gratitude would be equal to the triumph she felt at besting Leicester. This could well mean a promotion to a better position at court. The possibility of restoring Nick's title through fair means hovered just beyond his reach, then slipped away.

To win favor, Mistress Anne would have to dance and dance well, indeed. 'Twas far-fetched to think they could cram a lifetime's worth of lessons in less then three months. Still, if he wanted her alone and vulnerable, he had to appear as if he believed the feat possible.

"She'll hardly separate our heads from our necks for failing," he protested. "Nay, the worst that can happen is we'll be relegated to the ranks of the invisible. Now, I'll have no more of this nay-saying. You'll dance and do it well come July's end. Set your eyes upon success, and trust me."

His conscience screamed in protest over his choice of words. Until this moment he hadn't realized how much he could hate himself. By July, she'd be deflowered and driven from court. The only positive in all of it was that he'd be dead. Since he was no longer a follower of the Roman faith and not quite a faithful Protestant, he supposed he'd find himself in hell. 'Twas just punishment for his sins, and would, no doubt, leave him beyond caring over the harm he'd done to her.

"Nan?" Mistress Mary cried. "Nan, are you here?"

Anne started at her cousin's call, then pressed a finger to her lips to bid Master Christopher to silence. When she glanced over her shoulder, she gave thanks that the branches were thick enough to shield them from Mary's view. Not that her kinswoman would tell tales, but 'twas unseemly to be discovered hiding with Master Christopher. Despite the queen's assurances, Anne would have to be far more careful about who saw them and where.

"Nan?" Mary's voice was more distant, suggesting she had moved away from their bower.

"Let me go first," Anne quietly commanded her dancing tutor. "I'll not have Mary think ill of us."

Master Christopher bent his head toward her in agreement. "But, of course. Anything to please you, mistress."

"So you would say," she retorted.

Turning, she darted out onto the path, and stopped

to glance up and down the thread of colored tile. There was no sign of her cousin. From the distant stables, horses whinnied and grooms shouted as they prepared for the hunt. Nearby, spades scraped into earth as the gardeners set to their daily chores.

"Mary?" she called.

"Nan?" Mary called back, having moved farther from Anne's hiding place. "Where are you?"

"I'm coming to you," Anne cried. Lifting her skirts to follow her kinswoman's call, she left the path and made her way over a tiny hillock. Mary caught sight of her and turned to meet her. As she crossed beneath a brace of trees, they showered her with moist petals.

Mary laughed and swept them off the shoulders of her green hunting doublet as Anne joined her. "I vow this place is too wild by half. 'Tis almost indecent."

"You sound like Patience," Anne replied as she linked her arm through her kinswoman's.

"Are you calling me ill-tempered and narrow-minded?" Mary cried.

"You know I am not." Anne smiled as they matched their strides and made their way back to the path. 'Twas a joy to walk alongside a woman who had no liking for mincing steps. She glanced over her shoulder. Master Christopher had left their hiding spot. Gentleman that he was, he headed toward the opposite side of the garden.

When she looked back to Mary, she found her kinswoman's eyes alive with the thrill of prying out secrets. "I may have found something."

"About Lady Montmercy?" Anne lowered her voice into the tones of conspiracy, even though she was certain they'd not be overheard. To date, she'd had no luck finding anyone willing to speak of the noblewoman.

Some of the sparkle left Mary's eyes. "Well, not precisely about her. 'Tis about the old lord from Master Williams, the earl of Pembroke's secretary."

"So tell me," Anne demanded quietly, knowing this was the prod for which Mary was waiting.

"It seems there was bad blood between the old lord and Sir Amyas some years ago, when they were both serving on the Court of the Wards," Mary said. "Master Williams said they nearly came to blows more than once, requiring the ushers to part them."

Anne frowned. Although this was interesting, it wasn't the answer she needed. "Is there more?"

"It seems that Lord Montmercy had a gift for ferreting out his enemies' secrets, then using them to his advantage." Mary glanced up as a pair of wee birds darted from one tree to another. "Moreover, he hated the Protestant lawyers who gained power in court."

"Of which my grandsire was one," Anne murmured, then she sighed. "While this is reason for my grandsire to despise old Lord Montmercy, there's nothing here that might make him fear the lady."

"Nay," Mary agreed. "There is something more. It has nothing to do with your grandsire, only Lady Montmercy, but it's a trifle odd."

"What's that?" Anne asked as their progress along the path startled a squirrel. The creature leapt up a sapling to chitter at them in irritation.

"It seems Lady Montmercy surprised all the court when shortly after our mistress's ascension to the throne she asked that her son be given over to royal wardenship."

Anne considered this a moment. Lord Andrew had been born just before his sire's death, in the last year of King Edward's reign. "He would have been, what,

six years old then? Although 'tis a bit young, there
are pages of that age in court right now."

"Aye, that's true." Mary's expression filled with curiosity. "Still, Master Williams made a point of saying
how devoted Lady Montmercy seemed to the lad
throughout all of Queen Mary's rule. Then, of a sudden, she gives him into royal care and assumes a place
at court."

"Maybe, the lady has strong Protestant leanings?"
Anne suggested.

Mary made a face at this. "She hardly seems the
religious sort."

Anne shot her kinswoman a smiling, sidelong
glance. "Perhaps she but used the boy as an excuse
to avoid Queen Mary's company? More likely she'd
her fill of motherhood. She doesn't strike me as one
who would have room in her heart for much more
than her own self-interest."

"That much is true," Mary said with a laugh.

"Do you think we could speak to Lord Andrew
about his mother?" Anne asked. "Maybe he'd have a
clue to this conundrum of mine."

Mary giggled. "Have a care you do not approach
him at the darkened end of a chamber. He's all hands
and a ready cock."

"So I've heard," Anne replied, remembering the
lordling's complaints over his warden removing his
doxy at the maying. "Will he be hunting? If so, perhaps you and I can ride near their party."

"Aye, that we can." Mary's eyes filled with delight.
"Then, once the picnic begins, we'll sit with his company and ply him with questions."

"We can do that?" Anne asked as her heart leapt.
Master Christopher wore the Montmercy badge.

Would he be riding with his lordling companion this day?

Mary shrugged. "But of course we can. 'Tis the hunt, and there's no order in that. Now, hie, or we'll be late!" She grabbed up her skirts and dashed toward the gate.

Anne laughed as she ran. 'Twas just as well that she'd have Mary as her chaperone. She wasn't entirely certain her dancing master wouldn't be all hands and ready cock himself, or that she wouldn't enjoy it if he were.

Chapter Fifteen

There could be nothing so glorious as a headlong gallop through a fragrant and budding parkland, even if the day was marred with misty rain. It didn't matter that the breast and long sleeves of Anne's green hunting kirtle were sodden or that the hem of her brown underskirt was thoroughly splattered with mud; her hat might never again be the same. Who cared, when in the melee she and Mary had attached themselves to Lord Montmercy's party?

'Twas a great bevy of roebuck the queen and her court chased. Save for their small size, the dainty deer was worthy prey, the roebuck being a cunning beast. Twice had the bevy escaped their pursuers, and twice were they found again. When last their group had spotted them, the deer had lost their leaps and fallen into a flat run, their sides heaving.

"Hold, now," Master Fayrfax bellowed, looking all the more massive in his woodland attire as he called the six of them to a halt.

They drew their mounts together. Above the snorting of their horses, there were distant shouts. The hounds belled, the sound so fractured by the trees and low-hanging clouds that Anne couldn't guess at their direction.

In his fur-trimmed brown coat, Lord Montmercy

looked every inch the nobleman, his dark steed as arrogant as he. "Which way?" he demanded.

"East, I think," said Sir Edward Mallory, smiling against the day's pleasure. Now that he was away from those he wished to impress, the young knight's face had relaxed out of its somber lines, revealing another man, this one surprisingly boyish and merry.

Anne had earlier swept him from her list as one too ambitious to care for marital harmony. Now she wondered if she'd been too hasty. Nay, he was too much of a popinjay for her. Or, rather, he had been when he'd ridden out of Greenwich's gate. Beneath Sir Edward's dark coat, the many bows that prettified the front of his doublet had all been undone by the wind, the ribbons now streaming down the garment's front in a wild tangle.

"Listen," Master Christopher commanded, his eyes narrowing as he strained to hear. Beneath him, his horse danced, eager to run once more. 'Twas a fine sight he made, with his legs clad in tall brown boots gartered atop leather breeches. Beneath a sturdy brown coat, his doublet was the color of a fir tree. This made his eyes seem all the greener. Anne vowed to herself that when she was his wife, she'd see he dressed in no other color.

"There," he pointed. "They are to the west of us."

The huntsman's horn sounded again, piercing the leaden sky like a clarion call. It came from the west, as Master Christopher suggested. They listened to the bleats; the rhythm said the deer were finally at bay.

"Away!" Mary shouted, jabbing her heels into her mount's sides. Her horse lunged, sending her hat slipping to the side. Even as she grabbed at it, she was leaning forward in the saddle, urging her mount to greater speed.

Master Fayrfax bellowed at the thought of missing the hunt's end and turned his horse's head. Lord Montmercy whipped his steed into a full gallop, his coat flying. But 'twas Master Christopher who took the lead. As he leaned low over his saddle, his horse shot from the pack, as eager to be at the kill as his rider.

"God's wounds, Kit, you'll not best me this time," Sir Edward shouted after him, driving his own mount into its fastest pace, his ribbons streaming.

Laughing, Anne leaned low in her own saddle as her mount raced over hillocks and through the sparse trees. The belling of the dogs grew louder. Folk shouted in exultation, the few female voices threading like silver into the roar of masculine thunder.

The queen's party had trapped the dainty beasts in a narrow hollow. Amid the feathery new grass and budding birch, the rascals turned and sidled, seeking escape even as they faced their doom. Elizabeth loosened her bow and took the biggest of them, a full roebuck.

Once she had hers, the others of high rank closed in for their kills. On this day none were spared, not the does, kids, or gerles. As the deer dropped, the harrying hounds circled and cried for their meat, while the watchers shouted their approval.

It was all over too quickly for Anne. As the fire was built, she dismounted and watched the huntsmen give the dogs the roebucks' feet. How could she ever have found any enjoyment in her quiet life when there was so much excitement to be had? 'Twas sad to think that in only a few months she would leave all of this behind her. The next minute she frowned. What was happening to her that she should put her own pleasure ahead of her mother's needs?

As the huntsmen carried away the carcasses, the

roebuck's meat being prized as a healthy food, the
trailing servants had found their noble masters. They
brought with them food and blankets, then laid out
the feast with care even though no one was likely to
tarry long in this weather.

With their congratulations given to their mistress,
Mary and Anne were free to stroll. They chose a me-
andering course through the many groups, offering
greetings and polite conversation to each. It wouldn't
do to insult or appear obvious as they made their way
to Lord Montmercy's party.

A shiver shot through Anne as they drew near.
Sprawled upon his patron's blanket, his body braced
upon his elbow and a cup caught in his hand, Master
Christopher looked relaxed, indeed. Like many of the
other men, he'd opened his collars to reveal the strong
column of his neck. He was watching her, his need for
her nigh on pulsing from him. Surely if he were already so hot, it wouldn't take but a few of their lessons before he was ready to forget his need to remain
free in trade for that kiss. Ah, but once she'd tasted
his lips, would she be content to do no more?

Lord Montmercy looked up as she and Mary
stopped at the edge of his blanket, his dark blue eyes
showing pleasure that they should, again, come his
way. If his face was reddened from their ride, he'd
left off some of his arrogance with his coat. "Mistresses, will you honor us with your presence?" he
asked in formal invitation.

Anne blinked in surprise. He sounded different with
his voice hoarse from the shouting and the wet. Indeed, in its roughened state there was something in
his tone and cadence that plucked at memory's string.
Someone else she knew sounded like him. Even as

she reached out to grasp that one's identity, the whole slipped from her fingers.

"Please," the lordling went on with all the open-handed generosity expected of his rank, "come, break bread with us this day. There is plenty."

"There is, indeed," Mary replied with a laugh as she surveyed the feast. Lord Montmercy had done better than just a bit of bread and meat. There were boiled eggs, cold fish, pickled eels among other delicacies to tempt the tongue.

"Could we, cousin?" Anne asked of Mary in keeping with their planned mummery. "Would such a thing be appropriate?"

"I am not certain," Mary replied, her brow creased.

"But of course it would," Master Fayrfax said in encouragement. "We are all in the open here."

"Master John is right. There's no harm in it," said blond Sir Edward as he once again offered them his boyish grin. Every one of his bows had been retied.

Mary and Anne glanced at each other, then smiled. "We are convinced," Mary said, speaking for both of them as they curtsied to the young nobleman. "My lord, we would be honored to sit with you."

"You must sit here, mistresses," Master Fayrfax said, rising to offer his corner of the blanket. His broad face held a hungry look as he watched Anne. 'Twas as if he hoped to devour her instead of his cold meat pie.

"I expect that means I'll need to move," Sir Edward sighed in pretended inconvenience. He rose with Master John to leave the corner for the women. "Ease over, Kit, and make room for us," he said to Master Christopher.

Kit. Anne rolled his pet name against her tongue. She liked its feel in her mouth.

The queen's maids drifted down to sit in a pretty pile of petticoats. Once settled, Anne glanced at Master Christopher. He half smiled, then turned his attention into his cup.

Anne's eyes narrowed. So he thought to pretend disinterest, did he? She looked at her host. "I must confess, I was hoping you might invite us to sit with you, my lord."

"Glad I am to hear it," he said, Lord Andrew's tone suggesting he believed any woman would be glad of his invitation.

"Indeed," Anne went on, ignoring his pompous pride as she manufactured the jab she meant to send Master Christopher's way. "I only now realize my selfishness in claiming so much time of my kinswoman. I wholly forgot how devoted Master Hollier is to my cousin."

"Nan!" Mary cried, blushing. "He is not devoted to me."

"Did I say aught amiss?" Anne cried, playing out her prank for all it was worth. "But, Mary, at the maying he fair swooned over you, calling you beloved. Was I wrong to take his words to heart?" She glanced from her cousin to her victim.

If Master Christopher's eyes were narrowed in the promise of retribution, his mouth quivered in laughter. He looked at Anne's cousin. "Speak for yourself, Mistress Mary. I *am* devoted to you, just as I told Mistress Anne."

From his new seat behind Master Christopher, Master Fayrfax's face darkened as he caught a hint of the private undercurrents in this jest. Anne took the gentleman's jealous reaction as good advice. To show too much preference for Master Christopher in public would set tongues to wagging, and that wouldn't do at all.

"Have you heard the latest?" Master John asked, seeking to bring himself to Anne's attention. "I think Sir William Cecil is trying to curry Norfolk's support by aiding the duke with his suit in the Court of the Wards." His voice lowered. "With our royal mistress's secretary at his side in the Wards, you can be certain Norfolk will strip Leonard Dacre of both title and inheritance."

"The duke can do this?" Anne asked astounded.

"Lord Thomas is rich and powerful enough to do anything he wants, save marry the Scots queen," Sir Edward retorted.

"He could do that, too, if he could get Cecil to champion the idea to our queen," Master John retorted, certain his tidbit made him seem important to Anne.

"Nay, Sir William's too canny to put his head in such a noose," Sir Edward replied with a scornful snort, "knowing Elizabeth is dead set against the marriage, even though it could solve the problem of what to do with an exiled queen."

Anne looked from man to man, then glanced at Master Christopher and shrugged in confusion. He smiled.

"Enough of politics," he said. "Let us ask instead how our Mistress Anne enjoyed the hunt."

" 'Twas wondrous," Anne replied, with a sigh. "Everything at court is so much more active and interesting than anything I've previously known. I fear I will find it difficult to leave when the time comes."

Lord Montmercy looked shocked at this. "Why would you go?" he asked.

"Spoken like a man who's lived every day for the

past eleven years in his queen's court," Sir Edward teased. "Because she is the sole heiress to her grand-sire's estate, Mistress Anne cannot long stay a maid. She must wed."

Stung, Lord Montmercy reclaimed his arrogance and frowned at the young knight. "Does marriage mean she can no longer come to court? When I wed, I'll keep my wife close at hand."

"I doubt 'twill be you who chooses to keep close," Master Christopher laughed. "I think me your wife will want to keep you near to hand so you'll be less inclined to stray."

The youth had the grace to blush. Mary giggled, his companions laughed. Anne turned her smile into her lap, not wanting to insult her noble host.

"As for your husband, who is it your grandsire has chosen?" Sir Edward asked.

Anne's head snapped up. "No one, as far as I know. Why do you ask?"

The young knight looked startled. "I beg your pardon, but I thought—" he paused, then frowned. "Well, now, this is strange, indeed. Sir George Fulmerson said he approached your grandfather with an offer. Sir Amyas turned him away, saying another had been there before him." Sir Edward shrugged. "Perhaps he only said so to reject Sir George."

"Perhaps," Anne lied, working to hide her emotions. She well knew who that other was. Slow anger grew at Sir George. How dare he approach her grandfather without even asking her preference.

"It must be," Mary said. "Surely your grandsire would have spoken to you before arranging anything. It would hardly do to leave you uninformed, as you might unwittingly entertain other offers."

"Sir Amyas doesn't strike me as one to keep such

a thing secret," Master Christopher said, watching her with an odd sort of concern in his eyes. "Indeed, I'd guess him more likely to trumpet the man's name to all the world, then yank our Mistress Anne from court to make the arrangements for the wedding."

As the rest of his companions laughed at this, Mary clapped her hands to get their attention. "Pay heed, now," she demanded. "I am changing the subject.

"Anne and I have set ourselves the task of trying to understand her grandfather, since she knows so little of him. My lord, we think you may be able to help us in our quest. 'Tis said that your father and her grandfather had much discord between them."

Lord Montmercy looked surprised at this. "I couldn't tell you if it was truth or no. I never knew my father as he died just after my birth. Do you know aught of this, Ned?" He glanced at Sir Edward. As the young knight had just taken a bite of a cold meat pasty, he could but shake his head to the negative.

Master Christopher paused, his cup lifted to his lips. "Old Lord Montmercy hated everyone, or so my father was fond of saying," he said. "There were rumors that Montmercy believed he could displace the Seymours and rule England throughout the boy-king's childhood."

"What of your mother, my lord?" Anne asked, following the pattern of questions she and Mary had planned between them. "Does she ever speak of my grandsire?"

Master Christopher shifted suddenly, drawing his long legs in as he lifted himself into a sitting position. Anne glanced at him, a little startled by his abrupt movement. He brushed at his doublet, having dribbled wine upon it. "Damn me," he muttered.

Lord Montmercy's expression closed. "If you want

any information about that coldhearted bitch, you must ask her yourselves." Although he sought to make his words harsh and uncaring, his pain was so deep, tears started to his eyes.

Stunned that a simple question could have wrought so intense a reaction, Anne set aside decorum and reached over to lay her hand on his. "Pardon, my lord, I meant no harm by asking."

"You couldn't know," he muttered, striving to regain control. When he failed, he came abruptly to his feet and started away from the other picnickers without a word.

Master Christopher rose. "I'll go after him," he said, turning to follow the youth.

"My pardon, Sir Edward," Anne cried to the knight. "We truly intended no harm."

"Aye," Mary agreed, her voice echoing the same distress Anne felt.

Sir Edward offered a rueful grin. "He's right when he says you couldn't have known. 'Tisn't common knowledge, but his mother will not have even the smallest words with him. When he came to my brother as his ward, 'twas all my sister-in-law could do to staunch his tears, so deeply did he mourn for his lady mother. Yet the months, then the years passed, and she would heed no call and reply to no letter."

Anger flared in his fine-boned face. "She discarded him as if he were no more to her than some ruined gown."

Anne stared in disbelief at the young knight. Having only known her mother's love, despite the wrongs she'd done, she couldn't comprehend such cruelty. What could have happened those eleven years ago that had caused Lady Montmercy to hate her son so?

Chapter Sixteen

Neither Lord Montmercy nor Master Christopher returned to their meals, nor did they appear as the hunting party gave way to the rain and retreated. Anne's guilt nipped at her all the way back to Greenwich.

Once within the palace walls, most of the higher nobles and their parties retired to their own accommodations, be that chambers in one of the compound's royal residences or one of the jumble of jagged roofed houses that filled the palace grounds. To their minds, their day was done. Not so for Anne.

As a maid of the Presence Chamber, 'twas her duty to attend her royal mistress for the remainder of the day as Elizabeth did what business there was. Anne rushed to her own chamber in the waterfront building to shed her stained hunting attire. Nay, she couldn't call her room a chamber; 'twas too small for that.

As Anne and Mary were a good deal older than the other maids, who slept together all in one large room with their servants beside them, Mistress Eglionby insisted she and Mary own a bit of privacy. In Anne's case this amounted to a tiny closet coming off the larger room. There was barely enough space within its four walls for her bed and the clothing chest she and Patience shared. Indeed, with no space for her own cot, Patience slept across the foot of her charge's mattress.

Once more dressed in her brown garments of the morn, Anne entered the Presence Chamber. Here at Greenwich it was a long room, with a low, beamed ceiling and plastered walls hung with tapestries depicting hunting scenes. Tall windows were cut into the river wall, allowing a view of the Thames as it made its sharpest bend.

A day spent out-of-doors and the absence of the highest nobles left those who remained in attendance, even the queen, more relaxed. Some folk gossiped, while still more gamed with cards and dice, taking their seats upon cushions or the floor's plaited matting despite that they were once again dressed in their courtly best. Her business done, Elizabeth delayed retiring to her Privy Chamber to let her gentlemen entertain her. They brought forth their instruments and, to a bouncing tune, set to singing a song about the drinking of ale and the taking of a maid, much to the queen's amusement. Elizabeth plied her needle while they sang, her maids expected to occupy themselves with the same.

Anne found a spot near a window, where the light was good. Her project was to decorate fabric with a floral design for a chair cushion. Although she tried to concentrate on her stitchery, her mind kept slipping to Lord Montmercy and his mother. Every moment or so, she glanced toward the door, hoping Master Christopher might appear.

He didn't, but Lady Montmercy did. Like Anne, she was completing her own day's duty as a lady of the Presence Chamber. The noblewoman wore blue and yellow, with a large, sapphire-studded brooch pinned to her doublet's breast. An attifet sat upon her head, the cap's heart-shaped frame displaying her clear-cut features to an advantage, its snood containing her fair hair.

With her entry came the memory of Lord Montmercy's sarcastic advice that Anne should ask her questions directly of his mother. Staring at the woman, she chewed her lip as she considered the option. 'Twas strange that Lady Montmercy's face could be so beautiful and so lifeless in the same moment, but then what should she expect from one who had so casually destroyed her child's happiness?

As if she heard Anne's thoughts, Lady Montmercy looked in her direction. Anne let her gaze fall back to her needlework. What went on between the lady and her son was none of her business. She had her own troubles to pester her.

Although Anne managed a few stitches, Lady Montmercy's presence still pulled at her. She lifted her head. Like iron to lodestone, her gaze was drawn to the noblewoman.

Lady Montmercy watched her in return. As their gazes met, the lady lifted her chin and started across the room toward Anne. Well, that settled it.

Anne rose and offered her better a small curtsy as Lady Montmercy came to a halt before her. "My lady, you honor me with your presence."

"Mistress Blanchemain," the lady said in greeting. "I saw you watching me from across the room. Is there something you want of me?"

"I beg pardon if I have offended, my lady," Anne replied, "but you are so lovely. I fear you draw my eye, wherever you are."

"Is this flattery I hear?" the lady laughed. "What a clever girl you are." Although this should have been a compliment, it sounded more like a warning.

At that moment the gentlemen-turned-musicians began to pluck out a new tune, bringing the queen up from her chair, ready to dance. Each man in her troop of admirers cried out that he should be the one to partner her. Their pleas rumbled against the chamber's flat ceiling.

Lady Montmercy shot a glance over her shoulder. "In another moment we'll not be able to hear ourselves think," she said as she looked at Anne. "Come."

Catching Anne by the arm, the noblewoman led her into the room's farthest corner. As they stopped, Anne hid her questions behind a smile. Where to start? She settled for something banal. "You were not at the hunt this day. Do you not find the sport to your tastes?"

The noblewoman's smile took the tiniest twist. "I cannot say I'm fond of rattling about atop a horse. Nay, there are far more entertaining sports to be had within doors." She paused, the lift of her brows owning a touch of lewdness.

Scorn filled Anne. Given the lady's reputation, she could but think this was a referral to bed games. If Lady Montmercy meant to shock, she failed.

"I am startled to find there are many like you, who find more pleasure in a deck of cards and a wager than the fresh air and the out-of-doors," Anne replied. Let the lady decide if she'd been misunderstood through innocence or intent.

"But not you?" the noblewoman asked, a hint of sneering superiority in her tone.

Anne smiled. "While I do enjoy a hand or two, why sit within walls when there are so many other things to do and see?"

"So the country mouse finds this new life of hers

alluring, does she?" With no kindness in Lady Montmercy's tone, what could have been a gentle tease
was, instead, a stinging taunt.

Anne hid her irritation behind her smile. Apparently Lady Montmercy owned her dead husband's hatred for the Blanchemains. If this was to be a battle,
she may as well unsheathe her sword and have at it.
She studied the woman to gauge what sort of question
would be best.

No emotion warmed the depths of Lady Montmercy's dark blue eyes. Such control suggested it wouldn't
be easy to pry secrets from her. Then again, all need
not be revealed this evening.

Anne began her probe cloaked in innocence, asking
a question anyone might have over family history.
"My lady, I must admit, I've another purpose in attracting your attention. I mean you no insult, but I've
heard you're none too fond of the Blanchemains."

"Good heavens," Lady Montmercy said without
passion, "someone has been filling your head with
nonsense. What little I know of your family would fit
into a thimble. That, my dear, is hardly enough to
constitute acquaintanceship, much less create a foun-
dation on which to base dislike."

Anne sighed as if relieved. "Glad I am that the
rumor is unfounded. You see, I know my grandfather
is not a subtle man, may God bless him always. The
number of those he's insulted is legion."

This made the lady laugh, the sound hollow against
the more full-bodied amusement of their royal mistress across the room. "After his performance last
week at Whitehall, I'd offer that saying your grandsire
lacks subtlety is to announce you've just discovered
grass is green," she said.

Of a sudden Lady Montmercy's eyes widened. "Ah,

but I think I know the source of this rumor of yours. 'Tisn't me, but my lord husband who had discord with Sir Amyas." 'Twas a fine act, but an act just the same.

"God's truth, my lady?" Anne asked, playing her own role in their wee drama. "You've remembered something?"

"If you like, I can tell the tale," the beauty offered.

"Aye, pray do," Anne begged as prettily as she knew how. "I know so little of my grandfather, and he will not answer my questions, saying 'tis rude of me to pry." Or so she was certain he would say, had she ever asked.

Lady Montmercy laid her hand on Anne's arm in what should have been a friendly gesture. "If I am right in my remembering, 'twas a score of years ago. Nay, more. I was but ten and six when I wed my lord husband, and this event occurred in the first year of our union."

Here, she paused to smile, the look in her eyes distant. 'Twas the first honest expression Anne had seen upon her face. "How long ago my arrival at court seems now," the lady said with a wistful laugh. "Everyone was so old, the king, his courtiers, my own lord. All but Queen Catherine, the first queen I served as a lady-in-waiting."

Anne caught an excited breath. Her mother had served the last two of King Harry's queens. She recalled how Lady Frances had chided Sir Amyas for his lack of manhood. Was it possible her mother knew even more? There'd be a letter winging its way to Owls House on the morrow against that possibility.

"Poor Kate Howard," Lady Montmercy was saying, sadly shaking her head. "We were of an age, she and I, and how I pitied her. Although my husband was old, he wasn't fat, gouty, and ill-tempered like the king. Ah, but you asked about your grandfather, not a feckless and long-dead girl. Let me think a moment."

This time when the lady paused, she tilted her head to peer up at the dark beams that crossed the ceiling, her mouth pursed, her forehead creased. Anne's eyes narrowed. 'Twas an actor's portrayal of deep thought and, as such, shattered the noblewoman's claim she knew the Blanchemains only a little.

"Was Sir Amyas not an undersecretary in the Court of the Wards at one time?" Lady Montmercy finally asked.

"Indeed, he was," Anne answered, her voice appropriately encouraging.

"Aye, my lord husband also served upon the court. There, would their knowledge of each other have been formed. I must admit, my lord had no liking for those whose roots were in trade, as, I believe, your grandsire's are. He claimed such commoners were all honorless thieves, bent on taking places and positions rightfully belonging to nobler men." Although aimed at Sir Amyas, the lady meant for this to prick at his granddaughter, as well. This blow was not as subtle as the first, suggesting in its bluntness that speaking of the past was causing her pain.

"As I recall," the lady went on, "the actual source of the discord arose over the purchase of an abbey. My lord husband had offered for it, but your grandsire offered more, paying every fee and bribe to steal it out from under him. How my lord shouted and cursed over that. You can imagine how he felt when one of those he despised took what he coveted. Well, shall I say my lord never forgave your grandfather for the loss of that property?" She aimed a tight smile at Anne.

"This must be the source of the rumor," Anne replied, then tried a probe of her own. "My grandfather does own abbey lands. 'Tis the property he most prizes. No doubt he cherishes it because of his battle with your lord husband as he sought to buy it." This was an outright lie. Amyas had given the property to Walter, Anne's recently deceased cousin, for his use.

"Is that so?" Lady Montmercy murmured as if she considered Anne's comment an interesting, but unimportant, bit of information.

Had it not been for the years Anne had spent deciphering her mother's unspoken messages, she'd never have seen the flicker of pain that passed through the lady's eyes. Triumph rose. The connection between this lady and her grandfather had naught to do with business dealings gone badly. Nay, 'twas far more intimate than that.

Anne bowed her head to hide her excitement. "Thank you, Lady Montmercy," she said with what girlish sweetness she could muster. "I know it cannot seem like much to you, but I am grateful for your memories." With a final curtsy, she returned to her stool by the window and her handwork.

Chapter Seventeen

There was a tap on Anne's chamber door.

"Coming," Patience snarled, shoving her mistress's black velvet headdress at her.

As the slight woman worked her way past Anne and the bed's corner to the door, Anne stared at her keeper's back in dismay. Patience's ill mood was her fault. In her worry over how her governess was going to react to this morn's private dancing lesson, she'd turned the act of dressing into an ordeal.

Nothing felt right. Skirts were presented and rejected, sleeves tossed aside, gloves thought either too thick or too thin, with Patience all the while lecturing on the sin of vanity. At last and mostly because there was nothing left from which to choose, Anne settled on a modest black bodice and overskirt worn atop a scarlet underskirt with full black sleeves slashed to show their red and yellow lining.

Not that time wasted on clothing brought her one step nearer to a way to winning her keeper's cooperation. It wasn't just Patience's cooperation she needed; her governess would have to blind herself to the forward behavior Anne intended to ply against Master Christopher. Anne's mouth turned down in defeat. She was doomed.

Patience threw open the door. 'Twas Mary. "Good

morrow, cousin," she cried. Even though Patience stepped back as if to allow her entry, Mary stayed where she stood. There simply wasn't space for a third body in Anne's chamber.

"Nan, I'm sent to tell you and Mistress Watkins to hie yourselves directly to the park gate. There's drizzle today, so wear your boots and carry your shoes. Your walk will take you beyond Greenwich's walls, and the road is mucky." There was just enough sparkle in Mary's eyes to suggest she had either guessed or knew of the queen's scheme to best Leicester.

Suspicion tightened Patience's expression. She crossed her arms over her brown bodice. "Beyond the walls? Just where are we going?" she demanded.

As one who believed in treating servants with a firm hand, Mary frowned at such impertinence. "That is none of your concern, Mistress Watkins. Take a lesson from your better, who asks no questions, but goes where her royal mistress sends her."

"The queen has arranged for my dancing lessons to begin," Anne said to Patience as she tied on her headdress, pulling her plait through the tube of her shoulder-length veil. "I suspect we're off to some quiet place that offers a modicum of privacy in which to practice."

"This is strange, indeed." Patience glanced narrowly between the two maids as if she feared a hoodwinking. "Why would the queen send you so far from her protection? Who is to be our escort?"

Since Anne knew nothing of the arrangements, 'twas Mary who spoke. "I'll not answer on why our queen's majesty chooses to send Mistress Anne where she does, nor should you ask," she chided. "As for escorts," she went on, "there are the musicians, although as tradesmen I cannot say in any truth they can be called an escort. Master Hollier went ahead to make certain the place is ready for footwork, so he cannot serve. However, he left his serving man to walk with you."

"Oh!" The word leapt from Patience's mouth as quickly as her hands went to her head to smooth her hair. No matter that it was already taut against her skull, wound into a tight curl at the nape of her neck. In the next instant her eyes flew wide, and she glanced frantically around the room.

"Oh, dear," she cried, then slipped past Anne to squeeze between wall and bed and stop before their shared clothing chest. Its lid banged against the plastered wall as she threw it open. Panting, Patience dug through the stacks of clothing she'd only moments before refolded, complaining loudly over having to do so with each garment.

Anne looked at Mary, astonished. Mary shrugged as surprised as she, then retreated, closing the door as she went. "Patience," Anne called, "is all well with you?"

" 'Tis my coif, Mistress Anne," the woman replied, still bent over the chest as she sought her close-fitting white cap. "I set it aside, thinking to don it after you were dressed. Now I cannot find it."

Surprise grew. It seemed impossible that Patience didn't know where her headgear was. After all, she'd snarled at Anne when Anne had laid her cloak upon it. Lifting her outer garment from the bed's corner, Anne caught up the coif to hand it to the woman. "Here, Patience," she said. " 'Tis right where you left it."

The thin woman came upright with a start. Relief gusted from her as she claimed the cap from Anne. "My thanks, mistress. I couldn't have gone out without it." She clapped it upon her head, tucking in non-existent stray hairs as she loosely tied the strings beneath her chin.

That Patience should be so agitated over a missing cap was utterly beyond understanding. Anne frowned at her and sat upon the bed's end to kick off her shoes. "Bring my boots, will you?" She'd yet to give her keeper a direct order, fearing Patience's vengeance would be tales told to Sir Amyas.

"Aye, mistress," she replied, her tone as sweet as sugar, when only a moment before it had been all vinegar.

Grabbing Anne's boots from beneath the bed, she handed them to her charge, taking the shoes in trade. In the time it took for Anne to don these sturdy items, Patience had her own boots on, her cloak over her shoulders, and her prayer book in her purse. Snatching Anne's cloak from the mattress, she thrust it at her charge. "Make haste. They are waiting for us."

So much enthusiasm for something that should have sent her governess into a fit of nagging, if not complete refusal, was worrisome, indeed. Anne eyed the woman. "Does this mean you no longer have any objections to the lesson?" She cringed at the hopeful note in her own voice. Even if Patience had no objections, that didn't mean she wouldn't report the goings on to Sir Amyas.

"Where the queen commands, you cannot refuse" came the response, as if Patience had always claimed the queen's laws above God's.

Anne threw her outer garment around her, and fumbled with its single button. Patience stood at the closed door. The hems of her brown skirts jiggled as she tapped her toe, displaying the antithesis of her name.

"Swiftly now, mistress," she said as she darted out the door into the maids' larger chamber. " 'Twould be unkind of us to leave them waiting in the wet."

Anne stared at her governess's back. There was something desperately wrong here. She followed Patience through Mistress Eglionby's domain, then descended the stairs to the waterfront building's exterior door and out into the misty morning near the palace's tiltyard. 'Twas Patience who set the pace, her stride at the uppermost limit of propriety.

Through the passageway between the royal residences they strode, then along the back of the queen's residence, where the air was redolent with the smells from the kitchen. The rain had teased up scents from the cooking herbs filling the lower garden, rosemary and peppery thyme the strongest among them.

With no wall around it, Anne could see all the way across the lower garden to its far end and the park gatehouse. Made of stone, with two peaked roofs and a tall chimney, the massive structure spanned not only Greenwich Palace's wall, but Woolwich Road; anyone making their way east or west upon that thoroughfare had to pass beneath it as they went. A single, cloaked figure stood near the gatehouse. As he caught sight of them, he threw back his cloak hood. It was the pretty man, the one with the bright blue eyes and careless tumble of dark curls.

"Patience, who is that man?" Anne asked. "I saw you speaking to him at the maying."

"Why, 'tis Master Babthorpe, Master Hollier's servant," Patience replied, her voice suddenly warm and soft. "He came to walk with me, after you and the others left me alone and unescorted in the meadow." There was a hint of accusation in her voice.

Anne's heart twinged. She'd been too interested in Master Christopher to pay heed to Patience.

"Master Babthorpe wished to make my acquaintance as he'd heard from his master that I was a woman of faith." In saying this Patience indulged in the sin of pride. "He is a man who has come to value a godly life, after years of being lost to sin. I pray I am capable of instructing Master Babthorpe on the true path to righteousness. So far his lessons have proved him a clever student."

Anne's brows rose. For the first time in the month or so she'd known the woman, Patience's mouth almost curved into a smile. The change was so startling it was yet another moment before Anne comprehended what her governess had just told her. She gasped, shocked to her core. "You cannot mean you've been meeting with him since the maying?" she cried out.

"Not every day." The words came so quickly from Patience's lips that she hadn't time enough to wash the guilt from them.

"Since I have not been your chaperone, Patience, who has?" Anne demanded.

"No one," Patience replied in a small voice.

Anne's eyes narrowed. It was one thing for her to stretch the bounds of propriety. After all, she had the potential exposure of her spoiled state to prevent any straying to where she dared not go. Patience was quite another matter. Although Anne knew the woman had been married, she seemed so vulnerable when it came to men.

Beside her, Patience drew herself up to the full limit of her slight height. "There is no need of a chaperone, not when the purpose of our meetings is religious study." 'Twas an attempt to justify what was, by the standards of her own beliefs, unjustifiable.

Laughter dared to bubble from Anne. "Why, Patience, I believe you're fond of him!"

"I most certainly am not," the woman retorted, the heat of her response suggesting just the opposite. "I see in Master Babthorpe an opportunity to spread our Lord's Holy Word."

"Have you succeeded?" Anne asked. "Is he papist no longer?"

"He was never a papist, mistress," Patience replied with a shake of her head, "nor is his master. Although 'tis true the family was once corrupted by the Roman religion, as were all our families before we found the truth, only Master Hollier's brother yet clings to sin."

Anne's heart leapt as one barrier to her union with Master Christopher fell by the wayside. "Now, that is a relief, indeed," she said. "I think my grandsire would not object so to my taking lessons from Master Hollier, were he aware of this." She loosed a long, slow sigh.

Ah, but the path was hardly clear. Anne set herself to removing another barrier to the man she wanted. " 'Tis a shame we cannot tell him."

This made Patience frown. "We cannot?"

"Nay." Anne shook her head sadly. "My grandfather, may God bless him always, can be a mite set in his ways. Look upon how he deludes himself over Lord Deyville, thinking the man a friend when he is not. Nay, Master Hollier would have to make a public profession of his faith before Sir Amyas believes him anything but recusant. Not that it matters. Once my grandfather learns the queen has commanded me to take these private lessons, I fear he'll take me from court." She paused here, so her next words might have emphasis. "And you along with me."

Patience looked to the garden's end where the man she tutored in godliness stood. Master Babthorpe smiled, his beautiful face alight with eagerness as he watched them approach. He lifted a hand in greeting. New color came to life in her cheeks, only to drain away with the next breath. She blinked as the breeze sent rain spattering into her face.

"Were I to leave court now, Master Babthorpe would remain ever more locked in the darkness of his soul." Her tone was quiet and worried.

"It seems a shame, that," Anne agreed. "He looks to be a very fine man."

"He is," Patience sighed, then caught firm hold of herself. "I mean, he is a very serious student and will most likely be revealed as one of God's elect."

"I suppose my grandfather doesn't need to know about this," Anne offered, making her tone both hesitant and considering as she sought to convince Patience that a little more self-delusion wouldn't hurt. "After all, we know Master Hollier is no papist and you will be my chaperone, just as I will be yours. That is, if you were to combine Master Babthorpe's studies with my dancing lessons."

Even as the words left her mouth, Anne conceded defeat. This was too devious for Patience to accept. She'd have been better off suggesting they lie outright. Waiting for the explosion that must follow, Anne glanced at her keeper.

Rather than chide or point out that her charge had just proved with her words that the devil lived in her heart, her governess smiled. 'Twas no weak or watery movement of the mouth. Nay, 'twas a wide opening

of lips that displayed a nice set of teeth and proved
Patience almost as pretty as her student.

"But, of course, mistress," she replied. "Nothing
else makes sense, does it? We can hardly leave Master
Babthorpe caught in sin's darkness. Nor could there
be any wrong with which Sr. Amyas might find fault.
As you point out, we will chaperone each other."

Patience inclined her head to one side, a tiny frown
between her brows. "Now that I think on it, mistress,
I see it is the only answer. Indeed, if Master Babthorpe can be brought to find the better road, we may
well be able to do the same for Master Hollier. Such
a conversion can but please Sir Amyas."

Anne stared at the woman. Was this her Patience?
Had she just heard her governess try to sweeten her
into agreeing to the same devious plan Anne had
suggested?

"Ah, but of course," Anne stuttered, "you are right.
Indeed. It is the only sensible path." That was, it was
the only sensible path to take if one wanted to justify
spending time with a man.

Patience didn't notice Anne's reaction. Instead she
turned her head into the spattering rain, her gaze
locked upon the man waiting for her at the gate.
"Come, mistress. I vow the weather worsens. This is
no time to dawdle." With that, Patience set herself to
a very forward pace.

Worry speared at Anne as she lengthened her stride
to keep abreast of her maid. Oh, Lord, but what had
she done? Patience wasn't just fond of Master
Babthrope, she was head-over-heels in love with him.

Chapter Eighteen

Kit stood in the open door of this, their first secret practice venue, awaiting his student's arrival. Just beyond the structure's eaves a fine rain was falling. He looked to the horizon. The gray was weakening. Another hour or two, and they might actually see the sky.

Shifting in his stance, he glanced across the short expanse of grass to the neat array of houses, all white-washed walls and dark timber with thatch for roofing, that was the village to the east of Greenwich. Smoke lifted and curled from chimneys, the smell of burning wood twining into the tangy spice of the nearby Thames. Shouts rose from the river's bank as boats came and went. These folk were as much fishermen as farmers.

With nothing to do but wait, Kit let his thoughts drift back to his previous night's dream. It had started as his usual nightmare, with him a child once more. Nick had appeared, and they'd once again begun fighting their childhood battle. Much to his surprise, Mistress Anne had joined them in his dream kitchen. With that, the nightmare had softened into something far more provocative. As grateful as Kit was for escaping the horror of his past, there was a touch of guilt

at the thought of Mistress Anne coming between him
and Nick, even in a dream.

The mud-speckled party appeared and started
across the grass, heading for the wide, cobbled apron
that fronted this doorway. Such was Bertie's vanity
that he couldn't bear to deny the world his beauty;
he'd thrown back his hood, and his black curls
gleamed with moisture. The rest had their hoods
pulled low on their foreheads. Even still, Kit could tell
who was who.

With their instruments strapped to their backs beneath their outer garments, the musicians looked
humpbacked and misshapen. As for the women, the
brown skirts peeping through her cloak's edges placed
Mistress Watkins on Bertie's left. Mistress Anne
strode at his man's right, her cloak gray and skirts,
black. She was close enough now that Kit could see
the pale oval of her face beneath her hood. Her smile
flashed. Whatever she said caused Bertie to look at
her, the pleased movement of his mouth leaving a
deep dent in either cheek.

Jealousy's sword thrust through Kit. This was the
smile Bertie saved for the women he most wanted to
bed. Anger followed. He'd kill him if Bertie dared
touch his Nan.

Kit caught his breath. May God take him, but he'd
settled this matter with himself only yesterday. She
wasn't his; she could never be. Especially, not now.

Yesterday, when Ned had told the tale of Sir Amyas
refusing an offer for her hand, then asked about a
contract for marriage, she'd lied. Not only did Mistress
Anne know that such a contract existed, she knew
who it was her grandsire intended as her husband. If
he'd read her reaction rightly, she was none too
pleased over his choice. Kit's stomach tightened as he

imagined the sort of man Amyas would have chosen for her. No doubt it was a parched, pale preacher, all passion given to God, someone unworthy of Anne's fire and wit.

As the party reached the foreyard, Kit stepped out onto the cobbles, and opened his arms in invitation. "Do come in," he called, every inch the jovial host.

Leaving Bertie and her servant to pass her, Mistress Anne stopped in the courtyard and threw back her hood. The morn's chill walk had put pink in her cheeks and made her dark eyes sparkle. Kit grinned as she stared in consternation. He'd felt no differently when he'd first set eyes on this place.

"A barn?" she cried. "We are to practice in a barn?!"

Waving the musicians on inside, Kit crossed the slick stones to stand beside Mistress Anne and once more study the tithe barn hired on their behalf. Made of stone with well-kept thatch for roof, it was the village's collection point for what they owed their landlord. Six bays thrust out along each long side, with a tiny, square window cut in each extension to provide for air's circulation.

"This is not a barn," he chided her, " 'tis an adventure. Today we go east. On the morrow 'tis west. Who knows where we'll be the day after?" He paused to offer her an arch look. "It could well be in someone's moldy storeroom."

"I pray not," she laughed as he offered his arm. She wound her hand into the crook of his elbow without hesitation. As had become her habit, Mistress Anne leaned against his arm in a most agreeable way. In what he hoped would become his habit, he drew her closer still. She accepted this nearness with a smile.

He led her to the door, letting her stop to peer into

the barn's musty and dim interior. Short slatted
wooden walls, extending from both sides of the barn
and reaching only a third of the way across the structure's width, separated each bay one from the other.
The middle third of the structure stretched, open and
uncluttered like a long corridor, from door to door.

The musicians had shed their cloaks and set their
folding stools near this end of the barn; they were
now rousing their instruments. The drummer tapped
his tambour, his ear held close to the membrane, while
teeth-jarring sounds came from the two viols as bows
sawed against gut. The fourth man plucked and
twisted the pegs atop his lute's neck.

"Are you certain this is where we're to be?" she
asked him after a moment's study.

"Indeed I am," Kit replied. "This is the perfect
place to teach you the pavane's stately footwork and
careful paces. The floor's fairly even and, although
we'll have to leave the doors open for light, the day's
not so cold as to make this uncomfortable. Besides"—
he smiled at her—"we'll be too busy dancing to notice
anything else."

"If you say so," Mistress Anne replied, yet un-
convinced.

Releasing him, she crossed to one of the dividing
walls and stripped off her cloak. Kit gaped in disbelief
when he saw her attire. Where he wore a well-worn
and sleeveless cream doublet over his shirt, a sturdy
pair of brown breeches and his most comfortable
shoes upon his feet, she dressed as if this were the
Presence Chamber.

"What is this?" he cried.

"Do you not like it?" she asked, offering him a
mocking curtsy.

Nay, he didn't. Yesterday's brown had suited her

far better. The only good about her outfit was that beneath her ruff her shirt lay open, exposing her cleavage.

" 'Tisn't a matter of like or dislike," he said. "We're conducting dancing lessons, not serving the queen the dinner she never eats. On the morrow you'd be well advised to wear something you wouldn't mind having torn or stained."

She shot him a wry smile. "My grandsire swore I'd have no need for those sturdier garments I brought with me from Owls House. My thanks for the advice.

"Patience, my shoes," she called to the barn's opposite end. Bertie and Mistress Patience stood in the opening, gazing toward a nearby copse of yellow-green willows.

"Aye, mistress," her servant replied, her voice far more feminine than Kit expected.

Mistress Patience walked slowly up the barn's length, her damp hems collecting last year's grit as she went. A pair of shoes dangled from one hand, while the other held her prayer book clasped tightly to her breast. Kit glanced at Bertie.

His man was watching her. No hint of his previous complaints over these hours of enforced study remained, instead Bertie's face was filled with a sort of quiet admiration for this severe little woman. Kit freed a breath of amazement. Bertie had missed his calling. He could have made a right fine living as an actor.

The maid held out the shoes. "Mistress, while you practice, Master Babthorpe and I thought we'd sit near the far door. That will give us light and keep us dry, while we remain out of your way."

As Mistress Anne took her footgear and nodded, the maid whirled to return to the door. When Mistress

Patience saw Bertie watching her, she smiled. Kit's eyes widened. And a right pretty smile it was.

Beside him, Mistress Anne had grasped the wall. With the one hand left to her, she was trying to both lift her skirts and slip the shoes onto her stocking-clad foot. He bit back a smile. It appeared Bertie has having some affect on Mistress Watkins if the servant could be so careless with her charge. All the better for him and what he planned.

"Here," he said, taking hold of Mistress Anne's elbow to offer her the balance she needed.

"My thanks," she replied without looking up as she slipped on her shoes. "As inappropriate as my skirts may be, I didn't want to dirty them by sitting."

She straightened to look up at him. Her expression was sober, all the spark gone from her eyes. A tiny crease marked her brow.

"Mistress?" he asked.

"Yesterday you and Lord Montmercy never returned," she said, her voice low.

Nay, they hadn't. The lad had been astride his horse and riding hell-bent for Greenwich before Kit could stop him. It had taken half the distance to the palace before he'd caught up to Andrew. "He didn't wish to depress the spirits of those around him. I would have returned, but I felt it best not to leave the lad alone."

He'd stayed with the youth until a servant brought the round and rumpled lass who'd been warming his bed for the last months. Within minutes Lord Andrew was thrusting his pain into the maid, both of them groaning in a different sort of agony. At the back of Kit's mind, he offered Andrew a mental salute and wished something as simple as constant coupling would give him respite from his guilt over Nick.

"I am so sorry," Mistress Anne sighed. "Had I

known speaking of his mother might so upset him, upon my word I'd have held my tongue."

"Have no fear," Kit said. "He knows your intent was innocent. No permanent harm was done."

It wasn't only Montmercy she'd upset with her question. Christ, but he'd almost tossed the contents of his cup down the front of his doublet when she'd asked after Lady Montmercy. For the hundredth time since that moment, guilt nagged that she knew of the contract, even though Kit was certain 'twas impossible. Not even Lord Andrew knew what he held in his possession. As much as he wanted to ask Mistress Anne why she was interested in Lady Montmercy, he could think of no way to broach the subject without throwing suspicion on himself. Instead he smiled. "Now, remove your gloves, and we'll dance."

She looked askance at him over this last. "One does not wear gloves while dancing?"

"Have I not removed mine?" he touched the items, already tucked into his belt, then caught her hand in his. Warmth shivered up his back as his naked fingers slid between her gloved ones. 'Twas odd that the sight and feel of something so mundane could stir his blood.

Leaning near, he put his lips so close to her ear he could almost feel the velvet of her headdress. "The truth is," he whispered, "I'd just like to feel your hand in mine, with no fabric between us."

Laughing, Mistress Anne snatched back her hand. "You!" she cried out, her protest belied by the pleasure in her voice. "The gloves stay."

This time when Kit caught her hand, 'twas to lead her out to the center of the barn. "Now, then, we'll do again what we did at the maying."

He quickly found it best to lead her through the whole dance, calling out the steps as they took them.

Then, while the musicians rested, he drilled her on the precise execution of each step. This required that she lift her skirts so he could see the positioning of her feet, giving him cause to ogle her shapely ankles.

Although the dance was a slow, stately one, the constant repetition made for heat. This took its toll on her attire. First, her black oversleeves were untied, then removed entirely and left to hang on the wall next to her cloak. Her gloves and ruff went next. Soon her sleeves were rolled up onto her forearms. Best of all, her collar's strings had loosened with her movements and her shirt had begun to gape. With every glance he could see more of her chest from her shoulders to her bodice's top.

Two hours of activity made changes in his own attire. His doublet was now unbuttoned, hanging open from his shoulders, and his shirt collar was spread wide.

At last she maneuvered herself through the whole dance without him calling the steps. Kit smiled. "Well-done," he told her. "Now that the steps are in place, the grace will follow."

"May the angels in heaven begin their rejoicing," she gasped, fanning at her flushed face with a hand.

"One more time, to set it forever in your memory." He caught her by the elbow to turn her for another parade up the barn's length.

"Nay, I cannot," she moaned, and fell against him. Her arms latched around his waist as she rested her head upon his shoulder. "My feet ache and my head spins with double rights and lefts, sidings and kicks."

So startled was he by her unexpected embrace Kit lost all ability to think. Sensations flooded over him. With his collar undone, he could feel the softness of her veil against his bare throat. There was naught but the thin fabric of their shirts between them. With every breath her breasts moved against his chest.

His shaft filled. Aye, what he needed most was to have her lying beneath him—now. Just as he lifted his arms to embrace her, she stepped away from him, swabbing at her forehead with a hand.

Retreating to the nearest dividing wall she glowered playfully at him. "This is your revenge over how I teased you about Mary, I know it, aye. Well, you've bested me. Now, let me die in peace."

As she leaned back against the wall, her collar strings finally gave way and opened. Her shirt parted, leaving the top of her chest bare to him.

Kit thought his heart would break. He gazed at the exposed slender line of her throat, then traced the outline of her breasts, bared to their crests, as they thrust up above her bodice's top. How he wanted to touch his lips to those sweet mounds. His hands curled as if to close about them.

His gaze lifted to her face. Dear God, but she was beautiful. As they'd danced, the band of her headpiece had slipped back allowing a few, fine hairs to escape its confinement. They curled against her cheeks, touching places that he ached to touch.

Once again, the tiny mole at the corner of her mouth called to him. Aye, he'd start his kiss at that spot, then slide his mouth atop hers. Her lips would be soft beneath his as he plied them and waited for her to moan for him to take her.

Her gaze met his, her eyes seeming as dark and soft as the velvet of her headdress. New heat woke in their depths as her lips parted. Kit shuddered. Christ, but he'd die if he didn't love her this very moment. He took a step toward her.

"Master Hollier, shall we go?" the drummer asked, a touch of laughter in his voice.

Startled, Kit jerked. Mistress Anne's hand leapt to her chest, her fingers splaying over her bared skin. She loosed a quiet yelp, then snatched at her collar to draw her shirt closed.

He wheeled to face the musicians. Two of the men stared into the rafters, while the drummer and one violist smirked. The violist dared to chuckle. Kit shot the sniggering fool so evil a glance all four instantly sobered.

"Aye, you may go," he snapped, taking the coins he needed to pay them from his purse. Before the morrow's lesson, he'd see to it three of them were paid to stay away, while the last was paid double for coming and keeping his eyes closed.

Tossing the coins to the drummer, he watched them gather their belongings, his fingers pressed to his pounding head. If only it were as easy to still the other throbbing. Turning, he looked to where Mistress Anne had been; she was gone.

Panic tore through him. She knew what he wanted and had run! All was lost.

"Patience?" she called from the barn's opposite end.

He whirled, then squinted. The sky above the willow copse was a brilliant blue with not a cloud in sight. Neither were Mistress Patience and Bertie.

"Where are you, Patience?" Mistress Anne called, standing just outside the barn's door her eyes shielded with a hand.

Rage tore through Kit. He knew where Bertie was. His man was off laying with that woman! By God, he'd kill him, for no other reason than Bertie was enjoying the release his master had been denied.

Kit's jaw clenched, his teeth gritting. Christ, but this was utter madness. If he didn't find some way to tame his lust, he was doomed, indeed.

"In a moment, mistress," her maid cried, her voice rising from somewhere beyond the willows.

"I really must talk to her," Mistress Anne said, turning toward him with an irritable huff. "I vow, she has no sense at all."

Kit thought there should have at least been a quiver to her voice. Instead her tone was steady as a rock, as if nothing unusual had passed between them. How could she be so unaffected, when his knees were weak?

May God damn her, but she wasn't unaffected. She couldn't be, not when he'd seen the heat in her eyes. He was certain that if he took her in his arms and put his mouth to hers, she'd melt against him. Ah, but he dare not grab her.

She strode past him for the bay where she'd hung the bits and pieces of her attire. Yet struggling to master his own body, Kit could but watch as she put on her ruff, then pulled on her outer sleeves. Since there was no possible way for her to tie these into her bodice by herself, she turned to him. "Would you mind?"

"Not at all," he said, everything in him screaming against the agony of frustrated desire.

He tied one sleeve into her bodice, then reached for her wrist to fasten its cuff. What he hadn't noticed while they'd danced, he now saw. The bruises Deyville left were now but dull purple spots on her wrist.

This punctured his lust, leaving behind the need to see to it Deyville never again attacked her. "They've faded," he said.

"Aye, so they have," she replied, her voice far away and sad.

"Hey, now," he asked, yet holding her hand in his. "What aches in you that you should sound so?"

She looked up at him, her eyes wide. "You saved me from him once. Would that you could do it again." Her voice lowered. "But that will not be possible, not once we're wed."

"Wed?" Kit scoffed, stepping around her to fasten the other sleeve. "If that's the source of your worries, then be reassured. You cannot wed him, he's married already."

"His wife is dying," she whispered.

Her words sent him back from her a step. "You cannot be serious!"

She freed a short and bitter laugh. "Would that I were not."

Kit's head reeled. Christ! What sort of man planned his next wedding before his current wife was buried? And what sort of guardian was Old Amyas if he meant to give his heir to such a man? At the thought of Anne trapped forever in Deyville's clutches, a wholly new rage tore through him. Not his Nan.

"This is an abomination. You cannot wed him," he snarled.

"However much I cherish your outrage," she said softly, "there's not much to be done about it. My grandsire has made his decision." If her expression was sad, her demeanor was calm.

'Twas beyond Kit's comprehension that she could so easily accept this. "Do you intend to do nothing while this is arranged for you?"

"What would you suggest?" Mistress Anne shot him a wry look. "Perhaps, you would like to marry me in his stead?"

"Me?" Kit cried out, staring at her in surprise. From

the back of his mind came a tiny voice saying that marriage to this woman would be a fine thing.

She sighed. "You needn't worry so, 'twas only a jest. I daresay my grandfather would kill us both if we dared such a thing." A touch of anger flashed through her gaze. "Beyond that, I have no other choice. Should I resist my grandsire's will, I fear he will vent his rage on my mother."

Behind them, Mistress Patience and Bertie entered the barn. "Speak no more of this," Anne whispered to him. "Patience knows none of it and so would I keep the matter."

"As you will." Kit nodded, his attention shifting to her servant.

Mistress Patience beamed, her prayer book once more clasped to her bodice front. A tiny nosegay of windflowers now bobbed atop its closed pages. Where she smiled, Bertie glowered. Whatever they'd been doing, 'twasn't coupling. It was gratifying to see the same aching in Kit reflected in his man's eyes.

"Come, then, Patience," Mistress Anne called to her governess. " 'Tis time for our return to Greenwich."

To keep the queen's secret, Kit would wait a time before departing. Thus, he stood aside as the troupe left the barn, then went to stand in the doorway. Only when he could see Anne no more did he comprehend the new urgency her revelation gave his quest. If he didn't lay with her before Deyville's wife died, his opportunity would be lost. Once her grandsire made the announcement of their engagement she could spend no more time alone with him, queen's wager or not.

So how was he to rush her into coupling? Kit smiled without amusement. Another day like this one, and he'd take her, no matter how many people watched.

Once he did, she was doomed to a life of torment.

Breath escaped him in a slow steady stream as he stared out into the now bright day. The sun's heat teased tendrils of steam from the damp sod.

If Deyville would kill him for trespassing, Anne couldn't expect so easy an escape. Nay, since the nobleman would want to keep Old Amyas's properties, he wouldn't dare let the heiress die until she was brought to bed with his child. Kit had no doubt she'd pay in pain for her sin until that day.

'Twas with his heart aching at the thought of Anne suffering that he lifted his gaze to the road. The group was now nothing more than a distant blur. The answer seeped slowly up from his soul. She wouldn't suffer if she went into marriage with her maidenhead intact.

Kit stiffened, shocked at himself. What was happening to him that he could even consider betraying Nick to secure what could be only a temporary reprieve for some sweet-faced chit?

Deyville had always been a brutal man. Old Amyas had to know that, and still he promised his heiress to the man. If Amyas didn't care what happened to his granddaughter, why should Kit? But he did care.

He stared out across the vibrant landscape. This had all seemed so simple and clear-cut when Lady Montmercy laid it out to him. He waited for his guilt over Nick to rise and save him from this fatal softness of his. Instead there was only the question of whether Nick's title was really worth an innocent woman's life.

With a sigh Kit leaned his shoulder against the barn's door frame and closed his eyes. It was too late to save himself. Death waited for him, no matter what he chose to do, but he didn't need to use Anne to achieve his purpose. If he died, Nick would still have to wed, even though his wife might not be Lady Arabella and the amount of her settlement less than enough to restore the title. 'Twas success enough for Kit that Nick's line would continue.

It was decided, then. He'd leave his Nan virgin for Deyville and let Lady Montmercy vent her wrath on him.

Chapter Nineteen

"Mistress Anne?"
Anne started, her idle needle slipping from her fingers to fall onto her now almost finished cushion cover. So deep was her melancholy she'd not heard anyone approach. 'Twas a page, one of the older lads. He bowed to her, then rose with a cheeky wink and a grin.

On a different day Anne might have teased him over his behavior. Not today. How could a full six weeks of service to her queen have passed and left her yet unmarried?

"Aye, Master Phillips?" she asked, working to tame her depression.

" 'Tis Sir Amyas, mistress. He's wanting you."

"He's here?" she cried out.

Panic exploded in her. Lady Deyville was dead! Her grandfather had come to take her into his custody to hold her close for Lord Deyville's sake. Her frantic gaze darted around the Presence Chamber, as if seeing her grandsire might confirm or deny her fears.

These were the hours the queen held court, making herself available to those courtiers without the rank for access to her Privy Chamber and doing business. Elizabeth sat in her chair at the room's far end, dressed in scarlet and green, with ruby-headed pins to hold her curls in place. The hunting had been good this week, the weather kind, and her admirers especially attentive. All this left the queen in a fine humor. Just now she was speaking in Latin to an old man wearing black robes and a scholar's flat cap upon his head, offering congratulations on the book he'd written in her honor. There was no sign of Sir Amyas.

"Where is he?" Anne demanded of the page.

"He waits outside the door, mistress," he replied with a snort of snide laughter. "Master Bowyer has been commanded to refuse him entry, thus Sir Amyas asks that you come out to speak with him."

Anne stared at him in shock. Oh, dear God, what had her grandsire done this time? Who cared! If he couldn't come in, he couldn't petition for her release from the queen's service. Fool! He didn't need to petition in person.

So roiled her thoughts, panic battling relief. She set aside her needlework and rose, straightening the folds in her brown skirts as she stood. "I'll go to him. My thanks, Master Phillips," she said, starting for the door.

If this was a reprieve, it wouldn't last for long. She freed an irritated breath. Nay, idiot that she was, she'd doomed herself to marry Lord Deyville. With that, her spirits descended into melancholy.

Once she owned Patience's cooperation over the lessons, she could have taken her time, steadily teasing Master Christopher closer to her. Instead she'd thrown aside subtlety and used every weapon in her arsenal on him that first day. May God have mercy on her, she'd even allowed her shirt to slip open.

Her lips took a wry twist. It had almost worked. In that moment Christopher's desire for her had been so great he'd have broken any vow to press his lips to

hers. But the musicians interrupted and she'd panicked, nigh on asking him to wed her before she could
stop herself. Since that day, he'd made no attempt
to touch her. 'Twas time to begin her search for a
husband anew.

Even as Anne's heart groaned at this, relief grew.
At least she'd never have to reveal her spoiled state
to Christopher. Such a thing would dishonor her affection for him, even as it destroyed whatever it was
he might feel for her.

A tiny smile touched her mouth. All that made failure bearable was the fact that Patience was no happier
than she. A week ago Patience had discovered her
beloved Bertie in another woman's arms. She'd spoken not a word to the man since.

The usher stood near the Presence Chamber door,
gleaming jewel-bright in his blue and red attire. "Mistress?" he asked as she stopped before him; virgins
that they were supposed to be, maids-of-honor didn't
usually flow unescorted in and out of the room.

"My grandsire has requested a few moments to
speak with me," she replied. "I shouldn't be long."

Master Bowyer nodded. "I thought as much," he
said with a smile, as if commiserating with her over
her grandfather's hopeless behavior.

Turning in the doorway before departing, Anne offered the room and her Royal mistress the honor of
a curtsy. As she rose, her gaze once more darted
across those gathered here. By God, but she was as
hopeless as her grandfather; she was looking for Christopher, even though she knew he was in London on
business today.

Angry at herself, she stepped out the door. The
small space between the Presence Chamber and the
stairs leading down to the courtyard held about a

dozen people, all without rank enough to enter the queen's presence. They waited to be called by name, should their petition for a hearing be granted.

Her grandsire stood at the landing's far end. Gone was his black attire, worn to mourn Walter's passing, leaving him dressed in somber gray beneath his leather jerkin and slashed leather breeches. His features were rock-hard, his eyes narrowed. A muscle along his jawline worked, no doubt against the insult of being denied his monarch's presence.

Beside him stood a small, round woman, wrinkled of face and bright of eye. This one was dressed all in dark brown, with a white partlet tied over her bodice. Everything about her, from the simple coif upon her head to the toes of her shoes, suggested she was another who believed as Sir Amyas did.

'Twas a new sort of panic that shot through Anne. Her grandfather knew Patience was enamored of Christopher's servant and sought to replace her! Her heart fell at the thought of seeing Kit no more.

As Anne stopped before them, the old woman's eyes widened, and she smiled a nearly toothless grin. She seemed a cheery sort for one of Sir Amyas's coreligionists. After a month of curtsying to those above her rank, the bend of Anne's knees was automatic.

"Well, now, this is an improvement," her grandsire said in reaction to even this small show of respect, his tone as cold and harsh as ever.

Anne snapped upright, forgetting all else in the rush of irritation his words awoke. May God damn him, he was seeking someone on whom to vent what boiled in him and she was in no mood to play his victim. "Grandfather." Her voice was as cool as his.

Sir Amyas shot a harsh look at the woman beside

him. "You, over there," he commanded, pointing to the stair landing a few feet away.

"Aye, Sir Amyas," the woman said with surprising good humor, given the rudeness of his command.

As soon as they were private, Sir Amyas bent an almost approving look upon his heiress. "Here I was concerned that courtly life might leave you so emboldened no man would want you, our monarch being who she is. Instead I find you more humble than when I left you."

Teeth gritted, Anne sucked in a quick breath. " 'Tis my royal mistress who has wrought this change in me, so fine an example does she set." She left it to Amyas to decide if this was something to be cherished or feared.

"You would say so and be wrong about it," he snapped.

Anne's eyes narrowed, but she struggled to control her desire to best him in this battle of theirs. Then her mouth lifted. She didn't have to argue with him, especially since he couldn't follow her into the Presence Chamber.

"Grandfather, I cannot long remain out here," she said, reaching for his arm as if to wrap her hand about it in preparation for escort. "Why not come speak with me inside and at our ease?"

His breath left him in a furious stream. "I cannot. Cecil has forbidden me access to her"—he jerked his chin toward the chamber door and his queen—"until he feels I've mastered my rage. Her Majesty remains steadfast in her refusal to replace that papist Hollier with a righteous man."

This teased a spark of humor from Anne. Elizabeth had good reason to refuse, since Christopher's removal would render the royal wager null and void. "I had no idea," she murmured.

With what was almost a sigh, the anger in his eyes dimmed. "I tell you, 'tis a sad day when a man's friends turn on him. Where I say he must push her, William refuses to hear reason, claiming the queen wants no more of this subject. Well, if he thinks this matter finished, he's wrong. 'Tis Leicester I've come to see this day. If any man can help me in this, he can."

Anne wanted to laugh aloud. Poor Amyas was doomed, for he could but get the same response from Leicester he got from the queen.

The potential of her grandsire's defeat in any issue lent Anne the courage to pry. "Grandfather, I haven't seen your friend, Lord Deyville, at court these last weeks. As I recall, he mentioned his wife was gravely ill. I find myself wondering if she's died, although I am certain such a thing would have been announced." She chased all expression from her face to hide her knowledge of his plan, then wondered why she bothered. Sir Amyas didn't believe any woman possessed intelligence enough to decipher a man's intent.

"Nay, his wife yet lives," he replied without hesitation, a bitter edge to his words.

That meant there was still time. She should take this day as a warning to hurry and find herself the man she needed. Still, the urge to cling to Christopher persisted.

"As for what keeps him," her grandfather was saying " 'tis the marriage of his daughter. Once she's wed, he'll return to court."

"Glad I am to hear that it wasn't his wife who'd passed," Anne said, and truly meant it. "To lose both son and mate in one year seems hardship beyond bearing."

Amyas made a noncommittal sound. "So you would say. I'm off to speak with Leicester."

"With that, he turned and strode for the stairs. Anne stared after him. He had called her out of the Presence Chamber merely to chat?

"Wait, Sir Amyas," the old woman called after him. "Where and when shall I meet you?"

Her grandfather turned, his brow clouded in irritation. "Have you no decorum? You shout like a fishwife in the marketplace. My party will be ready to leave in two hours' time. Be out upon the Lawn," he said, referring to the wide field of grass that lay beyond the palace walls, "if you wish an escort back to London."

As if only just remembering what his purpose had been, Sir Amyas looked at his granddaughter. "This is Mistress Alice Godwin. Your mother's steward wrote to me, requesting that I bring the woman to you," he said, unaware that her mother's steward did nothing save at his mistress's command. "She was your mother's governess and now seeks to make your acquaintance." His duty done, he descended the stairs to make his way to Leicester's chambers.

Chapter Twenty

The old woman stepped forward, her grin so broad it looked to hurt. "Ach, I cannot believe this," Mistress Godwin cried. "If you haven't got her coloring, you have my Frances's pretty face." Her smile took a sly twist. "Nor was I so far from you that I couldn't overhear your conversation with your grandsire. I'd say you have her fire as well," she added in approval.

"Mistress Godwin," Anne said, offering the old woman the show of respect she hadn't wanted to give her grandsire. "How pleased I am to make your acquaintance. Did my mother send anything with you?"

"Indeed, she did," Mistress Alice said, pulling from her purse a fold of paper tied with string. "Frances said in her letter to me that I must mention to no one that I carried this for you, especially not your grandsire."

Anne tensed in excitement. If her mother had tendered such a warning, this must be the response to her questions about Lady Montmercy. There was subtle irony in Amyas unwittingly serving as escort to such a message. Taking the packet from the old woman, she tore it open.

There were three pages, all scribed in Lucy Malvin's clear hand. This was an extravagance indeed, and not just for the cost of the paper. It must have taken a full day for her mother to spell out so many words on her alphabet board.

Anne skimmed the greetings, her gaze catching on the assurances that her mother's health was yet good. This was news to savor, but not now. There'd be time later to peruse the whole from beginning to end.

Seeking information about Lady Montmercy, she scanned the lines. A sentence jumped out at her. *My beloved daughter,* Lady Frances wrote, *I am wondering if your heart yet beats swiftly over this Master Hollier, or has your fancy moved on to another?*

Anne stared. How did her mother know she felt anything for Christopher? In the next instant her cheeks flushed as she understood the source of her mother's intelligence. It had become her habit to write a daily description of her activities, including the folk who peopled them, in the hopes her mother might find a little entertainment in the doings of the royal court. These notes went their way to Owls House as often as there were messengers riding in that direction. Only now did Anne realize how large a part Christopher had played in them.

Embarrassment washed over her. It would pain her dearly to admit to her mother she'd foolishly pinned her heart and hopes on the wrong man. Clearing her throat as if by doing so she could clear her heart of Kit, she read on. What she wanted was at the end of the missive.

You have asked about Lady Montmercy, Lucy wrote for her mother. *Although you were right that she and I both served the last two of King Harry's queens, I knew the lady only well enough to think her a sad lass. As I have nothing to offer you, I send instead Mistress*

Godwin, who was my governess until I wed with
your sire.

Whilst Alice and I lived at court, she formed an affection for Lady Montmercy. So strong was their liking
for each other that upon my marriage, the lady hired
my Alice to become governess to her daughter, the
Lady Arabella. I recommend Mistress Godwin to you,
promising that you may take every confidence in her,
spilling to her the secrets you have not shared with me.

Anne made a face. Would that her mother were
half as witless as Sir Amyas thought her. Folding the
papers, she tucked them in her purse for later enjoyment, then looked upon the old woman.

"I have much I would like to ask you, mistress,"
she said with a smile. "A moment please, as I must
win some time in which to do so."

The old woman laughed at this. "As I can think of
no better way to spend my afternoon than with my
Frances's daughter, I suspect I'll wait."

Anne slipped back into the Presence Chamber. Although it took more than a moment, when she again
left the room she had the whole of the afternoon to
dedicate to her unexpected visitor. "Come," she cried,
catching the grandam's arm in hers, "the day is a
lovely one. We'll walk in the garden as we speak."

It was to the wilder of the gardens that she led
Mistress Godwin. May's blossoms were gone now, the
trees having set their fruit and donned their summer
raiment. The tiled pathways were dappled in light, the
air sweet with the smell of the wild roses that grew
against its enclosing walls.

As they strolled away from the gate, the old woman
looked about her. "So many years and so little has
changed," she said with a smile. " 'Tis just as lovely
now as it was in my day."

"And, just as private, no doubt," Anne replied. "Glad I am for that. I think it wouldn't do us any good for someone to overhear what we say. Moreover, I've not seen Lady Montmercy today. I cannot believe she'd much like to find you speaking to me." This was all the more so since the lady was aware of Anne's curiosity in her, although not the purpose behind that interest.

"Have no fear on that account," the old woman said, her smile tightening into what was almost a grimace. "I happen to know the lady is in London. That's why I came to speak with you this day."

"God be praised for that much," Anne breathed, then smiled at Mistress Godwin. "I know time is short, but speak to me first of my mother. I have only known her since—" Anne caught back *since my birth left her crippled*. "Since she's been without movement and tongue."

"So you have, you poor thing. Well, I expect I can tell you a thing or two." Mistress Godwin lifted her head, looking into the distance as her eyes misted with fond memories. "My Frances was like you, all cheek and brass. Aye, so lovely and daring was she, I feared she might catch the old king's eye." She sighed against the danger of attracting a monarch's eye. "I gave thanks, if she did not, when the last of his Catherines insisted on her removal from court. 'Twas then that her father accepted Sir Amyas's offer of his younger son for her."

Mistress Godwin glanced at Anne. "No insult intended, but I always felt the squire could have found someone better for her. Sir Amyas's son was an overbearing braggart and Frances, well, Frances was who she was. But her father was certain Sir Amyas's star was rising, and my Frances was a second daughter."

"No insult is taken," Anne laughed. "If I never knew my sire, I know my grandfather and can imagine the son he produced. I think Mama was content to manage the estate, only tolerating her husband's infrequent visits."

According to Lucy, her father had come to Owls House only at Sir Amyas's insistence, then stayed just long enough to set his seed in his wife's womb. Four daughters in a little more than as many years, there were. When Anne's birth left her mother as she was, her sire had visited no more.

"I say your father died as he deserved," Mistress Alice said with a certain satisfaction, "surrounded only by servants in his father's London home." She paused to sigh. "Had I been free to come to Frances then, I would have done so, but I knew she was well cared for, while Betta needed me more."

"Betta?" Anne asked, grateful that the conversation was moving away from her birth and its consequences.

"Lady Montmercy," the old woman replied in explanation. "If your mother was unhappy in her match, Betta was barely surviving hers." Here, the old woman fell silent.

Thinking she needed time to gather her thoughts, Anne strode alongside her for a few moments, content to let the fragrant breeze play in her skirts and to feel the sun's warmth upon her shoulders. When the quiet between them continued, broken only by birdsong and the gentle drone of insects, Anne glanced at her. "Mistress Godwin?"

"I am waiting," the old woman said.

"For what?" Anne asked in surprise.

"To hear why it is you have an interest in my Betta. What I have to say is beyond private and could well see lives destroyed. Before I spill the tale, I'll know to what purpose you intend to put my words. That, and you must pay my price by telling me why you pry." Mistress Alice looked at her former charge's daughter, her gaze cool and calculating.

Anne studied her visitor, considering how much she could afford to reveal, then loosed a breath of defeat. Chances were her mother had guessed a good part of what Amyas was about and why Anne sought information about Lady Montmercy; Lady Frances would have written as much to Mistress Alice. Between that and what the old woman had overheard in her conversation with Sir Amyas, a falsehood here could cost her the information she might need to save herself.

"My grandsire would have me wed with Lord Oliver Deyville, whose wife is dying as we speak. That I will not do," she said.

Mistress Godwin loosed a snort. "Why? Because you do not like the man? This seems a selfish reason to destroy another woman's life."

"Nay," Anne protested, " 'tisn't just that I have no liking for the man, although I admit I do not. Who could care for him, when he is another like my grandsire, cruel and uncaring? It's my mother. Not every man would include her in his household, and I cannot, nay, I will not abandon her to spend her life alone among servants. I am all the family she has left, and she needs me."

"So you'll not marry Lord Deyville for your mother's sake. Have you a man to put in his place, one who might accept my Frances as she is?" the old woman asked.

"I thought I had." Anne offered her a small, sad smile.

"But he has refused your mother?" Mistress Alice cocked a brow.

Anne sighed. "Nay, of all the men I know, I think him most likely to not only accept her, but cherish her for who she is. Unfortunately, he is not interested in marriage, not to me or any woman."

"Ah, so he is a man who likes other men," the old woman said, a slight sneer on her face.

The need to defend Christopher against such a charge sent words tumbling from Anne's lips. "Nay, Master Hollier is not like that. 'Tis some promise he's made that makes him keep his distance from me."

This turned the corners of the woman's mouth. "Hollier, is it? Would that make him the grandson of Lord Graceton?" At Anne's nod, the woman's smile widened. "Now, there was a stubborn old man if ever I saw one. He was fortunate he didn't lose his head as Sir Thomas More did. If your Master Hollier is in any way like his grandfather, he'll keep that promise of his to the death."

Anne's heart cried at this. So she also believed. 'Twas for Owls House and her mother that she strove to put aside her care for Christopher. "Given time, I will find another," she said to the old woman, "but 'tis time I do not have. This is what I seek from you, a device that will not only force Sir Amyas to wait while I find the man I need, but make him accept the one I choose."

"And the search for this weapon of yours has led you to my Betta?" Mistress Alice turned her gaze to the movement of her hems as they walked.

"Aye," Anne replied. "At my presentation there was a strange interplay between Lady Montmercy and my grandsire. Sir Amyas, who despises all women, seemed to fear her."

Mistress Godwin's brow creased as she pondered what Anne had told her. After a long moment she nodded. "Aye, then, we'll speak of the past. First, vow to me that you'll keep the tale I tell between you and I, should you find no other use for it."

"I so vow," Anne replied without hesitation. Not even Lady Montmercy deserved to be so casually destroyed.

"Then, I will begin by saying old Lord Montmercy was a monster, and Betta wasn't your mother. She lacked the heart to resist his evil."

Disbelief woke in Anne at such a description of the noblewoman, the emotion strong enough to cause her to interrupt. "That I cannot imagine. Lady Montmercy seems so cool and controlled."

The old woman gave a sad shake of her head. "The woman you now see is not the Betta I knew and loved. What now resides in that body is a creature who owns my pity, but not my heart. Lord Montmercy destroyed her, for it wasn't a wife he wanted when he wed with her, but a tool. He used her youth and beauty to seduce his enemies and tease their secrets from them."

Anne stopped still in the pathway to stare at the woman. "Are you saying she made herself a whore for him?" she breathed in horror.

Mistress Alice's gaze was warning-sharp, suggesting she did more than pity Lady Montmercy, despite her protest to the contrary. "She made herself nothing. 'Twas the old lord who used cruelty to force a fine young woman into evil. There were beatings if she refused and handsome rewards when she complied. The rewards grew greater when what she brought him resulted in the destruction of one he hated. Those sapphires of hers were a gift after her greatest success. As I said, she had not your mother's fire, or yours, to deny him."

"What of his heirs?" Anne asked, struggling to un-

derstand and all the while thinking of herself and Lord
Deyville. "Did not the old lord want children from
her to hold her property as his?"

"Nay," Mistress Alice shook her head. "Betta
brought him little in the way of lands, and he was
content to use her properties for his lifetime, caring
nothing for her bloodline. As for his own estate, he
had an heir, or thought he did, in his son by his first
wife, who was already wed and producing children."

Anne's head spun. Such horror seemed impossible
on a day when wildflowers nodded their brightly colored heads to them along every turn in the pathway.
At last her thoughts fixed on one idea. Mistress Alice
said that the old lord had used his wife against his
enemies. Amyas had been one of his most despised
foes. "Do you know if any of those men Lord Montmercy made his lady bed might have been my
grandsire?"

"I fear I cannot say," the old woman replied. "The
shame she shared with me, but not the names. Indeed,
so great was her shame that I feared for her sanity.
That was, until Lord Montmercy let her keep her
son."

"Let her keep?" Anne demanded.

From the bend in the path ahead of them, there
came a woman's laugh. A man's deeper chuckle followed, the sound filled with lust. Anne gasped. Together, she and Mistress Alice turned, walking back
along the tiled path to where it branched. When they
were walking in this new direction, Anne looked at
her guest.

"What did you mean by 'let her keep'?"

"Now, girl," Mistress Alice chided in quiet amusement, "you do not strike me as one so innocent as
that. A woman cannot go from bed to bed without

occasionally bearing fruit. Only once was the old lord
unable to force my Betta's body to shed the child that
grew within it. That one, a lass it was, he took from
her, refusing to say where he went with the little one
and whether the babe lived or died. Everyone else
was told the babe had been stillborn."

"May God have mercy," Anne said, her eyes closing
as she offered up a prayer for the innocents old Lord
Montmercy had killed. "So why did he allow her to
keep her son?"

" 'Twas in the last year of King Edward's reign.
Lord Montmercy knew he was dying. There'd been
plague the previous year, the outbreak catching in its
first wave the lord's son and his family." Mistress
Alice shot Anne a vengeful look. "The Lord's retribution for Montmercy's evil, of that I have no doubt.

"At any rate, it didn't suit the old lord's hatred for
his brother to allow the estate to fall to that man, so
he took to laying with Betta, something he'd not done
before. When she proved fertile, he let that child stay
where it had rooted." Alice leaned close and lowered
her voice. "In all truth, I'm not certain he knew the
child wasn't his."

"You believe it wasn't his spawn?" Anne asked,
both shocked and fascinated by this tale.

"I know the child is not," the old woman replied
with not a little satisfaction in her voice. "My Betta
knew whose seed grew in her, and it wasn't her lord
husband's."

Anne's head reeled. Lord Andrew was a bastard.
What if he were Amyas's child? Excitement tried to
rise. Was it Amyas she'd seen in Andrew's strut and
heard in his hoarsened voice?

Her hopes collapsed. It couldn't be. Worse, however

intriguing Mistress Alice's tale, there was still no proof of Amyas's connection to Lady Montmercy.

"Until the last year of his life, the old lord had taken care to see his wife formed no affection for those she used," Mistress Alice was saying. "But in those last months he was too ill to watch. All I know is that my poor darling was happier than I'd ever seen her. Whoever her son's father is, she loved him with all her heart."

Anne pulled a face. If she was looking for proof positive that it wasn't Amyas, there it was. How could any woman love him?

"Of one thing I am certain: the man is a devout Protestant," Mistress Alice continued, "for he went into exile upon Queen Mary's coronation."

"As did my grandsire," Anne mused, trying to imagine Lady Montmercy and Sir Amyas as lovers. The pieces were there. Only the proof was missing.

The old woman nodded. "At any rate, even though my Betta was then a widow and could have had another husband, she held firm in her affection for this one, believing him just as faithful. Five years it was she waited, until Queen Mary lay dying, with her Protestant sister set to take the throne. What saddened some made Betta nigh on joyous."

Mistress Alice shot Anne a quiet, sidelong look. "And why not, since a Protestant queen would allow the return of all those exiled during the Catholic queen's rule? Betta went to serve the new queen, all the while watching for the one she so desired and doting on her son." The old woman shook her head against the memory, her whiskered mouth twisting into a small smile. "How she cherished that lad."

"Aye, so I'm told," Anne said, the inklings of understanding stirring within her. "That is, until the day your Betta gave her son to a warden and turned her back on him. 'Tis said she'll have naught to do with him to this day."

Mistress Alice sighed. "In that, I fear the lad pays for his father's sin." She stared ahead of her, the look in her eyes once again distant. 'Twas sadness she viewed in the past.

Anne's heart clutched. Even though she was already certain what the answer would be, she asked, "What happened when Betta's lover returned?"

"He rejected her," the old woman said in a quiet voice. "In doing so, this man achieved what Lord Montmercy had not. Something in my Betta broke with his desertion. She threw away his son and became what you see when you look upon her now."

Here was the cruelty of which Anne knew her grandfather capable. She breathed out, imagining the pain of having endured a husband's torment with only a lover's promise of happiness to keep her sane, then to be tossed aside by the one she trusted. "How horrible for her."

"You, my sweet, cannot afford to pity my Betta." The old woman's voice was tight.

That brought Anne out of her musing with a start. "What do you mean?"

"Come now," Mistress Alice taunted. "Having heard my Betta's sorry tale, do you think your need to escape marriage to Lord Deyville enough to cause me to spill it? When your mother wrote to me, I plied my Betta with subtle questions and liked naught the answers I received. Nay, you hear what I know because my love for your mother cannot countenance your destruction . . . and that is what my Betta plans for you."

Chapter Twenty-one

'Twas in the house where he and Lady Montmercy had first met that again Kit sat, once more using the barrel-cum-chair. With summer upon them the shutters were thrown wide, allowing the sun to flow into the forechamber. The bench before the fireplace gleamed a warm brown, while the wee copper pot standing upon the brick hearth glinted. Gone was the fine writing desk, suggesting it had belonged to the lady, not the householder.

It was rage he expected and found in Lady Montmercy. The noblewoman paced the length of the room from doorway to the wall separating foreroom from bedchamber. Gone was her doll-like blankness of expression. Instead her skin seared bright red along her cheekbones, while her mouth was held to a thin line.

"I'd not have thought you so limp of prick," she snarled, throwing the insult like a spear. "Did you forget to tell me you could not couple like a normal man?"

Even as her charge stung his pride, Kit bit back his challenge that she try him. Proving his manhood to this woman wouldn't protect Anne, and her protection had become his all. He hadn't had a nightmare since that day in the barn. 'Twas as if shielding her from harm somehow balanced the wrong he'd done to Nick, all those years ago.

Lady Montmercy whirled, her dark blue and gray skirts hissing and snapping against the floorboards as she returned toward the street door. "Have you nothing to say?" she demanded.

"What can I say?" he replied. "You wanted to know if a Puritan miss is as easily seduced as any other maid. I am here to report that she is not. Mistress Blanchemain holds tight to her virtue."

She jerked around to glare at him. "This is your defense, that she is a virtuous woman?"

Kit shrugged. "Am I to be blamed if there are women in the world who will not give way to sin?" He tossed this out as repayment for her insult.

The lady's chin snapped up. "You dare?"

"Nay," he replied, "I but report. I even set my man to seducing her maid in the hopes of winning some aid in that direction. Like her mistress, the servant holds tight to virtue."

'Twas a fact that left Bertie much humbled, very frustrated, and utterly unwilling to admit failure. This, despite that Mistress Patience had refused to speak with him the whole of last week over some slight he'd done her. Indeed, this failure seemed only to have strengthened Bertie's determination to have the maid.

Bracing his elbows on the chair's arms, Kit rested his chin upon his steepled fingers. "Madame, I am dismayed that you would expect success so soon. You are too eager."

"Over a month, and you call me too eager?" she shouted at him. "How much time did you think to take?"

"As long as I need," he snapped. "We never discussed how quickly I was to achieve your goal."

"Sir Amyas could die before you've used her," she nigh on shrieked. "You fool! He wants her married. No doubt he's already planning her wedding."

Kit shook his head. "Nay, Mistress Blanchemain tells me her grandsire has received several offers for her hand and has refused them all." Aye, Amyas was yet waiting for Deyville's wife to die, while that god-forsaken woman clung stubbornly to life.

"Take heart, madame. If Mistress Anne's not yet willing to yield to me, know that she's sorely tempted." So deep was Anne's need for him that her every touch blistered his skin with her wanting. This kept his own desire for her simmering barely under control, despite his cause.

Lady Montmercy whirled at the doorway to the bedchamber, her sapphire earbobs dancing. Frustration seethed in her gaze. "Be gone from me. I'll find me another to do what you cannot and see you in prison for your failure."

Kit waved away her dismissal as the empty threat it was. "Set a new man in my place, and he'll only have to begin at the beginning, going where I have already gone. Who knows how much longer that might take?"

"If you cannot seduce her, then force her," the noblewoman shouted.

"Where?" he sneered. "In Greenwich's hall whilst I school her in dancing with half the court to witness my attack? That's where it must be done, since I've no other access to her."

Her eyes narrowed, and her mouth twisted into a vicious line. "You are not the first man who thought he could play me for a fool. Like the others, you'll pay the price for your arrogance. I know of those secret lessons of yours."

It took all Kit's will to keep surprise off his face. "We have no private meetings," he lied, his voice hard.

She was but probing, she had to be. Not even Leicester, who had pried, knew of their private lessons. Anger followed.

This wasn't the first secret thing Lady Montmercy had discovered about him; there was that contract written before their initial meeting, yet addressing the very issue that so plagued him. Someone, someone who knew him intimately, was talking too much and only to her. Even as he put his finger upon the only man it could be, he shied away from the thought. Bertie couldn't have betrayed him.

Her eyes widen until he could see a ring of white about her irises. "Ball-less man," she spat out. "Since you're not man enough for it, and say seduction will take more time than I would wait, I think I'll hire me one with a bolder cock than yours to force her. Rape is such a simple thing, three minutes and 'tis done."

Here was the threat Kit had come prepared to face. Rising from the chair, he strode to stand before her, using his greater height to carry home his point. "Have a care with the man you choose," he retorted coolly. "He must either have a position like mine, giving him legitimate access to the heiress, or be a man close to Amyas. Anyone else, and it won't be revenge you win, not with Parliament's temper just now. Instead Amyas will make a martyr of his granddaughter, using her to decry the queen's court as wicked and immoral. Every member will echo his charge, making of Mistress Anne a rallying point as they again try to force our queen to wed. Instead of Amyas's destruction, you'll but turn court and country's sympathy in his direction."

Rage drained from the lady's face as he explained to her what she already knew. With a gasping breath she buried her face in her hands. "May God damn you," she cried into her palms, her voice edged in hysteria.

When she lifted her head, her face was once again composed, her eyes expressionless. 'Twas with Anne's safety neatly achieved that Kit returned her look.

"I will give you until the court begins its summer progress." Her voice was lifeless and dull. "If she is yet virgin at July's end or affianced before that date, you'll find yourself in the Fleet for your debts where you will die."

"And if I should offer to pay them?" 'Twas a pointless question; he knew what her answer would be.

"You can try," she said coldly, "but I find I'm not in a generous mood. I want what was originally promised me in return for my loan."

Kit offered her a quick bow. "My lady, do your worst, knowing that I, and I alone, hold in my hands all you hope to accomplish."

Turning, he strode from the room. The end of July. Lady Deyville damn well better have died by then. If not, Lady Montmercy would have no reason to arrange his demise. He'd have already expired, having eaten himself alive for want of Anne.

It was a short walk to the alehouse where Bertie waited. 'Twas an old establishment, the plaster between its dark beams gray and spotted with mold. There was no glass in its windows, and with the lower floor's shutters all thrown wide to welcome in so fine a day, Kit could see nearly all the public room.

Bertie sat by himself at the farthest table, his cup before him. His shoulders were bent, his head bowed. Kit's heart clenched. Bertie had the look of a man

stewing in guilt. Lord, but it hurt to think he'd been
betrayed by a man he'd known since his sixth year.

Two steps took him down into the alehouse's main
room. He strode across the room and set his hand on
his man's shoulder. Bertie nearly leapt from his skin.

"God Almighty, Master Kit," he gasped out, "I
didn't see you enter. You're back more swiftly than
I expected."

The corner of Kit's mouth lifted at this. "So I am.
Fetch the horses. I'd be at Greenwich before the evening meal."

Once they were mounted and traveling, there was
too much traffic along London's narrow streets to
allow for conversation. That much Kit expected, but
Bertie's morose mood continued well after they'd left
behind the urban noise and stench. Worry grew. Kit
sighed.

The need to ask after Lady Montmercy was strong.
So was the desire to avoid Bertie's answer. If his man
admitted betrayal, Kit would have no choice save dismissal. He couldn't imagine life without Bertie at his
side. 'Twas too fine day, what with the sky clear and
the sun warm enough to tease up rich scents from the
fertile fields, to contemplate such an event. Perhaps
there was a way to tiptoe around the issue.

Kit glanced at his man. Bertie was muttering to his
saddle, the words owning a measured cadence. He
was praying!

'Twas this that spurred Kit into action. He leaned
over and slapped Bertie's thigh. His man's head
snapped up, bright blue eyes wide in surprise.

"What is it with you, today?" Kit demanded, his
voice seeming overly loud and accusatory against the
quiet of the countryside.

Bertie drew a shattered breath and threw back his

head, his eyes clenched shut and his fists closed at his sides. "I cannot believe what I have done," he cried out to the sky above them, his tone as heartbroken as any man might be in confessing that he'd betrayed his master.

'Twas pain, not anger that snaked into Kit's gullet. "What is it you've done?" he demanded.

Bertie turned in his saddle to look at him, his eyes wide in desperation. "Master, I asked Patience to wed with me," he cried.

This knocked the breath from Kit's lungs. "You did what?"

"I asked her to wed," the man whispered, head hanging.

As Kit's shock ebbed, amusement rose. "You," he dared to taunt, "who vowed no female would ever lead you about by your nose, have let that wretched woman ring you?"

Anger clouded in Bertie's eyes. "Patience is a woman of great faith, good morals, and the owner of as sweet a heart as any man might want in a wife," he shot back. "I'll not have you speaking so about her."

This lover's defense only egged Kit on in his need to tease. "But marriage, Bertie," he protested with a laugh. "You as a husband, now there's an image quite beyond my ability to concoct. How could this happen to you, you the master of all women, the one who swore Mistress Patience would be writhing beneath you in under two weeks time?"

Rather than mount a defense or give way to outraged pride, Bertie's expression drooped. "Master, I am so ashamed of myself. 'Twas wrong of me to ever contemplate seducing my Patience. Worse, I've now made my proposal without admitting what I'd first planned for her. To trade vows before confessing my original evil intent will befoul the affection I now feel for her."

His words resonated in Kit, waking his own shame. What sort of man signed a contract framed to destroy an innocent woman? His well-trodden honor chose this moment to raise its head from the muck of his soul and demand he make a similar confession to Anne.

"Would that I were not so great a coward," Bertie went on, very real worry staining his blue eyes. His voice lowered. "I fear if I tell her, she'll cut me out of her life forever."

Kit grimaced as his heart descended to ride in the heel of his boot. 'Twas his own fate he saw reflected in Bertie's fears. By God, Anne would kill him when she heard the story of that contract, and rightly so.

"So what will you do?" he asked, curious for his own sake.

"I don't know," his man cried, heartache in his voice. "Master Kit, I never knew it possible to crave a woman's mind and soul more than her presence in my bed, but so it is with Patience. This last week, whilst she refused to talk to me, I thought I'd die. No quick tumble is worth the possibility of losing her."

Kit's brows rose at this. "Is that what you did to anger her? I wondered."

A sheepish grin twisted Bertie's fine mouth. "Aye, she caught me with another maid. I tried to explain that all men need release and just because I laid with that woman didn't mean I loved her. Rather than soothe her, this only made her angry." Astonishment colored his every word.

A laugh caught in Kit's throat. "More fool you for attempting honesty."

Bertie gave a pained shrug. "She'd filled my heart

and mind with her teachings, making me forget she is a woman like any other. I tried telling her that 'twas on her behalf I'd laid with another woman at all, since she was driving me mad with the wanting of her and I didn't wish to befoul her with my sinful lusts. Rather than see the compliment, she cried as if I'd killed her." Befuddlement filled his face.

"From the frying pay into the fire," Kit groaned.

"Aye," Bertie agreed with a sorry nod. "Then, last night when Mistress Anne arrived for your dancing lesson, there was my Patience, smiling at me as if ready to forgive. The words leapt from my mouth before I could stop them."

Kit shook his head at his love-struck servant. "So ringed you will be. Well, I suppose she can take up residence in my London house, but how will she feel when court moves and you must attend me elsewhere?"

Bertie's gaze flickered away from him to stare across the verdant roll of hills. "Actually, I'd thought of returning with her to Graceton to take up residence with my mother," he muttered. "There's too much temptation for me at court."

"Ringed and castrated," Kit hooted.

Bertie glowered at him. "I was going to invite you to our wedding. Perhaps, I will reconsider."

" 'Tis probably best," Kit said. "I fear I'd ruin it all by rolling upon the floor whilst you spew your vows."

Now that his spleen was clear of what troubled him, Bertie's shoulders lifted and his face came to life in relief. Again, thoughts of Lady Montmercy filled Kit, bringing with it the terrible need to confront his man.

"Bertie, do you know Lady Montmercy?" Kit's voice rang in his own ears.

His servant frowned. "Nay, not the lady herself, but I know of her, through Nell."

"Nell?" Kit prodded.

"Aye, Nell was once that lady's maid, although I think she now serves the viscountess of Hereford. I met her when you and I first came to court. Our affair didn't last long, for Nell was far more interested in you than me. I fear I don't tolerate competition well." 'Twas a weak jest, given Bertie's soon-to-be married state.

Here was the confirmation Kit hadn't wanted to find, even though it was four years old. Bitterness filled him. Did Lady Montmercy investigate every man who came to court, or had he somehow caught her eye?

"Do you recall speaking to this Nell of life at Graceton?" he asked, then grimaced. He sounded like an inquisitor.

Only now did Bertie comprehend there was more to his master's questions than simple curiosity. The man straightened in the saddle as a pinched line marred the perfection of his brow. "I suppose I might have, Master Kit, as those first few months found me often longing for home," he said, then loosed a deep sigh. "Given how little I liked Nell all those years ago, I cannot imagine why I ever agreed to rekindle our affair."

"You what?" Kit stared at the man.

Bertie's mouth took a bitter twist. "Nell's path and mine crossed again some two months back. At the time it seemed convenient, since we knew each other and all," he shrugged, shame flickering through his gaze once more. " 'Twas with Nell that my Patience found me."

Blame for Bertie's betrayal came to rest squarely

upon Kit's shoulders. In keeping his servant ignorant of his involvement with Lady Montmercy, he'd left Bertie vulnerable to the manipulations of that viper in silk.

"Is something amiss?" Bertie asked, his concern growing.

Kit was no more ready to tell his man of that contract than he was Anne. Nor did it matter. Now that he knew the lady's conduit, he could guard against it. At least he had the assurance that Bertie was no Judas, only a loose-lipped, if pretty, fool. "Nay, I was but curious."

"Master, if I've done wrong by laying with Nell, know I've already vowed to Patience that I'll do so no more." Bertie held a hand skyward. "As God is my witness, Master Kit."

"That is like a fish vowing to never again swim," Kit scoffed, then readied himself for what was sure to be a long and pleasant argument over Bertie's newly strengthened morals.

Chapter Twenty-two

Although it was well into the evening, the sun yet hung hours above the horizon. So it was in late June, the days long and sweet when the weather was good, and this day had been as fine a one as Anne had ever known. Here in the wilder of Greenwich's gardens, those creatures living within its walls were busy using these extra hours of light to their best advantage. Aye, and why not? None of them had to marry Lord Deyville.

Anne blinked back tears as she strode along the tiled pathway. Sir Amyas's note had arrived late yesterday, his message contained in but two terse lines. The first said he'd accepted an offer for her hand in marriage, although he didn't reveal her intended husband's name. The second informed her to be prepared to leave the queen's custody in the near future. This could only mean Lady Deyville was dead and she was doomed. In the past month Anne had come no nearer to finding the solid proof she needed to make Mistress Alice's revelations useful. Nor had she had the opportunity to begin again her search for a new husband. This brought her to an abrupt halt. That was a lie. There'd been time. But instead of taking action, all she'd done was dance the days away with Christopher.

Guilt rolled in like the tide. Only this morn she'd

had another letter from her mother. Lady Frances reported that Mistress Alice wrote highly of her, calling Anne a true and loving daughter. Aye, so true a daughter was Anne that she'd let her heart settle upon Christopher to the exclusion of all others.

How could she have abandoned her mother so? Anne sighed. Because she loved Christopher and wanted to marry no one else. The thought of never again feeling his hand on hers, or his arm around her as he led her through the patterns of a dance, tore her in twain. She fought her tears. Nay, she'd not cry, not when this might well be her last night with him. On the morrow, he left court on the queen's business.

"There you are," Patience whispered as she stepped out from the wee copse of willows that served as their hiding spot.

The shock of Patience's attire was enough to startle Anne out of her black mood, at least for the moment. "What are you wearing?" she cried quietly.

Patience smiled and turned a circle, her arms wide to better display her new bodice. 'Twas a pretty greenish-blue, the hue dark enough to make her eyes glow the color of Lady Montmercy's sapphires. "Do you like it?"

"I do, indeed," Anne replied, but 'twas Patience she liked more. Gone was the pale, pinched spy. Love for Bertie Babthorpe had brought to the surface a fine woman with shimmering eyes and a mouth that ever curved into a pretty smile.

" 'Tis a wedding gift from Bertie," Patience said, fair glowing. On the morrow, she and Bertie left for London, where they were to be joined by Patience's uncle. Patience's family, Calvinists all, paid no heed to banns and required no celebration of the event.

Anne let her governess's joy lift her from her own

cares. "I think it wasn't a bad thing for you to catch him in that other woman's arms," she teased gently.

Satisfaction filled Patience's smile as she ran her hands down the new bodice's front. "A woman does what she must to get what she wants, is that not right, mistress?" Then she caught Anne by the arm and drew her in amongst the willows. "Come, now, let's get you changed. Bertie and the musician must be waiting."

At the center of the drooping branches was a small open space. The bundle of Anne's practice garments lay on the moist ground. Christopher, worried that someone might discover their secret lessons, had come upon this strategy. Anne strode into the garden as a maid-of-honor, changed into these far humbler garments, then departed, looking more like a servant than a woman of consequence. The process was reversed at the lesson's end. 'Twas also for concealment's sake that Patience now walked with the musician, while the disguised Anne was escorted by Bertie. Aye, and neither Patience nor Bertie knew where they were off to until the last moment.

Easing around Anne's back, Patience tore at the lacings that held her bodice closed. "Is all well with you, mistress?" she asked as she worked. "You seem out of sorts this day."

Even as Anne opened her mouth to tell her governess what had happened, she caught back the words. She wanted nothing to spoil Patience's joy. "In all truth," she lied, "I long for home, being sick of this place and its stench."

Patience laughed as she pulled off Anne's bodice, leaving the sleeves attached. "Aye, two months here with so many people and not enough river to wash away the offal has made it foul, indeed, even to one such as I, who has lived all my life in London!"

As the woman folded this garment, Anne shucked her skirts, along with farthingale and all the underpinnings. Her ruff and corset followed, leaving her dressed in only her shirt.

Anne pulled it closed over her bare breasts as Patience handed her the one-piece garment country girls wore. 'Twas a combination of both skirt and bodice, the bodice's front scooping low beneath her breasts. Dyed a pretty red, it had served Anne well on cleaning days at Owls House. Once it was on Anne discarded her black velvet headdress, braided her hair, and tied on a coif, not unlike the one Patience wore. That left only her shoes. Anne leaned against a tree trunk to don them, while Patience wrapped the expensive court attire in the oiled cloth against an unexpected shower.

When the bundle was set aside, Patience turned to look at her mistress. "Where do we go today?"

"Duke Humphrey's tower," Anne replied.

"Right, then. I am off to meet the musician," Patience said as she stayed where she stood.

Anne looked up. Her servant smiled, the movement of her mouth sad. "Each time you step out with no one at your side, I think of the maying and Lord Deyville's attack," she whispered. "I worry for you every second, mistress." With that, she slipped from the glade.

Anne stared at the swaying branches. She was worried for herself, as well.

Kit stood in the tower's gateway, dwarfed by its thick walls. Duke Humphrey's tower, an old defensive structure not unlike the one that crumbled at Graceton's heart, stood at the top of the hill behind

Greenwich Palace. 'Twas a marvelous spot. Looking one direction a man could see the hodgepodge of buildings that filled the palace compound. Looking another, he could see the rooftops of London. That was, if the day was clear and the man was looking.

'Twas through gritty, burning eyes that Kit stared blindly out upon the gentle, rolling landscape. Last night, for the first time in two months, the nightmare had returned, all the more stunning for its long absence. With a sigh he leaned against the cold stones of the gateway. He knew why. The queen had commanded him home.

'Twas royal fear over a Catholic uprising that sent him to Graceton. Although indebted and yet without his rightful title, Nick's holdings were substantial and his Catholic leanings well-known to his queen. Elizabeth wanted assurances that Graceton's squire wouldn't encourage those who lived on his lands to rise against her. Unfortunately, Kit's nightmare was no respecter of causes. It knew only that Kit was returning to the source of his guilt.

A couple emerged from the park gate. Kit watched them cross Woolwich Road, then the grassy expanse that was the Lawn. They started up this hill, confirming they were of his party. Kit freed a bitter breath, torn between anticipation and frustration.

These lessons had become sheer torment. No longer was it only lust for Anne that plagued him. Somehow his need to protect her had twisted into an emotion Kit didn't care to name. This was dangerous, indeed, tempting him into thoughts of permanence, even though he knew such a thing was impossible.

The couple was halfway up the tower's hill now. Kit frowned. The lute player he recognized, but who was that woman at his side? She wore a pretty blue bodice atop her brown skirts, while beneath her coif soft wings of brown hair framed a fine, oval face. As she chatted to the man beside her, her hands dashed and darted in lively punctuation.

He straightened, eyes wide. Mistress Patience? As if she'd heard his thought, she looked up the hill and smiled. Kit gaped in astonishment. How could she have changed so, and he not notice? No wonder Bertie was in such a hurry to wed and bed her.

As she and the musician strode into the tower's gateway, Mistress Patience offered him a respectful bob, while the musician more touched than doffed his cap in deference to Kit's gentle status. "A fine evening, master," the man said. "so where's it to be tonight?"

"In the garden," Kit replied. "Tap upon the gatehouse door," he pointed to the opposite end of this tunnel-like passage, "and the caretaker will show you the way."

As the musician strode past him through the shadowed gateway into the courtyard beyond it, Bertie's bride to be stayed where she stood. The maid watched him, her look intense. Kit shifted uncomfortably under her scrutiny, then tried to smile. "Is there something I can do for you?"

A small frown creased her brow. "Master Hollier, am I right in thinking you hold some affection for my mistress in your heart?"

'Twas the probe Kit expected from her in May, but spewed with none of the harsh accusation he'd envisioned her attaching to that question. Now, as he opened his mouth, 'twas an admission of love that crowded onto his tongue. Kit choked it back, stunned at himself. Where had that come from? He cleared his throat and tried again.

"Mistress Anne has become a good friend, well liked by me for her wit and humor. Does that satisfy your question?"

"Indeed, it does," she replied, her smile beautiful. "Bertie was right in thinking you'd not speak the whole of it, only skirting around your true feelings for her."

This sent a start through him. Bertie had spoken to her of him? By God, the man was worse than a sieve!

"Nay, now," Mistress Patience said as she all too rightly read his outrage, "you mustn't think Bertie spilled some secret. 'Tis by what he said to me in passing, that you were a private man and not one to share your inner thoughts with others, that I judge your words."

"I can only hope marriage to you will teach him better manners," Kit replied, only a little soothed by her attempt.

"I'm sure it shall," Mistress Patience promised with a surprisingly wicked twinkle in her eyes, then she sighed and sadness chased the smile from her lips.

"Master Hollier, 'tis against your fondness for my mistress that I now presume to tell you something, praying you will keep my words in confidence. Sir Amyas writes that Lady Deyville departed for her heavenly home yesterday. Once Lord Deyville has spent his proscribed two months mourning her, Sir Amyas intends for Mistress Anne to wed him."

Kit stiffened at this news. Anne was his! Deyville couldn't have her.

With the next breath his shoulders dropped. Nay, she wasn't his. She couldn't ever be his. If he dared to wed Anne, she'd be a widow within a week, whether 'twas Lady Montmercy, Sir Amyas, or Lord Deyville who did the deed.

"Why do you tell me this?" he asked, his voice carefully neutral.

"Because, she cannot wed Lord Deyville," Patience replied, a frantic edge to her voice. "You saw him at the maying."

So he had. The image of that nobleman trying to force himself on Anne turned itself into a vision of his Anne suffering beneath that godless lecher on her wedding night. Emotions tumbled in him.

"Now, mistress," Kit said, attempting to soothe them both at the same time, "what we saw that day was a man worried he would lose the one on whom he'd settled his affections." He cringed inwardly with that word. 'Twasn't affection Deyville had for Anne. "He'll not treat her so, once they're wed."

"So you would say, being a man," Mistress Patience retorted with surprising spirit, "but I have a different experience with one much like that nobleman. Bowing to my father's will I agreed to wed a man he called his friend. Within a month I came crying to my parents of abuse. Rather than heed me, my father blinded himself to my bruises, saying they were my fault. He wouldn't"—she paused to draw a ragged breath— "nay, he couldn't believe ill of his friend. Instead he abandoned me to my marriage, just as Sir Amyas will do to my poor mistress."

She stepped closer to lay a hand upon Kit's arm, the need to protect her charge flowing into him from her slender fingers. "Sir Amyas will come soon to claim her. If you care for my mistress at all, Master Hollier, you'll not abandon her."

The woman's mouth set to trembling as tears swam in her eyes. She turned abruptly on her heel as if embarrassed to have revealed so much about herself to follow the musician and caretaker to the garden's gate. Her shoulders were square, her spine pike-straight.

Kit watched her until he could see her no longer. What sort of world was it that offered his Anne naught but abuse, yet left him incapable of saving her? What sort of coward stood idly by while the woman he loved entered into marriage with a monster? His dream's impotence closed around him. This was worse than watching Nick fall into the fire, for he knew his brother had survived. He doubted Anne would fare as well.

Depression swirled in on him. Once again, someone he cherished was going to be destroyed. Once again, there was nothing he could do to stop it, for not even his death would save her.

Chapter Twenty-three

Duke Humphrey's tower was massive, squat, and square, rising high above its thick enclosing walls. Tall, arched windows pierced its stony sides, the glass glinting in its westward face. Above the crenellations that edged the tower's top like giant teeth perched a steep, conical roof, lead tiles the color of pewter. 'Twas quite a building, like nothing Anne had before seen. Then again, all she'd seen of the world was Owls House and its nearby village, her grandsire's London house, a glimpse of Whitehall and Westminster, and now Greenwich.

She glanced to the side, thinking to ask Bertie about this place and its history, only to catch back the question. Christopher's servant had the look of a man going to his execution. His brow was clouded, his gaze aimed at the hillside a few feet ahead of them. Anne fought back a laugh at the thought that Patience should beam so over marriage, while her husband-to-be walked beneath a cloud.

Christopher appeared at the center of the tower's arched entryway. Anne set aside all worry over her future to drink in the sight of him. Against the evening's warmth and their upcoming activity, he'd shed his doublet, cap, and gloves, leaving him dressed in naught but his full-sleeved white shirt and a pair of brown breeches, with dark stockings to display his well-made legs. The evening's breeze made free with his hair, tossing the golden-brown strands. She frowned. There were dark circles beneath his green eyes, and his face was drawn and tight.

"Is your master ill?" she murmured to Bertie.

"What?" The startled servant glanced at his employer. "Oh, him. Nay, he's well," came the man's distracted answer. "Just tired. That nightmare of his kept him from his rest last night."

"Nightmare?" Anne asked, hoping for Bertie's explanation, but she was too late. He was once again lost in his own thoughts.

As they strode into the entryway, Anne smiled at her tutor. "Good even, Master Christopher."

When he returned her smile with his own, Anne sighed. How she loved that slow turn of his lips and the way it made his eyes glow with whatever 'twas he held in his heart. Right now what lay there was pleasure at seeing her.

"Where is she?" Bertie asked in what was nearly a demand, his voice echoing oddly in this short, stone tunnel. He fell silent as if startled by the effect, and began anew. "Where are we to be tonight, master?"

"In the garden through yon gate," Christopher replied, pointing but taking no step in that direction.

As Bertie moved off like a sleepwalker, Anne waited for Christopher to follow. When he didn't, subtle pleasure flowed through her. It seemed he intended to have a moment alone with her. Once again, the breeze set to toying with his hair.

"You are looking very windblown this even, my fine tutor," she said with a smile, lifting a hand to straighten his hair. "There."

Golden sparks came to life in his eyes. "My thanks, mistress. Shall we?" He extended his arm.

"You look tired," she said as she accepted his invitation, daring to lean against his arm as they started for the garden's gate.

"I am, a little." He drew her nearer.

"Bertie tells me you suffered with a dream last night."

Surprise flashed in his eyes, then Christopher's brow furrowed. "Bertie spoke to you of my dream?" he snapped.

Anne's heart hit her toes as she recognized how intrusive her comment had been. May God damn her, but she'd just ruined their last evening together. She released her hold on his arm. "My pardon, I didn't mean to pry."

His anger disappeared, leaving only regret in its place. "Nay, the fault isn't yours." Christopher turned his gaze toward the tower's courtyard and watched Bertie disappear into the lush foliage of what was surely the garden. "It's only that it seems my servant speaks of me to every woman he knows."

A discussion over their servants was not what Anne wanted from him this night. Nay, what she wanted was to feel all of him against her. Shame followed so lewd a thought. All in all, she thought it far better to die at Deyville's hands for her lack of purity than to suffer Christopher's scorn over it.

She started when Christopher caught her hand, his fingers entwining with hers. His palm was hard, his touch gentle. She shivered when he moved his thumb atop hers in a subtle caress. The pleasure returned to his eyes.

"Come dance with me, Nan," he invited, his voice

low as he claimed the use of her pet name. 'Twas love for her she saw in his face.

Even as joy filled her, Anne's heart broke. Why couldn't this have happened a month ago? In the next instant she shook free of such mournful thoughts. If now was all she had, then it would have to do.

"I will, Kit," she whispered. He smiled, as pleased as she by the sound of his shortened name on her tongue, then led her into the garden.

This evening was one meant to tease the senses. Clouds filled the yet-blue sky like a herd of newly washed sheep. A warm breeze, blessedly free of stench, tousled the tall trees that lined the garden's four walls. Beneath them roses and hawthorn grew, thick and tangled. At the garden's center was a neat square of grass. This bit of lawn was level and lined by spicy-smelling stock and pinks, making for a fragrant dance floor.

'Twas a galliard they practiced this night. The fast-paced dance required much footwork and a good amount of leaping on the man's part, or so Kit claimed. Anne stumbled her way through the steps long after she knew them by heart, because each time she pretended to fall, Kit caught her close. For that brief instant, she'd lean her head into his shoulder and imagine he was hers. Then, before her ploy became obvious, she'd push away with a laugh at her clumsy footwork.

As one hour became two, all the bouncing loosened Anne's braid, while her coif slipped back to dangle by its strings between her shoulder blades. Her collar, however, stayed primly tied. With no corset and a bodice cut so low, the opening of her shirt would reveal far more than she was willing to display.

The last hour's passage was marked by the colors

on the tower's western face, the gray stones glowing golden-orange, then lavender. In the other direction, twilight's deep blue velvet curtain lifted above the eastern wall. Bats began to flutter from the tower's cap.

Anne's heart wrenched in panic. There was no more than a half hour's light left to this day. How could their time together be ending when there was yet so much she needed from him?

"Master Hollier," the musician called out, flexing his fingers as he paused, " 'twill soon be too dark to walk home."

Anne willed Kit to command the man to play on. Instead he stopped and released her hand to glance in surprise about the garden. "I had no idea it was so late. I'll get your pay."

As Kit went to fetch his purse, Anne glanced to where Patience and Bertie had been seated in study. They were afoot and waiting to depart. Regret so deep she swore she'd die from it filled Anne. 'Twasn't fair that this was all she'd ever know of her Kit.

Patience's expression was soft and sad. Anne drew a startled breath at what she found in her governess's eyes. She knew Amyas was coming for her!

Of a sudden Patience leaned her head toward Bertie and whispered something. His eyes widened, his brows high upon his forehead as he looked at Anne. A touch of a smile came to life on his face. Together, they turned and started through the trees for the garden's gate.

With that the liking Anne knew for the woman she'd once so despised burst into love. 'Twas privacy Patience was offering her, a chance to share some time alone with the man she loved. So unexpected and precious a gift made tears sting at Anne's eyes.

Coins jingling in his hand, Kit turned and started back toward Anne. He tossed the coins to the musician, who snatched them out of the darkening air with ease. His swift movement teased a ringing thud out of his lute, the instrument now hanging across his back.

"Go you on ahead," Kit told him. "We need a few moments to catch our breaths. For this night Mistress Patience can walk back with my man."

"My thanks, Master Hollier," the man said with a salute. There was a musical rattling of the strings as he walked away through the trees.

"Where have Mistress Patience and Bertie gone?" Kit asked after the man was gone. "I vow they were here just a moment ago."

Fearing the truth would cause him to hurry their departure brought a swift lie to Anne's lips. "I expect they took a last stroll."

"Well, they'd better be quick about it. The caretaker will be wanting to lock the gates in another few moments," Kit replied, reaching out to take her hand. "Yesterday, you spoke of the La Volta, wanting to try a few steps. Shall we do so while we wait?"

Nay, Anne wanted to scream. Her interest in the La Volta had died with Lady Deyville. Dancing was the last thing she now wanted to do with him, but *I beg your pardon, Master Hollier, but I'd really rather lay with you,* hardly seemed an appropriate alternative.

"Aye, that would be fine," Anne heard herself say. "Perhaps, if you but lifted me once and turned? Every time I watch our queen's majesty do it, I think it must be like flying." Dear God, she was prattling like some featherhead, while her need to feel his mouth on hers grew all the more urgent. Who knew how long Patience would wait before she called?

"As you will," her Kit said with a smile. "Put your

hands on my shoulders. You must brace yourself, holding still as I turn."

Nodding, Anne drew her hands along the strong line of his shoulders as she sought the right spot. Her palms came to life with the feel of him. A new, warm throbbing woke deep in her being. Perhaps this wasn't wholly a waste of time, after all.

"Are you ready?" he asked, a new huskiness to his voice as he set his hands at her waist.

A thrill shot down Anne's spine. His eyes were alive with wanting, his mouth soft in desire. If she touched her lips to his, it wouldn't be gentle sweetness she found in that melding, but something more substantial.

"Aye," she whispered.

He lifted her. Beneath her hands, Anne felt his muscle tighten as he held her aloft. 'Twas a quick circle he turned. She gasped in surprise as her skirt flew. Her braid, already half undone, fell open, and her hair spilled free about her.

"It does feel like flying," she laughed.

His second, even swifter turn, caught Anne by surprise. Her hands slipped, and she dropped against him with a cry, latching her arms around his neck as she fell. He caught her close.

'Twas all of her that was pressed to him. Anne's body tingled against their contact. The beat of his heart was hers. Heat tore through her, her need for him so deep she shuddered. Their mouths were close. It would take but the smallest movement of her head to touch her lips to his. Even as she warned herself what she wanted could but win her Kit's hatred, she turned her head.

"Kit," she breathed, her lips moving against his as she spoke.

A low, deep sound rumbled from him as he caught

her mouth with his. His lips slashed across hers, demanding her response. Anne's arms tightened around his neck as she gave him what he wanted and triumphed in what he shared with her.

Then his arms relaxed, as if to release her. Anne loosed a quiet sound of despair and tightened her hold on him to pull herself closer still. 'Twas her turn to take his mouth.

A great breath shuddered through him. He caught her face in his hands to kiss the corner of her mouth, her cheek, her brow, then her ear. She moaned in soft delight, the sensations he made in her every bit as wondrous as she'd dreamed they would be. As he kissed a line down her throat, she placed her hands against his shirt, then smoothed her palms over the masculine swell and fall of his chest. Even with fine cotton between her hands and his skin, the feel of him was enough to set fire to her core.

He loosened her collar. She trembled. When he kissed the spot where her neck met her shoulder, she gave over caring what he might think of her were he to discover her secret. All that mattered was that he should make himself one with her.

Never, Kit swore to himself as he worked at the ties on Nan's collar, then kissed her exposed shoulder, had he known pleasure like this. If it was the months of wanting her that heightened his senses, then he was glad for it. Sensation surged in him as he stroked a hand down her side, then curled his fingers around the fullness of her breast.

Heat tore through him as she arched into his caress, offering herself to him. He brushed his thumb against her breast's peak. Even through fabric, he felt her nipple tauten. The need to place his lips against it exploded in him, driving him beyond any other consideration. He tugged her shirt apart, then drew a shaken breath as her breasts were exposed, his to see, to feel, to taste.

Rather than a cry of shock, Nan arched again, her hips pressing to his in eloquent invitation. He lowered his head and brushed his tongue against her nipple. She moaned softly, her fingers threading in his hair, urging him to caress her so again. A tremor rattled him as he did her bidding. Closing his mouth upon the peak of one breast, he cupped his hand about the other.

Her breath came in panting gasps. The sound of her passion sent his own need spiraling. When she traced the curl of his ear with her finger, waves of pleasure flowed over him, teasing him into sucking like a babe. She cried out and moved her hips against his, then lowered a hand to the top of his breeches.

Even as Kit felt her fingers working at that garment's ties, he knew this was wrong. They had to stop. If they didn't, she'd be doomed to torment in her marriage.

He swore he meant to lift his head from her breast and tell her to cease. Instead he closed his eyes and waited. When his breeches slid down his legs, she reached beneath his shirt to find his shaft. He shuddered as she trailed her fingers down its hard length, then gasped against her breast as she closed her hand around him to play this game in earnest.

With a growl of need gone too deep to care about right or wrong or witnesses, he straightened. Kicking aside his breeches, he yanked at the ties to her bodice. As it loosened, he pulled at her shirt's front opening wanting all of her against him.

Nan released him and stepped back. Kit's cry of

disappointment blossomed into a breath of awe as, in one lithe motion, she shed bodice, skirt, and shirt. She stood clothed in naught but her stockings, gartered at her thighs, and her unbound hair. 'Twas love for him that softened her face and glowed in her dark eyes.

Dear God, but she was lovely. Evening's silvered light gleamed against her pale skin and turned her dark brown hair into ebony. He marked the dark strands as they clung to the curve of her cheek, trained down the slender line of her neck to spill across the swell of her breasts. His gaze descended, following those tresses to where they curled at the generous turn of her hips.

As his attention came to rest upon the dark hair that cloaked her most private place, a sliver of sanity cooled what boiled in him. He had no right to her. Anger shot through him. If not him, then who? 'Twas he she'd chosen that first day in the Presence Chamber. Still, his conscience nagged.

"Nan, we cannot do this," he said, his voice hoarse as he put the only barrier left to him between them. "Bertie and his bride might return at any instant."

She gave the smallest shake of her head. "Nay, they won't. They await us beyond the garden walls." In the next instant she sighed as if her heart were breaking. Tears glistened in her eyes. "Do you love me, Kit?"

"Aye, Nan, I do." 'Twas her pain that wrested these words from him, even as he yet strove to resist them.

"Then, love me now," she begged softly.

All resistance died with her plea. He tore off his shirt. By the time it had fallen from his fingers, she'd shed shoes and stockings. She gave him time enough to remove his own leg wear, then closed the distance between them.

Laying her hands against his chest, she stroked her

palms downward. Although he groaned against her caress, 'twas no longer touches he wanted from her. Kit caught her by the hips and pulled her against him. Her skin was like silk against his. When she breathed, he could feel the movement of her breasts against his chest.

Boldly she lay her arms over his shoulders and drew herself up onto her toes. Kit shivered as his shaft was pressed against the source of her womanhood. With a quiet moan of pleasure, she buried her head into the turn of his neck and moved against him in elegant parody of what they both wanted.

Taking her chin in his hand, he raised her face to his. He touched his mouth to hers, his kiss a declaration of his need. Her hips moved against his, and the promise of pleasure turned his inner heat into an inferno. He drew her down onto the soft grass until she lay upon her back beneath him. Settling on his side next to her, he braced himself above her.

"You are beautiful," he said as he drew his fingers down along the outline of her breast.

She smiled, her eyes closing against his play. Her hips shifted, as if to draw his taunting fingers in their direction. He couldn't resist.

Placing kisses against her ear, his fingers found their way down below her waist until he touched the folds of her nether lips. Her warmth and wetness fed what boiled in him. She trembled and arched beneath him, then opened her legs to offer him what he most desired.

His breath caught. Shifting atop her, he settled between her legs, his shaft poised at the entrance to her womb. "Stop me," he told her even as his need for her ate him alive.

Her eyes opened. She reached up to lace her fingers

behind his neck. "Nay," she breathed. "Only remember that you love me." Her voice was soft and almost frightened.

Before he could react to this strange plea, she thrust up against him, taking all of him within her in one stroke. Kit gasped, the pleasure of her bold move too great to allow for surprise. Instead he simply thrust again.

Anne cried out as his entry sent a wave of pleasure flowing over her. She threaded her fingers into his hair and forced his mouth to hers. With a groan Kit lowered himself full atop her, his kiss telling her of the passion she woke in him. His desire could only match her own.

Again, she lifted her hips. This sent that wave of pleasure crashing over her again. 'Twas ecstasy she'd have of him and right quickly, too. She arched beneath him.

He tore his mouth from hers, panting. "Cease, love," he growled, "else I'll spill my seed this instant. Let me please you as I will."

Anne gloried in his words. Although he must know her secret, he yet called her his love. She relaxed beneath him to give him his way with her.

Touching his lips to hers in small and taunting kisses, he teased her with slow and steady thrusts, until what grew in her was so intense she quaked beneath him. He groaned, then his breathing grew ragged and shallow. His movements quickened. Anne caught her arms around him, meeting his thrusts with her own. 'Twas as one that they found their joy.

As he relaxed atop her, Anne's ecstasy ebbed into something even better. Until this moment it seemed she'd been but half a person. Now, as she held Kit close, she felt whole.

Tears again filled her eyes. Would that she need never lose him. She stroked her hands down his back, loving the feel of him. The shiver her caress wrung from him evolved into a steady shaking of his shoulders.

"Kit?" she asked at this strange reaction.

Managing a muted sound, he rolled onto his side, taking her with him as he went, so they lay face-to-face. Shame filled her. Now that passion had dimmed, was he angry over her lack of maidenhead? She buried her head into his shoulder, incapable of looking at him.

He pressed his lips to her cheek. "For shame, my love," he breathed against her skin, "you were no maid."

'Twas laughter, not rage, that filled his voice! Startled, Anne lifted her head to look at him. What was left of day's light was just enough to show her he was grinning. Indeed, his smile was wide and carefree as fits and starts of amusement yet bubbled from him. Of all the reactions she'd expected from him, this was not one of them. Against his odd behavior, the words of explanation she hadn't meant to offer escaped.

"I was but ten and four, and Owls House is so isolated that, well, we, he and I—" She wrapped what little pride she had left about her. "It just happened. When it was done, I sinned no more. That's all I'll say about it," she finished in warning.

Still smiling, he tucked a strand of hair behind her ear. "Love, I care nothing for your past sins."

"You can love me despite what I have done?" she cried, unable to believe what she saw.

"Indeed, I think I prize you all the more because of it." He winked.

Anne stared. He still loved her. So certain had she

been of scorn and so great her relief when she didn't find it, tears started to her eyes. She tried to stop them, but they wouldn't be halted. He loved her still. At last she but turned her head into his shoulder and wrapped her arms around him.

Chapter Twenty-four

The irony of being doomed to failure long before he'd signed that contract was almost more than Kit could bear. 'Twas the thought of so many men and one woman all chasing after what no longer existed that tickled him. It wasn't until he felt the warmth of her tears against his skin that he realized what he found humorous must have been terrifying for her.

Pulling her closer still, he stroked her hair. "Ah, my poor love, how this must have weighed on you," he murmured.

"You cannot know," she cried against his throat. "When my grandfather came to fetch me, saying he had me a court position, I thought I'd die. I didn't dare tell him."

"I expect not." The words left his mouth on a bitter breath. "Somehow I cannot envision him forgiving you for this."

Nay, 'twas more likely Amyas would have murdered her, for no other reason than the shame her sin had done his name. He marveled at how much she loved and trusted him. It was her life she'd laid into his hands as she revealed her secret to him.

She lifted her head from his shoulder to look at

him, wiping away her tears with the back of her hand. "I was trapped no matter where I turned."

Kit dared a tiny laugh. "So you were. God knows Elizabeth would never forgive you the deception, were she to learn of it. And then there is Deyville." Fear for her tore through him as he realized how close she'd come to disaster. "Christ, but he would have killed you for this! May God damn me, I nearly helped him in it."

"What do you mean," she asked with a final hiccough. "You haven't helped him."

"Have I not?" he laughed, the sound harsh with anger at himself. "These past two months, all that stood between you and what we've done this night was the knowledge that you were intended for Deyville. Rather than find some way to rescue you from that godforsaken union, I stood idly by, telling myself that if I left you untouched you'd be protected against his abuse."

Silence followed his words as she lifted herself above him on an elbow. Her mouth bent slowly into a crooked smile. "Oh, so that explains it."

"Explains what?" he asked.

"You. You cannot know how hard I've worked." When he frowned in confusion, her smile widened, then filled with wicked amusement as her brows lifted. "Think you a woman's shirt opens of its own accord?"

Her words brought with them the memory of their first dance in the barn. Kit's eyes widened. "Why, you little imp. You were trying to seduce me!"

"Aye, so I was, much to my despair," she chided, much aggrieved. "Do you have any idea how my esteem has suffered with my failure?"

By God, but he did, indeed. With a laugh Kit caught her close and again claimed her mouth with his. He let his kiss fill with all the heat she inspired, then rolled onto his back, dragging her atop him.

Anne gasped against his lips, then shifted to lay just where they both wanted her to be. When the kiss was done, she crossed her arms on his chest to brace her chin upon them and gaze into his face. "How I love you," she told him with a sigh.

"Why me?" 'Twas a lover's demand, Kit's heart aching to know why she found him special above all others.

She didn't deny him. "If I must list the reasons, then I'll start from the first. You are kind. That I knew the moment I laid eyes on you. Where every other man at my presentation looked at me and saw only the heiress with her fields and houses, you saw a friendless stranger. 'Twas pity you offered me against their greed, wishing to make me feel at least a little welcomed."

He smiled. Her interest in him had awakened the very lust that even now simmered in his gut. Raising a hand, he drew his fingers down the curve of her cheek. "It wasn't all welcome."

With a smile, she shifted her hips, drawing a quiet gasp from him. "Nay, it wasn't, and I'll not beg your pardon for desiring you," she retorted with a smile.

"Did I ask for it?" He raised his hands in protest. "Nay, not me. So it was my kindness that set you to seducing me, eh?"

The amusement faded from her face. "If you would know from whence that sprang, then 'tis best I tell you the whole truth. While my grandsire wanted a titled man for my husband, a man of great pomp and prominence, I meant to catch me a man who would accept my mother as she is. Your brother is crippled.

Once I heard from your own lips that you loved him, despite his infirmity, I knew 'twas you I must have.''

She paused, a touch of shame showing in the twist of her mouth. "I know you are reluctant to wed. What choice had I save to set myself to seducing you, hoping to break your barriers?"

Kit tensed beneath her, his emotions writhing. How could it be that she valued him for Nick and the wrong he'd done his brother? One instant, he wanted to rise and run from her, the next he was overcome by his need to hold her close and sob against her shoulder, just as she had his.

'Twas she who settled it. She touched her mouth to his. Gone was the heat of the previous moment. Instead her kiss was sweet and filled with her love for him. He, of all men, had no right to such affection, not after what he had done to his brother.

"Someone told you wrong." His voice sounded harsh, even to his own ears. "My brother is not crippled, he is scarred from burns suffered years ago." He meant to say no more, but the rest erupted from his mouth before he could stop it. " 'Twas my fault, for 'twas I who sent him tumbling into the hearth."

Kit froze against what he had revealed. His eyes closed as his heart stilled and his lungs ceased to fill with air. He was dying even before he owned her scorn for what he'd done.

A quiet sigh left her. " 'Tisn't fair that we cannot wed, when we are so alike." Her voice was sad. "If you are the cause of your brother's scars, I am at the root of my mother's crippling. 'Twas my birth that left her as she is, voiceless and immobile. Despite that, and all the other wrongs I've done her, she loves me still, just, I think, as your brother must love you."

It wasn't forgiveness she offered him, but understanding. Aye, and in offering it to him, she did what Lady Montmercy's contract could never have done. She released him from his past.

Life poured back into Kit. His pulse rushed. His lungs craved air. As he filled them, his eyes opened and he looked upon the only woman in the world for him. 'Twas his soul she owned, just as he held hers.

"Dear God, how I love you." The words left his lips touched with wonder. "I never knew I could feel this way," he told her, nigh on drowning in what filled him. "How could I live so long and never know this?"

"Because you've only just met me," she replied, as if this explained all.

He grinned. "But of course that is the reason," he taunted with a laugh, then kissed her. "What a clever girl you are. Lovely, as well. And you love me!" He kissed her again, then tore his mouth free, spirits soaring against what he held in his heart for her. "Marry me, Nan."

"Now you ask, when 'tis too late," she said with a sad shake of her head. "My grandfather has already promised me to Lord Deyville."

"Deyville cannot have you," Kit growled, clutching her close to him. "I'll die before I let him touch you."

"You'll die if you wed me," she retorted. "Or so my grandfather has sworn, should we dare to trade vows."

Yet giddy with his heart's affection for her, Kit scoffed at such a threat. "Let him do his worst. I would rather be wed to you for a single week, than exist the rest of my life without you."

She smiled at this and caught his mouth with hers. Her kiss spoke of how much his words had pleased her. Then, she was sliding off him to kneel beside him.

With a finger she traced the line of his face. "Fine sentiments, my love, and I cherish you all the more for them, but I say a week is not enough. Kit, I want you for all my life. If marrying you will do nothing more than guarantee both of us die, then I'll not do it. Instead set your mind to finding some way to force my grandsire to accept you."

This brought Kit upright with a sigh. He scrubbed at his face with his hands. "Never has there been a union more hopeless than ours. What you want is impossible. Not even if my brother offered him a contract, in which he named me his heir and promised our title's restoration would your grandsire have me."

Anne eased to sit with her legs crossed, tailor-fashion. Kit savored the look of her framed against the black velvet of the sky, the moon's light laying silver shadows on her skin. Her hair pooled on the ground around her hips.

" 'Tisn't fair," she said, her arms crossed beneath her breasts. "Why must the only man I would have as my husband be the only man my grandsire would never allow me to wed? It's all the more unfair, when I know he has another heir."

"What?!" The word exploded from Kit's mouth. "How can you say so, when you are the last?"

She shook her head. "I didn't say this other one was legitimate or that I could prove he is my grandsire's get. Or that proving it would do us any favor. Nonetheless, in my heart I'm certain Lord Andrew Montmercy is my grandsire's son."

"Who says this is so?" Kit demanded, needing to defend Andrew from such a slur.

"No one," Anne replied, her tone hopeless.

"Then, why would you accuse Lord Andrew of bastardy?" Kit demanded in confusion.

Anne peered at him through the gathering shadows.

"Do you recall my grandsire's strange reaction at my presentation?"

Kit drew a slow breath, not certain how much he wanted to admit to having observed between Lady Montmercy and Amyas. "He did seem overwrought at having me named your tutor."

"Nay," she said with a shake of her head, "not then, but afterward, when we'd left the queen's presence. He was in a strange state, muttering about biblical temptresses and saying he was warned against any plot *she* might send his way. I was certain it was Lady Montmercy he referred to, so I set myself to seeking out the connection between them, hoping to use it to guarantee the man I wed was the one I chose."

Would that such a thing were possible. "So what did you find?" he asked.

"Mistress Alice Godwin," she replied, "who was my mother's governess before she went into Lady Montmercy's employ. According to the tale she tells, Andrew is not his father's son, but was sired by a Protestant who went into exile upon Queen Mary's rise to the throne."

"Just as your grandsire did," Kit offered.

"Aye. So, too, does she say that Lady Elisabetta's lover was to have wed her upon his return to England, or so the lady expected. Instead he rejected her."

Understanding swept through Kit as the logic fell in place. "And in revenge the lady rejected Andrew, knowing him to be the son she'd borne this man," he mused, "just as she now plots your destruction to deprive Sir Amyas of his only remaining heir. Could it be she hopes to force him into acknowledging her son as his own?"

Even in the darkness he could see Nan frown. She

set a hand upon her hip. "How is it you know Lady Montmercy plots against me?"

Kit grimaced. Christ, but he was as bad as Bertie. So which was it to be? Lose a chance to rescue Anne from marriage to Deyville, because he revealed no word of that contract, or lose her to rage over how he'd plotted to destroy her? This was no choice at all.

A foul and filthy feeling crept over him as he cleared his throat. "Now that you've exposed your deepest secret to me, is there room in your heart to forgive me my sin? Vow to me you'll love me still, despite what I have done."

Although startled by his request, she lifted her shoulders in a quick shrug. "I so vow."

Kit launched into his tale, barely clinging to the hope she would keep her word. "Before you came to court, I entered into a contract with Lady Montmercy in which I agreed to seduce you, then reveal I'd taken your maidenhead to all the court. Her intention was not so much to destroy you, but to ruin your grandfather."

"Now, why in the world would you agree to do such a foolish thing, when the queen is certain to want your head for it?" she asked with a quiet laugh.

"Because I am a debt-ridden, misbegotten idiot, who has since discovered himself incapable of doing the evil he planned," he offered in apology. "That, and I wanted my brother's title restored. Marriage to Lady Montmercy's daughter provides income enough to achieve that." He stopped, waiting for some reaction from her. There was nothing.

"You're not angry at me?" he asked after a moment.

'Twas a scornful sound that left her lips. "Over what? A seduction you did not do? Nay, I'm not angry, not when what she did made it possible for me to love you. As you have forgiven me my sin, I will forgive you yours. Rather than dwell on our wrongs, tell me how we can use this contract of hers to force my grandfather to accept you."

Better that he conjure up some way to use that contract to prevent the lady from murdering him. Kit shook his head. "I cannot see how it can help us. Even if your grandsire were to acknowledge Andrew as his own, Andrew would be his bastard, while you remain his legitimate heir."

Kit gave breath to a bitter laugh. "Pity poor Andrew. Not only has the lad lost his mother, if what you believe is true he'll also lose his title and his name. Nay, he'll lose his very identity." He wondered if this wasn't at the back of Lady Montmercy's twisted brain when she'd written out the contract, thus leaving a trail to be followed. What a paradox. The old man already owned the title he so craved for his bloodline, but only as long as he never acknowledged his son.

Anne's shoulders slumped. "I couldn't bear to hurt him more, but what of us? If we cannot use this, we are doomed for certain."

"Mistress Anne!" Borne on the night's sparkling breeze, Patience's voice floated to them from the garden's far edge.

" 'Tis time to leave. The caretaker would lock the gates."

"Nay!" Anne cried, even as she leapt to her feet and grabbed up her garments.

Owning more time than she, Kit rose to watch her dress. She was right. It was forever he wanted from her. More than that, he'd be damned to hell before he let her go to Deyville.

She pulled her outer garment on over her shirt, then

fumbled with her bodice lacing. Her fingers trembled so badly she couldn't manage this simple task.

"Shall I?" he asked, not waiting for her reply to take the laces from her fingers. There was great joy in doing this humble chore for her. 'Twas then he vowed to himself that he would find a way to do this for her as her husband.

She looked at him. Sadness marked every line of her face. "I do not want our time to end." Her mouth took a wry bend. "To think, all this practicing and we'll never have a chance to dance before the queen."

Kit started at her reminder of the queen's wager. With it came the foolish hope of winning royal favor. He damned himself as thrice an idiot. Even if Elizabeth delayed Anne's marriage to accommodate the wager, there was no guarantee the finest rendition of the La Volta would garner them more than a pretty smile from their monarch.

Anne gathered up her stockings and garters, then thrust bare feet into her shoes. Again, she fought to smile. "I daresay there'll be no invitation for you to attend my wedding."

Kit's eyes narrowed as he shook his head. "You'll not marry Deyville."

"Kit," she cried in soft protest, "we've just determined there's no way to stop my marriage."

"Ah, but there is," he replied, the need to protect her from Deyville burning like a holy cause within his heart. "That nobleman will die before his wedding day, on this you have my solemn oath."

"Nay!" she cried in protest. "If you kill him, it will mean your life. I cannot bear the thought of you dead."

"Mistress, you must come now." There was a new,

worried tone to the maid's voice. The garden gate loosed a rusty groan as it opened.

"I come," Anne called back, then threw herself at Kit wrapping her arms around him.

He pulled her close. Her kiss was desperate and filled with her love for him. As he released her, he caught her face in his hands to look at her. The moonlight turned the trails of her tears to silver.

"Do not mourn yet. There is still time," he told her.

"I cannot help myself." She turned her head to press a kiss to his palm. "I must go." This last was a forlorn cry.

"Then go, taking my heart with you," he told her as he released her, "and know I cherish yours above all else. We will find a way, I know it, aye."

"Would that I could believe you," she cried, then whirled.

Kit watched her disappear into the night. Only when he could see her no more, did he turn to gather up his own attire. She was right not to believe him. There was no hope at all.

Chapter Twenty-five

'Twas late evening on his second day of travel before Kit reached the grassy parkland surrounding Graceton Castle. Not once on either day had the sun made its appearance. Instead he'd been accompanied by a steady rain falling from a leaden sky. 'Twas heaven crying for his hopeless cause.

As night overtook him, the world around him seemed trapped in a hushed and drear dullness where the rattle of harness rings and the snort and sigh of his horse were the only sounds. Turning his face into spattering drops, Kit looked at the place of his birth. Graceton Castle sat on a sharp lift of land caught in the river's bend. It wasn't a house by any reckoning, but centuries worth of stone towers and stretches of ancient wall remade into a residence.

From this angle, he could see the river wall. Ivy clung to its gray stones, leafy lines snaking upward to frame the small square windows on the house's lower level. More graceful, arched openings marked the second and third storeys, where the hall and family quarters were located. There, the house's roofline lifted slightly above the wall's crenellation, each one of these square stone teeth wearing an archer's cross.

Along the river's bank, the summer's growth was lush and thick, as if in desperate reaction to the previous winter's unusual cold. That left little to be seen of the village across the water. Here and there, Kit caught the glint of light or the darker curl of smoke against the blackening sky.

He started onto the narrow, tree-lined lane that led to the house's gate, his thought as muddy as the path beneath his horse's hooves. For two days he'd pondered the conundrum of how to keep his life and marry Anne. If the answer yet eluded him, Kit was certain it turned upon Lady Montmercy's hatred for Old Amyas. He freed a quiet breath. What good did all this thinking do him when there was no way to make use of it?

The lane let him out before the mossy, massive gatehouse on the north wall. 'Twas here, on the outside of the walls, that Nick kept his stables. Wisely so, as it prevented the befouling of the air near the house.

Even before Kit dismounted, a stable lad was running to announce his return to the house. He watched the lad sprint off into the darkness. This guaranteed there'd be a greeting party of at least one, Nick's housekeeper, a woman nigh on as old as the house. Mistress Miller had served the Holliers since their grandsire's time. For reasons beyond Kit's ken, she retained a persistent fondness for Graceton's prodigal son.

Sodden cloak dragging on his shoulders, he set across the grassy expanse between gatehouse and the main doorway. As always, his gaze was drawn to the ancient keep tower. Left where it stood as a reminder of the Hollier's permanence, the broken and crumbling structure glowered down upon the house from its mound.

From this vantage point Graceton Castle looked more resident than fortress. The kitchen lay in the

corner nearest the gate, along with the house's brew-
ery. A cheery glow flowed over the short wall that
enclosed that area, bringing with it the distant sound
of laughter and conversation.

The hall soared three storeys above the service
buildings. Four long windows marked its courtyard
face. Only the barest shimmer of light escaped the
thick glass. Kit didn't bother listening for sound;
there'd be none. Since Graceton's squire spent no time
within its walls, neither did his servants.

Beyond the hall the house thrust outward into the
courtyard to accommodate its living quarters until it
melded into the far wall. The gallery clung to the
house's second storey, stretching its length from hall
to the opposing wall, a long, square stone box pep-
pered with graceful windows. Meant to allow access
to the upper chambers, it also served the inhabitants
as a place to walk on the all-too-frequent rainy days.
His gaze followed the gallery's length to where it
melded into the corner tower.

'Twas here that Father Roger, his and Nick's
priestly tutor, had endured the torment of his students.
Kit loosed a startled breath. He hadn't thought about
his and Nick's school days in years.

The door in the hall's sheltered entryway flew open.
Mistress Miller stepped out onto the top step, her
bracing cane in one hand and a lighted taper in the
other. In the candle's glow her face, framed in her
kerchief and high-necked white partlet, was as round
and wrinkled as a dried apple. Her grin was wide and
nearly toothless. Kit gave another sigh. He'd be lucky
to come away from this greeting with only one pinch
to his cheek.

"Master Kit, whatever brings you tapping on our

door so late?" she called, her age-deepened voice echoing against the tall walls that surrounded them.

"Royal command," he replied as he climbed the three short steps leading up to the door.

"Even if 'twas that Protestant she-devil who sends you, I'll praise God for it, Master Kit," she said, being too old to care upon whose ears her opinions fell.

"Enough of that," he said in mild warning. She reached for his cheek. He lifted his head. "And that as well," he laughed, kicking the mud from his boots. "How is my brother?"

A morose breath gusted from her as she tottered back into the hall. "As well as might be expected for a man in his condition. If you're thinking to see his lordship tonight, you're too late." Like many of the older servants, as well as a good number of the villagers, Mistress Miller cared nothing for the legalities of Nick's title or lack thereof. All that mattered to them was that he was the eldest son of the previous lord, making him lord in their eyes. "The damp and that woman of his chased him into bed early this evening."

Kit glanced over her shoulder to the hall's screens, behind which stood the stairs to the family quarters. "Is Master James about?"

"Nay, he's gone off to London to do Lord Nicholas's business," she replied. "Now, no more talk. You're sodden, through and through." She latched a gnarled and wrinkled hand onto his arm. "You should have sent word you were coming. I'd have seen a decent meal laid out for you, instead of just a bite and a sup. Come, then, I've sent a lass to wake the fire in your chambers. Up you go to warm yourself."

It was nearly noon the next morning before Kit tapped on the door to his brother's suite. He wore his most comfortable attire, a brown doublet, the sleeves left off, atop a pair of well-worn leather breeches. This was home, a place to toss aside courtly affectations and live the simple life.

With Jamie gone to London, Kit expected Nick to call for him to enter. Instead Cecily Elwyn opened the door. "Good morrow, Master Christopher," Nick's woman said in greeting, her golden eyes alive with pleasure at seeing him again. Aside from her odd yellowish eyes, there was nothing remarkable about Cecily. She was round of body and narrow of face. Strands of black hair escaped her widow's kerchief, while her blue bodice and brown skirts were a little haphazard in their arrangement.

"Good morrow, Cecily," he said as he stepped within the chamber. "Is Nick ready to see me?"

"He is," she replied, still smiling. "Come along, he's in the bedchamber."

As Kit started across the suite's forechamber, he shook his head. Once again, papers were strewn across Nick's desk, the tables heaped with precious tomes. 'Twas only as Kit saw Cecily and the room together that he realized Nick's room was very much like Nick's woman, both of them being comfortable in their disorder. The comparison made him smile.

"I vow, Cecily, he hasn't changed a whit since our youth. At least this clutter of his appears to be an organized mess."

"So he claims," she said, "forbidding us all from straightening, fearing he'll find nothing after."

"Is that you, Kit?" Nick called out, the cost of raising his voice a cough as he appeared in his bedchamber door.

"It is, indeed," Kit replied as he and Cecily stopped before Graceton's master.

Nick wore a long black robe not unlike those affected by older gentlemen at court right down to the belt about his middle. Day's bright light streamed past him from the windows behind him. Even in so thick a robe, his form was gaunt. Still, he seemed no thinner now than he'd been on Kit's last visit.

"If you two are to talk, I'd best be on my way," Cecily said. With a smile to her lover, she started to turn. Nick caught her by the elbow to hold her in place.

"There's no need for you to go. What Kit and I have to say isn't private," he said softly, the affection he knew for her filling his voice.

Kit glanced between the two. 'Twas the same love he felt for Nan he saw reflected in Nick's green gaze. Nor was there any doubting that Cecily cared as deeply for Nick. It fair glowed in her narrow face.

"Huh," she replied, her attempt at scorn defeated by that softness. "You only wish me to stay because you're greedy for my company. You'd not be so lonely if you'd come out of these rooms."

Nick only shook his head, his gaze smiling at her if he couldn't. "Nay, I daren't come out, else you'd never again come in to wake me. You are a wondrous sight in morn's light." He lifted his bony fingers to her face, turning his hand to draw the relatively unmarked skin of its back down her cheek.

"So says the scarred man of his plain woman," Cecily laughed, then gasped as Nick wrapped his arm around her to pull her against him. She shoved free of his embrace. When he reached for her again, she slapped at his hand. "Nay, now, you'll not do me so with your brother standing right here."

"What? Do you think Kit a child in need of protection from what it is men and women share?" Lust and laughter filled Nick's voice.

Cecily crossed her arms and narrowed her eyes. Her show of anger couldn't belie the pretty pink stain pleasure left upon her cheeks. "Nay, you'll not draw me into one of these sorts of arguments. I'm going now, but you remember your vow," she warned with a shake of her finger. "I'll know if you've dumped it."

A touch of chagrin flashed through Nick's green gaze and was gone. "Just because I wouldn't drink that last is no call to go doubting my word. I vowed I'd keep it a full twenty-four hours, and so I shall."

"Until this even, then." Standing on her toes, Cecily pressed her lips to Nick's scarred cheek. She turned and made her way across the suite, shutting the door behind her as she left.

Once she was gone, Nick sighed. "She won't wed with me, you know."

"You've asked her?" In Kit rose all the harsh prejudices his forefathers held against noble marrying peasant. He shook them away. Here was a woman who loved and accepted Nick, in spite of his scars. What right had he to deny his brother happiness?

Outrage followed, over the hurt Cecily's rejection did to Nick and the insult it dealt his station. Kit frowned at the door. "Why should she refuse you? She ought to be thrilled to move from that woodland hidey-hole of hers and become dame of this fine place."

"She claims there's no point to our wedding, not when she knows she's barren," Nick started, only to have a spate of coughing overtake the rest of his sentence.

Kit's frown deepened. So Cecily wished to leave Nick free to wed and beget true heirs. And rather than betray the one woman who accepted him, scars and all, Nick looked to Kit to carry on their family's line and name. Shame filled him.

Why had it taken him so long to see this? Fie on him for daring to toy with his brother's life and love. Now if he couldn't find a way to escape the murder Lady Montmercy had planned for him, Nick would have no choice but to set aside Cecily and wed another.

Nick finally caught his breath to finish his thought. "In all truth, 'tis cries of witchcraft she fears most. Cecily says the villagers are uncomfortable enough with her, what with her strange eyes, her herbal knowledge, and her mother's madness."

"Her mother wasn't mad," Kit replied out of long habit, having spent many an hour in their woodland cottage as Nick recovered. Cecily's dam had but owned a hermit's personality, liking as little contact with others as possible.

"So you and I know, but others don't see it so. Cecily fears shouts of black magic if she, a poor cottager, should wed the local gentry. Enough of that." Nick lay a hand on Kit's shoulder in invitation. "We'll sit while we talk."

Kit followed his brother into his bedchamber. "Mistress Miller tells me Jamie's gone to London. What's he doing there?"

The sound of Nick's amusement was made husky by his ever breathless lungs. "Business with regards to Graceton Castle. He didn't want to go, saying London is fetid this time of year."

That made Kit laugh, as well. "He's right in that," he said as Nick claimed the chair closest to his private altar. That left Kit with the nearer one. He was barely between its arms before he reared back out of its depth, eyes stinging and gasping for breath.

"Christ, Nick! What is that stench?" Whatever it was, its source was the pot hanging over the slow-burning fire on Nick's hearth. Kit coughed and turned his head aside in the hopes of escaping the pungent air.

Nick loosed a helpless sigh. "This is the source of Cecily's scold. It's a concoction meant to loosen my lungs. She's worse than you for fussing over me, but I say I'd rather die from lack of breath than live with this stink." Even as he raised a scarred hand to wave it beneath his nose, his green eyes glowed with laughter. "Only the fact that I gave my word is keeping me from dumping it out the window and into the river. Thus her chide, for she knows I'm counting the hours to eventide. Give it a moment. It gets easier as you become accustomed to it."

Already breathing more freely, Kit smiled at his brother. Never had he seen Nick look happier. Indeed, contentment etched itself into every line of his brother's thin body as he sprawled in his chair. Nor had he ever seen Nick look healthier. He had good color where his skin wasn't scarred; his eyes fair glowed with health.

A tension Kit didn't even realize he owned eased from him. He sighed against its departure, his heart lightening. All in all, this was turning out to be a most surprising and marvelous trip home.

"It's good to see you looking so well, Nick."

"I am well," Nick replied without hesitation, then surprise darted through his gaze. "I didn't hear you shout last night, Kit." 'Twas a careful reference to the dream.

"That could be because I didn't shout," Kit said.

Wonder swept over him again, just as it had when he'd awakened this morn. For the first time in forever, he'd slept through the night here at Graceton without a single dream, much less that nightmare. "I suppose travel in the wet left me tired enough to sleep like a rock."

"Aye, and our Lord Jesus tells me he returns on the morrow," his brother retorted, eyes narrowed in scorn. "What happened, Kit?"

The urge to speak of Nan and how her love had changed him filled Kit's mouth. He swallowed the words. How could he tell Nick he was finally ready to wed, but certain death followed his marriage? He couldn't, not when the only woman Nick wanted was barren and beneath him. "I wish I knew," he finally lied.

"Well, whatever it is, I'm glad for it," his brother said. "Aye, and I'm just as grateful Jamie wasn't here. Why, he could have sat for hours upon that landing waiting on your appearance." 'Twas a gentle tease.

Kit smiled at the thought of Jamie sitting in the dark. The image brought with it long-forgotten memories of their school days, before the accident. He leaned back in his chair, fingers laced behind his head. "Do you remember Father Roger and how he made us sit?"

Amusement bubbled from Nick's scarred lips. "God's love, but I haven't thought of him in years. Do you know he once wrote our lord grandfather suggesting we'd be better off drowned, as we were certain to bring dishonor to his name?" Vindictive pleasure filled Nick's gaze. "When I found that letter, I added him to my prayer list, knowing my words would annoy him no matter in what realm he now languishes."

Mention of their Catholic tutor brought with it the

reminder of his reason for returning. Kit glanced at the massive crucifix hanging on his brother's wall. As always, illegal candles burned upon Nick's private altar, their twining streams of smoke bearing heavenward his even more illegal prayers. "Nick, the queen sent me to you."

"Let me guess why," Nick interrupted, his eyes bright with intelligence. " 'Tis the state of my loyalties she sent you to probe, hiding her intent behind the guise of you helping me count Graceton's men and weaponry."

This set a curl to Kit's lip. "I tried to assure her there's no reason to doubt you, but she trusts no one. 'Tis the fear that Norfolk yet intends to wed with the Scots queen that has her so shaken."

His brother's scarred brows rose to their limit of mobility. "And shaken she should be," he said, words carrying far more than their simple meanings.

Kit moved to the edge of his chair. "What is it you know?" he demanded.

"Do you mean beyond the fact that Norfolk has sent the Scots queen a diamond as a token of his promise to wed her?"

Kit grimaced against this bit of news. "I'd not heard that. Who says so?"

"I've had letters," Nick said with a shrug. " 'Tis for the good of the country, or so they say, that our duke must wed the *sweet*"—he gave the word a sarcastic edge—"Mary Stuart. Much mention is made of our own queen's heretical and Protestant advisers, evil men who are stealing from the nobility their hereditary positions and honors. England must purge its government of these men, so our misguided Elizabeth can be returned to the Pope's fold." Nick almost managed a scornful look.

"Or else," Kit bit out, "they'll put their Catholic queen and her English consort upon our throne."

Kit truly hadn't thought Norfolk and the recusant barons would go so far. So repugnant was the idea of civil war that he came to his feet and strode to his brother's window, needing to see that the world beyond it hadn't already been laid waste. Below him the willows swayed in the breeze. From the rushes along the bank, a family of swans appeared, gray cygnets caught between their white parents, then floated gracefully downstream. He watched them until he could see them no more.

"Who was it that wrote to you?" he asked without turning.

"Well, now, 'twas the strangest thing," Nick said. "The ink ran, obscuring the author's name."

Kit whirled to stare at his brother. "You would protect traitors?" Even before he spewed the question, he knew his brother wouldn't answer. Nick couldn't, not trapped as he was between his deeply held faith and his belief that God, Himself, had set Elizabeth upon England's throne.

"Nay, 'tis dreamers I protect, not traitors," Nick replied with a sigh. He rose and came to stand beside his taller brother at the window, laying his scarred and bony fingers on Kit's arm as if to comfort.

"Kit, leave it be. No man should be judged by his dreams, any more than 'tis right to peer into a man's soul to discover what beliefs he holds there. On that issue, our Protestant princess and I are in accord."

"How can you be so certain there'll be no war or usurping of the throne?" Kit asked.

"Because these plotters cling to a time when men asked no questions, only followed their sworn lord in battle because he led them," Nick replied. "I think

me those days died before our grandsire did. Shall I
tell you how I replied to my correspondent?"

At Kit's nod Nick's eyes narrowed with amusement.
"I asked him why I should replace this fine Tudor
queen, a woman who's given me ten years of peace
in which to prosper. I reminded him that Catholic or
not, Mary Stuart has already proved she can start a
war on one side of the border and looks to be fo-
menting another on our side. Me, I'm hungry for ten
more years of peace and all the wealth that might
bring."

As he read the astonishment in Kit's face, laughter
rumbled from Nick on a cough. Turning, he retreated
to sit in his chair, looking more prince than prisoner
as he stretched out his legs before him and steepled
his hands atop his chest. "What? Did you think I was
one with our grandsire, ready to defend the true faith
unto death? Nay, as long as our sweet Elizabeth leaves
me in peace and none of those Puritan preachers again
befouls my village with their tripe, I couldn't give a
farthing for the rest. You"—he pointed a bony finger
at his brother—"do not come home often enough if
you thought anything other of me."

Kit grinned. "Then, I shall assure her majesty you
will not rise against her."

Nick snorted. "You can tell my dearest, fairest,
sweetest majesty that she owns my loyalty, along with
all the pikes, poles, men, and arquebuses I own, for
as long as I continue to profit under her rule."

With a laugh Kit returned to sit in the chair opposite his brother. "You are right, I don't get home often
enough. I've never seen you so at ease."

"I am no different today than I've been in years,"
Nick said softly. "God's love, but you're looking at
‿," he whispered, his tone almost awed.

Kit shot him a puzzled look. "Of course I'm looking at you. I'm sitting across from you in a chair and cannot help it. Why do you always go on about this?"

"Because, until this moment, all you've seen were my scars. At last you look at me, the man beneath what the fire and steam laid upon my face."

His words twisted in Kit, but where before there had been horror, now there was only sadness. What had festered was well on its way to healing.

"I have never told you how sorry I am for what happened," he said, his words a bare whisper.

His brother groaned, then coughed. "Kit, you've begged my pardon so many times that I am heartily sick of hearing it, especially so when it was I who did this to myself."

That shocked Kit. "How can you say so, when it was my foot that sent you tumbling?"

"Think," Nick insisted, "do you not remember how angry I was? I was furious that our lord father was sending me away, while you were allowed to stay. I set out to hurt you in that battle of ours. When I couldn't, I cheated. All you did was try to even the score between us."

Sorrow glowed in his eyes. " 'Tis I who should beg your pardon. No one would heed me when I tried to explain; instead our lord father, our lady mother, the others, they all turned on you. So heavily did they ladle their blame and hatred upon you that your every night came to be tortured with that dream. By the time I came into my own, with knowledge enough to see what they were doing, 'twas too late. You'd taken up where they'd left off."

Kit frowned. He remembered the ache of his shoulder where Nick had struck him, while from his mind's recesses came the angry echoes of the child Nick's words. The horror paled, then the memory sank deep into him, shrouded as if for burial. He loosed a bitter breath. Aye, who had time to think on the past, when the future loomed and it was none too kind?

Nick shifted uncomfortably in his chair. "So now that I've told you we're prospering, you've no questions over the status of our accounts?"

"Why should I?" Kit asked, startled by this odd change of subjects.

"I thought perhaps you might be ready to ask me for that loan, at last." Nick's tone was cautious, his gaze was considering. He had more to say, but hesitated to share it.

"Nay, I need nothing. I managed to satisfy my debtors, at least for the time being," Kit said with a shrug, staring at his folding hands. 'Twas his blood Lady Montmercy wanted in return for what she'd loaned him, not coins.

Silence woke between them, growing until it was beyond uncomfortable. Kit looked up. "What is it, Nick?"

An uneasy laugh rumbled from his brother. "I hadn't meant to tell you, but now that I see this change in you, I find I have no choice. Among other things, I've sent Jamie to the queen to ask that our title be restored. This is to be done on the condition you be recognized as my heir and serve as my proxy."

The breath whooshed from Kit's lungs, and he leapt from the chair. "You've done what?!"

Nick held out his hands as if to stave off attack. "Now, Kit. Even if you rode day and night, you'd be too late to stop him."

Kit stared at his brother, not certain whether to murder him or hug him. On one hand, this put him on near an equal footing with Deyville, freeing him to attack the nobleman if need be. On the other, he now bore the responsibility for Nick's lordship. Not that he'd live long enough to be of any use to Nick as a proxy. As the weight of it settled upon his shoulders, Kit dropped back into the chair. Bracing his elbows upon his knees, he stared at the floorboards between his feet. "Why now?"

"Well, there's quite a story in that," Nick replied, the cadence of his words slow and careful. Kit glanced at him. Nick was leaning his head against the chair's back to stare up at the plastered ceiling.

"Only two weeks ago, a gentleman tapped upon our gate. He had the oddest following, one man a clubfoot, another missing a hand, still another with a slit ear."

This brought Kit upright in shock. "You received these men!"

Nick turned his head to offer his brother a scoffing glance. "I know when it's to my best value to open my door. After all, 'tisn't every day so important or irresistible a bit of business drops into my hands. At any rate, the transaction they presented to me had as one of its conditions the restoration of our title. Jamie suggested 'twas unfair of me to do so without speaking to you."

With a sigh Nick straightened. "I knew then he was right, but truly, the offer was beyond my resisting. I fear I set my name and seal to their paper, then sent Jamie riding for Greenwich to present it and my request for the resumption of the title to our queen. If I've hurt you in doing this, then I beg your pardon."

Kit waved away his brother's apology, more than a little confused at Nick's odd manner. "What sort of contract would require you to reclaim your title?"

"Ah, well," Nick's brows rose to the limit of their mobility, " 'tis a merging of two properties, one over which I claim control and the other belonging to the second party, at least to some extent."

Odder and odder. "Who is the second party?" Kit asked.

His brother shook his head. "I'd rather not say until the matter is completed to our satisfaction. There's reason to believe an outsider who claims some ownership of the one property might work to prevent this merging, unable to see it's in the best interest of all to allow it."

"Nick, none of this makes any sense," Kit protested.

"It did to me," Nick said, somewhat stiffly. "Only promise me you'll not go do something rash and idiotic because of this."

Kit smiled. 'Twas too late for that. "Dear brother, if you deny me rash and idiotic, there's naught left for me to do."

His jest made Nick cough in laughter. "God knows that's true enough. So"—his voice took on the tone of casual conversation—"tell me of court and your doings."

Ah, here was a safe subject. Kit blinked, only now realizing he'd never spoken to his brother about his life at court. It wasn't for lack of trying. 'Twas just that they never got this far before the arguing started.

"If gossip is what you want, then Elizabeth once again beams at the earl of Leicester, having toyed with Sir Thomas Heneage long enough to punish her earl for fathering a bastard on Lady Sheffield." Kit gave a derisive snort.

"Old news," Nick said, waving away his words. "The gossip I get through Jamie's uncle. I want to know of you. What have you been doing these last months?"

"Dancing," Kit replied with a laugh.

His brother stared at him. "You? You, who owns all the grace of a duck on ice?"

This piqued Kit's pride not a little. "To that I say, it takes one to know one. I was skillful enough to win my position from Elizabeth when I first came to court. I'm far better now, after two full months of daily practice."

"And why do you dance so excessively?" Nick asked, enough sourness in his gaze to suggest the thought of such exertion interested him naught a whit.

Kit paused, considering how much of the queen's wager he dared tell, then threw aside his concerns. Who would Nick tell? "Because, I, dear brother, am now the tutor. Two months ago the queen took into her service a new maid-of-honor, a lass who had never danced a day in her life. By the strangest chain of events, it came to be my chore to educate her."

At the question in Nick's gaze, Kit held up his hands. "Don't ask, the events are too complex to explain." God knew that was true enough since explaining meant divulging the details of his contract with Lady Montmercy.

"At any rate, what followed was a wager between the queen and Leicester as to how swiftly the girl might become competent in her footwork. Leicester said not before the Yuletide, while the queen counts on the La Volta by July's end." Kit shot his brother a quick smile. "The queen intends to make certain she wins this bet of hers. 'Tis she who's set us to our daily practice, a bit of information to which Leicester is not privy."

Nick's mouth thinned in scorn. "What sort of a backward lass knows nothing of footwork?"

The need to defend Anne roared through Kit. "Nay, Nick, she's not backward, only untutored and for a good cause. Her mother, who once loved to dance, is now crippled, made so by the circumstances of Nan's birth. 'Tis to honor her mother that Nan never pressed to learn."

"Nan?" Nick's brows tried to rise at so intimate a referral to the maid.

Kit warned himself to have more care with his affection. Even though 'twas only Nick who noticed, he couldn't afford to make this a habit. Such a breach of etiquette at court might lead to questions too difficult to answer.

"Aye, she's Mistress Anne Blanchemain," he said in explanation.

"Blanchemain." Nick lowered his head to stare into his lap. "Now, there's a name I know from Jamie's uncle. Isn't there a Sir Amyas Blanchemain, a Puritan who keeps close company with Throckmorton and his band of zealots?"

"Aye, Sir Amyas is Mistress Anne's grandsire." Kit laughed. "I'll have you know, he's none too thrilled at having me, who's related to a Catholic like you, close to his heiress."

Nick looked up, his eyes glowing with his smile, then he shook his head. "God's love, but it must be tedious for you to be trapped in the presence of so pious a lass."

Kit laughed. Tedious and pious weren't words he would ever apply to his Nan. Passionate and sensual—they were a set that fit her.

"Mistress Anne would lay scars upon your scars for thinking her the shadow of her grandsire," he chided. "In all truth, I've never known a woman quite like her. She's charming, clever, and bold far beyond anything I thought I might admire." And she loved him.

His heart sighed, pleased to own the affection of so wonderful a woman.

"But ugly as the day is long," Nick said with such conviction that Kit frowned at him.

"Why would you say that?"

His brother looked startled once again. "I beg your pardon. I only thought she must be, since you've said not a word as to her appearance. Generally when a man speaks highly of a woman's character without mentioning appearance, 'tis because she's no beauty. Either that or he wishes to convince another man to take her off his hands."

"How would you know how one man speaks to another?" Kit retorted. "Your experience with the world is confined to these rooms."

"You're right, I don't know," Nick agreed. "No doubt she's beauteous beyond bearing."

There was just enough scorn in his brother's voice to make Kit's eyes narrow. "It so happens that Mistress Anne is beautiful. She is dark of hair and eye, with this wee mark right here."

As he touched the corner of his mouth to show Nick where, the memory of pressing his lips to that spot as he kissed her shot through him. The embers of his desire burst back into flame, bringing the memory of Nan's other assets. Kit drew a quick breath. Dear God, but even in remembering their joining, his passion for her was whetted anew.

"Good God," Nick said quietly.

Kit started, scrambling out of his mind-numbing lust for Anne, to return to his conversation with Nick. His brother was staring at him, elbows braced upon his chair's arms, hands folded across his midsection.

"Kit, I vow you're smitten!" Nick cried out. "And I thought you owned an iron heart too hard to be softened by any woman. So do you intend to ask her to wed with you?"

Kit's mouth opened to confess that he already had. He caught back the words. If he said that much, he'd have to spill the rest, and that would hardly do. "I cannot. Not only does her grandsire's hatred for me make such a union impossible, he's already promised her to another."

Laughter marred Nick's clear green gaze. "What a pair we are, Kit. I want a woman who won't have me and you desire a woman you can't have."

He rose. "Come, then, I'll show you what weapons and men my books say we can claim, then leave you to count them for your queen."

Chapter Twenty-six

"Nan, you're paying no heed and making it too easy for me to win." Mary scooped up the playing cards from the cushion's center.

Anne gave what she held in her hand to her kinswoman, who sat opposite her on the floor, the cushion between them serving as a playing table. Mary was watching her, a worried frown marring her smooth brow. "My pardon, Mary," she said, "but watching the hawks circle all morn left me dizzy in my thoughts."

That was a lie. 'Twas nerve-wracking anticipation, not hunting with birds, that left Anne addlepated. It had been five days since she'd said farewell to Kit and Sir Amyas had yet to come. This only left Anne stewing in a terrible mixture of hope and horror. If the horror had its roots in the thought of Kit dying because he'd killed Lord Deyville to prevent her wedding, the hope grew out of a childish dream that Kit would return, bringing rescue with him.

"Play on, Mary," she said with a sigh. "I promise I'll pay greater heed with the next hand."

As Mary shuffled the deck, Anne looked past her cousin's shoulder at their royal mistress. Elizabeth wore a bodice of brown so thickly studded with jewels the fabric almost couldn't be seen. Her skirts were brown and yellow, her dark sleeves trimmed with bright yellow bows. Rather than her usual jeweled pins in her fiery curls, she wore her hair caught in a pearl-studded caul, with a pearl droplet to mark the center of her forehead.

'Twas the business of giving audiences that occupied the queen this afternoon. Anne glanced to the chamber's door, hoping the man presently backing out of the queen's view was the day's last petitioner. Instead the usher once again stepped into the chamber.

"Master James Wyatt, steward to Squire Nicholas Hollier," he called.

Anne's heart shucked its exhaustion at the mention of Kit's surname and she leapt to her feet, brushing the wrinkles from her blue overskirt. She and Mary were once more wearing their blue and white attire from the maying.

Master Wyatt crossed the room toward his monarch's chair, papers tucked beneath one arm and a wooden box held out before him. Silence rolled over the watchers as everyone turned to feast their eyes upon this newcomer. So it was each and every time a stranger of note made an appearance at court. Nor did Master Wyatt disappoint.

Deep auburn hair framed a handsome face. His brow was broad and smooth, his nose straight, his chin square and clean shaven. Set beneath sharply peaked brows, his eyes were a clear blue, the color of a winter's sky. Tall, although not as tall as his squire's brother, he wore a brocade doublet the color of autumn oaks. His rust-colored breeches were conservatively cut as befitted a man from the country. Embroidered in golden handwork, brown garters held brown stockings to his well-made legs.

"Oh, my," Mary said in open appreciation of the fine figure he cut.

Anne turned her head to whisper, "What do you wager our mistress gives him all he wants, just because of his face?" Mary gave a coy lift of her shoulders as Master Wyatt knelt before England's queen.

"Majesty," Master Wyatt said, his voice pleasant. "I bring you greetings from Squire Hollier, presenting to you this token of his affection for you." He extended the box.

'Twas little Dorothy who took it, the youngest of the maids curtsying deeply as she opened the lid to display the contents to her royal mistress. Elizabeth made an appreciative sound as she lifted the item from the box. She held it out for those who were nearest to see. 'Twas a square brooch, larger than the queen's hand. A great pearl hung from its underside. Elizabeth apparently thought well of this gift, for she smiled.

"The squire hopes this pleases you, Majesty," Master Wyatt said. "It's meant to represent the two fish and two roses that tradition says the lord of Graceton owes in yearly tribute to his monarch."

"Does this mean he has at last decided to reclaim his title?" Elizabeth asked, her tone noncommittal.

"It does, indeed," the man replied.

That brought the queen's brows high upon her forehead. She set the bejeweled pin back into its box. "How does he dare send a servant to do what he knows can only be done if he kneels before us on his own behalf?" This was more demand than question.

"Madame, the squire cannot come. A childhood accident has left him too frail to travel and so scarred that he feels himself unfit for social interaction."

This sent a murmur over the crowd. Beside Anne, Mary gasped, her cheeks coloring in shame. As often as she'd pried at Kit over his vow not to wed, she'd also tried to tease information from him about his reclusive brother.

Anne's heart warmed. What Kit had told no other, he'd shared with her, lifting her above all others. This only worsened her longing to see him again and tell him just how much she loved him.

In her chair their royal mistress straightened in surprise. "If he is thusly done, how does he intend to fulfill the duties required of his title?"

"Through his brother, Madame," the squire's steward explained, his voice loud enough to reach every corner of the now quiet room. "The squire will accept the title, as his father's will requires. Once he owns it again, he will name his brother, Master Christopher Hollier, as his heir. As such, Master Hollier will become his proxy in all matters of business pertaining to the lordship."

Elizabeth eyed the handsome man, her face carefully blank. "What does the squire intend to do once he marries and has children of his own?"

Master Wyatt shook his head. "Madame, the squire doesn't intend to marry."

The royal brows shot up at this. "The squire's scarring leaves him incapable of fathering his own heirs?"

The question made Master Wyatt shift uncomfortably on his knees. "Squire Nicholas feels he would make an unacceptable husband. As such, he refuses to wed." This answer neither confirmed nor denied the man's ability to make his own children.

A number of parties around the room set to a nervous stirring, men belonging to the earl of Northumberland converging upon their fellow Catholics in the earl of Arundel's party. Only then did Anne understand. Squire Nicholas might as well have given his title to Kit. This meant a Catholic landholder of some note was ceding power to his Protestant brother.

Nor had Elizabeth missed this implication. There was a new light in the queen's gaze. Anne guessed she thought this a more precious gift than that brooch.

"Madame, all is explained in these." Master Wyatt held out the papers he carried. "I pray you peruse them with care, understanding that those mentioned within them have no knowledge of what goes forward on their behalf. If further explanation must be had, I am authorized to speak for the squire in all matters. In that case, however, I most humbly request that any discussion be done in a venue less public than this."

Mary leaned close to Anne. "Glad I am I didn't wager with you over this," she breathed. "He will have his private interview, and not just because of his face."

As Elizabeth skimmed the papers, her brow clouded. "You vow you can explain this?" She demanded, as if what she read irritated her.

"All of it, Madame," Master Wyatt promised. "If you find it a trifle complex, be assured it is necessary, given the state of the squire's health and the reluctance of some of the involved parties to cooperate with his desires."

Elizabeth nodded once in sharp agreement. "You will stay at Greenwich until I have had a chance to study these." She motioned to the usher. "Master Bowyer, see that this man has a chamber, one that befits the status of his master, the squire." As pages were dispatched, a quiet moan rose from those dependent on the queen for housing. At least one gentleman would lose his chamber to accommodate the outsider.

"My thanks, Madame," the handsome man replied, relief touching his face. He rose and offered as courtly a bow as Leicester might have managed, then stepped politely backward out of his queen's presence.

Anne watched him retreat from the chamber door, hoping once more that the day's audiences might be finished. Instead Master Bowyer announced yet another man, a scholar from Oxford. Sighing, Anne was turning back to Mary and their card game when she caught a glimpse of movement in the doorway.

'Twas Sir William Cecil who slipped in without announcement. The queen's secretary looked more careworn than usual this morn, the lines carved into his well-made face deeper, the pinched crease on the bridge of his nose tighter. At his side strode Sir Amyas.

Anne's heart plummeted. Against Sir William's sober green and black attire, her grandsire's clothing seemed almost festive. His doublet was a greenish-gray beneath his short gray coat, his gold chain massive. His breeches were made of black and gray strips of fabric, while his finest ruby pin trimmed his black velvet cap. Amyas was smiling as Sir William carefully steered him through the crowd toward her. That his grin was broad enough to reveal the gaps where he was missing teeth could but mean Anne's doom.

She and Mary bobbed as one as the two came to a halt before them. "Sir Amyas, Sir William," they said in unison.

"Mistress Mary." Amyas gave the maid a bare nod of his head. The only greeting Anne got was, "You should have more care. You've creased the fabric of that skirt."

"Mistress Anne, pray tell your grandsire just how it has been these last days." Although Sir William's voice was fraught with frustration, he kept his words low enough so as not to draw his royal mistress's attention. "Pray tell him, since he'll not heed me, that there has been a frantic note in Her Grace's voice, that she hastens to and from this task and the other without ever settling fully upon anything she does."

Startled that the secretary should want her confirmation on what all the court knew, Anne looked at her grandsire. "Grandfather, 'tis true. Of late, she has been very nervous and quick to lose her temper. 'Tis worry over the Scots queen troubling her, now that the earl of Murray has made it clear he'll only have his half sister returned in chains. That, she cannot abide, anymore than she likes keeping the Scots queen in our kingdom."

"Amyas," Sir William went on, lowering his voice as he spoke, "I beg you, heed me in this. Go home and wait another month."

Her grandsire's jaw set to its most stubborn angle. "You would have me leave my granddaughter for another month near that papist?"

"Master Hollier is no papist," Sir William said, although his protest lacked any force, as if he'd long ago given up convincing his friend of this fact.

"So you would tell me, thinking to soothe me into accepting the unacceptable," Amyas said, his eyes narrowed in refusal. "I'll not do it, William, not when it was wrong of Her Grace to force him on me in the first place. Nay, this is my granddaughter. I'll have her in my custody, as is my right," he stressed these words.

Sir William pressed his fingers to his temple as if to stop an ache. "You're not hearing me, Amyas. It isn't a matter of right. Her Majesty hasn't seen the contracts, she is irritable, and in the past your words have grated on her so many times that she may refuse you for refusal's sake."

Hope soared in Anne at this. As wrong as it might

be, she willed her grandfather to ignore his friend. If there was one thing of which she was certain, Amyas Blanchemain was capable of annoying his queen.

Outrage flashed in her grandfather's dark eyes. "I am as careful as the next man with what I say. 'Tisn't me who is at fault here, but her. All the world knows a woman is incapable of dealing honestly with a man. This regiment of women is an abomination in God's eyes."

Both Anne and Mary gasped as Sir William's eyes widened in dismay. "Do you know no better than to quote Knox within Her Grace's hearing?" the secretary whispered harshly. "What has happened to you, Amyas? There was a time when you owned subtlety and perception, when you were sensitive to the currents around you. 'Tis as if you wish to bring your house crashing down around your ears. I tell you, exile changed you and not for the better."

Amyas's face could have been carved from stone, but beneath that hard exterior Anne caught a glimpse of the same pain that had driven him to attack her mother. "Are you quite finished?" His words dripped ice.

Insult begot insult. Sir William stiffened, the friendship of the previous moment departing from his gaze. "As God and these two maids will witness, Amyas, I tried to stop you. If you'll not heed me in this, then badger me no more for favors. I've already wasted enough of my precious time trying to drive sense into your hard noggin."

Regret dashed through Amyas's eyes, and his face softened. "You mean well, William, but what I want is nothing more than my right to control my heiress."

If this was an attempt to placate, it came too late. Sir William whirled on his heel, putting his back to the man he'd tried to aid. "Nay, old man. I'll hear no more of your complaints and protests. Find another to harass."

The queen's secretary glanced at Anne, hurt and confusion mingling in his gaze, despite his harsh words. "I beg pardon for involving you, Mistress Anne. You cannot know this, but when I first came to court, your grandsire was a man most worthy of my admiration and emulation. Would that you had known him then." The words were meant for Amyas. Sir William strode away without a backward glance.

'Twas a bare breath later when the usher called out, "Sir Amyas Blanchemain."

"Ah, so she did see us enter. Good," her grandfather said, his eyes alight with approval. "Come, I want you close at hand." Reaching out, he grabbed Anne by the elbow, just as he had at her presentation.

As he drew Anne toward her royal mistress, all conversation again stopped in the room, as the occupants turned their gazes toward throne and queen. If it was to be another battle between the queen and her most irascible subject, they'd not miss a word. Amyas knelt before his queen, doffing his cap. Anne dropped a deep curtsy, then moved aside to a place where she could clearly see both combatants.

"Why, Sir Amyas, whatever brings you back into our presence, after you've kept yourself aloof these past weeks?" Elizabeth asked of this thorn in her side. Although her tone was filled with simple curiosity, 'twas a trap. She knew full well why her secretary had forbidden Sir Amyas from her presence.

"Majesty, I am an old man," her grandfather said, his head bent. "Between my years and my labors on your behalf in my own shire, I fear I haven't the energy to keep up with so youthful a court."

"Is that so?" No emotion touched the smooth lines of Elizabeth's face. "Then, it must be some great event which causes you to expend what little strength you have in store to visit us this day."

Amyas missed the sarcasm as he raised his head to beam upon his queen. "Indeed it is, Majesty. I have contracted for my granddaughter's marriage."

So many were the men who groaned at this that the room thundered with sound of their disappointment. Elizabeth sent a questioning look at her newest maid. Anne bowed her head as if she had no opinion at all in the matter. However bold the queen might be, she didn't care for the same behavior in her maids. 'Twas the gentle obedience God's Word said women owed their fathers that Elizabeth expected of the females who served her.

When the room was again quiet, Amyas added, " 'Tis my age that now brings me here, begging you to release her to me. I need her aid in the planning of her wedding."

"Why have we not seen your contracts?" Elizabeth's words were icy.

"I have only now delivered them into Sir William's hands," Amyas returned, his tone as humble as that of the lowest petitioner.

"Then, your request is premature," the queen snapped. "You cannot plan the wedding until we have reviewed the contracts and approved the union. We will call you to us when our decision has been made." Her tone was final.

Tension drained from Anne, leaving her senses reeling in earnest this time. To still the spinning, she lifted her head from her meek pose. Once again, her royal mistress watched her. In Elizabeth's dark eyes lived the promise to keep her newest maid close to her.

'Twas that wager! Elizabeth wasn't going to let her go, not until after she'd danced at July's end. If that was now only two weeks distant, it was two weeks more with Kit than she'd dreamed to have.

Before his monarch's chair, her grandfather reared back on his knees. "You will not release her?" he cried out half in outrage, half in surprise.

The queen's slender fingers curled about the arms of her chair in what Anne now knew was a certain sign of the coming storm. Once again, her grandfather's timing was poor. Elizabeth no longer cared about alienating this Protestant, a man whose extreme beliefs and bad behavior rankled her. Why, when she'd only moments before replaced him with Kit, a far more valuable Protestant, one who had already served her well and would now sit in the House of Lords?

"Has your age also left you deaf?" Elizabeth snapped. "We said you may not have her now."

Amyas's face flattened. His eyes darted from side to side, as if seeking aid from some invisible companion. Despite all the warnings, it seemed he found his queen's refusal so wholly unexpected he couldn't think of a way to combat it. Just when he shouldn't have done it, he opened his mouth.

"Madame, all I want is to take my heir into my custody as is my right."

The hush in the room was so complete, Anne could hear the shrill cries of the gulls on the river. The day's stiff wind battered at the windowpanes. If it was sunny outside these walls, 'twas a thunderstorm that filled this chamber. Two spots of color came to life on Elizabeth's cheeks. Her mouth narrowed to a thin line, while her dark eyes tightened to mere slits.

"How dare you, sir!" The words exploded from her.

"First, you belabor our poor secretary and pester my lord of Leicester to force Master Hollier's removal as Mistress Anne's tutor. Now that this has failed, you speak of your *right* to remove your granddaughter from our court, talking of contracts we have yet to see. You abdicated your rights to her when you offered her to us, thinking to use our court as a marketplace in which to display your heiress. We will accept no contract you would offer us for Mistress Anne's hand at this time. Leave us."

Even Amyas was not so blind that he couldn't see another sound might destroy his prospects of ever seeing his granddaughter wed to Lord Deyville. The old man came to his feet and backed carefully from the room. As he went he left his shattered pride, his hopes of catching a title for his bloodline and, most likely, his career on the floor before his monarch's chair.

Chapter Twenty-seven

He was back! After seven days, her Kit finally returned. His note came to her by a circuitous route, from Kit to Bertie to Patience to a page to Anne in the Presence Chamber.

Thinking she might well expire in happiness, Anne read again the words from her beloved. Kit meant to join her in the Presence Chamber, once he'd washed away the muck of travel. Even as she chafed at the delay, Anne knew she'd see him no sooner. No man entered the presence of England's queen save in his best.

Tucking the note into the purse at her belt, she turned her attention back to the evening's entertainment, her heart whirling apace with dancers across the room. 'Twas the queen, dressed in blue and gold, her jeweled cap gleaming in the bright glow of so many candles, who led the romp. At her side was her favorite, the earl of Leicester, looking fine indeed in scarlet. They kept the galliard's quick pace to perfection, laughing as they went.

As the tune ended, Leicester drew Elizabeth close. The queen leaned her head near her earl, letting him pass a word in private to her. Whatever he said, 'twas quickly done. When they separated, Elizabeth re-

treated to her chair, while the earl started across the
room, moving toward Anne.

Apprehension's tingle made Anne glance from the
nobleman to her monarch. The queen was watching
her, wicked humor filling her dark gaze. A lift of the
royal brows was enough to convey that the nobleman
again meant to test the fledgling dancer. This was
Anne's cue to forget all she knew of dancing. Anne
bit back a smile. It had become quite a game between
them, one she could in all honesty say she enjoyed as
much as her mistress.

As the tall nobleman stopped before her, she curtsied deeply, waiting until her amusement was well hidden before rising. In the midst of his third decade,
Lord Robert yet owned a slim, broad-shouldered
form. Framed by closely cropped brown hair, his face
was handsome, his nose straight, his jaw strong. 'Twas
a fine mustache that clung to his upper lip, outlining
a sensitive mouth.

Now that Anne knew him better, she understood it
wasn't only his appearance that caught him his queen's
affection. Etched beneath the surface of his skin was
a hint of sadness, a reminder that he'd lost father and
brothers to the axe, and lived for a time under the
threat of death himself. 'Twas another survivor Elizabeth saw when she looked upon her earl, a man who
understood her need to be cunning and devious, because to be anything else might be fatal.

Candlelight made the jewel in Lord Robert's ear
sparkle as his brown eyes filled with appreciation beneath the smooth arch of his brows. "Well, now, Mistress Anne, I think we are a pair, this night," he said,
the wave of his hand indicating Anne's red velvet kirtle with golden brocade underpinnings, the same attire
she'd worn for her presentation.

The urge to tease welled in her, growing beyond her ability to thwart it. "If that be true, my lord, than I am your poorer twin." She looked askance at the golden beads trimming the slashes in his scarlet doublet and the diamond buttons holding them closed. Her gaze shifted to his brocade sleeves, the fabric's pattern outlined in pearls. "I have no idea how you bend your arms in those sleeves."

"There's no power in the world to prevent their bending," he retorted with a laugh, "not when there's a beautiful woman within their reach."

With that, he took a step nearer to her until he stood a breath too close. His eyes warmed with something more than appreciation, and his smile took a wholly different bend. 'Twas a potent reminder that the nobleman found her attractive and didn't mind pleasing himself with sly touches under the pretense of testing her dancing skills.

He reached out as if to straighten the brooch that held her kirtle closed at the waist, the backs of his fingers brushing the line of her bodice near her breasts. "In all truth, mistress, there's not a woman in the chamber who can match you in those colors."

It wasn't what he said, but how he said it that made Anne feel as if she were the only woman in the room. Aye, and each time Lord Robert did this to her, she understood why Lady Sheffield had given way to him to the detriment of her marriage and her repute. Ah, but to do more than trade verbal taunts with this man was to court her own destruction.

"My thanks for your compliment, my lord," she said, working to set things on a different path. "To what do I owe the honor of your attention this night?"

The heat died from his gaze. 'Twas a woman who lost herself to passion he sought, not one capable of restraint. Control was the one thing he had in abundance in his royal lover. He winked at her. "I have told Her Grace that 'tis time again for you to display what you've learned of footwork."

"Nay, my lord, I pray not," Anne cried in pretty protest. "I vow I'll die in embarrassment if I fall as I did in our last dance. 'Tis only fate that saved your toes that time." Although the queen had given her leave to trod upon her favorite's foot, Anne had yet to breach that boundary. What Elizabeth offered and what she accepted were not always the same thing.

He smiled at her feminine distress, then extended a hand in invitation. "Come, now, what are a few toes between friends?"

"I will call you mad, my lord," she said with a shake of her head as she set her hand into his. "Just remember my warning when you are hobbling on the morrow."

He laughed and bravely led his dancing partner to the head of the newly formed procession. When they were in place, the musicians started a slow tune, chosen for Anne's benefit. As always in these tests, Anne began on the wrong foot, then laughed and did a quick shuffle to correct herself.

Up the room's length they went at a slow, stately pace. Anne concentrated on the steps, but not because she didn't know them. Nay, the more skillful she became at dancing, the harder it was to make missteps. When the music's beat indicated 'twas time for the couples to separate, each side turned away from the middle to walk back down the length of the procession. Anne turned the wrong direction.

Mary waved at her from near the queen's chair. "Nan, the other way," she called out with a laugh.

Freeing her very best shocked yelp, Anne whirled.

As she hurried to regain her place, she nearly collided with the viscountess of Hereford. The queen's fiery-haired cousin gave Anne a laughing shove. "To the front, mistress," Lady Lettice directed in encouragement.

"Fly, Mistress Anne," the queen cried from her chair, getting double the pleasure from this particular piece of entertainment, "else my lord of Leicester will grow aged and infirm as he waits for you."

By the time Anne found herself again facing Lord Robert, she was breathless with her attempt to befuddle. "I am so embarrassed," she said softly as she took his hand again.

"Nay, do not be," he replied. If his voice was kind, his eyes were alive with the certainty that his wager was won. "I think me you are doing better. After all, I still have my toes," he teased.

"My thanks," she said, linking her arm in his as they began the series of steps that would take them back up the room's length.

Anne shot a look over his shoulder at the chamber's door, hoping for Kit. 'Twas Lord Deyville she found instead. Dressed all in black as befitted mourning, the nobleman was watching her, his pale eyes afire with rage.

Lord Robert's turn caught Anne yet staring at Deyville. With a surprised cry, she whirled, only to fall hard against the earl's chest. The queen's favorite caught his arm around her as if to steady her, then pleased himself by pressing her tightly to him. Gasping at what he dared, Anne fair leapt back out of his arms. 'Twas fear that prickled up her spine against the possibility that her royal mistress had noticed his embrace. She glared at him. He grinned.

His triumph over having stolen a bit of pleasure

from her was so like what Deyville meant to do to her, and had done to her at the maying, that Anne's anger woke. By God, but she'd had enough of men who thought to use her without any care for what might happen to her as they did so.

"If you're steady, again, mistress," her partner said, lust and laughter living in his brown gaze, "hurry your steps a bit, or we'll be too late to turn at the head of the room. Remember, the men will circle first, the women after."

In her anger Anne forgot to hide her skill. Up the room's length she went without a single misstep, standing aside with her fellow female dancers as the men circled, then clutching hands with the other ladies as they turned. 'Twas only as she once more caught her arm into Lord Robert's and saw the startled surprise in his eyes that she realized what she'd done.

It was almost too late to correct the error, for even now they were making their final turn. Anne's mouth narrowed. There was no help for it; his foot would pay the price.

With a mummer's gasp of confusion, she turned the wrong way and pretended to stumble. He reached out to steady her. Just as expected, he tried again to pull her too close. Anne moved her foot directly atop his shoe, then stepped with all her might.

Lord Robert loosed a bellow of pain and hopped out of line. The dance ground to a halt as participants and musicians alike burst into laughter, the room echoing with the sound of amusement. Anne clapped her hands to her cheeks in horror. "And I was doing so well until this moment," she cried out to the room.

As Lady Lettice flew to take the earl's left arm, supporting him whilst he tried to set his foot upon the ground, Anne came to take his other. "My lord, a thousand pardons." Her words rang with a distress she didn't feel. "I was concentrating so hard upon my steps, I forgot which way to turn."

Lord Robert managed a smile. In his gaze lived the acknowledgment of the message she'd sent; there'd be no more grabbing on his part. "Give it no more thought, Mistress Anne," his words were uttered through clenched teeth.

"Bring him to us," the queen called from her chair.

Anne drew a breath in fear against what her impulsive need to punish might cost her. Turning, she and Lady Lettice aided the hobbling man to his royal mistress's side. It wasn't until the queen offered a swift, sidelong glance that Anne relaxed; there was no anger in the royal face.

"My poor Eyes," Elizabeth said to her earl, her lips curving into a smile. "Has my backward maid broken your foot?"

He smiled. No matter what many said of him, or what Anne knew about him, 'twas true affection Lord Robert carried in his heart for the woman who was his queen. Anne saw it in the curve of his mouth and the softening in his face as he looked upon Elizabeth.

"It matters naught, as long as my wounding gave you a moment's entertainment," he told her.

"I'll not take joy from your pain," Elizabeth replied. "Since you're done with dancing for the evening, so am I. Come, you'll take my arm. I've work to tend to, and you have bruises that need treatment."

As the queen rose from her chair, the Privy Chamber usher beat his staff against the floor to call the room's attention to their monarch's departure. If Lord Robert's injury and Elizabeth's hold on his arm excused him from it, there was no such reprieve for others. Across the room men pulled their hats from their heads and bowed. The ladies and maids, Anne included, dropped into curtsies, not to rise until the queen had passed them for the chamber door.

"We bid you all a good evening," England's monarch called out to those who attended her.

As she passed out the door, Mary and the other ladies of the Privy Chamber rose to follow her. 'Twas Anne's lower rank that kept her bound in the more public room. In departing, Mary offered her kinswoman a pleased smile, more than liking the injury done to the man she so despised. The last to follow were those noblemen yet seeking to press a final word of flattery on their monarch, leaving only a few of their fellows behind them.

One who stayed was the duke of Norfolk, dressed in subdued blue. Rather than follow where he, above all other men, had the right to go, he but stared hungrily after Leicester as the earl led his queen through the Privy Chamber door. It always seemed odd to Anne that no matter how many men the duke gathered around him, he ever wore a solitary air. 'Twas as if his higher rank didn't raise him above others as much as it isolated him.

"What now, Mistress Anne? Pining after a widower placed more highly than me?" Lord Deyville nigh on breathed his angry words into her from his stance behind her.

With a startled cry Anne turned, only to gasp as the nobleman grabbed her arm. The rage she'd seen in his face while he watched her dance yet colored his features. "You were toying with Leicester," he snarled.

This comment took her by surprise. "I was not," she retorted, wanting to add that if she were, it was none of his concern, since the queen had refused his contract. Such a prod wouldn't serve.

"Nay?" Jealousy burned bright in his cheeks, bringing vicious lights to his gray eyes. "You would say so, but I saw you dancing with him, letting him fondle you."

She yanked on her arm. "He but steadied me after I stumbled," she lied, since it couldn't do her any good at all to admit to Leicester's interest. This bit of gossip would fly to the queen's ear.

"Liar!" His fingers tightened until she flinched. "Where others might be blind, I know what I saw. He grabbed you, holding you until you thrust away from him."

Anne wanted to scream in frustration. "Then, how is it you accuse me of interest, when you admit you saw that I don't encourage his attention?" she snapped, looking over his shoulder in the hopes of aid from some quarter.

The only one near enough to overhear was Lady Montmercy. Curiosity glimmered in the lady's usually blank gaze. This could but mean the noblewoman's interest was piqued, indeed. Worry shot through Anne. Lord Deyville's tirade would only add fuel to Lady Montmercy's plan for her destruction.

"You'll free me this instant," she commanded her thwarted suitor.

"I think not," he replied with a twisted smile. "Indeed, it seems I must be even more vigilant if I'm to keep what's mine, and," he continued in warning, "you are yet mine. What your idiot grandsire has put wrong can be rectified and our contract will stand. I am here to see no one steals you from me in the meantime." He raised his free hand and brushed his fingers down the curve of her cheek.

Anne turned her face to the side, then stepped back
to the limit of her arm. Her breath hissed from her in
a heated stream. "Only when that contract is approved
by our queen, will I be yours. Know you, I will do all
I can to see that day never comes."

"Is that a threat?" His mouth lifted in an unholy
smile. "If so, then I can do you one better. I think
me I'll take you, spoiling you for any other man. Thus
will I force our queen's hand in the matter of the
contract. Once you're maid no longer, she'll have no
choice but to wed us, wishing to save what's left of
your repute."

Anne glared at him. Perhaps Kit was right, 'twas
better to die with him, than enter into marriage with
Deyville.

Chapter Twenty-eight

Once more dressed in his courtly best, this time his blue doublet over gold and brown breeches, Kit reached the Presence Chamber. The silver trim on the scarlet uniforms of Elizabeth's lifeguards gleamed against the light of a hundred candles pouring through its door. 'Twas the sound of as many voices that flowed out with the light, so loud Kit could barely hear the music that was so much a part of the queen's idle hours. As always, the guards' pikes were held to block the door's opening, deterring the lowly and unwanted from entering.

Kit nodded to them, knowing only one, Will. The man was one of the two guards whose tongue he'd dampened with ale after Anne's presentation. "A fine evening," he said in greeting.

Will smiled. "It would have been a better evening if we'd not had our backs turned."

"Aye," the other added, "we only heard my lord of Leicester's bellow when your student trod upon his foot."

Kit laughed as he took up his role in this, the queen's sly game. "I try, the Lord God knows how hard," he sighed, every inch the long suffering tutor. "As a dancer, I fear Mistress Anne may well be hopeless."

Still chuckling over the thought of his Nan bruising the earl's toes, he moved toward the door to await the usher. Across the room stood Lady Montmercy. Kit frowned. Her face was alive with interest. He followed her gaze. Lord Deyville stood nearby. 'Twas his Nan's arm that foul nobleman held.

Rage burst to life in him. "Let me pass," he hissed to the guards.

As he'd done before on Kit's behalf, Will's pike lifted. Kit ducked beneath the other man's weapon to enter the room unannounced. His gaze locked upon Deyville's back, he closed the distance between them.

Even as his hand went to his belt where his sword should have been, he caught back the urge to do murder. Their cause couldn't be helped with an open display of his love for Anne. Nay, 'twas control he needed now more than ever. By the time Kit came to a halt next to Deyville, he'd hidden his seething emotions under a courtier's polite veneer.

'Twas his finest bow he offered the nobleman. "My lord, condolences on the recent loss of your wife," he said in the sham of regret.

Deyville's jaw clenched, his eyes narrowed. Ah, but no longer did they meet as inferior to superior; now that Nick had publicly named Kit his heir, they were far closer to being equals. It seemed Deyville knew this for, with a furious hiss, the nobleman released Anne and leaned close. "She's mine. Touch her, and you die," he muttered.

Kit grinned. 'Twas too late for that. He'd already touched her and was more than prepared to die for what he'd done.

"My lord, I heard you well enough the first time you offered me that warning." His words were a reminder that he'd already bested the peer once, albeit in a verbal battle, as well as a promise to do the same again.

Deyville glared at him. Kit acknowledged his anger with a lifted brow. At last the nobleman whirled to storm from the room. As he passed Lady Montmercy, the lady's usually circumspect gaze gleamed with consideration. Even as the oddness of this struck Kit, he set it aside to look upon the woman who held his heart.

"Did he hurt you, Mistress Anne?" If he dared not speak words of love, he softened his voice, letting his tone and his smile say what he could not.

"Nay," she said, her eyes alive with the affection she held for him. "Do you know, Master Christopher, you are most handy to have about for rescues. I think me, I'll keep you close for some time to come."

As she renewed her promise that 'twas he, and he alone, she wanted, Kit's love grew until he felt giddy with it. "Mistress, I am at your service for as long as you will have me," he promised in return.

Joy filled Anne's face. Her lips parted, inviting his kiss. Even as the need to accept what she offered nearly overtook him, he caught hold of it. "Have a care," he whispered in fond warning. "This glow of yours simply will not do. Folk will talk."

The desire, but not the love, left Anne's expression. " 'Tis a good thing I am a woman of great control," she said, "else I would give them plenty to talk about."

"And I would let you, were I not man impervious to seduction," Kit laughed. "Bertie tells me the queen declined to even look upon your grandsire's contract. If that is so, what did Deyville want of you?"

"He wished me to now he yet intends to make me his," Anne said with new worry. "I fear I lost my

temper with him and said too much. He threatened
rape to force the queen's hand in the matter of our
marriage."

Even as her words sent anger soaring again, a warning bell clanged at the back of Kit's brain. He glanced
to where Lady Montmercy stood. She was gone.

As he stared at that empty space, terror rose in him.
Lady Montmercy had overheard Deyville's threats
against Anne. How long would it be before the lady
found a way to use Deyville to do the deed Kit had
refused? He drew a sharp breath. Christ, but with
Deyville as her tool, Lady Montmercy would achieve
more than just Sir Amyas's destruction. Once Anne's
lack of maidenhead was exposed, they'd all be destroyed—himself, Anne, Amyas, Andrew, even Lady
Montmercy.

Across the room the musicians launched into an almain. With a rowdy burst of laughter, a new set of
dancers gathered to enjoy the tune. Now that the
queen had retired, they broke ranks to include even
servants in their midst.

"Kit!" John's deep voice rose over the music and
general buzz of conversation to reverberate against
the stone walls.

Kit turned. John and Ned were leading young Lord
Montmercy toward them. Anne leaned close, and Kit
forgot all to let his senses fill with her nearness.

"I cannot help myself," she whispered with a tiny
laugh. "I have the most horrid urge to call him uncle."

Having not seen the lordling since Anne's revelation, Kit now freed an astonished breath. Striding
toward him, holding his shoulders in the same stiff
fashion as his sire, was the connection between the
lady and the knight. The rusty red color of Andrew's
doublet enhanced his olive skin tone. His dark hair

was the same color as Anne's, while they shared the
same shape of eye, although Andrew's were a deep,
brownish-blue. 'Twas Old Amyas's mark that showed
in the length of the lad's nose and the squaring of
his chin.

As Andrew stopped before them, Kit bowed. Now
that he was convinced Andrew was Amyas's son, it
felt wrong to offer the lad such respect. After all,
Amyas was the son of a tradesman and Andrew
naught but his bastard.

Anne bobbed. "My lord."

"Mistress Anne," Lord Andrew said, then turned
his attention on Kit. "But here is the man who will
soon be my equal."

"Ah, so Master Wyatt has been here, has he?" Kit
said, trying for a casual tone. It felt awkward to speak
publicly about being Nick's heir.

"Master Wyatt is still here," Anne corrected. "Your
brother's steward waits on a personal interview with
our royal mistress."

"Aye, so he does, and much to my detriment," John
said, with a touch of irritation. "His coming cost me
my quarters, leaving me and two others sleeping at
the top of the servant's hall."

Ned sniffed. "It but proves you're not quite as
clever as you thought when you appropriated a better
man's accommodation." John had maneuvered himself
into one of the small house-like residences that sat
beyond Greenwich's tiltyard.

As the others laughed, Ned glanced at Kit, new intensity in his gaze. "Something interesting happened
while you were gone. I have it from an usher that
Norfolk addressed our queen's councillors, and won
an agreement among them that Mary Stuart should
be wed to an Englishman."

Kit shook his head. "Norfolk but lays the ground-work to announce what he's already done." He leaned forward and lowered his voice to keep what he said next private. "The duke sent the Scots queen a diamond as a token of his intent to wed her."

"Nay!" Anne cried out, worry creasing her brow. "He had no right to plot and plan so behind my mistress's back. Someone must tell her what is afoot."

"Better you than me, mistress," John said. "I want to keep my head attached to my neck."

With that, the conversation flowed from politics into hunting and hawking. All in all, it evolved into a most pleasant evening. They stayed until the candles were guttering in their sconces and most all the others were at their rest. At last they started from the Presence Chamber.

Although the guard at the door had changed, Kit was surprised to see Will yet remained. The guardsman leaned against the wall, watching the door as he waited. As he saw Kit exit, he straightened and lifted a hand. "Master Hollier, a moment."

With a shrug to his friends, Kit stepped to the side to see what he wanted. "Take heed, master," Will whispered when they were close. "At the base of the stairs are two men. They're bailiffs from the Fleet, come to claim you on behalf of your creditors."

Eyes wide, Kit reared back from him, nigh on choking against this news. Lady Montmercy wasn't going to wait for the end of July to take his life. Gratitude followed. 'Twasn't just his life Will had saved, but Anne's as well. Without Kit to guard her, there was no one to stop Deyville.

"I owe you more than a cup of ale for this," he told the man, his voice thick with thanks. "You are a friend and true!"

"I thought it only fair that you be warned," Will said with a lift of his shoulders and a wink. With that, he descended the stairs to find his own rest.

Kit stared after him. Of a sudden he gave thanks that the queen had kept Jamie waiting. Chances were the lady had told her bailiffs where his quarters were, but not his connection to Jamie, or where Nick's steward slept. Aye, but how to reach that residence before the bailiffs caught him?

As Kit rejoined his party, he glanced at Anne. Worry touched her dark gaze. This only strengthened his need to escape the noblewoman's trap. Kit offered his friends a sheepish grin.

"I fear I'm having a bit of a problem with my creditors. Philistines that they are, they've set the bailiffs on me," he said. "Will's just told me they await me beyond the door."

If Anne gasped, John and Ned groaned in commiseration, both having made brief stays in that foul place for the same reason. Lord Andrew puffed out his chest. "Well, they'll not have you. I'll promise to pay what you owe."

"A thousand thanks, my lord," Kit said, wishing coins could solve his problem, "but coins I can get from my brother through Master Wyatt. I need you to keep the bailiffs at bay long enough for me to make my escape to Master Wyatt's quarters."

John's deep laugh echoed in the stairwell. "I think we three are stout enough to deter two."

"What of you, Mistress Anne?" Kit asked of his love, feeling her fear for him cross the space between them. "Will you think me a coward should I make a dash for it?"

"I should think you a fool if you didn't," she retorted, her carefree smile ably hiding what ached in her. Would that there were some way to tell her he'd send word through Bertie of the outcome. Ah, but there was, or rather he could at least leave the hint.

"John, you say you're sleeping in the servant's hall?" At the man's nod Kit continued. "My servant, Bertie Babthorpe and his new wife have taken to using that hall. If you'd be so kind, have your man awaken him and send him to me?" As he spoke, he glanced at Anne. Much of the worry left her gaze; she'd wait for Patience to come to her.

"Aye, I can do that," John said.

It took but a moment for the party to reorganize. Anne took Lord Montmercy's arm and descended the stairs with Ned and John on their heels. Kit took up the rear, already wishing Jamie's quarters weren't at the eastern end of the palace compound, near the orchard.

Ned pulled open the door. Kit peered out over the false lordling's head. Sure enough, the moon's bright light gleamed upon the faces of the waiting men. Anne and Andrew stopped just outside the door. John and Ned spread themselves across the doorway to shield Kit as he ducked and crept out behind them. When he was ready, his breath drawn for the run, he tapped the big man on the shoulder.

"Now!" John bellowed, lunging around Anne to catch one of the men. Ned leapt out on the opposite side. Kit saw no more as he raced down the length of the waterfront building. The bailiffs' shouts echoed after him, loud enough to set shutters to banging against the wooden walls as courtiers and their servants peered down on what went forward in the courtyard.

These residences were much like London town houses, being tall and narrow, each with its own sharply peaked roof and doorway. Down the wee lane between two banks of buildings Kit went. He didn't slow until he reached the door to the residence allotted Jamie.

Gasping for breath, he pounded on the door. He dared not shout, for fear of drawing attention. There was no response. Christ! What if Jamie wasn't here? He threw himself against the door. 'Twas barred, meaning someone was within.

From the far end of this stretch of dwellings came the ringing echo of a running man's gasping breath. One of the bailiffs had escaped his captors. Again, Kit pounded.

The door flew open. 'Twas Jamie's servant, Tom Lowndes, who stood in the opening. Dressed in only his shirt, his fair hair stood on end as if Kit had roused him from a deep sleep. He yelped in surprise as Kit shoved past him, slammed the door, and dropped the bar.

"Master Kit," the man cried, only to have Kit grab him close and cover his mouth to still his tongue.

"In a moment, Tom," Kit whispered.

He listened. Whoever followed ran on by without pausing. Kit's relief was so deep it left his knees shaking.

Releasing Tom, he turned his back to the door. The room was so tiny that Tom's bed, naught but a simple mattress with a blanket, nearly reached from wall to wall. Two more mattresses, occupied by Nick's staring footmen, filled what space remained. At the far end of the room was a stair, although to call it such was unfair. 'Twas more ladder than steps.

Standing at its base, caught in the circle of his candle's light, was Jamie. Like his servant, Jamie wore naught but his shirt, however where Tom stared,

Nick's steward grinned. "Well, now, Kit, to what do I owe the honor of your visit? If you've come for a bit of a loan, 'tis useless. I've already tried."

Kit frowned at him. "What do you mean?"

"In preparation for his title's restoration, Nick wished to see your debts repaid. I fear the lady won't take your coin, Kit. It's your hide she's after."

Kit stared in shock, then his heart dropped through the floorboards. If he and Anne hadn't been doomed before, they were now. "Christ, you don't know what you've done!"

"I don't understand any of this," Bertie cried out in confusion. His voice echoed hollowly in Jamie's nearly empty bedchamber, to whence they'd retreated upon his arrival. 'Twas clear Jamie hadn't intended to spend much time at court; Nick's steward had brought no bed with him, leaving him sleeping on the same simple mattress his servants used.

Jamie sat upon the folding stool he'd brought with him, while Kit stood near at the hearth, his elbow braced upon the plain wooden mantelpiece. With July nights too warm for a fire, 'twas two candles that stood in the room's center, their flames flickering against the fetid fingers of air that pried through the shutters. Their meager, golden illumination reached out to encircle Bertie. Kit's servant stood near the stairs, confusion printed on his face.

He glanced from one gentleman to the other. "Let me say it this time, to see if I have it right. Lady Montmercy has set the bailiffs on you, Master Kit, because she refused Master James's attempt to pay your debt to her. She doesn't want the coin, but your life instead."

"Aye," Kit said with a nod.

"So, at dawn on the morrow, you'll allow them to arrest you." Bertie paused to cross his arms, a look of harsh skepticism on his face. "Then, they'll take you to their prison, where you'll die."

Jamie loosed a small and bitter laugh at this. "Nay, Bertie, he'll not be in that cell long enough even to take on fleas. I'm to follow on his heels with coin enough to bribe the jailers to release him. He allows the bailiffs to take him only to convince Lady Montmercy that he's been incarcerated."

"Once Master James has released me," Kit continued, "he and I, along with Graceton's men, will come riding back to Greenwich to hide in the garden at Duke Humphrey's tower."

"Where Lord Deyville will later go to attempt the rape of Mistress Blanchemain," Bertie finished for him, his voice weakening as befuddlement overtook him once again. "Tell me again. Why will Lord Deyville go to the tower to misuse Mistress Anne?"

"Because," Kit told him, "Lady Montmercy will send him there, knowing the nobleman wishes to have his way with her. Now, Bertie, pay close heed to this. There are two things the lady needs to believe if she's to urge Lord Deyville to make his attack. First, she must think no one knows I've been taken by the bailiffs and, second, that Mistress Anne and I planned a dancing lesson in the garden for the morrow's afternoon."

Bertie blinked in thought. "Ah, this is why you'll let the bailiffs catch you in the early morn, before there's anyone about to see them do it and spread the gossip. But how are we to let the lady know about the dancing lessons?"

Kit knew what he must say next wouldn't sit easily on Bertie's soul. Crossing the room, he lay his hand upon his servant's shoulder. "She'll trust the information because she'll have it from the same source that has always filled her ear with my doings."

Bertie shook his head against this. "And what source is that, Master Kit?"

"You Bertie," Kit said as gently as he could. "You will tell Nell, who will carry our lie to the lady's ear, just as she has done all the summer long."

Bertie's face whitened to a deathly pallor. He staggered back until he made contact with the plastered wall behind him. Crumpling against it, he slid down to sit at its base, tears in his eyes.

"Foul me," he cried, his voice broken. "How could I not see that bitch was using me?" Gasping for breath, he came upright far enough to kneel, his head bowed. "With all my heart, I beg your forgiveness, master," he managed in a trembling voice.

Kit crouched down beside him, laying his hand atop Bertie's folded ones. "There's no need for forgiveness. 'Tis as much my fault as yours, for I never told you to beware the traps Lady Montmercy might send your way."

His servant looked up at him, shame and self-hatred marring his handsome face. "I'll not fail you, Master Kit, even if what I do means I lose my Patience."

This made Kit smile. "Nay, now, I'm not asking that you bed Nell, only see the information she must give to Lady Montmercy set into her hands."

Relief gusted from Bertie, then he frowned in consideration. "Aye, 'tis simple enough to say I'll not lay with her, but hard to avoid when 'tis coupling she'll expect from me." He paused in thought.

"I have it! I'll go to her as if all is normal, only to draw back confessing I'm newly wed. Guilt will seem to gnaw at me. I'll pace as if battling my urge to do

sin, spilling the information in the process." His eagerness to play his new role washed all the shame from
his face. "Better and better! I can also add I fear
Mistress Anne will go to the tower and be disap-
pointed because I cannot find you."

Coming to his feet, Kit shrugged. "If you can do
that without making it seem contrived."

Bertie shot him a narrow-eyed look. "Master, as I
now sleep in the servant's hall, while you rest in your
quarters, I have no way of knowing what you're about.
Should you be gone before I arrive to see you dressed,
I can only wonder in whose arms you are sleeping and
when you might next appear. She'll believe me."

"Aye, then," Jamie said, drawing their attention
back to him, "all that needs doing is to convince Mistress Blanchemain that she must walk to the tower
with naught but her maid and Bertie at her side. Once
she's there and while she's yet uncertain as to whether
rescue awaits, she's to allow Lord Deyville to tear at
her clothing."

Kit whirled on him with a gasp. "She'll do no such
thing. She needs only to tease him into making plain
his intention to use her, then we'll leap from hiding
to take him."

"Nay, Kit," Jamie said as he rose from his stool and
came to stand near Bertie, " 'tisn't so easily done as
that. If the nobleman doesn't tear at her garments,
this plan of yours will be all for naught."

Rage tore through Kit at the thought of allowing
Deyville to treat his beloved so. "You ask too much!"
he shouted.

"Nay, he's right, master," Bertie warned. "Threats
he can deny. If he doesn't touch her, all you'll have
accomplished is to warn both him and Lady Montmercy against your plots."

Kit looked from Jamie to Bertie, his breath catching in disbelief. They were both against him in this. "Nay," he pleaded, "I cannot let him touch her."

They but stared at him, waiting for him to acknowledge what he already knew, there was no other way. Nor did he have a choice. Fate had set these events into motion the moment Nick sent Jamie to repay his debt.

When he made no reply, Bertie asked, "What shall I tell Mistress Anne to expect once we've exposed the nobleman?"

Kit left Jamie to outline the details of carrying Deyville to Sir William with Anne's defeated attacker. No matter how he tried, he couldn't banish the image of Deyville trying to force himself on Anne at the maying. To twiddle his thumbs whilst Deyville once again hurt his Nan burned a hole in his heart.

When Jamie fell silent, Bertie reached out to touch Kit's arm. "Master, all will be well."

Kit tried to smile. " 'Tis I who should say this to you. Unfortunately, I find I'm not near as fond of this plan as I was a few moments ago."

Bertie grinned, then turned to the stairs. "Until the morrow in the garden, then," he said by way of a farewell.

Once he was gone, Jamie eyed his employer's heir. "I would call you well and truly smitten," the man said, laughter staining his voice.

This startled Kit out of his morose thoughts. "Say that before Sir William on the morrow, and you'll see Mistress Anne ruined."

Jamie cocked his head, a brow lifted in question. "Our queen is so jealous of her maids?"

Kit sighed. "Our queen is jealous of everything,

wanting to be the center of all. If there's a love match to be arranged, it must be she who does it."

There was an odd flicker of pleasure and worry in Jamie's pale blue eyes at this. "Then, I shall take great care in my words," he replied, stretching as he prepared to return to his interrupted sleep.

Kit caught him by the arm. " 'Tis more important that you take care of that paper of mine you're to claim from Lord Montmercy. Fetch it before you come chasing after the bailiffs, for I want it next to my heart as we meet with Deyville. I pray you see that the seals on it aren't broken. There can be no question of forgery when it comes into Sir William's hands."

Kit made his tone urgent. It was vital Jamie didn't see what lay upon that paper. There was no great liking between him and Jamie. If Nick's man saw that contract 'twas entirely possible he'd try to destroy it, thinking he was saving Nick from the queen's wrath. Not that Kit was looking forward to enduring royal rage, but there was no help for it. All that would stop Lady Montmercy from extracting her vengeance on either Anne or himself was exposure.

"As you will," Jamie said, his eyes narrowed in mistrust. He leaned down to snuff out the candles. "Now, 'tis best we both get to our rest. 'Tis quite a day we face upon the morrow."

Kit retreated to the room's far end, where he used poor Tom's pallet. There was naught for him to look forward to save endless hours contemplating his rash and idiotic plan. They were doomed for certain.

Chapter Twenty-nine

Anne stood before the massive walls of Duke Humphrey's tower, feeling smaller than a sparrow. Did the caretaker open the gates every day, or had Kit been here to tell him to do so just for this event? The desire to shout out his name grew in her. Aye, but what if it wasn't him who called in reply?

Her stomach souring at that thought, Anne looked down at herself. Beneath the blue of her outer skirt, the cheery little flowers embroidered on her white underskirt stared up at her. An hour ago it had seemed appropriate that she once more wore her maying attire. Now she knew she'd been a fool to don it. Deyville could but see it as a taunt.

"This is utter madness," she said, staring into the gaping mouth that was the tower's gateway.

" 'Tis," Patience agreed from beside her, her arm clutched into Anne's. Bertie's new wife wore her bridal bodice, but her hair was once more caught into its tight bun, as if so severe a style were some sort of armor against attack.

"I have a dagger strapped to my belt," Bertie offered, his face no less pale than those of the women beside him.

Anne glanced at him. "Tell me again what it is Master Christopher would have me do."

"You must let Lord Deyville begin to tear at your clothing," Bertie said, no confidence in his voice. "If he doesn't, there'll be no proof of his attack. Once he's left you in disarray, Master Christopher and Master James will leap from hiding to affect your rescue. They'll bear him to Sir William Cecil to complain against his attempt to force you." Bertie tried to smile.

"This is good," Anne said, working to convince herself of this, just as she had the dozen other times she'd heard the plan since they started up the hill from the park gate. Surely 'twas better to face Lord Deyville with the hope of rescue than to come upon him unaware in some darkened corner. Moreover, once he was exposed, his threats would be done.

"And his confession will expose Lady Montmercy, who plots against my master," Bertie added.

These words set the seeds of courage into Anne's soul. She'd do this to keep Kit safe. Even as she took a step toward the gateway, those new sprouts wilted. What if Kit weren't here?

As the need to run screaming back to Owls House filled her, she turned to peer toward the rooftops of London, visible in the distance. Woolwich Road was empty, save for a single horseman, coming toward Greenwich at a gallop. A single man wouldn't be Kit.

Patience turned to look with her. "We shouldn't do this without Sir Amyas to witness," she said.

Anger shot through Anne at this suggestion. Like as naught Amyas would hold her down as he urged Lord Deyville to do his worst. Courage blossomed against anger's heat. Be damned if she'd turn tail and run like some cowardly dog!

Anne turned to face the open gateway, eyes narrowed and heart bolstered. "I am ready."

Passing through the tower's gate, they entered the

garden. Anne loosed a bitter laugh. 'Twas wrong to plan a rape in the same spot where they'd consummated their love.

As they strode for the small lawn at the garden's center, Anne peered through the thick trees and growth. Ah, but Kit wouldn't be here. It would be in the tangled bushes at the far end that he'd find a hiding spot.

They stepped from the trees into the square of grass, and Anne's heart simply stopped beating. Lord Deyville stood at its center. Worse, he had two servants with him, burly-looking men dressed in leather jerkins with swords strapped at their sides.

Panic shot through her. If Kit wasn't here to stop him, these men guaranteed Deyville would have his way with her, no matter how Patience and Bertie protested. She turned, thinking to run.

Another man just like the first two now stood between her and escape. She glanced at Kit's servant. Stout of heart he might be, but he knew when he was outnumbered. Patience was ashen against this unexpected threat.

Fighting her fear, Anne turned back to face the nobleman. He was ready for the task he'd set himself, his doublet and hat lying not far from where Kit had set his own attire the previous week. The fine cotton of his shirt clung to the powerful line of his shoulders, no doubt to remind her of how easily he'd held her at the maying. The sun gleamed off his bald pate, and glittered in the jewels decorating his sword's hilt. That was four swords to Bertie's single dagger.

"Why, Mistress Anne," Lord Deyville said, smiling at her. "I cannot imagine how we come to meet like this."

Since there was no longer any point to politeness,

Anne gave free rein to her tongue. "I expect you would not, being a man of little imagination."

"The vixen shows her claws," he chided, his gray eyes coming to life with pleasure. "Let us be civilized about this. I realize you came here to tryst with one man, but as he is unavailable"—his smile widened as he referred to Kit's arrest—"come lay with me instead."

Anne drew a sharp breath. 'Twas worse than she thought. Lady Montmercy had hinted that Anne and Kit were lovers. No doubt the lady meant this as an additional goad to drive Lord Deyville into doing her will.

The nobleman extended a hand toward her. "I promise I'll be gentle, that is if you are yet in need of such care." There was a vicious twist to his mouth as he said this. "Tell me, my sweet, are you the same woman you were when you came to court?"

Anne wanted to laugh. She was, indeed. Instead she sneered at him. "Such impertinence, especially since the queen has refused your contract for my hand."

"What spirit," he said, still smiling. "If you are yet the virgin you claim, I'll have you first so no other wants you. If you're not, well . . ." He paused here and lifted his shoulders. "It would be better for both you and Master Hollier if you haven't given to him what is mine. Come, then, let's embark upon our voyage of discovery."

"Nay, my lord," Anne replied, fixing her feet into the earth. "I'll not freely give you what you want."

The nobleman leered. "Better and better. We will like each other well, wait and see," he crooned, taking a step toward her.

Anne forced herself to hold her place. "You'll do

this with these two"—she waved a hand toward Patience and Bertie—"to witness?"

"But, of course. 'Tis far better if they do," he replied. "The more who know you're spoiled, the sooner we'll be wed."

Rage returned. "Is that so? Then, come for me. Are you man enough to try me on your own? Nay, I doubt that. 'Tis why you brought these three with you. You'll have them hold me while you use me like the foul coward you are."

Dangerous lights sparked in his cool gray gaze. Two steps brought him to stand before her. "Do you dare to call me coward?"

"Are you so old you cannot hear?" she retorted.

His hand closed around her throat, beneath her ruff. Anne gagged, her fingers tearing at the lacy circlet as she tried to pry off his hand. Stars flickered at her vision's periphery as blackness encroached.

"Say it again," he whispered to her, his lips moving against her cheek. "You cannot know how your defiance excites me."

"Nay, you'll not do her so!" Bertie shouted, drawing his dagger. Birds, startled from the treetops by his cry, cheeped in distress as they circled and flew.

Deyville lifted his head from Anne's to look over her shoulder at Kit's servant. Naught but casual interest filled his gaze. "Silence him," he said to his man.

Gasping against Deyville's grip, Anne couldn't help but listen as Patience screamed, then began to sob. Behind Anne, steel clashed against steel. Men panted. Feet slid and pounded against the grassy earth.

Certain that Kit and his force would leap out of hiding to save Bertie, Anne waited. No rescuers shouted to announce their arrival. Bertie cried out in pain, then choked. Patience's voice rose in a shrill, short yelp.

Anne's eyes closed as fear ate up all her anger. Kit was not here. She was doomed.

"Bertie," Patience sobbed, the rustle of her skirts loud against the ensuing silence. "Do not die," she pleaded to her new husband.

'Twas Patience's pain that saved Anne; she'd not let Deyville steal the woman's newfound joy. As the lord lowered his head to lay his mouth atop her, she bit down with all her might and brought her knee up between his legs. She tasted his blood in her mouth, but between farthingale and petticoats, her other attempt was useless.

"Bitch!" Deyville snarled, jerking back, his hand opening in reflex reaction to her attack.

Gagging and gasping for breath, Anne stumbled back from him. She turned, moving for the gate. Deyville caught her by her caul, his fingers digging past its pearl-encrusted surface into the thickness of her hair.

Yelping, Anne twisted against the pain, kicking and thrashing as he drew her back to him. "Let me go," she tried to cry. Her voice was barely a whisper as the words tore at her bruised throat.

He dragged her with him across the grass to where Patience sat, crooning and sobbing. Anne's heart ached. Bertie's head lay in his wife's lap. His eyes were closed, red stained the breast of his blue doublet.

Reaching down, Deyville removed Bertie's dagger from his limp fingers. "Shall we see who draws more blood?" he asked her as he straightened.

The knife's tip pressed to Anne's lower back. She gasped. There was a tearing whir as he drew its sharp blade up her bodice's lacing. Her bodice sagged open, hanging from her arms by the ribbons that held her sleeves to it. Once again he set the dagger to her back, this time to her corset's lacing.

A terrible roar echoed from the garden's back. "You bastard!" Kit screamed.

Deyville whirled, dragging Anne with him as he turned. Anne's eyes teared as she saw Kit racing toward them, his naked blade held in his hands. His eyes were wild, his mouth pulled back into a grimace. At his heels came Master James and three more. Hissing in surprise, Deyville tossed Anne to the side as he turned to meet this threat.

Her breath left her lungs as she hit the earth. Still, she kicked at one of Deyville's men as he tripped over her. There was great satisfaction when she saw one of Master James's men skewer him. Rolling to the side, her bodice clutched close to her chest, she crawled to Patience. As if nothing went on around her, Patience was carefully combing her husband's dark hair with her fingers, whispering a child's lullaby as she did so. Anne caught the woman close, her gaze yet locked onto Kit and Lord Deyville only a yard distant.

The sun flashed on their blades as the weapons clashed. So fast did they make contact and retreat, Anne could barely keep pace. The rasp and grate became a steady beat. Her love flinched as blood darkened the sleeve of his blue doublet.

Around them, all of Deyville's men had dropped their swords. One clutched his arm, another sat holding his seeping thigh. The last was unhurt and wished to stay so.

Panting, Kit thrust again. Deyville stepped back, his blade moving to ward off the attack. He stumbled on his downed man. With a cry he lurched to the side, then fell.

'Twas the need to do more than draw blood that

darkened Kit's face. Panic shot through Anne. He was no peer. If he killed a nobleman, he'd pay with his life, no matter the excuse.

"Nay," she tried to shout, but all that left her throat was hoarse whisper.

Kit lunged, the sun glinting on steel as he stabbed toward the nobleman's back. Master James's blade flashed as the gentleman dared prevent his master's brother from doing murder. Kit staggered back, from Lord Deyville. 'Twas time enough for Master James to signal his men into forming a circle about the nobleman as he sat up, his chest yet heaving in exertion.

A raging sound escaped Kit as he once more threw himself toward the man he would see dead.

"Nay, Kit," his brother's servant said, holding his sword at the ready.

Even as Kit halted, his face twisted in hatred for this intruder. "I am my brother's heir. You have no right to interfere," he hissed, raising his sword's tip to place it where Master James's head joined with his neck. "You'll stand aside," he commanded, his voice cold and hard.

Master James didn't move, save to drop his blade. The weapon clattered dully onto the grass. "I am unarmed," he said gently. "Do your worst to me, Kit. When you're done, your need to spill blood will be sated."

Kit stood still as stone, his sword yet pressed to the steward's throat. The silence that followed was broken only by Patience's soft sobs and the harsh breathing of tired men. At last a sigh shuddered through him. His hand opened, and his sword dropped to bounce away from him on the ground. Then his fist closed. Kit swung. Master James nigh on flew off his feet to land atop Lord Deyville. The two of them sprawled backward to lay as if dazed.

Kit shook his hand as if it pained him. "That is for

daring to stand between me and what is my right," he
snarled at his brother's servant.

Spitting blood, Master James sat up. "I'll not apologize, not when it got me what I needed to clear you of
your idiot troubles and spare Nick more of your grief."

Kit whirled and came striding toward her. His gaze
darted to Bertie, pain filling his green eyes. He
crouched beside her, reaching out to touch her cheek.

Anne drew back from him. "You must not," she
croaked. "Too many watch. I'll not have it charged
you were forward with me, whilst I am in this state."

'Twas a new battle he fought, the need to hold her
warring with the demands of propriety. Propriety won,
as they both knew it must. "You are unharmed?" he
asked.

She smiled. "Aye, save for some bruises."

His fingers descended to rest against Bertie's throat
as he sought his servant's pulse. He breathed in relief.
Catching Patience's fingers to still her stroking, he
shook her hand to awaken her from her shock. The
woman raised her head to look on him, her eyes dull,
her cheeks stained with her anguish.

"Patience, your husband lives," he told her. "You
must bind his wound, before he loses more blood.
Come, now, gather your wits for Bertie's sake."

The garden's gate groaned as it opened. The sound
of running footsteps echoed into the grassy square.
Anne's grandsire, hatless and without his usual chain
and coat, burst out onto this wee battlefield. Sir Amyas's dark eyes were afire, his face pulled into lines of
unholy rage. At his back was Sir William, with five of
the queen's guard behind him.

"There is the debaucher," Amyas roared as he
pointed to Kit. "Take him and cut out his heart!"

Chapter Thirty

Anne sat at the end of her bed and stared at the door. Everything had gone wrong. A helpless sound escaped her as the vision of Kit being borne away between two guardsmen again filled her. No one heeded her when she'd tried to say 'twasn't he who'd done wrong.

Nay, no one heard her. No one could. Anne tried again to swallow. Her throat was bruised below her ruff. As for speaking, the best she could do was croak.

Thanks to Mary's maid, she now wore her tawny brown gowns, and her neatened hair was confined beneath the black velvet headdress. All that needed doing was for the queen to call. If that didn't happen soon, Anne would surely die.

There was a tap, then Mary opened the door. Anne leapt to her feet. Her kinswoman tried to smile, but there was too much worry in her face for that. "She's called for all to come. Beware, Nan. She's fair beside herself over this."

Mary's warning only sent Anne's terror spiraling. If their royal mistress raged, there was no hope for her or Kit. Anne followed Mary across the maids' chamber. Once they'd descended the stairs, exiting the building so Mary could lead Anne to the royal chapel.

From the chapel they made their way from chamber to chamber until they reached the queen's apartment.

Anne stared at its door, behind which she had never been. "She sees us in private?"

Again, Mary tried to smile. "She does this for your protection. If there's no blame to be placed on you, she wants no stain left on your name."

Even as Anne tried to take hope from this, it died. 'Twasn't every day Sir William had the guard dragging a courtier into the palace walls. There'd be no stopping the tongues or the speculation.

Mary opened the door, standing aside to allow Anne to enter first. Tapestries covered every inch of the chamber's walls: their blues, reds, and golds brilliant. A great arched window looked out onto the river. Through it, Anne could see the water's surface gleaming in the setting sun, as bright as any diamond.

A desk was standing near that window, lighter of design than a man's and decorated with pretty woodwork. Papers were strewn across its surface, but its chair was missing, having been moved to the room's center, where England's monarch sat.

Elizabeth's face was rigid, her eyes narrowed. Anne glanced to the queen's hands. A touch of relief woke. The royal fingers were yet relaxed against the chair's arms. Wroth her royal mistress might be, but she was still prepared to listen. Aye, and then she'd spew what boiled in her.

Kit knelt close to the queen's chair, dressed in his green doublet with its gold spangles. Master James was nearby, again wearing his rust-colored attire. The skin along his swollen jaw was purple. Lord Deyville, again in mourning black, was on his knees to their far side. Anne's grandsire knelt still farther back, closer to the door. At Amyas's side stood Sir William.

Wondering if she should take hope from their arrangement in the room, Anne stepped within and dropped into a curtsy. So deep did she bend, her head bowed nearly into her skirts. Mary did the same alongside her.

"Bring in your kinswoman, Mistress Mary," the queen called, her voice hard and cold.

"Madame," Mary said, not yet raising her head, "she must kneel close to you. I fear she is without voice."

Anne heard the queen's sharp intake of breath at this. "Then, bring her near." There was no change to the royal tone.

Head bowed, Anne rose and strode across the room, choosing a spot where she might be within Kit's line of vision. This meant she could see the others as well, all save for her grandfather. As she knelt, her head again bent over folded hands, Mary went to stand behind her royal mistress's chair.

"We would hear from your lips who it was that did the attacking, Mistress Anne." This was a regal command.

" 'Twas Lord Deyville, Madame," Anne managed in her croak.

"God's eyelid," the queen said more softly. "Lift your head, lass, then open your collar so we may see it all."

Anne did as she was bid. When her ruff was removed and her collar open, anger blazed in Elizabeth's dark eyes. "You say Lord Deyville did this to you? A nod is good enough."

Anne nodded.

Confusion flickered through Elizabeth's gaze. "If he is the attacker, then what explanation have you for the note Sir Amyas bears?"

"What note?" Anne asked, startled.

The queen lifted a scrap of paper from her lap and read aloud. " 'Greetings to you, my good and kind employer. You must come this afternoon at three of the clock. I fear Mistress Anne is set on a private meeting with the one you so despise, the appointment to be at Duke Humphrey's tower above Greenwich.' " Elizabeth peered at her maid from over the note's top. " 'Tis unsigned, however we can but assume from its contents this was written by your governess."

If Anne hadn't just learned how much it hurt, she'd have throttled Patience for this. Why couldn't the stupid chit let well enough alone? Patience's determination to protect Sir Amyas from Lord Deyville had only made more problems for them all.

"Madame," Anne brought out in her croak, "might I let Master Hollier speak for me? He knows the whole of it."

This request pleased the queen naught at all. Her nostrils flared, but she nodded. "Tell your tale, Master Hollier," she commanded.

Kit didn't raise his head as he spoke. "The note, Madame, was but an attempt on Mistress Watkins' part to protect her mistress. She knew Sir Amyas had settled on Lord Deyville as Mistress Blanchemain's husband. As such, she believed Sir Amyas deaf to any complaint against the nobleman. Thus she formed her note in such a way that her employer would be certain to come and witness with his own eyes that Lord Deyville is not a decent man."

Lord Deyville shifted and glared at Kit. "I'll not stay still and listen to these insults," he snarled, trading on his rank to look boldly upon his queen.

"You'll stay where we command you," Elizabeth snapped, then her gaze shifted between Anne and Kit.

"God's teeth, but we find it galling that this mere servant dares to decide to whom her employer may or may not marry his heiress."

Anne raised her head. "Madame," she said, straining to make her words clear, "you must understand that Mistress Watkins had witnessed the nobleman's first attack against me at the maying."

Elizabeth rocked back in her chair, surprise chasing all else from her expression. "He did what!"

"He did what?" Sir Amyas echoed from the back of the room.

Anne glanced over her shoulder to her grandsire. He almost sounded concerned. Perhaps she had wronged him in thinking he intended to allow Lord Deyville free rein over her.

Leaning forward, her elbow braced upon the chair's arm, Elizabeth's eyes narrowed in suspicion once again. "If this is true, mistress, why did you say nothing to us of it?"

" 'Twas but my third day at court, Madame," Anne said, offering her queen a helpless look as she stopped to clear her throat. "I feared Your Grace might send me away for the shame of it, or worse that I'd not be believed. Lord Deyville is a man placed high above me and can say what he will, while I am but a maid with no defense to offer, save my word."

" 'Tis none of your shame when another assaults you," her royal mistress declared.

"No harm was done, Madame," Kit continued on her behalf, "for by coincidence, Your Grace sent me to find Mistress Blanchemain at that same instant, wishing her returned to your presence. When confronted, Lord Deyville retreated. If I did wrong when I bowed to Mistress Blanchemain's request to remain silent on what I'd seen, I humbly beg pardon."

"Hold your pleas for mercy until all is said and done," Elizabeth retorted stiffly. "This does not fully explain the note. Why should this servant know the exact hour of the attack?"

"Madame," Anne tried again, "only last night Lord Deyville again made his threat of rape against me. 'Twas his intent—" Her voice would go no further. She stopped and looked in frustration at Kit.

He was waiting for her signal. If he dared give no other sign to her, his green eyes were soft with his affection. Once again, he took up where she'd stopped.

" 'Twas his intent to spoil Mistress Blanchemain for all other men, thus forcing Your Grace's hand in his petition for her hand in marriage. To that charge, Madame, both I and Master Wyatt can testify, for we heard him utter it again at the tower."

"He said that?" Amyas's sharp cry rang against the dark beams that crossed the chamber's ceiling. Anne turned her head to look at her grandsire. He was glaring at the nobleman.

"Not now, Amyas," Sir William hissed in warning.

'Twas useless. Amyas leaned forward on his knees in accusation, his gaze locked on the man he'd meant for his granddaughter to wed. "You'd have used her, with no guarantee that you could wed her? What if our contract didn't stand? You'd have left me with a spoiled maid as an heir, that's what."

Lord Deyville raised his head and sent icy rage in Amyas's direction. "You'll not speak so to me, not when 'twas your idiocy that left us with no other option."

"Be still!" Elizabeth's command rattled the panes in the window. Both men bowed their heads and held their tongues. "Why," her voice was yet raised near a shout, "should the governess know the exact hour of the attack?"

Anne cringed, her head lowering once more. She sent a sidelong glance at Kit. He offered a brief and crooked grin. From this point on, explanations became a mite more difficult.

"Madame," Kit said, "given the nobleman's previous attack, his new threat left Mistress Blanchemain fearful of being surprised whilst alone and unprotected. Thus, we arranged the meeting, thinking to expose him."

Elizabeth's gaze shifted to her maid. "Prove to us you are as intelligent as we believe you to be by saying you sent no note to Lord Deyville to lure him to this trap of yours."

"I sent no note," Anne replied without lifting her head, her voice as strong as possible. "I have no idea how Lord Deyville knew of my location." That was true. She knew Lady Montmercy had carried the message, but not how the lady had come into possession of that knowledge.

"Thus we move our attention to you, my lord." There was a new sneer in the royal voice. "As our maid-of-honor says you had no note from her, how is it you knew she was to be at the tower at the appointed time?"

Anne again glanced at Kit. Excitement filled his gaze. 'Twas the queen herself who would draw out the accusation against Lady Montmercy.

"Madame," the lord raised his head, his brow creased in anger. The sun had set far enough to turn his bald pate a ruddy hue. "I again protest this whole inquisition. None of my accusers are fit rank to bring a charge against me."

Elizabeth's chin lifted as her brows rose. "It was

our maid, a young woman under our protection, upon whom you left your bruises. The charge you face comes from this chair"—her index finger drilled into the chair's arm—"and nowhere else."

The nobleman gave an angry toss of his head as his lip curled in scorn. "I'd have left no bruises if Your Grace's maid had been as forthcoming with her favors to me as she has been to Master Hollier. I say she got no more than she deserved for toying with me," Deyville snarled, throwing his own accusation.

Once again, Amyas's cry rang out, but 'twas Elizabeth Anne faced. Fiery anger filled the queen's dark eyes. "Have you given up your maidenhood to Master Hollier as Lord Deyville accuses." This was no question.

Fear tore through Anne. Which would it be? Lie to her queen, or speak the truth and earn naught but ruin for it?

Of a sudden, Deyville's earlier words echoed in her head. She straightened on her knees and looked boldly into her monarch's face. "Madame, I vow to you upon my mother's life, whose existence I hold most dear, that I am the same woman now as I was the day Your Grace accepted me into your service." The words filled the air around her, ringing with the truth, because they were.

"As for Master Hollier"—Anne again bowed her head against the possibility her royal mistress might read something she shouldn't in her gaze—"he's been naught but honorable in his behavior toward me. Not once has he forced a touch upon me or made any sly suggestion." She coughed as she fell silent, daring to peer up from her meek pose at her monarch.

Elizabeth's face was more relaxed as her gaze returned to the offending nobleman. "It appears you are mistaken about our maid's morals, my lord. Now, how is it you knew where to meet Mistress Blanchemain?"

Lord Deyville's spine was stiff. Outrage marked his expression at being thwarted in his attempt to turn accusation away from him. There was a long moment of silence.

"Speak, my lord." 'Twas a whip crack of command.

" 'Twas Lady Montmercy who informed me of the maid's destination and when to meet her there."

Amyas's gasp was deep and pained. Anne looked at her grandsire. His face was wan as he sagged back to sit on his heels, his lips moving as if in prayer.

"Why is it we are not surprised to hear her name mentioned?" Elizabeth said, glancing from Anne to Kit. 'Twas the memory of the events surrounding the naming of Anne's dancing tutor that flashed through her eyes. Her sharpened interest showed as she eyed Kit.

"Sir William," the queen called to her secretary without looking up from her gentleman, "put your head outside the door and tell our page to bring the lady here. I think we must needs ask her a question or two."

Chapter Thirty-one

Anne's knees grew numb as they waited. Elizabeth drummed her fingers against her chair's arm, the tempo increasing as her impatience grew. Anne dared but once to glance at Kit. He tried to smile, but worry marred the attempt. As the sun settled into its bed for the night, Mary set to lighting the many candles in their sconces and their branches.

At last the door opened. No sign of worry touched Lady Montmercy's face as she stepped within and closed the door behind her. She glanced at the room's occupants. Candlelight played against the jewels in her small cap and gleamed in her fair hair. Her ruff glowed like snow against skin only a little less pale. When she was but a step into the room, she drifted down into a deep curtsy, her silken skirts flowing around her, her sapphire earbobs glinting.

"Madame, you called for me?" the lady said, her head yet bent.

"Aye, my lady," her monarch responded, her words chipped from ice. "We would know why it was you sent Lord Deyville to attack our maid."

Anne eased to the side to better see the noblewoman. A wee frown touched the lady's perfect brow as she shifted into a kneeling position. "Madame, I did no such thing." The woman played her role to perfection. Rather than outrage, which might have been suspect, 'twas confusion that filled every word.

Across from Anne, Kit loosed a bitter breath. Sour amusement twisted in her. Had he truly believed Lady Montmercy would walk into the room and admit all? She watched as he undid the middle buttons of his green doublet, then pulled a small packet from its resting place against his shirt. At his sign, Mary came to take the fold of paper from him.

"Majesty," he said, as she carried it to the queen and placed it in her hands for him, "perhaps, this will help to clarify matters."

The queen turned the packet in her hands, touching the wax that sealed it. "Whose signets are these?"

"Madame, they are mine and Lady Montmercy's," Kit replied.

Only then did Anne understand this must be Kit's contract. Even as fear for him filled her, she glanced at Lady Montmercy. The noblewoman maintained her humble pose, head bent and eyes focused on her clasped hands.

"That cannot be, Madame," the lady said without raising her head, a touch of sharpness to her tone. "I've never had occasion to use my signet when Master Hollier was present."

"Is that so?" the queen replied. The faint line of her red brows rose. "Shall we look upon what it is you haven't set your signet to?"

As she opened the paper, Mary stepped close with a branch of candles. The queen scanned the contract, then her breath hissed from her. She threw the paper from her.

"What is this foul thing!" The words dripped like venom from her lips. She glared at Kit.

He kept his neck bent. "Madame, there is no way to explain myself, save to say I was a desperate man, hounded by my creditors. My only defense is that after I signed that sheet, I discovered myself incapable of doing what it was the lady required of me. To this end Mistress Blanchemain has already attested. Nor would she release me from this, threatening vengeance if I did not comply."

"This is so, Madame," Master James seconded. "When I tried to repay the sum she expended on Master Hollier's behalf, she refused my coin."

The queen's gaze shifted to Lady Montmercy. "What have you to say of this?"

"Madame," the woman said meekly, her head yet primly lowered, "I know nothing of what lies upon that paper. Ask anyone. I am barely acquainted with Master Hollier. I cannot imagine why the gentleman should go to such efforts to impugn me."

"So 'tis forgery you'd charge, is it?" Elizabeth's expression stiffened. "You'd vow you never asked Master Hollier to take Mistress Blanchemain's maidenhead in trade for the payment of his debts and the marriage of your daughter to Squire Nicholas Hollier?"

Master James made an odd gagging sound at this, and wobbled on his knees. From the back of the room, Anne's grandfather's voice rose to a keening cry. 'Twas so terrible a sound that she turned to look, fearing the same fit of madness that had taken him after her presentation. Moaning, he buried his face into his hands and rocked on his knees.

Sir William crouched down beside the old man. "Amyas, what is it?" he said, catching the old man by the wrists to still his movement.

Amyas drew a shuddering breath and let his hands

fall. Against her will, Anne's heart filled with concern for him. Pain etched deeply into his face. His gaze was fixed on Lady Montmercy. The lady didn't look up from studying her twined fingers.

"So does God strike another blow against me," Amyas said with a shuddering breath. "She is a temptress, a Jezebel." This was more aching cry than accusation. "She drew me into sin. In retribution, our Heavenly Father has done to me as he did to Job, stripping me of all I held precious and more."

Anne's brows rose. Did he count the deaths of her sisters and her cousins as his payment, or was it only the loss of his manhood he bemoaned? She shot a glance at Kit. He met her gaze with astonishment at her grandshire's blatant loss of control.

Elizabeth's brows drew down, and her mouth tightened until 'twas but a narrow line. "God's teeth, what's he babbling about, Sir William," she demanded.

"I know naught, Your Grace," her secretary said with a shrug as he returned to his feet.

Anne cleared her throat. "Madame," she said, forcing the words from her throat, "I do. My grandsire and Lady Montmercy were intimate many years ago. I suspect he promised marriage to her upon her widowhood," she said, editing Mistress Alice's tale to protect Andrew. "When the lady became available, he rejected her. Thus her plot. She seeks to wreak her vengeance on my grandfather through me."

Lady Montmercy gave a single, sharp cry as she raised her head. Panic replaced her blankness. She pressed a fist to her chest. "You cannot know this," the noblewoman cried, eyes wide in disbelief.

"Indeed, I can," Anne said. Despite the wrong the lady meant to do her and Kit, pity woke. There was no victory in revealing that the only one this lady yet

trusted had betrayed her in order to foil the very vengeance she sought. "My lady, you've forgotten that
Mistress Godwin was my mother's governess before
she came into your employ."

"Nay," the noblewoman whispered as horror shot
through her blue gaze. Even as she understood she
was revealed, her shoulders tensed in resistance. "This
is but another lie." What should have been a protest
of outraged innocence was a shaken breath.

Elizabeth slammed her fist against her chair's arm.
"Will you say again, my lady, that you didn't tell Lord
Deyville where to make his attack against our maid?
By what means did you ferret out that information?"

Lady Montmercy shivered as if suffering the ague.
"Madame, I said nothing to Lord Deyville, nor do I
have any means by which I would know where and
when Mistress Anne might be."

"Lying bitch," the nobleman shouted at her, loud
enough to make her flinch. "Tell Her Grace the truth!
'Twas you who overheard me speaking with the maid
in the Presence Chamber, or so you said when you
came this morn, offering the very opportunity I
wanted."

"Nay," the lady cried out, control slipping from her
grasp with this assault.

"Your Grace," Kit said, addressing the queen even
as he kept his gaze on the noblewoman, " 'twas because I refused to comply with the terms of her contract that Lady Montmercy sought out Lord Deyville
to serve her foul purpose."

Lady Montmercy pressed her fists against her tem-
ples and squeezed her eyes shut as she sought to escape her accusers. "I know nothing of this, Madame."
Her voice shook like a leaf in a storm.

Elizabeth stood, every line of her body afire with

outrage. "How dare you persist in your lies, when it seems 'tis only you who could have done this? Sir William, we'll have her Tower-bound for planning the assault of one of our maids."

A strangled sound left Lady Montmercy. She threw back her head. Her lips were drawn back into a vicious snarl, her pale cheeks blazing. Leaping to her feet, she turned on Sir Amyas.

"I loved you," she shrieked, throwing herself across the space between them. Her fists fell. Even as Amyas cried out, he made no attempt to shield himself from her blows.

Sir William caught her from behind, holding her by the arms. "My lady, you must not," he commanded her.

The noblewoman only leaned forward against his grip to put her face near Amyas's. "I bore your son! How could you return and call me Delilah? You said what I felt for you was sin, and I must wipe you from my heart as you had removed me from yours." As the last word dropped from her lips, she sagged against Sir William's grasp, sobbing.

Anne's heart broke for Andrew. She dared a glance at her royal mistress. 'Twas disappointment, not surprise that filled Elizabeth's eyes. This could only mean the queen had suspected Andrew's bastardy, but hadn't wanted to acknowledge it. Now her hand would be forced by what the lad's mother revealed.

"Take her from our presence," Elizabeth commanded her secretary, her gaze shifting to the nobleman who'd been the lady's accomplice. "Attempted rape of one of our maids is a serious matter. Lord Deyville, we command you on your honor to present yourself to the Tower, content to wait there for our decision as to your punishment. Leave us, and do no more harm to those around whom we have set our hand."

Even as Deyville's face twisted in rage, he yielded to his monarch's command. "I am at your mercy, Your Grace." Rising, he backed from his queen's presence, until he could throw open the door and storm from the room.

Sir William turned. Sobbing, Lady Montmercy lay limp against him as he bore her from the chamber. Mary followed to shut the door after them. When she'd closed it, she set her back against it and faced the room.

Amyas's panting breaths echoed against the walls as he sat upon the floor. His legs were sprawled out before him. His head hung, his hands lay, open and upturned, in his lap. His shoulders shook.

It didn't matter that her compassion might never be returned; Anne couldn't bear his pain. "Madame," she said to her royal mistress, "might I go to my grandsire?"

'Twas the promise of the coming storm that darkened Elizabeth's face. "Aye. See if you can settle his senses. We must speak with him as regards his son."

Taking care to step backward until she reached her grandsire, Anne dropped to kneel beside him. Since her touch had once before stirred him from a similar state, she lay her hand upon his shoulder. "Grandfather, you must gather your wits."

He raised his head. His gaze was unfocused, his tears laid their tracks upon his stony cheeks. As Anne stroked her hand down his arm, a sigh escaped him. His gaze slowly centered on her.

"She set Lord Deyville to use you," he muttered, "and I in my arrogance would never have seen the evil he intended."

'Twas more apology than Anne ever expected from him. She offered a small smile. "Aye, but she did not succeed. You must give your thanks to Master Hollier, who not only refused her evil, but stopped Lord Deyville from doing his," she said, hoping the queen could hear her. It wouldn't hurt to remind her royal mistress that Kit had contemplated wrongdoing, but done no wrong.

"Now, give your attention to our queen's grace. She must speak with you about Lord Andrew Montmercy."

The mention of Andrew's name sent pain flowing through her grandfather's gaze. 'Twas proof he knew Andrew was his son. Anne bit at her lip in fear for the lad, wishing there were aught she could do to stop his destruction.

Amyas watched her, as if seeking to decipher her reaction. Anne caught her breath. He wasn't going to claim Andrew. Since he'd lost the title he so craved for his legitimate line, he meant to see his illegitimate line kept its peerage. A certain stiffness followed, as if Amyas expected her protest.

Anne let the corners of her lips lift in approval. Surprise started in his gaze, then his face softened. Lifting his hand, he touched his fingers to her cheek as if in thanks. Her smile grew. 'Twas his acceptance he offered her, just as she'd given him hers. They weren't much, these last two Blanchemains, but they were all each other had.

Drawing a deep breath, Amyas struggled to right himself on his knees. Anne caught his arm to aid him. "Majesty," he said, his head bent and his voice yet thready with pain.

"Sir Amyas, is Andrew Montmercy your son?" Harsh and uncompromising, Elizabeth's words rang in the room.

Amyas drew a shuddering breath. "Majesty, he is not."

"You can say so after the lady's claims and her hysteria?" There was frigid skepticism in his queen's voice.

Raising his head, Amyas stared boldly at England's monarch. "Madame, I admit the lady and I did sin, but our affair ended before she came with child. If it is proof you would have from me, then I can offer it. I cannot be the boy's sire; I am impotent. 'Twas this that God demanded of me in retribution for my adultery with the noblewoman."

Overcome by the shame of his admission, his eyes rolled up into their sockets. Even as Anne was grabbing for him, he toppled back onto the floor.

Kit stared in shock as Amyas sprawled, senseless, upon the floor. By God, the man had opened himself up to the worst of shame to save his son's title. Forgetting the right and wrong of what was done, Kit couldn't help feeling new respect for him.

Anne looked up from his prone form. "Have no fear, Madame," she called out, "he is but fainted." Her royal mistress was no lover of illness or death near her person.

With that assurance Elizabeth turned her attention to Kit. New color touched her cheeks, her eyes blazed. There was nothing left of her lips, so taut was her mouth. She set her hands on her hips.

"God's eyelid, but you are a miserable piece of misbegotten manhood!" she shouted at him.

"Aye, Madame," Kit agreed. Satisfied now that he'd achieved Anne's safety, he readied himself to take the full brunt of his monarch's rage. She didn't disappoint.

"We are *appalled*! To even consider so foul a plan besmirches your honor and your estate. We should have you drawn and quartered. All that saves you is our maid's testimony that she is yet untouched." Her words thundered in the room.

Kit flinched at the thought of such a death. "I am at your mercy, Madame," he said.

"That's God's own truth," she raged, moving to her desk. "Both you and your godforsaken brother had best acknowledge 'tis our mercy you beg for and our mercy you do not deserve for your plots and plans!"

Grabbing a handful of paper, she thrust it toward the branch of candles that stood upon the desktop. Beside him, Jamie made a choking sound. Kit's eyes widened. Nick's contracts! May God damn him, but he'd destroyed Nick's hope of regaining his title!

Just as one edge began to brown, England's queen gave a muted shriek and snatched the papers away from the flame. Tossing them toward the room's corner, she whirled and stormed to the window. Fists clenched, she stared out into the darkness, her back to the room.

"Take your sorry hide out of our presence," she commanded. "July's end! If you fail us on that day, so help us, we'll do with those contracts as we threatened! Out! Be gone with all of you!"

July's end?! Kit stared at her back in astonishment, then wrenched around on his knees to look at Anne. Her eyes were round with the same surprise.

From the door Mary motioned frantically. He needed no second hint. Grabbing Jamie's arm, he yanked his brother's steward to his feet. Even though her back was turned, they made their bows to their queen, then backed swiftly to where Amyas lay. Lifting the old man between them, they followed Anne and Mary from the room. There was no one in the

Privy Chamber, save for the maids and ladies who waited on their mistress's call.

As Mary closed the door behind them, she sighed as if in relief. Kit looked at Anne. Now that her surprise had ebbed, her gaze was filled with sadness. Kit's heart joined hers in despair. If there had ever been any hope for a union between them, 'twas dead now.

Aye, and if they didn't win that wager for the queen, Nick's hopes for his title's return would be just as dead. Despair worked its way into shame. He'd never even had a chance to offer his brother's compliments to the queen.

"May the devil take your soul to hell and keep it there for all time," Jamie hissed, glaring at Kit from over Amyas's yet limp form. "What sort of worm-eating bitch's son tries to force marriage onto the one to whom he owes his obedience? By God, if she'd burned those contracts of his, I'd have seen you dead for it!"

His words pricked into what was rapidly becoming a festering wound in Kit. "I am your better. I'll take no criticism from you."

"Be still, both of you," Mary cried, shoving at Kit as she urged them both across the Privy Chamber's width toward the Presence Chamber door. "You've no idea how fortunate you are! Aye, she's raging, but as angry as she is, she knows you've given her far more than you've hurt her. She's sent you out of her presence to prevent herself from doing aught that she'd regret."

As they reached the exit from the Privy Chamber, Mary caught Anne's arm. "Hear me now," she said lowering her voice as she glanced between Kit and Anne, "whatever else, do not lose that wager for her. If you do, she'll remember every bit of what you've done wrong and none of the right."

Chapter Thirty-two

Richmond Palace was a sweet place. Its huge orchard, placed between the palace and the Thames, was just now coming into fruit as July became August. So, too, were its acres of gardens, caught within its curtain walls, yielding up their bounty. The meals emanating from its eighteen kitchens were flavorful, indeed.

Just as important, at least to Elizabeth's courtiers, Richmond's three courts offered decent lodgings. Kit and Master James were sharing a spacious set of chambers built into the brick walls surrounding the wardrobe court. Kit was borrowing the use of Master James's manservant while Patience nursed Bertie back to health in Kit's London town house. As for Anne, she'd hired a new maid, and they stayed nearer to the queen, in the inner, Privy court. Their rooms consisted of a forechamber for this lass, and an inner good sized bedchamber for Anne. Not that it mattered.

Standing in the gallery's bay window, Anne stared down into the privy gardens and willed her life to end. Nothing mattered, not when there wasn't the slightest possibility that today would bring happiness to anyone, save the queen. Tonight Anne would win Elizabeth's wager for her.

The last two weeks of dancing practice with Kit had

been sheer torment, touching him, all-the-while knowing he could never be hers. Still, for his sake, she put
her heart and soul into those lessons. If there was
nothing else she could give him, Anne meant to see he
won approval for those contracts Elizabeth had nearly
burned. Her concentration had been profitable; she
was now as competent a dancer as anyone at court.

"I was wondering where you were," Kit said from
behind her.

Anne drew a sad breath and turned. He looked fine,
indeed. Another two weeks of summer had left his
skin even more sun darkened, which only enhanced
the green of his eyes. Ah, but 'twasn't their color that
thrilled her. As always, his love for her filled his gaze.

Reaching out, she lay her hand against his chest to
finger one of the golden spangles that decorated the
front of his green doublet. By agreement, they'd tried
to match their attire. Thus, she wore her golden presentation attire, pairing it with brown sleeves and
overskirt, then borrowing a small brown cap decorated
with golden beads from Mary. This complimented his
brown breeches and the golden garters at his knees.

"I couldn't bear to watch the others dance, knowing
what awaits us," she said, trying to smile.

His face softened against a pain they shared. "Dare
I say I know what you feel?"

Anne wanted to cry out against the unfairness of it,
but she had no chance as Mary thrust her head from
the Presence Chamber door. "Hie you two," she
called. " 'Tis time."

"Come," Kit said, extending his arm in invitation.
As Anne caught her hand into the bend of his elbow,
he pulled his arm close to his side, so she walked as
near to him as possible.

"Are you nervous?" he asked, sending her a side-long glance as they matched their strides.

"How can I be, when you are to be my partner?" she replied, letting her need to win him the queen's forgiveness overwhelm all else. "I daresay we shall astound them."

He offered her that smile of his, the slow movement of his mouth sending a shiver down her spine. "You will, at least."

Together, they entered the Presence Chamber. Like many of the other royal chambers at Richmond, not an inch of the wall showed, so thickly was it hung with tapestries. The ceiling was plastered, the white lime wearing a clever pattern on its surface. Tall bay windows let the late afternoon light into the chamber, teasing brilliance from the jewels and silks worn by the courtiers.

Near one window stood Master James, the gentleman again wearing his russet attire. As he met Anne's gaze, he offered her an encouraging smile. And so he should, since the resolution of his master's business hung upon her footwork.

Elizabeth sat in a fine chair beneath a golden cloth of state. Today, the queen wore blue, the color displaying her pale complexion and fiery hair to perfection. A great diamond broach caught two thick ropes of pearls to one side of her bodice. She waved her maid toward her.

"Here is Mistress Anne," England's monarch called out, her voice overly loud and owning a brittle edge.

So it had these past two weeks and not because of what Lord Deyville and Lady Montmercy had done. Nay, 'twas a reflection of the tension that filled those around her. It seemed everyone now knew of Norfolk's plans, save Elizabeth, who was left to react helplessly to what she sensed. Anne couldn't rid herself of how wrong it was that no one, not even her spies, would tell England's monarch the truth about her noblest subject.

"Look, my lord," the queen called to the Earl of Leicester, who stood only a few feet from her. Her dearest wore again his scarlet attire. " 'Tis Mistress Anne, come to show us what she's learned thus far in her lessons."

"Have a care with your toes, Master Hollier," the earl called out in a good-natured tease. " 'Twas days before I could don my shoe."

Anne's cheeks burned against this, but she had no time to think on it. The musicians started into a pavane, having been warned ahead of time to begin with the slowest, working their way into the La Volta. Kit claimed her hand, and she took her place beside him at the head of the chamber. 'Twas to be just the two of them dancing before all the court.

They flowed into the movements of this stately dance. As they worked their way up and back the room's length, Anne glanced across the courtiers—and started. Amyas, who'd sworn to have no more to do with court, stood near the door. He wore black, as if in mourning. His face was drawn, his skin sallow as if his former lover's plot had sapped him of all vigor.

The pavane was ending. Anne tore her gaze from her grandsire and concentrated on the next dance, an almain. Letting her senses fill with Kit's nearness, she cherished his every touch as the movement of his body beside hers teased her senses. She barely noted when this tune ended and the next began.

They moved smoothly through her repertoire, but it wasn't until they were hard at the fast-paced galliard that she realized they'd become the center of attention. A wide circle had formed around them as everyone watched.

She glanced at the queen. Elizabeth was beaming, her face alive with pleasure. Anne's spirits soared. Kit was saved!

Giving way to the pressure of her joy, she threw back her head and laughed, then put all her heart into the steps. She even dared to lift her skirts, just a little, so all could see just how well she performed her kicks.

Kit grinned. 'Twas a challenge he threw her by nodding at the musicians to step up the tempo. Smiling at him, she kept it.

They started into the La Volta. Anne loosed a wild and happy cry as both Kit and the music swept her up. The crowd clapped, calling "La Volta," the signal for Kit to lift her. Each time he did, she held herself above him and looked into his face, letting her expression tell him just how much she loved him. Her desire for him spiraled, until the heat between them had naught to do with dancing.

At last the music stopped. 'Twas in triumph that Kit turned once more with her in his arms, then set her feet onto the floor. Laughing and gasping, Anne reached out to catch his hand in hers. Together they faced their monarch. As he offered his finest bow, Anne dropped into a deep curtsy.

Applause thundered across the room. Elizabeth came to her feet, shouting her approval. "I knew she would be a quick student," she crowed to her earl.

"Aye, and I think I've been hoodwinked," Lord Robert pretended to complain. Wise man that he was, he knew 'twas always best that the queen won her wagers.

Kit's hand tightened on Anne's as he looked upon victory. Nick's contracts were safe. Never had he loved

his Nan more. His heart broke. From now on she'd
no longer be his.

"Come forward, Master Hollier and Mistress
Blanchemain," the queen called, yet clapping against
her admiration for their feat. He led Anne forward,
then knelt with her before their royal mistress. Once
they were in place the queen again scanned the
audience.

"Come you as well Master Wyatt. 'Tis your contracts we'd discuss now."

Jamie knelt beside Anne and Elizabeth sat. Her
movements were easy and relaxed as winning her
wager lifted her out of what plagued her, at least for
the moment.

"Master Hollier," she said to him, "are you aware
that your brother has requested the restoration of
your family's title?"

"Aye, Madame, I am," Kit replied, still breathless
from exertion. "The squire spoke of it whilst I was at
Graceton gathering the information Your Grace sent
me to acquire. I regret circumstances haven't allowed
me to convey to Your Grace the message my brother
sends you. He would have you know he wishes for
ten more years just like the last ten you have given
him, complimenting your kingship and saying no other
prince in all the world is your equal in supplying the
peace in which an honest man might prosper. You
own his loyalty, for he'd have no other upon England's
throne." He peered up at her when he was done.

Elizabeth basked in the words, pleasure begetting
more pleasure. "He is an interesting man, this reclusive brother of yours. Having said that, we think you
do not know the whole of what the squire requests in
his title's restoration. Although he accepts the lordship
as he must by the conditions of your father's will, he

doesn't intend to keep it. Instead he relinquishes the title and all the duties of his lordship to you. The property he will hold until his death."

"Nay!" Kit reared back on his knees in surprise. "He said I would but be his proxy!"

Even as he resisted, the logic of it filled him. Why muddle the business of the title, when Nick had no intention of marrying and siring his own children? It eased Kit's heart some to know Nick intended to keep Graceton, as was his right. Aye, but he couldn't bear to accept this without protest. He'd not have anyone think he was eager to take what belonged to his brother.

"Madame, I must accept, because I know 'tis what my brother wills for me, but I do so under protest. I would rather that the title passed to heirs of the squire's body."

"We expected no less from you," Elizabeth said in approval. "After much thought, 'twas this intent we finally discovered in that paper of yours." There was new softness in her voice.

She turned her gaze on Jamie. "As for you, Master Wyatt, we would have the squire know 'twould have been far easier if he and Master Hollier had resolved their differences without involving us. Their maneuvering nearly resulted in an innocent woman's destruction."

Kit frowned at this, glancing from his queen to his brother's servant. Jamie kept his gaze focused on the silk embroidery that decorated the queen's hems. "I can but agree, Madame," the steward said. "Master Hollier had no right to try and force his elder brother's marriage through such underhanded means."

"Indeed, he did not," England's monarch agreed.

"But the squire was no more right to resist our royal command that he resume his title."

"Nick resisted his title's restoration?" These startled words leapt from Kit's lips.

The queen's attention swung in his direction. "Aye, Master Hollier. He only now requests it because he wishes to coerce us into accepting his contract for your marriage."

"My what?!" Rage raced through Kit, but the wave of Elizabeth's hand silenced him.

"Master Wyatt," she said to Jamie, "we have decided to approve the squire's requests on one condition: he must wed and attempt to breed his own heirs. In this Master Hollier is right. The squire owes it to his father to see the title continues in his line. If he fails at siring children after two years time, he may cede the title to Master Hollier. Until then Master Hollier will be his proxy in all matters to do with his lordship."

"Madame," Jamie cried in protest, "Squire Hollier is not fit for marriage. There's no woman who'll have him."

"Odd," the queen said, her voice growing stronger by the word, "it seems to us that both Lady Montmercy and Master Hollier believed that Lady Arabella Purfoy would have him. We intend to ask that same lady if she is amenable to such a marriage. We feel she will agree as the match is an advance for her."

Kit sagged. He doubted if Lady Arabella would be given the opportunity to refuse. Nay, she'd have to agree, thinking to either win royal favor by separating herself from her mother, or to try and win some mercy for her dam, who now sat in a Tower chamber.

With that, the image of Cecily pressing her lips without hesitation to his brother's scarred cheek, her smile filled with love for Nick, filled him. Christ! This was no victory, but punishment worse than being drawn and quartered. Not only had he lost Anne, but he'd just forced Nick into marriage, which might well cost him his love.

"Madame," Jamie tried again.

"If he wants his contracts approved, he must agree," the queen said again, her tone final.

Kit looked up, his heart dead in his chest. The queen signaled to her usher. Stepping forward, the man called out, "Sir Amyas Blanchemain."

Beside Kit, Anne started in surprise. It was a moment before Amyas made his way to his queen's throne. Kit frowned. Lady Montmercy's revenge had been effective even without being complete. The old man was nearly shuffling, his head hanging.

Sir Amyas knelt a short distance from Jamie. "Madame, I am here."

"Sir Amyas, we have received a contract for your granddaughter's hand in marriage."

"How can that be?" the old man asked, his voice lacking both its arrogance and its power. "I submitted but one contract, and Your Grace saw fit not to consider it."

"This offer was made by Squire Nicholas Hollier to Lady Frances Blanchemain for the marriage of his heir, Master Christopher Hollier to her daughter, Mistress Anne Blanchemain," the queen said, her voice flat, but not cold.

Kit's senses spun. Beside him, Anne made a tiny sound, that might have been a squeak of joy.

"In this offer," Elizabeth was saying, "Lady Frances suggests you have another heir upon whom to gift your wealth, making Mistress Anne Lady Frances's sole heir. If this is so, then she would indeed have the

right to wed her daughter where she wills. We find
ourselves wondering over this other heir of yours. If
you have none, say so and we will refuse this contract
on your behalf."

Kit tensed. Anne looked up, her eyes alive with
panic and despair. 'Twas another trap to force Amyas
into naming Andrew his bastard. To protect Andrew,
Amyas would refuse. Aye, and as Amyas did what he
must, all chance of marriage between Kit and Nan
ended.

The old man shifted on his knees, then lifted his
head to look at Kit. Gone was the hatred, leaving only
peace in his dark gaze. Once again, he bowed his head.

"Madame, I say again I have no other heir than
Mistress Anne." The words left him on a sigh.

"Then, shall we refuse the squire's offer?"

Amyas shook his head. "Madame, Sir William as-
sures me Master Hollier is no papist. So, too, was it
Master Hollier who saved my granddaughter from
shame and ruin. A man would have to be mad to
refuse such a husband and a title for his only heir.
The contract may stand."

Anne thought for certain she'd died as she heard
her grandfather say these words. She lifted her head
to stare in astonishment on her royal mistress. 'Twas
amusement and pleasure that filled Elizabeth's dark
eyes.

"Do you object to this match, mistress?" the
queen asked.

"Nay," Anne gasped. "I find it satisfactory."

Her royal mistress made a moue of disappointment.
"We do not. We have discovered in you an interesting
maid and don't much like losing you so swiftly. Vow
to us that you'll remain to serve us until your marriage, then return after, as our lady-in-waiting."

A smile crept across Anne's face. This was favor, indeed. Aye, and 'twas more than possible. Her term of duty lasted but four months, meaning they could dwell at Owls House for eight months of the year. Then, while she served the queen, her mother could take up residence in Kit's London house, with Mistress Godwin to bear her company.

"Madame, I would be honored to do so," she replied. "Your Grace and this court has so dazzled my senses, I fear I can never again be content with simple country life."

This compliment put even more warmth in Elizabeth's smile. "As your mother is an invalid, we will make ourselves available to aid in the planning of your wedding."

The affection Elizabeth showed her in this made guilt leap in Anne's heart. She didn't deserve the honor, not when she knew the duke of Norfolk schemed behind Elizabeth's back, but was too great a coward to share that information. The need to tell her queen what she knew overwhelmed Anne.

"You are kind beyond my deserving, Madame," she said. "Against such generosity, I feel I must speak to you of something that has been troubling me." As she paused, waiting for permission, Kit shot her a worried look.

The queen's brows rose in sharp surprise. "Speak, if you must."

"Madame," Anne said, raising her head to look upon her monarch, "it has come to my ears that the duke of Norfolk has given the Scots queen a diamond against his pledge of marriage. I feel 'tis only right that you should be told."

A gasp rolled over the courtiers. All color drained

from Elizabeth's face. Her eyes widened, then her mouth twisted in something between rage and terror.

"He's done what?!" Elizabeth shrieked and leapt to her feet. Grabbing the cushion from her chair, she threw it into the room. The chair toppled behind her.

Courtiers scrambled. The earl of Leicester was backing from the room. Anne cringed.

Elizabeth turned to look upon the higher of those who served her. Tears filled her eyes, while fury colored her cheeks bright red. Her hand was at her jeweled belt, as if seeking a sword. When she found no weapon, she tore the belt from her waist, and threw it at the window. It clattered against the thick glass, then snaked to the ground.

"Cowards!" she shouted at her courtiers. "How long have you known? Yet none but this maid has the courage to tell me! By God, I'll separate all your heads from your necks for this," she roared.

Amyas touched Anne on the arm. "Come, lass, 'twould be wise for you and your new husband to leave."

Anne looked at Kit. He watched her, both awed and stunned by what she'd done. Then, the corner of his mouth lifted and he reached for her hand.